SHADOWS & ASH

AUTHOR
PARTNERS

The Shadowless series by J. P. Cane

For the most enjoyable experience, be sure to read *The Shadowless* series in order.

Dedication

For Mom and Dad
All my love

part
I

one

Lily and Reed

A wife bent in prayer. A husband lifeless, but not dead.

At her bedside vigil, Lily Martin Williams holds the small crucifix near her moving lips, unable to let go of the irrational thought that her husband is truly dead.

In the eerie stillness, her soft breath whispers prayers, while Reed has no breath at all.

Her eyes cast over to the windows blacked out by layers of garbage bags. A defense against even a single ray of light slipping in and… and… What? What exactly would the sunlight do? Would Reed burn?

She knows he'll awaken. She knows vampires sleep coma-like during the daylight hours. This is how their life will have to be for now.

She knows.

But her heart gulps in despair. Unable to eat since breakfast, she has spent the morning running errands then rushing back here only to spin in the suspended moment till the sun goes down. Not knowing what to expect, she paces Reed's one-bedroom apartment, end-to-end, while thumbing through websites, trawling for any kind of information that may help her.

VAMPIRES

REAL VAMPIRES
HOW TO SAVE A VAMPIRE
CURE FOR VAMPIRES
HOW TO TURN A VAMPIRE BACK TO HUMAN

Lots of links to movies and novels, costumes and conventions, undead make-up how-tos and do-it-yourself fangs. Below the sponsored ads, results link to articles on vampire lore and legend; haunted and macabre Philadelphia attractions like the Eastern State Penitentiary and the Mütter Museum; an occult shop in Manayunk. She marked some for further investigation. Then noticing the waning sunlight, she moves to Reed's room for the evening's verdict.

Under the glow of the nightstand lamp, she folds back the coverlet and puts her ear to his chest. Before, whenever she had snuggled up with him in his bed or hers, she enjoyed that steady tattoo of life.

Now, not a single reassuring beat.

A mannequin instead of her groom. Not even married a week and frantically apart nearly half that time.

He remains warm though. Warmer than she expected. As though his cotton tee shirt had been plucked off a clothesline under an August sun.

Returning to her prayers, her eyes study Reed. He lacks the pallor typical of the movie stills and artistic renderings that had appeared in her search results. Men and women with chalky, almost translucent skin; arresting eyes with irises that glared red; and snarling mouths with predatory teeth. In some, crimson smeared their lips, in others blood coated the lower half of their faces as though they bobbed for hearts in a barrel.

Those last gory images had shaken her. Too real for Lily, she rubbed her arms to soothe away the memories of last night when real vampires, with real fangs, bled real people to death. And intended do the same to her.

Even now, she reminds herself that she is safe, whole, unhurt in her husband's home. With tenderness, she touches Reed and fixes his hair.

"Come back to me."

And he does. Signs appear in his face when his eyelids tighten, brows crease, and jaw flexes.

Then Reed's brown eyes spring open. She launches herself at him just as he sits up, embracing him, sharing her relief.

Smelling like his old self, Reed's encircling arms put her into the safest place in the world. He's the warmest, coziest blanket. She releases a breath she hasn't realized she is holding.

Pulling her closer, he says, "Morning. You're better than an alarm clock."

"Evening. Actually."

"Oh. Yeah. For a second, I hoped it was all a very bad dream. Are you okay? Have you been out?"

She had dressed down to joggers and a sweatshirt today. She nods. "Better now. I was so worried that you wouldn't wake up. How are you feeling?"

"You know...? I feel pretty rested, ready to go, but I don't want to." With a wink, he says, "Let's just stay in the here-and-now." He reaches for her, then hesitates. His eyes down.

She follows his gaze to the necklace and the crucifix resting on her skin. "I'm sorry. I should have left it at home." She feels terrible for being so thoughtless.

After a moment, Reed shakes his head and draws his eyes to hers, "No, I want you to wear it. Never take it off, Lil."

They adjust themselves on the bed. She tucks her head on his shoulder after he props himself up on several pillows.

Cradling her, he says, "It feels so good to hold you again."

She presses a kiss into his skin. "I wanted to be here when you wake up."

"How about we don't leave this room?"

"I don't want to either. But Ky-"

"No, don't say his name."

"He's coming and you need to get ready."

He's quiet and looking away. Stubborn. Seeing that he's unhappy with this, she relents, "All right. Five more minutes, then you have to get up."

"And a kiss," he says looking back to her.

"One." Tender, the kiss fills the time and her heart.

***

Per their domestic routine, the first one out of bed brews the coffee. In the kitchen, fresh ground roast greets Reed. And fresh from the shower, he's dressed in his casual style of white undershirt, flannel top, and dark jeans.

Already seated at the small round table, Lily warms her hands with her coffee mug. He pulls up a chair. Looking at his own mug, his lips twist. The scented steam mocks him.

His wife makes a face, maybe realizing her mistake. "It's liquid—does that count?"

Instead of the inviting dark brown swirling in the mug, he sees a flash of arterial red. He jabs the mug away, "I don't want any." He taps the table, "Don't let yours get cold. Drink up."

Between sips, she fills him in on her day: Running necessary errands, researching online, and checking in with their new French friend, Aleron. The older man had been a part of the harrowing past few days and nights, having both saved Lily's life and reunited her with Reed.

"The super will be by tomorrow. He'll replace the window, but it'll have to be during the day. You'll need to be elsewhere."

"Our new place," he says.

"Exactly. I brought your old air mattress and frame over." They hadn't had time to move into their new apartment before the wedding.

Reed smiles. "We can camp out. Build a little fire and make s'mores. Listen to the stirrings of urban creatures."

Lily says, "Sounds fun. It is the season for spooky stories."

He has forgotten about Halloween. He likes this time of year. Grinning pumpkins, haunted hayrides, crackling campfires. He scratches for a memory. Something to do with the season and Lily. Something they had done together. But he can't grasp it.

He lets it go. They can make new memories, and he's all the more grateful for another night with her. After all that has happened, they have come through it. His heart has been stitched back together, all but beating with renewed desire to be her man.

His smile lifts watching her simply doing the little things she's not even aware of. How she holds the mug in her hands when she sips, or her pinkie curling by her mouth when she considers something. And hearing her voice, her laugh, even her concern.

He wants to make the most of this time. He doesn't have long left till he has to do a necessary errand of his own tonight.

Not waiting for her to finish her coffee, he comes around to her and stoops to drape his arms over her shoulders, squeezing gently, assuring them both that they are in fact together, safe, and real. He noses her dark hair, taking in the light floral smell of shampoo, letting out a contented breath.

"Can we just go back to France? We don't have to pack. Just grab your passport and wallet and let's fly out of here."

Lily smiles and pats his forearm, "I have both in my purse."

"Yes. That's my girl," he says in a tone like a fist pump. "If we go right now, I promise foot massages every time we finish shopping and sightseeing."

"That is very sweet."

He straightens up, letting go, "Don't say, 'but.'"

"Reed," she turns in her seat to look up at him, "You know we can't. Not yet."

He knows.

He steps away.

He rakes his hair, then massages the back of his neck. He knows.

He can feel it. The lightest tremors disturbing his mood. A vital part of himself comes loose. He's slipping away. She's his rock, and he needs her.

She reaches for him, "We're going to fix this first. You hear me?"

Fix. Can this be fixed? Can he be human again?

By the certainty in her voice and the determination in her eyes, he is desperate to believe her.

He takes small comfort by how much of her he still remembers. There's that at least. Since being turned into the undead, he has been plagued by visions of crows stealing memories. He's a scarecrow, a figure of half-stuffed burlap from which they filch bits of straw, severing links to the people he loves. Moments of mischief with his brothers and sister, family celebrations, and dates with Lily.

Only recently has he realized that the crows skip skills he has built up over his lifetime as though they found such things skimpy, too ordinary to be appetizing. His firefighting training remains in his bones; his woodworking tools in his rough hands; his knowledge of local and French architecture etched in his brain.

As though picking up on his thoughts, she says, "Do you still have trouble remembering?"

He gives a reluctant nod.

"I have an idea about that." She comes to his side, holds out her phone, and brings up the gallery app. Photo by photo, she asks him to identify the people smiling from the screen. He knows a few, but others he's not sure about, including family members.

His agitation grows with each unfamiliar picture. In response, the heat in his chest rises. He and Lily have learned that instead of blood, vampires have ichor, a black substance that collects in the heart. And because he's an erif, it runs hot, a seething briquette. At a low flame now, the ichor flares up sometimes, turning discomfort into pain worse than heartburn. And when it's really bad, it radiates to his shoulders, down his muscled arms, to his large hands and calloused fingers waiting to ignite.

"Is that Mom?"

Lily smiles, offering encouragement.

He doesn't take it. "I only guessed because she's with Dad. I still remember what he looks like."

His fists clench and unclench. He doesn't even recognize his own mother!

Without a word, he breaks from her. The gaps in his memories have deepened into ravines. He fears that not only are his memories lost in those chasms, but he may lose his sanity. Like Marie had.

Marie de Telfour had been the one who crashed their honeymoon and threw them into this nightmare. She had become obsessed with Reed the moment she spotted him in Paris, then later made him a vampire and left Lily to be devoured by her vampire children. Even after he escaped home, she and her gang followed him across the Atlantic Ocean, determined to drag him back.

Lily steps beside him and rubs his back, "I'm sorry. I just thought it would help."

"Not your fault."

She snuggles into him and, after a moment, he snuggles back.

At least the birds haven't returned to take more.

Along with the amnesia, he's changed in other ways. Perhaps too much. And he senses that Lily knows this but won't let on. She says she's fine. She smiles and laughs the same. But he knows there's something just under the surface. Is she scared of him? How could she not be? Last night was a horror show. How can she be fine? He had killed Eddie, Marie's first child. And Reed came close to killing Lily. Are they to pretend that none of that happened? That with a new day or night, or whatever, turn the page, start fresh?

Here or in France, it's still their honeymoon. They should be enjoying themselves. And he's supposed to be a living breathing human being, not an undead monster.

Lily says, "When Kyle comes—"

"I don't want to talk about him right now," he says, sharper than he intended and regretting it.

Kyle Dowd. His sponsor. A guide to this vampire world Reed wants nothing to do with. Tonight, he will have to do monster things instead of human things. He'll need to drink blood.

"Fine." She takes their mugs to rinse out in the sink. "Aleron sends his regards."

"I'm sorry. How is he?"

"He's having a difficult time. I had to coax him out of my place so I could take him to breakfast. And we said our prayers at St. Patrick's."

"Why not our church?"

"Didn't want to be recognized. We're still on our honeymoon."

"Good thinking."

"After you leave, I'll shower, then get him out for dinner."

"Take him to get some cheesesteaks. Real Philly food."

She nods. "He leaves tomorrow. I wish we could do something for him. He's despondent."

"I feel for him. And I need to thank him for saving you."

"After all the grief I gave him. I thought he was a crank at first."

"Understandable, don't you think?"

"Can either of us say we truly understand any of this?"

"No."

"We trust in God to help us through this. But what do we do? What do we tell our families?"

"Nothing. They can't know."

Lily's eyebrows jump, "Why can't they know? I know."

Reed crosses his arms over his chest, "Think about it. This has been a secret for centuries. At least. Do you think that's by accident? They only tell those who need to know and who will never say or do anything about it."

Lily says, "Kyle helped save my life. He's not going to kill me. That doesn't make sense."

Reed shakes his head, "It does. He's not who we thought he was. I think he's hurt a lot of people."

Lily says, "But you still need his help, right?"

Now weaving his fingers together behind his head, Reed says to the ceiling, "I'm a probie again. But for a monsters club instead of the fire department."

Lily says, "That's not who I saw last night. I saw Kyle do everything he could to prevent people from getting hurt. He's not a monster and neither are you. Don't talk like that. It's not funny."

Reed looks at Lily, arms extended, "Even if you're right, he doesn't call the shots. There's this Devlin guy who's movie-monster-level creepy. He might seem like a normal guy, but the way he talks and the clothes he wears. I was told he's as old as the Constitution. Can you believe it? This guy lived when the country was founded here? He should be the one giving tours of Independence Hall. I can't get my mind around it."

Lily curls a finger by her mouth.

Finally, she relents with several nods, "You're right. We won't say anything." Then a hopeful shrug, "If we get you better soon, there will not be anything to tell."

A huge 'IF.'

Suddenly, Reed frowns, leans back to peer outside the kitchen toward the front door of the apartment.

A moment later, the doorbell rings.

"You said his name too many times."

***

Lily peeps through the fisheye lens in the apartment door before opening it. Mr. Kyle Dowd appears as well put-together as last night and just as serious with an all-business expression.

When the door opens, Kyle says, "Is this a good time?"

Lily says, "Yes."

"No," Reed says from behind her.

Ignoring Reed, she welcomes Kyle inside.

"Thank you, Mrs. Williams."

"Lily, please."

Dressed in a suit, Kyle looks like a gentleman. From her family and their social calendar bursting with black-tie galas, weddings, and fundraisers, she knows menswear. Perfectly fitted, his is tailor-made and the light blue necktie complements both the taupe wool fabric and his red hair.

In comparison, she feels unfashionable in her lazy attire, but dismisses this self-conscious impulse. Kyle has seen her worse.

Kyle's vigilant eyes seem to note everything and everyone. Just as he had last night in the Whitpain Hotel suite, where she was held hostage, tied to a chair, as bait for Reed.

Behind her back, she rubs her wrists to assure herself the nylon cords of the hotel curtains aren't still digging into her skin.

Kyle says, "How are you and your French friend?"

"Aleron's managing. As am I. I'm very grateful to have Reed back. Thanks to you."

Barely managing. Grief-stricken, Aleron has said little, has had little appetite. Little wonder given how things turned out last night. Lily has tried to comfort him while contending with what she and Reed must now face.

Kyle hands her a slip of paper with inked writing on it. "This is the funeral parlor in Paris where Marie will be received. Please give this to him before he leaves."

She reads the Parisian address located in the 3rd *arrondissement*.

When she and Reed had been torn from each other by Marie and her vampire gang, she had never felt such terror. While Reed was thrown into a getaway car, Lily was tormented by the vampires left behind. After their cruel fun, she would have been their midnight meal. But then, like a shot, a Peugeot sedan rammed into her captors. Like a replay of what happened to Reed minutes earlier, the driver, Aleron, hustled Lily into his car and sped away before any of the vampires could recover.

As he would later admit to Lily, Aleron hadn't happened to be driving by, he was spying. He too loved someone who had been turned into a vampire, his fiancée: Marie.

In the living room, Lily offers Kyle a chair near the futon.

No one sits.

Reed says to her, "You know he stabbed me with a chair leg right here last night?"

Kyle says, "And yet, here you are, no worse for it."

Lily says, "Boys, behave. Kyle, can I get you anything?"

Reed mutters, "A throat, perhaps?"

Lily can't believe her ears. "Reed!"

Turning to Kyle, she holds up a finger, saying, "Please excuse us. We'll just be a moment."

Lips pressed together, she gives one look to Reed, who then follows her down the apartment hallway to the bedroom at its end.

After closing the door, she says, "What is going on?"

Reed points at the door, "I don't want him here. Not here and not now."

Lily says, "Well, he is here. What is bothering you? Really?"

Stepping closer to her, putting his arms on her shoulders, he says, "I want more time with you. We just got back together."

Lily softens. She wants more time too. "We're not going to lose each other again."

Reed says, "I can feel him in my head, just like Marie."

Lily still has difficulty understanding what that means. Before going to sleep before sunup, he tried to explain to her that because Marie is his sire, part of her is in him, giving her some control of his actions, like he was at the end of a leash she held. And because she had fed him her blood, he ended up with some of her thoughts and feelings. And having had fed later from Kyle, Reed's got some of him as well.

"I don't want to go out there. Out there, I will have to do things I don't want to do." Quieter, he adds, "I think he's killed people."

"What makes you think such a horrible thing?"

"You know after the fight, I had to... I was thirsty... More than thirsty."

"Yes, you drank Kyle's blood, or whatever it's called."

"Well, it's not like drinking a glass of milk. When drinking his ichor I got this picture of him, and a widow he's speaking to. I think he murdered her husband."

Lily considers this. "Talk to him about it, if you're concerned. The man did everything he could to save lives last night. Strangers' lives. Give him the benefit of the doubt. In the meantime, be nice."

After a quick kiss, they return to the living room.

Lily says, "We're doing our best under the circumstances, and we appreciate your help. This has been trying for both of us."

Kyle says, "I understand, and I wish I could say it will get easier. It will not. Not for a while anyway. When would you and Reed have returned home from your honeymoon?"

Lily says, "The Sunday after next."

"Till then, that's where you still are as far as your families are concerned. There's much for Reed to learn, some of which he will not be allowed to share with anyone, including you."

"Pardon?"

"Think of our Society as a corporation. We have trade secrets."

Reed wraps an arm around Lily's shoulders, "I'm not keeping secrets from her."

"You will have to. You're a lawyer or a doctor who doesn't share confidential client information with others. And that goes for you, Lily. You can't tell anyone what you already know."

Though she and Reed have already agreed to keep this between themselves, Kyle must know how impractical that will be the longer this goes on for. But Lily buttons up and simply nods her agreement.

"As I've said: you're on honeymoon. No one expects to hear from you, so keep a low profile. Don't let yourselves be seen, which shouldn't be a problem for Reed." Vampires hide in plain sight. Overlooked, as Aleron had put it. Like shadows.

Kyle continues, "What happens next depends on tonight and the nights that follow. You are each other's security. Understand?"

Her spirit sinks. "I'm beginning to understand all too well."

Kyle says, "I know it's difficult. We'll help you through it."

Stepping up to Kyle, Reed says, "I have a condition of my own: You're never to come to Lily without me. Not you, not anyone in your secret club. Not even a phone call."

Regarding Reed evenly, Kyle says, "Then you'll cooperate with us. You do as I say when I say. I don't want to threaten, or have to use the bond we now share, but these are the facts of the matter. Marie screwed up—she's responsible, but she's in no position to make it right, even if she wanted to. We're trying to contain the disaster she caused for you both. Selfishly on our part, yes. Being an erif makes you potentially powerful in protecting the Society from our enemies. But you're on probation, so keep in line. If you're more of liability than an asset, well, let's not think on that."

Reed scowls, "This is f—"

"Thank you for your honesty, Kyle," she says to smooth over Reed's rising temper. "What I'm hearing is that Reed will cooperate till he's human again. Then you won't have to worry about us any longer."

Kyle says nothing. His silence does not reassure Lily that this is in fact the plan. "Tell me this is the plan."

Kyle says, "At this moment Reed is a danger to the Society of Brandywine, himself, you, everyone. The plan is to begin teaching him what he needs to know to pass initiation. And once he's a member he will support the House when called upon in whatever capacity he is able."

"I don't want to be a member. I want out of all of this."

Kyle turns to Reed, "My help is contingent on you doing just that. The Society has much to offer its members, including access to information that may help you. I can't promise such information exists. I honestly don't know."

Lily blows out a breath, "This is difficult to hear. I'm glad you're his sponsor." Taking Reed's hand, she says, "We both are."

Kyle says, "So far, you're both doing the right thing. I genuinely wish to help, while being as truthful as I can." Kyle adjusts the cuffs of his dress shirt. He says to Reed, "Do you still have the tuxedo from your wedding?"

Reed looks at Lily expectantly. Another thing he's forgotten, it seems. She tells him, "You wore your dress uniform, which your father took to be cleaned. You were going to pick it up from him when we got back."

Kyle says, "Then how about a good suit?"

"Yeah. I've got one of those."

Kyle says, "You'll need a mask as well."

Reed looks askance, "I'm not robbing anyone. Or doing other crimes for you or the Society."

"For the masquerade tomorrow night. There you'll meet many more Society members."

Lily says, "I'll get you one. It's Halloween season, so there are plenty of shops that will carry them." Perhaps the one in Manayunk.

"Good. Let's get going." Kyle nods to Lily, "I promise to return him safe and sound, and that no one will else will get hurt. Good to see you again."

Reed says by her ear, "You'll be asleep by the time I get back. Then I'll be asleep when you get up."

She says, "Remember to go to the new apartment. Not this one."

"Right, right. But I'll need to drop off my stuff there."

Lily says, "I already did that. You'll have all you need. And I replaced the phone you lost. You can text me if you need anything."

"What's your number?"

"It's under favorites."

two

Beer Run

R eed says little during the car ride.
　　What's to say? They're out to get some blood. Like a beer run.
Find a store and snag a six-pack from the refrigerated case.

If only.

He's not squeamish. On the job and off, he has seen and treated
countless wounds and injuries. And his engine company has run a number
of blood drives. Reed must have donated pints and pints of blood over the
years. If he had only squirreled away some bags of plasma then...

They pass the Fishtown clinic on their way out of his neighborhood.
And finally getting the hint, Kyle drops his attempts to snare him into conversation. What could Kyle say? Can he explain what he had done? When
Reed drank Kyle's ichor, that crude oil oozing from his wrist, the fresh
impressions chilled him. Kyle deliberately killed someone. The who, the
why, and the how has faded away, but the disturbing feeling remains with
Reed. How can he trust this guy driving him who-knows-where?

What Reed had told Lily was no exaggeration. Without warning, Kyle
had slammed a piece of wood into Reed's chest, his heart, paralyzing him.
Part of Kyle's plan to rescue Lily. Didn't see fit to tell Reed about it before-
hand. But, despite everything, it worked. That's all that matters. And Lily
is a good judge of people. He will trust that for now.

If Kyle makes a left up ahead, they will eventually reach a hospital. Its name escapes him, but Reed pictures gurneys racing through the emergency entrance. He thinks a friend had been on one of those stretchers.

Kyle continues straight.

Reed is tempted to ask him which one they'll stop at. Or will it be a blood bank? Does Kyle have a pass or fake access badge to get in and get the bags? Casually glancing about the Audi, Reed doesn't see a cooler or other container for their haul. Maybe one is in the trunk.

Up Broad Street into North Philadelphia, university banners crop up above the scattering of mayoral campaign posters. People with backpacks walk and chat with each other.

Is there a bio-research lab on campus that they'd steal from? Another half dozen blocks, he's given up on guessing. Where are they headed? Shouldn't take this long to find a suitable place. There's no lab or hospital or clinic in sight. Reed has a sinking feeling that he is in for a long night and that this will not be a simple beer run.

***

Once out of the parked Audi, Reed recognizes the pearlescent purple body of Celestine, a '64 Impala, and the man leaning back on it. Lean himself, Michael appears younger than 33-year-old Reed, though he is actually decades older.

Reed has only ever seen him in formal wear when posing as a Latin playboy and an admirer of Marie as part of Kyle's rescue plan. Now he wears black jeans and a white linen shirt, partially unbuttoned, revealing a slim gold necklace and hairless chest. Michael could be a model in a fragrance commercial, tangling with a beautiful woman on a breezy beach.

Beside him, the taller Professor Malcolm Gold looks like he would be more comfortable after-hours alone in a library rather than running along the surf. Dark suit, white dress shirt, paisley tie, and loafers. None of which fits him well.

But he can speak French, which had been crucial last night. He not only interpreted what Aleron shared with them about Marie, but spoke for Michael when he had tried to convince Marie to let Lily go.

Michael says, "Ready, my man?" and offers Reed a chummy smile, which does not put him at ease.

Rush hour has long passed. Reed looks around. Several apartment buildings and businesses on their side of Diamond Street. Opposite, a corner bar, hardware store, hair salon. No blood bank in sight. Or even an urgent care facility.

Michael says, "Time to feed, Reed."

He looks around again. "I don't suppose we're going to a pet store?"

"Animals won't do," Kyle says.

"How do you know? Maybe it's different for erifs," Reed's desperate for a loophole. He had been told erifs are not too common so maybe in addition to having the ability to fry a henchman with his hands, he can get by on some hamsters.

Kyle says, "It is the same for all of us: Fresh and human."

"And by fresh you mean, what?"

Michael grins, "Right from the tap."

"Not so narrow and crude as that," the professor says, who is paler than Kyle. Also, lanky and awkward, his hands not knowing what to do with themselves, a bit clumsy overall. Wearing tortoiseshell glasses, he seems to be looking inward rather than at any one of them. "The nutritional aspect of the blood diminishes rapidly outside the human body. Though more expedient to drink directly from the person, the blood can be first collected into a cup or other vessel. By some, the method is considered to be a more refined mode of imbibing."

Turning to his friend, Michael says, "But practically—we're talking practical—"

"What you're talking about," Reed says, put off by how casual they are about what they expect him to do, "is that you want me to go up to a perfect stranger and take their blood." He looks to each of them "There's got to be another way."

Kyle says, "There are many ways. Violently. Voluntarily. In-between. You'll have to find your own approach and whom to approach. And we're here to help. Starting now."

This feels like when his older brothers used to egg him on some foolish dare. Childish stunts then, deadly serious now.

Malcolm says, "Avoid biting the neck unless you know what you are doing. You may kill them."

Malcolm's advice isn't helpful. Reed knows about the neck's vital arteries. In any case, Reed remembers his first-aid training should something go wrong. But he will not bite there. He doesn't want to think of his teeth sharpening to hurt another person, as he had nearly done to Lily last night at the Whitpain Hotel.

Kyle says, "You don't need to take much if you feed frequently enough. A couple of ounces. Tonight, just get a taste."

"Great."

"But if you go without for too long, you'll lose reason and control."

Reed once more glances around. Is he to just pounce on one of the pedestrians passing by?

"You have it all backwards," Michael says. He puts his arm around Reed's shoulders as though drawing him into a secret.

"I do?"

With a wise nod, Michael leads him away from the others. Past Malcolm's Impala and the next two cars. "You're thinking of an end. One possible end. A bad end."

"I'm not going to hurt anyone."

"Agreed. Me neither. I'm a lover. So put that bad end out of your mind. Far more, far better possibilities than that. Look? See the bar?"

Fixed to the windows of The Challenge, signs promise great times, games, and beer. "That's why you brought me here?"

Michael launches into his pitch—and quite a pitch it is. Winning grins, knowing eyes, and assured gestures cast a shadow play before Reed, nearly convincing Reed that not only can he do this, but that both he and whomever he's set up with will have a fantastic time. In fact, the blood will be the best part. Like the meeting of two souls. Reed need only be open to it.

Reed remembers the experience of drinking from Kyle—the ichor felt like an immersive movie, but not a summer action blockbuster, more like an intimate portrait that stays with you long after leaving the theater.

Still, despite Michael's compelling commercial, he's not convinced that this will be easy, or that he can do it at all. But what's the alternative? Lily?

No. Not her.

"And when it happens, oh *mi amigo*, the feeling is indescribable. Forget what you think you know. It's soul-to-soul. A communion. Deep waters. All the more reason to drink shallow for now."

He makes an emphatic nod to Kyle and Malcolm then to Reed, "You're ready."

While they cross the street, Michael says, "Ditch the ring."

Reed's eyes drop to the gold wedding band on the finger of his left hand. He touches it protectively. He will not take it off. "Never."

Michael yields, "You're right. Leave it on." Then seeming pleased with himself, he grins, "I have a better idea."

"You do?"

"You've got to learn to let go of expectations, man. Surrender. Go with the flow." Before reaching the door, festive with orange and black crepe paper ribbons, he says, "You're going to do great. Trust me."

***

Mid-October air shakes cardboard skeletons near the entrance door of The Challenge, a draw for college students seeking to blow off studies and steam, watch a game, hook up.

A decade older than many of them, age isn't the reason they veer around Reed without a glance as though he's nothing more than one of the decorative ghosts. Hovering and insubstantial.

But he notices them. Their carefree carousing. Hoisted glasses of hoppy draft beer overtopped with foam. Tables pounded for great plays, groans of lamentations for bad ones.

Young men and women chat each other up around high top tables; from the bar others watch the game, downing IPAs, and licking buffalo sauce from their fingers. He feels their warmth. He doesn't need his special sight to see the vitality each one possesses. A life force zips through them, a live wire that practically hums in his ears.

But absent in him. He's apart and he doesn't know if he'll get back what was true, what was real and solid and sure. He's forgotten so much, lost so much of himself.

Young men and women, laughing, eating, hugging, texting, whispering, arguing, grousing, play out a human story. One he's no longer part of. Beings he's no longer one of.

He's a vampire here for blood.

Michael has disappeared. Why is Reed even trusting him? Charming, yes, but the man's a little too slick. He wonders if this is a mistake. He knows this is a mistake. What choice does he have?

Reed slips into a booth. He busies himself by reviewing the laminated Happy Hour menu. Beers, nachos, sliders. Nothing on the menu appeals to him now.

While reviewing the rules of an upcoming costume contest taped to the wall, Michael arrives like a waiter delivering an order. Beside him, a woman in bold clothing, bright lipstick, and owl-framed glasses holds a puffy coat in a half-nelson under her arm.

But her expression doesn't match Michael's triumphant one. Wearing a thin smile, she looks at him as if he's a wounded bird.

"Ms. Eleanor Alamonte, may I present to you Mr. Reed Williams."

Suddenly in motion, the woman hops in beside him, laying one of her hands on his arm. A tender gesture.

"Michael told me what happened to your wife. I am so, so sorry."

Reed's eyes cut to Michael, about to throw some scorching words, but the man has already blended back into the crowd.

"To die unexpectedly, and so young," she says. Her other hand rises to her heart in sympathy. "Michael thought that you could use some company to help you get back on your feet. I told him of course I would. I'd do anything for a friend like him."

Reed considers the gold band on his finger, feels its weight in promises. To have and to hold. To cherish. To be faithful. Forever. This was Michael's plan? Use Lily to manipulate this woman? It's twisted. Genius. Twisted for sure.

Go with the flow.

"A friend?"

"Yes. And between you and me," she says quiet for the moment, "I almost forgot about him myself." She shakes her head, tossing waves of dark hair. "We lost touch after he moved to New Mexico or Arizona someplace." She shifts in her seat, "But then we run into each other here. Well, over there," she points to another area of The Challenge. "And it's like we never missed a beat." Smiling like all is forgiven, she says, "Crazy, right?"

Reed wonders if this is true. Michael seems able to ingratiate himself with everyone he meets. When Reed had met Michael, Reed too believed he was a friend from long ago and nearly forgotten.

What is Reed doing? Playing along with Michael's game? Already lying by omission. Does it have to be this way?

Part of him wants to tell her the truth. Part of him needs to suck down a cigarette or twenty. Out of habit, his hand hits his shirt pocket for a pack, but he finds only folded sunglasses, reminding him they're from Marie. He shudders at the thought of her. That first night as a vampire, he had worn the glasses to conceal his ichor-black eyes until he learned to change them back to human ones. Another creepy aspect of what he is now.

Eleanor turns to him, earrings dancing beneath her ears. "Do I look like her? Michael said that I could be her younger sister. But now I'm thinking the resemblance might upset you."

She looks nothing like Lily. Not a sister, not a cousin. "Not really." He frees his arm from her and slouches down the bench.

She lets him go.

Tapping a familiar groove, he says, "Can I order you a drink?"

Missing Reed's raised hand, one waitress passes their table. Then another.

Of course. Reed frowns. He's unseen. Vampires don't catch human notice. Unless they do something to call attention to themselves, they fade into the background.

Reed singles out a waiter pocketing change from an abandoned table. Fingers in his mouth, Reed whistles. Sharp and arresting. The waiter perks up. Good enough.

By the time the beers arrive, Eleanor has seated herself opposite Reed, her coat tossed into the corner. Her fingers encircle her beer, which, like his, remains untouched. The foam head slops down his glass and soaks into its coaster. Why had he ordered one for himself? A waste of money.

Leaning over the table, eyes soft with concern, Eleanor says, "Are you all right, Reed? If this is too much, if you're not ready, I can go. It's just that, I'm here. You know? Like Michael said, no pressure. If you want to talk about her, I can be a good listener. But if you don't..."

Reed doesn't like this. His brown eyes rise, "Her name's Lily."

"That's a pretty name." With the implied invitation to stay, she smiles. "Michael had said you two were close. So close, it made him jealous."

"Did he now?" The man can lay it on thick. Is this how Michael gets his own... donors? Now there's a word for it. More kind than prey. Less honest.

"We are very close." Once, he had believed, inseparable. Now, he feels that widening gulf between them. Almost as wide as here in The Challenge, and between him and Eleanor. As though he's observing this from the outside, instead of participating. Like a television show that he's half paying attention to. Do the others feel this way?

Eleanor's hands form a table for her chin to rest on. "How did you meet each other?"

He takes a moment to recollect, but the details aren't there for him to find. He lost so much since becoming a vampire. He keeps it simple. "There was a fire. I got her out of it."

The fire had branded her forearm, but rather than be self-conscious of the patch of blasted skin, Lily has made no effort to conceal it.

"Oh my, Lord, really?"

"It's hard for me to remember. I've been having memory issues."

A smile spreads across her face, "Romantic when you think about it. A hero!" Eleanor raises her glass to him, then drinks.

Reed shakes his head, motioning with his hands for her to cool off with that word.

"Michael mentioned that you are a firefighter."

"I am. I was. I don't know." He rubs his scalp unsure what to say. Another thing to sort out. "Look. Let's talk about you."

The waiter comes by to ask her if she'd like to order any food. She's good with the beer.

"Well, my studies keep me busy and I don't plan to stay here after earning my masters." The colorful crystals set in her brooch throw the light.

Between sips of beer, she explains that her parents had emigrated from the Dominican Republic and settled in Reading. Her mother's a registered nurse there, so Eleanor's always been interested in helping others.

"I admire my mother's dedication, but hearing her stories about pus, and bed sores, and wound care, always left me a little queasy." After shuddering with a sour face, she laughs at herself. "I'm more into numbers anyhow. And I love research. So, I took a different direction."

She has spent summers at a nonprofit back home. With a degree in policy, she envisions working with organizations in Harrisburg to influence healthcare policy state-wide.

He half-listens to her, being sure to offer a polite smile here and there. Laughter seems to come to her easily. She's sure of herself and personable.

Kindness in her eyes and warmth of her voice helps him to feel real. A tenuous connection. He's here now, in a booth, with a human being having a conversation.

"But, if the right person comes along…" she says, followed by a sheepish, "You never know."

"You never know." He gives a small smile. Is this flirting? Is this smart? *Don't overthink it.*

A pair of college-age women stop at their table on their way out of the bar. They're checking on their friend. Reed offers a small wave when Eleanor introduces him. He notes unspoken words between her and her friends. Taking their leave, one says, "You'll be okay?" and the other, "Call me later."

Reed doesn't wish to hurt her, but the point of being out here, chatting with strangers, is to learn to get blood. Just enough to keep the edge off.

With confidence he could do this as often as he needs so that he will never lose control of himself.

Fresh and human.

How is this going to work? He tries to envision what comes next. Take a walk that ends at her apartment. Get invited up and put on music. Chat. Laugh.

Reed considers Eleanor's throat, which totters with each swallow of beer. He's a clinician noting its broad sweep of skin, the pair of moles just off to the left on the way to the juncture of neck and shoulder. The faint blue traces beneath and the surging red blood cells within.

He pictures a caped vampire from the movies standing behind her, hands on her shoulders possessively, nose in her hair. Now it's Reed himself, his head beside hers. He soothes with his gentleness, relaxing her so that her eyes close with heaviness, while his own eyes scout for a place to bite below her ear, farther down her neck to her shoulders...

"Where are you?"

Reed hears Eleanor's words calling him back.

He apologizes for drifting, but she shakes her head: *No need for that.* "I can't say that I know what you're going through, but someone whom I care deeply about did lose his wife to cancer." She pauses to think what she wants to say. "It took time, but he found his way through the grief. And you will to. I guess what I'm trying to say is that you're taking a big step tonight. Don't be hard on yourself, and just as with my friend, your wife would want you to live, to go on, to smile again, to be happy again. I'll put you in my prayers."

He would want that for Lily as well, if... if he can't come back from this. If he ends up like Marie with no memory of her, he hopes she'll move on.

Never one to procrastinate, he leaves several bills under the coaster. Crap or get off the seat.

"Let me take you home."

chapter

three

Control

K yle Dowd does not fail to notice a rat following Reed and his female companion. Steps after they have left The Challenge, the rat had parted from a slash of shadow to pursue. Fascinated, Kyle wonders if he's seeing it right from his vantage on Diamond Street.

Malcolm certainly doesn't notice, absorbed as he is by his notebook while seated behind Celestine's steering wheel.

No mistake. Over a foot in length, this brown-furred rodent skulks along the block's stone and brick stoops and storefronts. Though the couple's conversational pace is casual, the rat's feet fly, nearing the sweep of the woman's skirt.

When the couple stops at the crosswalk, the rat does as well, casting up its head like an antenna array. Twitching ears, nose, whiskers capture the subtlest cues from the oblivious pair.

Once the traffic signal changes, Reed escorts the woman across the street, but the rat does not follow, having gained the intelligence it sought. Or lost interest. Its body rounds the corner, the tip of its bald tail slipping out of Kyle's sight.

Tempted to tag himself in, Kyle points his leather shoes west to follow Reed. He wants to be sure Reed's first hunt goes well. The man hasn't had any practice; only the little prep and pep from the three of them before Reed went into the bar. Much can go wrong.

Instead, Kyle restrains himself and removes his pocket square. Unfolding it, he draws the blue silk between his fingers. He will trust Reed and allow him the space to try things his way. In the nights to come, Reed will find his groove and work out his own approach to finding a blood source, the types of people he prefers, and how often to feed.

Stooping to touch up the leather of his shoes, he considers another reason: Intruding could jeopardize Reed's effort. Even if Reed never spots Kyle trailing him, he will sense Kyle is near due to the bond they share, drawing tighter the tenseness Kyle has felt since he picked Reed up at his apartment and Reed's icy silence during the car ride here. Kyle had felt uncommon surprise. He thought they parted on better terms the night before. He'll let Reed stew till he's ready to share.

He has rubbed the shoe leather many times over before the slam of the Impala door closing draws him from his thoughts. He glances up to Malcolm, who gazes in the bar's direction. Kyle stands to look as well.

Here comes Michael, leaving The Challenge, carrying a satisfied grin and delivering it to Kyle. No doubt he's pleased with himself. The gambler thinks he drew a lucky pair. He may be right.

Michael drapes one arm around Malcolm's shoulders. "We're going to be rich," he says to his buddy while looking at Kyle, rubbing his thumb over his fingers in expectation of the won wager. "What are you going to do with your half? Buy the university?"

With care, Kyle refolds his silk square and returns it to the breast pocket of his suit jacket. "Bet's not won yet."

Michael waves off Kyle's skepticism. "You saw Reed leave with that lovely *chica*."

"I did." He does not mention also seeing the hefty rat.

"Good as done. Couldn't have set him up better. Sometimes I impress myself. He'll be thanking me. Again."

Malcolm says, "If monetary compensation has been promised to that young woman, it will be deducted from your half."

"You know me well enough that I never pay for anything. Found her chatting with a couple of her friends. Listened. Made a few educated guesses about her, introduced myself, insinuated—"

"Falsified," Malcolm says.

"Suggested—suggested that we had studied together, then let her fill in the rest."

Kyle says, "And where does Reed fit in?"

"Oh, that it was fortuitous that she and I should reunite this very night." As though on a stage, Michael parts from the professor to enact the exchange. "*Mi amigo* was in great despair over the tragic loss of his dear, young wife." He holds a heavy heart in his hands, eying it with pity. "So sad. It was all I could do to get him out of the house." Bathed in an imaginary spotlight, Michael puts his hands together in fervent prayer, "Could you possibly keep him company, possibly show this grieving widower that he has much to live for? Show him the deep compassion and tenderness, I know you possess."

Kyle says, "He's not going to like that you did that."

"He liked it just fine."

Malcolm says, "Masterful, Michael. Such a gambit garners sympathy. Reed appears vulnerable, in need of consolation, while romantically unattached. And to answer your earlier question, I would like to purchase for Grace a jeweled necklace that sparkles like her voice, to use a trite simile. What will you purchase?"

"I will let Kyle answer. Kyle, what do you think I should spend your money on?"

"A large humble pie." If matched in proportion to Michael's self-assurance, the sliced-up pie could feed every university student in the area.

Kyle has only known Michael... well... for how long now? Time rushes faster than Kyle's grasp. Five years? Perched on his motorcycle, Michael rolled onto the Tamerlane estate, paying the customary visit where new arrivals announce themselves to the House. When they had met, Kyle mistook him as a near-forgotten pugilist. In the man's handsome Latin face, Kyle might have recognized Salvador Lopez, before years in the ring smashed the pretty out of it. Then he realized Lopez would have been retired, if even alive.

No, not him. Michael is a man from everywhere and nowhere, no accent to whisper a place, no memory of his human days. By his telling, he has traveled across many borders, over many miles, like a drifter from a movie western, but instead of a squinty eye and a trigger finger, he has a deceiving confidence and a disarming smile.

"Incorrect." Michael makes a game show buzzer noise. "I think I'll purchase some hotels on Park Avenue. Maybe buy the B & O Railroad and luxury train cars."

Though he is not ready to concede Michael and Malcolm won, he would gladly lose the bet. It would mean that Reed successfully obtained blood. And by doing this, Reed clears a daunting hurdle on his way to being inducted into the Society of Brandywine. Importantly for Kyle, the sooner Reed learns to fend for himself, the less complicated Kyle's life will be.

In a short amount of time, Kyle's respect for Reed has grown. He's a decent man who's facing up to very challenging circumstances. But he's also a pebble in Kyle's shoe. His routine, working on model trains, feeding his mice, watching a bout or bar game, has been disrupted for the foreseeable future. Not only does he need to teach Reed how to survive as a vampire and provide novice-level information about the Society of Brandywine, as his sponsor, Kyle is responsible for Reed's actions. Especially the screw-ups. Stubborn and short-tempered, ignorant and inexperienced, Reed risks endangering himself and self-sabotaging his probation.

Both of them have landed in unfamiliar territory. Kyle has never been a sponsor before. Till becoming one himself, with no say in the matter, Reed hadn't known vampires even existed. So, their shared path of initiation is not a usual one. Typically, the sponsored human learns all that is necessary for membership in the Society. The rites, customs, bylaws, obligations, history. And there's the preparation to leave the human life behind as neatly as possible. Resolving unfinished business, shedding familial connections, maybe getting a new identity before "dying."

Michael says, "Grace is a woman of sophistication and elegance, intelligence and beauty." Taking a moment to study Malcolm, he says, "What she sees in you…"

He peers at his pal as though seeking some elusive, endearing quality.

Kyle cannot guess either, since Malcolm speaks little of affection, intimacy, companionship. Not that Kyle has a romantic life to speak of either, nor a desire for one.

Michael says, "You just need a new style. A new wardrobe." He sighs, "A new body, really, but I suppose we'll stick to what's possible."

While the man picks apart Malcolm's workaday and monotone attire, Kyle notices the rat has returned. Or maybe its sibling. Again, across the street, teetering on its back legs, watching them. Watching him?

The way this one stares at him, like there's an intelligence behind its eyes, as though it's really chewing on a thought. A dark knowing.

Kyle doesn't know what he's doing. Without a word to his friends, he steps away. The brown bruiser, maybe five pounds, loiters between The Challenge and a hardware store. At the end of its triangular head, whiskers twitch in the air, and a beady eye fixes on Kyle.

Stalking rats and babysitting novices. Kyle would prefer helping his brother-in-blood, Alcott Ashton. Alcott and his capable human assistant, Leonard Webb, are investigating the death of Troy Dawson, also known as Blade. Troy, is—or was—the leader of a gang of vampires sequestered across the river in Camden, New Jersey. Some twenty years ago, Kyle had forged a truce between the Society of Brandywine and these outcasts. A truce that has held.

But for how much longer? If Troy's gang hasn't learned of their leader's death, they will soon. Then blame will fall on the Society. Unjustifiably, but understandably, Kyle will admit. With so much bad blood, having no motive to kill the upstart will little matter to them.

Troy's demise leaves Tommy Dutton in charge, assuming nothing else has changed. Kyle will likely need to reach out to him.

And he is here chasing rats. Once a SEPTA bus rumbles by, Kyle crosses the street. By the time he gains the sidewalk, he loses sight of the rat. It has scurried. Some place. His eyes cast up the block, down the block. Then he spots the rat's tail slurped like a noodle into the storm drain beneath the curb.

Kyle dashes over and bends to peer into the dark opening. He hovers, expecting those watchful eyes to appear out of the gloom. He thinks he hears tiny splashes receding.

Once, during Kyle's initiation period, Alcott had said to him in passing not to venture underground. In reply, Kyle said that Alcott didn't know him as well as he had thought, if he believed Kyle would ever have the impulse to reach for a lantern and rope to descend into such a dark, dank environment. Leather shoes squelching in muck, tailored suit splattered by offal, some sepsis-infused stew dripping into his red hair.

Kyle recoils when the present sewer smells reach him. He can almost taste its funk. The rat is welcome to it.

Just a rat anyhow. Kyle has let his imagination get to him. But he doesn't think so. Just as well, though. What would he have done had he caught it? Interrogate it?

After Kyle crosses back, Michael says, "What was that about?"

"That one may have been eavesdropping. Certainly, it was watching."

"A rat." Michael says, dubious. "Do you owe it money too?"

"Have either of you heard of vampires living below ground? Like rats that serve a queen or leader of some kind?"

Kyle jogs his head, wavering on whether he believes it himself. Pieces of gossip he had heard years ago.

Once, Alcott had alluded to them during that same talk. He spoke of being beneath the streets, though not for long. Long enough to know not to go there again, where the dark is almost palpable. "I had the sensation that a hundred eyes were fixed on me."

Alcott hadn't mentioned unusual rats then. Only obliquely that more than rats and other ordinary creatures make their homes there.

Later, at a visit to Tamerlane, from the periphery of a conversation broadly about documenting the history of First House, Kyle had heard more. A committee was compiling a who's who list, from the First to the Founders, the ichorists, and human notables.

Talk turned to sightings of creatures who dwell below. Second- and third-hand speculation. Some ways contradictory and altogether disturbing. Creatures, perhaps some stunted offshoot of a vampire lineage, perhaps of no vampiric relation whatsoever, perhaps born of some magic concoction, or hailing from eastern European lands, maybe places farther still, or maybe native to this soil. They live entirely beneath these streets less as individuals of a society and more the many fangs and claws of one cohesive body serving a queen living off animal blood or animal flesh or the worms of the earth, wriggling down there together.

Malcolm says, "Am I to infer from what you just said, that you believe the rat you pursued was an emissary of a supernal subterranean society?"

Kyle cannot completely discount that he recently saw that flash of intelligence, purpose. "I was told that they spy."

"They spy? On us? Or on you?" Michael says, tapping his chin. "Then why did it run away?"

"And why the interest at all?" Malcolm says.

Kyle shakes his head, "This wasn't the first time." Last night, outside a Wawa convenience store, Kyle and Reed had been chatting. When he noticed a rat loitering near them. He chased it away.

Saying this aloud makes the idea both more far-fetched and more believable at the same time. Kyle notes to bring this up with Alcott. It may help with his investigation. And he can get an update on how the search for Troy's killer is going.

Kyle says, "Reed's on his way." By the bond they share, he has felt the man's presence shift from a background hum into his awareness.

The psychic tether connecting one to the other formed when Reed had drunk Kyle's ichor last night. An unpalatable solution that didn't go down easy for either of them. The man already has a bond with his sire, Marie, as Kyle has with his own, Elias Devlin. The bond he has with Reed will dissolve soon enough while the bonds with their sires are permanent. Permanent, but for a ritual that can mystically server them. Moot now in Reed's case since Marie is incapacitated by the stake in her heart and will be shipped back to Paris.

Michael says, "What's next with Reed? Is it still your plan to set him up with Roxy Marchetti?"

"I haven't decided. Why do you ask?"

"Well, considering she's an erif and he's an erif. She likes fire, he sets people on fire...."

Kyle frowns, "That was an extraordinary situation. He found a resolution."

"Resolution? That's a take. He roasted the guy."

"That is why I'm considering contacting her." He doesn't know her well, and he's not inclined to reach out just yet. Alcott has described her as, "a lovely flame seeking gunpowder." So, handle her with care.

Michael continues, "He might have done the same to any of us."

"He was in control."

"Was he though?"

"Michael...."

"You didn't see what happened. Not like I did." His rising voice, betraying rare unease, strikes Kyle. Usually worry repellent, like rain on a fresh-waxed Celestine, Michael's concern dampens Kyle's own confidence in this matter.

Is Malcolm concerned as well? Kyle asks Malcolm with silent regard, but the professor offers nothing.

Down the way, Reed moves, not with a relaxed gait or Michael's swagger, but hustling quicksteps, his expression grim.

Michael is right, though. Kyle had been sidelined during the fight at the top of the Whitpain Hotel. He missed much of the melee. When he gained consciousness, Eddie was already lain out on the hotel room floor, charred flesh along the man's arms, chest, neck and lower face.

Michael says, "What he did to Eddie didn't look like someone in control."

four

Monster

Crossing an intersection, Reed says to Eleanor, "Who would be the right person?"

"Excuse me?" Eleanor says.

He walks between her and the curb. "Back at the bar, you said that you would stay if the right person came along." He needs to keep talking, keep walking to keep his mind off what comes next.

Eleanor begins her list, "Someone funny."

"I've never been that."

She looks up, "Is that so?" She stifles a laugh, "You're not off to a good start here."

Hands deep in the pockets of her jacket, she says, "Someone honest, who doesn't play games or play around."

"I play softball. Strike two?"

When Eleanor laughs, her whole body fizzes.

A glimmer of a connection stirs in Reed. She's human, and by her, he feels human himself. She's real. He can see her, reach her, grasp her. He wants to hold onto this.

He smiles a little. "Do you like the Phillies?"

She pins him with a serious look. "Who do you think got them into the Series?"

He had nearly forgotten that the team clinched the play-offs earlier this week. Both he and Lily have watched many of their season home games from their perch in her family's box seats.

Her smile returns, "Me and Papa have been saying our prayers, asking for St. Sebastian's intercession."

A wind snaps. She draws in a breath and pulls the zipper of her puffy jacket to under her chin. Reed has no jacket. Indifferent to the cold, Reed has played and worked outside in all seasons. Like his father, Howell, a man who often wears cargo shorts in wintry temps and piles of snow.

Reed remembers this. Can see his old man in those shorts stringing up Christmas lights across the sides of their house.

Maybe the birds are truly gone. Maybe some of his memories will return.

And maybe Reed will pitch for the Phillies.

Gone or not, the birds distract him, churning up anxiety he's unaccustomed to. They don't belong in his head taking memories that are rightfully his, picking apart his scarecrow body. Straw after straw, the more he loses, the more he forgets, leaving him stuffed with panic.

Alarmed, Reed had flailed about trying to describe these nightmares to Mr. Alcott and Mr. Webb, then Kyle and Malcolm. Not one of them had an explanation. Not one of them could put him at ease. Michael, least of all. He had lost his memories too, all at once. *Tabula rasa.* Just woke up a vampire one night in a 1964 Impala in southern California, Michael's human life a void. From what he told Reed, he's fine with it, doesn't need it, doesn't miss it.

Reed doesn't believe this. When he had married Lily, they pledged their hearts to each other. Should he ever forget her, his heart would still know, like a permanent ache from a lost limb. A deeper agony than the fiery ichor there now. He could never be fine with that. Could never live with that.

What now? Should he continue getting close to Eleanor? She has family in Reading rooting for her and her big plans after she graduates. Friends who want her to check in tonight. How can he possibly be close? He hasn't even been honest with her.

He wipes his face with a hand.

Reed checks himself as he and Eleanor stroll to the next block. Kyle had told him a sign of thirst was fixation on a thought or obsessively counting objects like sunflower seeds. He has a clear head for now. So at least there's that.

She asks, "Where do you live?"

"Fishtown."

"Really? There aren't any bars there?"

A really good question. A couple of miles separate here and there. "Michael recommended the place," which, luckily enough, is true.

Eleanor accepts this, then points in a southwesterly direction. "My apartment is on Gratz."

He will make sure she gets there safe and sound, say goodbye, and catch up with Kyle. He's not thirsty. He doesn't need to do this.

But he must do this. The truth is that he's in an impossible situation. He can call this off. Thank her for her help and wish her luck with school. But that only puts off the inevitable. If not this Eleanor, then it'll be another Eleanor another night.

He will do this one thing—one time—which will put off the moment he's really thirsty. And before that happens, he'll find a way back to being human. Before he hurts anyone. But how can he not hurt her? Is he a monster? Lily insisted that he is not. Is she right, or does she not know him any longer?

Along their way, the sky opens and brilliant gold pours in. Reed squints. The sunlight spreads over the rowhomes and stores studded with satellite dishes and now wooden frames like canted crosses. Rays spread farther over the asphalt now crusted with clods of dusty soil. From the pavement, stones erupt like molars.

Reed raises a hand to shield his eyes. After a moment, the sun's harshness dims. Spots of shadow blot the yellow-white sun.

He gropes for his sunglasses.

"Reed?" Eleanor returns to him, slightly amused. "You stopped walking. What are you looking at?" She cranes her head to scan the sky. She only sees what he sees now: The bright moon and the Pegasus and Sagittarius constellations.

"Thought I saw something," he says covering for his returning unsettledness. He's sure that, high above, he had heard crowing.

"I was asking how you know Michael."

He touches his shirt pocket, feeling the arms of the sunglasses through the fabric. Glancing to her, he guesses it would be odd to put them on now. "We met recently. Found we had a lot in common."

Did he just hear another bird call? Weirded out, he distracts himself by pointing out some architectural features, but without any heart. The distance has grown again. He's not human. He's a predator and she's prey.

They pass a number of three-story rowhouses, red brick atop brownstone. Handsome double wooden doors at their entrances, wrought iron guarding their windows. In their midst are churches, playgrounds, and bodegas.

Upon reaching the stoop of her rowhouse, Eleanor turns to look at him. "Thank you for the walk." She considers her words, "I can't say I know the grief you're experiencing, but I hope talking with someone has helped you feel better. I can give you my number if you ever want a listening ear."

"Yeah, I'd say you were a big help."

She takes a couple of steps up, turning back to see him at eye level. Looks like goodbye. He doesn't know what to hope for here. He can leave. Eleanor has survived an encounter with a vampire unaware and unharmed. Or he invites himself in and brings Michael's perfect layup home.

"Would you like to see a picture of her?" He slides his new smartphone out from his jeans pocket. Lily had purchased it earlier today since he had lost his in Paris. Thoughtfully, she added a wedding photo of themselves on the home screen. But it may as well be the kind of photo that comes with a new picture frame. The greatest moment of their lives and he remembers little of it.

"She was beautiful." Eleanor smiles over the picture and oohs over Lily's wedding dress. "Gorgeous. Elegant. Classy."

"She is." God, he wants to be honest. "She's still alive." When Eleanor's eyebrow raises a silent question, he adds, "To me."

She looks at him in sympathy before leaning over to hug him. They embrace, cushioned by her marshmallow jacket. Strands of her hair sweep his cheek and one of her hands gives a supportive rub to his back. It's little comfort. In fact, he struggles with himself.

If he lets Eleanor go, he'll never do this. Can he do this here? Her coat's zipped up. No access. Maybe her hands?

He decides to lean into the renewed feeling of estrangement. He's apart. Invisible. Insubstantial. Dead.

A sip. Just a sip. That's all for now.

He's killed a man. What's a bite? A bite is nothing. She'll be fine. Do it quick. One bite, one taste, then run off. She'll survive.

His tongue runs across his teeth. He can make them sharpen, and ready to pierce. Better to get inside, away from eyewitnesses. She hasn't mentioned living with anyone. Once inside, he would help her out of that coat, get comfortable, let her confirm with her friends she's home.

He breaks from her.

Ready to ask if he might come up for a cup of soothing tea, he feels something land on his shoulder. Alarmed, he staggers away from her. Behind those owlish glasses, her large, dark eyes blink slowly. Black feathers spread out. A beak sprouts. Soon a whole black bird emerges from the tree hollow that had been her face, launching at Reed, who falls away, terror-stricken.

Swooping just above his brown-brimmed hat, the bird leaves a chill in its wake. Reed ducks. Looking around himself, he's back in the last place he'd ever want to be. A nightmare returns, too real, too oppressive.

He's plunged into an expanse of what had been a wheat field and now has the stubble of reaped stalks. Golden light touches everything.

More birds strafe him with their beaks. He dives to the dirt. All around him, the field rolls gently, but he feels constricted, confined. He can't be here. This place isn't real. He was just with someone else. Someplace else.

His hands, gloved in worn leather, his body gaunt with skin of burlap. His perforated flannel shirt and corduroy pants are sunken in places where straw is missing, stolen. He's once again a scarecrow unfit for its duty. The only one scared here is himself.

Above the birds gather and glide. They peer down at him.

Given stick-thinness, he doesn't have much of himself left. How can he live after the last straw is taken from him? Would he cease to exist, or exist as discarded tatters, or transform into a phantom hovering over a barren field?

Then he remembers the lily and how it had helped him before. His clumsy fingers undo the top buttons of his shirt then grope within. From the bristly straw, he withdraws the flower. Its fresh white petals bring relief. Still there. The best of himself.

In unison the crows cry, spread their spectral wings and lunge for it.

"Reed!"

Reed feels a hand on him. Someone is shaking his arm.

"Are you all right?"

He's back. The field and sun and birds have all vanished. Eleanor—she's the one shaking him. She gasps and releases him as though one of the crows got loose from the other world and snapped its beak on her fingers. Stricken, she shrinks away. The back of her foot catches on a step. She stumbles and bangs onto the stoop, her cry caught in her throat. Her eyes shriek all the same.

Color gone from her face, her clothes ashen, her vivid brooch turned pewter. Her aura shimmers a bright blue.

Her wide eyes fix on his own. His eyes. Her expression. He instantly understands how he must appear to her. His brown irises obliterated by the darkness now there. A careful mask torn away.

Not human. A vampire. A monster.

***

Reed bolts back the way he and Eleanor had strolled minutes ago. Now the way looks different. Light pales to greys and shadows deepen. Fear of the crows must have jolted his vision, washing out all color but for the lively blue auras of the pedestrians he sprints past.

His unnerving eyes had spooked Eleanor. In a flash, her concern collapsed into horror; horror of him. The revelation that monsters are real and offer to walk you home.

He hasn't forgotten Lily's own reaction to his unnatural eyes. In a Whitpain Hotel penthouse, he loomed over her, on the precipice, urged to take a final step. *Kill her*, Marie demanded. With the bond, she could compel Reed to do most anything. Weak and thirsty, he couldn't fight her anymore. His teeth sharpened to bite into Lily's neck and slake his thirst for blood.

With her own beautiful eyes, Lily looked up at him, teary with anguish and fear but also resolve and faith. She forgave him for what he was about to do.

Then he had found the flower within himself. The lily recalled the best of himself, giving him the strength to refuse the chorusing crows and refuse the tyrannical Marie.

His hands bunch into fists.

Damned crows.

What memories has he now lost? Hard to put a finger on an absent tooth. He knows there are gaps, but not their shape.

He needs to do something about these damn birds.

As he draws within blocks of where he left the three men, Reed stops. Squeezing his eyes shut, he wills them to clear, to resolve to their natural brown. When he opens them, the subdued colors of Philadelphia at night return.

As does his awareness of Kyle. Their new bond has put Kyle in his head, though it feels different than the one he has had with Marie.

Mon lion, she had often called him. Her bond was a creepy intimacy as though she had curled inside his head, her elegant fingers plugged into his brain, at the controls. And despite his disgust of her, of her possessiveness of him, a part of him desired her and wanted to please her. He shudders to think what would have happened if he hadn't escaped from her grasp and took the next flight home. Would he have lost his will to her, become another of her lackeys, Eddie, Ron, Clarice, and Jean-Paul?

Kyle's bond, though more mellow, is still very much unwanted. A hook into Reed that Kyle could choose to pull any time he desired. Kyle wouldn't do that. He has been straight with Reed. Right?

But Kyle could. Kyle could make him do things. And the thought snares Reed's mind too.

***

In loose casual postures, Kyle and the other two, Michael and Malcolm, look his way. Straight to Kyle, Reed gets right to it. "The crows are back." He rubs his brow, "I thought I was done with them when Marie was staked."

"Why did you think that?"

"I don't know. She was in my head for the longest time. I figured the birds were part of it. Now you're in my head."

"That is temporary. I told you that."

"It had better be. I took Eleanor to her place, then I'm suddenly back in the field." He throws out his arms, "What do I do? I'll lose everything."

Michael says, "You were quick. How was Eleanor?" Hands out to receive, he says, "Give us the details."

Reed turns on Michael, getting in his face, "And you. Don't you *ever* use Lily in your setups again."

Michael's smile pedals away as he falls back against Celestine, "Take it easy, man. We backed you."

Heat blooms in Reed's chest. He grimaces. Upon seeing Michael's alarm, he gives Michael space, while keeping his words sharp, "What did you say?"

"I said we backed you, man. And it worked, right? Got you into her house, right?"

Reed backs off more, surprised how spooked Michael appears. Still pissed, Reed says, "No, it didn't work. The birds got in my head. Got in the way. They took me back to the field. Next thing I know, she's tripping over herself to get away from me. Saw my eyes. So, I ran."

Kyle holds out an open hand to Michael. "Cash only, please."

Michael shakes his head, "No way, man. You heard him. Interference."

Looking to each of them, Reed says, "You took bets on me?"

Michael says, "I believed in you, Reed. Malcolm and I bet you could do it."

"What the hell?" Hackles rise as Reed stalks before the three of them, "This is not a game. This is my life. And someone could have gotten seriously hurt."

He wheels away. With energy he doesn't know what to do with, Reed considers storming out of here. Just run.

Kyle steps in, "All right. You're worked up. Cool down."

"'Worked up?' You're not getting it. I'm losing my mind!"

"Come with me. We'll figure this out." Kyle heads to the driver's door of his Audi. The other two keep a safe distance.

Desperate to believe Kyle, Reed frowns, unsure. To the man's credit, he hasn't pulled on the bond.

Kyle says, "I promise we'll get answers."

chapter
five

Tamerlane

The tight-lipped chill from their previous ride together lifts with Reed's rising panic. Kyle prefers the man's previous silent treatment.

"Tell me you have a plan for this," Reed says, turning in his seat to face Kyle.

Kyle steers his Audi into traffic and recalls that Reed smokes. "Need a cigarette?"

"I quit last night. Now, tell me what to do about these damn crows before I lose Lily. She's all I have."

Turning the steering wheel one-handed, Kyle reaches out to Reed with the other. His cool hand presses flat on Reed's chest. Where he touches, the flannel feels hot out of a dryer. An overheated erif will damage his car. Again. "You'll get help. First, I need you calm. Take in a few breaths. Release them slowly."

Hand back on the wheel, Kyle looks expectantly at Reed who appears ready to protest. After a moment, Reed shuts his mouth and counts ten deliberate breaths.

Kyle says, "Good. Tell me what happened. You walked the woman back to her apartment…"

Reed describes his hallucinations, or whatever they are. One moment they had been chatting breezily, the next daylight broke over the sky and

41

buildings below. Dry earth replaced the asphalt. It was over in seconds when the woman pulled him out.

"Then when we get to her house, I'm back in that field down on my ass. The crows are all around me trying to get every last straw. I don't know how long I was there till Eleanor shook me out of it. She looked as scared as I was. And when I realized why." Here Reed worries his hair with a hand, "She saw, Kyle. You know, my eyes. So, I ran."

"That's why you have the sunglasses, which don't do anyone any good hanging out in your shirt pocket. I'm sure you will remember them next time." Even Marie had understood that well enough to give him the pair. Probably the only thing of hers that was worth keeping. "Did you hurt her?"

"No."

"Did you set anything or anyone on fire?"

"No."

"Did she record you?"

"No."

"Then let it go. Happens. Especially with novices." Even if the woman refused to believe Reed's dark eyes had been some trick of her mind, that she truly saw what she saw, what would she make of it? "In any case, who would believe her?"

Residences and corner stores, pedestrians and loiterers pass by as Kyle takes Reed south and west.

Kyle says, "What's happening to you, the memory loss, had happened to Marie. Isn't that what Aleron told us?"

By the end, Marie had no memory of her fiancé. In the penthouse suite, she shoved Aleron aside while he pleaded for her to stop her insane scheme. She refused. She was determined to have Reed.

"Right," Reed says, sitting taller and attentive in his seat. "She lost them all. But instead of birds, she was on a boat that went to pieces."

"And it took time. Months at least."

Nodding, Reed says, "I think so, but I don't have months. I don't have time left at all."

Kyle says, "But see my point? There's precedent. It isn't happening only to you. And maybe not only to Marie."

"So, what are you saying?"

"The Society has many members who have lived many lifetimes and learned many things. Odds are someone will know about the crows. But leave that to me. We need to find someone who can be discreet."

"Good. Good." Reed settles back into his silent state, head tipped against the glass, perhaps seeing the dark ribbon of the Schuylkill River or maybe not seeing anything at all.

After Kyle signals for an exit, Reed says to the glass pane, "We're going to Tamerlane?"

"Yes. Bound to be people there preparing for the masquerade. Remember the etiquette. Keep civil, be polite. You're not on a first-name-basis with them, so refer to members as Miss or Mister. Let them do the talking. Since you're the new one, there will be lots of questions. Be candid, except for one thing." Kyle pauses to ensure Reed is paying attention. "Do not, for your sake, do not speak to anyone there about your wanting to be human again. You want them to believe you've come around and will take the oath to join, fall in line, and be a good standing member."

"Why? I didn't ask for this. Let's call it a mistake, okay? Just undo it. Why should they care? I will tell them, look, I'm not going to make trouble, and I won't, Kyle. Lily and I won't tell a soul. And like you said, who'd believe us? Change me back and we'll forget it ever happened."

Kyle shakes his head, "You're not grasping a fundamental tenet of the Society: Being turned is voluntary. What Marie did to you—turning you without your consent—is not the way we do things here."

Kyle continues, "Undoing the change is not something that's been needed. I don't know, but maybe it's never been looked into."

"Lily had read online that when the sire is killed, all her children become human again."

"Online, huh? Well, that doesn't work. Believe me." The problem with the Rotters would have been solved long ago, if that were the case.

Reed says, "This is all crap. Right? Like you're all some regal, elite club, better than everyone. 'Exalted,' Alcott told me. But you're all killers. And you think because you have rules and etiquette that makes it okay?"

"You don't have to—"

"I know. I know. I don't have to kill, but you—" He cuts himself off. Quiet, he says, "Forget it."

"No, no, Reed. You've been chewing on this all night. Spit it out. Better here in the car than at Tamerlane. Finish what you were going to say. Tell me why you've been sulking since I came to your apartment."

Reed says, "You've killed before."

"A long time ago, yes."

"You murdered someone."

"Yes."

Kyle had known that by sharing his ichor with Reed he risked some part of his dark past coming to light. He isn't surprised Reed glimpsed such a memory, but he is more than disappointed.

Reed says, "Who was he?"

There had been countless men whose lives Kyle ended. But only one particular man Kyle had been thinking about last night.

Kyle brakes for the yellow light. "An accountant and a family man."

"You murdered someone with a wife and kids?"

Kyle only nods. Stanley Whittaker's creative bookkeeping had bought the rope from which he hanged himself. Kyle just delivered it coiled in a black leather bag.

But Mr. Whittaker was just a small stretch in the yards and yards of rope Kyle has bought for himself over the years. Rope long enough to hang himself from the top floor of Liberty Plaza. He has no illusions he will meet a more unpleasant end in time, but not before he makes right for so much of what he has done wrong.

Kyle says, "I am paying for it. And you're not the person to sit in judgment of me."

Reed says, "That would be Mrs. Whittaker. Does she know you're the one who killed her husband?"

Kyle grips the wheel tighter, "That's not your concern right now. Is it?"

Reed cuts his eyes at Kyle, "I want to know who I'm trusting—if I can trust him at all."

Kyle releases his fingers while waiting for green. "You trust me as I've trusted you. I saved your wife."

"You did, then you threaten her. See where trust is an issue?"

"I'm helping you now. Both of you. You both need to follow my plan or else I can't protect you. And like I told you before, I don't want to use the bond, but I will if it comes to it."

"I'm not sure about that either. I want to believe you, but back at The Challenge, you bet against me."

"No. I bet that you wouldn't go through with it. That you wouldn't drink from whomever Michael set you up with."

"How is that not the same thing?"

"You'd rather I believe you'd have no hesitation in hurting an unsuspecting stranger? An innocent person? That you'd bite them and drink their blood? You're a good man, Reed. Still. Even with all that went down. That's what I bet on."

***

On the grounds of Tamerlane, Kyle leads Reed to the rolling green between the old Georgian manor and the new house to its south. Between both, centuries-old maples and hickories shape an avenue that leads to the banks of the Schuylkill.

Like many initiates of First House, Kyle had not been aware of Tamerlane's existence until the approach of his Rite of Initiation. Few humans know of it either. Provided a daylight tour, Kyle noted the colorful gardens and fecund orchards, the stables that sheltered handsome horses, and a river landing. Coming here each time, even now, he is taken by the tranquility despite its improbable location within the city limits.

Though Lord Devlin has resided here for much of his and its own existence, he did not establish Tamerlane and never thought or cared to improve upon the manor. Either by design or some quirk, the antiquated building is a cell service dead zone.

Atop ladders human workers string lights through the boughs under the direction of Sebastian Milos and his wife, Vanessa. The pair throw entertaining galas for the Society of Brandywine, so planning and preparation for the masquerade is properly left to them.

When the couple notice Kyle and Reed approach, they leave the workers to their tasks.

Both are dark-haired and have Mediterranean complexions. Sebastian smooths his hair close to the scalp with pomade, while hers descends past her shoulders in waves. Taller than he, she's quite slender too, emphasized by the corseted waist. He's barrel-chested, the fingers of his large hands adorned by chunky rings and prismatic gemstones.

If the pair had told Kyle they had been the inspiration for Mr. and Mrs. Addams of the famed cartoon and television show, he'd believe them, less for their passing physical resemblance, and more for their affection for each other, from love pats to swooning embraces. Except for Society business that requires only him, they are always together. Though the Addamses are odd but wholesome, Kyle has heard that the Miloses are perversely wicked.

Speaking to Kyle, Sebastian tips his walking stick toward Reed, "I see that you have brought the fireworks."

So, word about what had happened last night at the Whitpain Hotel has gotten around. "Brother Sebastian, you wouldn't happen to have seen Brother Joseph around."

Vanessa says, "I am given to understand that Brother Joseph will not be attending. He is out of town."

Disappointed, Kyle considers who else can help Reed. "I'm going to make a call." He claps Reed's back, "Be gentle with him while I'm gone."

Kyle returns to his car and places a call.

When the other end picks up, he says, "Hello, Sister Emma."

"Why hello, Brother Kyle. An unexpected, but welcome call. How is your evening?" she says with her usual theatrical flair.

He says, "Fine."

"Perhaps it is the connection, but I am certain that I had heard a deep sigh beneath that syllable. I take it you are not calling to speak pleasantries with me as much as to ask for my insight on some matter. House business? I will listen in the vain hope that business turns personal."

"You read me well."

"Shall I say that I am hurt to be correct?"

"It isn't my pleasure to cause you pain, Emma."

"No, that is the Miloses' proclivity."

"Yes, well the call isn't for me, not directly."

"Hmm... does this pertain to your ward?"

"You already know about Mr. Williams?"

"Brother Thomas informed Sister Anne, who in turn informed Sister Catherine and word coursed through its usual channels."

"He needs your help."

"Dear me, the man isn't even a member and he already needs help? I would think you quite capable in your role as his sponsor."

"Would you rather come to Tamerlane or shall I bring him to your home?"

"I will be by once I change clothes—oh what shall I wear for you? Tell me what you are wearing. A suit, certainly, but what of its color and cut? I know you are partial to the herringbone pattern. I will find something complementary."

"Solid taupe, but you needn't dress especially for me."

"I most certainly will. We will need to do something about your penchant for earth tones."

"One night, I may surprise you."

"Indeed? And I expect to have your exclusive company at the masquerade. Agreed?"

"Emma—I'm not really ready for that."

He can hear hangers swish across a metal rod.

"Ah! I believe I have found what I will wear. Kisses."

chapter
six

Ms. Shipley

"You're a handsome one," Mrs. Milos says. She peers at Reed like a detached scientist cataloging her observations. Her husband does likewise, leaving Reed with the feeling he's a lab animal Kyle has donated for their experiments.

Their eyes keen, the couple approaches him; kids eager to learn by pulling apart.

His van Dyke beard oiled, black hair slicked back, Mr. Milos sizes him up, "Fit. Tall. Good jaw."

Reed doesn't believe anyone has remarked on his jaw before.

Her words accented, the woman says, "This is the impertinent one you had told me about?" Her eyes seem to take in every detail of him, counting each hair on his head.

In another language, perhaps Greek, Mr. Milos says something to his wife, then continues in English, "You should have seen his outburst before Lord Devlin. Whatever impression he made on Brothers Gideon and Alcott, I found myself astonished at his temerity. And I confess a touch of admiration. Devlin, however, did not appreciate, as he put it, the man's 'choleric disposition.'"

The woman's deep red lips curve into a smile at this, while her husband looks up at Reed, saying, "You dared Devlin to do his worst. Consider yourself fortunate for Gideon's intercession."

Reed says, voice dry, "Well, I wasn't in a good place then." In fact, he was at his lowest, believing Lily had been murdered. Possessed by fatalism, he didn't care about protocols and niceties and consequences.

The pair settle close together while their eyes move up and down Reed's body. Mrs. Milos says, "How are you and Brother Kyle finding one another's company?"

"Still figuring each other out."

"You understand that he is responsible for preparing you for your initiation? He is to educate you in the Society's customs, its Compact, the House by-laws, offices, and ranks."

Reed nods. "And how to survive on my own."

Mr. Milos says, "Certainly. Thus far you have survived on luck. Inevitably, however, fortune turns on its wheel. See to it that you learn from Kyle before you are crushed beneath it."

"I will."

"As the Master of Ceremonies, it will be I who will perform the initiation rites."

"When will that be?"

"When Kyle informs us that you are ready."

"Sounds formal."

"Formal, yes. Binding as well. Your oath will be held with the deepest trust among all."

The woman takes a step closer, arms folded, "I'm to understand your sire made you without your consent." With contempt, she adds, "The old way."

Reed shares the feeling, "Yeah."

"Yes." Her expression turns a degree sharper, "Do you believe you are well-suited for the gift given you, though you had no wish for it?"

Reed catches himself before sharing what he thinks of this gift. "I'm adjusting. Kyle is helping." *Where has he gone, anyway?*

Appearing to relax a touch, Mrs. Milos says, "Brother Kyle will instruct you on what the Society of Brandywine expects of its members. But it will be your choice to accept or not. It will be up to you to pledge loyalty, to promise to do what is asked, to sacrifice for the good of First House, and to commit yourself to our ways. This is not some civic club, lax and informal. We will not tolerate less than your utmost contribution."

Mr. Milos says, "Can you pledge your whole heart?"

"What?"

"Can you pledge your whole heart?"

"I will."

Mr. Milos absently taps his walking stick, "Hmm. We shall see."

Several workers, wearing identical coveralls and dark leather chokers, file away to another section, carrying toolboxes, ladders, and plastic buckets filled with cords and bulbs.

Mrs. Milos says, "Have you fed yet? Have you cut your teeth? Surely Kyle has helped you with this?"

"We're working on it."

"I recall my first feeding." Wistful, Mr. Milos plays at the curls of his mustache, "Young man. Dimitris, I believe. His blood sang with emotions—the right amount of pain and ecstasy. I do wish he were still living."

A shudder of revulsion escapes Reed.

"Oh, do not worry," Mr. Milos continues, "He died many years later as mortals do. A grandfather of twenty-three. His family had no earthly idea of their *pappoús*'s scandalous inclinations."

Turning to her husband, Mrs. Milos says, "Oh, remind me my love, who was that meal we had in the Orpheum?"

"You are speaking of the Vasilakis family. Crete, '64, if memory serves." He gives a laugh, "We dined for nights."

Her eyes drift closed for a moment. "Ah yes, their final performance."

While the pair reminisce in Greek, or whatever, with serene smiles, Reed considers the exits, tempted to slink away. *Where the hell is Kyle?*

Parting from her husband, Mrs. Milos circles Reed with measured steps, buff chippings of the Cotswold gravel crunching under her heels. "Brother Kyle seeks Brother Joseph. For himself?" When Reed turns his head, she continues, "Or for you? Are you having some difficulty? What distresses you? Won't you share with us?"

Hell, no. If Kyle had thought these two could be helpful, he wouldn't have walked off. To each of them, Reed says, "I'm fine."

Idly shining up the silver top of the stick with a scarlet handkerchief, Mr. Milos says, "Disturbing dreams, perhaps? You do not wish to say?"

Reed says nothing.

"An erif..." Mrs. Milos says at the edge of his field of view. "Indulge us please. Describe to us how it feels to be an erif."

Reflexively, Reed puts a hand to his heart. The heat is milder than earlier tonight. "Like my heart's sizzling in a pan when it's not roasting right in the fire."

She coos behind his ear. "Such delicious imagery," then moves on. "Do you enjoy pain?"

His head turns to follow her orbit. "No. Why would I?"

Picking up Reed's disbelief, Mr. Milos says, "Do not be so quick to dismiss. Pain instructs. It reveals weaknesses that must be fortified and limitations to be exceeded."

From behind him, Mrs. Milos says, "It's pleasure in another form. You may find it, as we do, most nourishing when drawn from others."

Both before and from behind him, they chatter in Greek like they are sharing a dessert, sweetness in their voices.

Mr. Milos smiles, "We are curious: Would you describe yourself as inclined to rashness?"

"No."

"Perhaps having a short fuse? Easily agitated as your behavior last night suggests?"

"Sometimes."

Mr. Milos says, "Do you like fire?"

His wife adds, "He is a fireman, my love."

With his admired jaw closed tight, Reed says, "To put them out."

Now at his other side, Mrs. Milos reveals sharp teeth. He winces, still finding it disturbing. Which is a good sign, isn't it? None of this is normal.

"Does fire not excite you? Quicken your blood?" By his shoulder, she peeks at him and her fingers dance, "Tell me you have not played with it."

He shakes his head, not liking the sudden twist in the conversation.

"Not even with a lover?"

"What the hell are you talking about?" He turns to see more of her.

She gives a coy shrug, "With candles, perhaps? Your partner holds one above you. Allows the wax to melt. Drip onto your skin. Drop by drop. Or..." She glides away, "Pass the candle under your feet, while its flame licks your toes."

Reed merely shakes his head.

She returns to her husband, who gives her a squeeze. "Not your pleasure?"

Mr. Milos holds his cane up to Reed's eyes. A stylized serpent embosses its silver top. "Perhaps your wife's pleasure then? Does she have a brand seared into her, marking her as yours?"

"Leave my wife out of this." His words fire off before he's aware of it. He cools his glare.

Far from being wounded, the pair smile even more. Mr. Milos says, "There it is. The spark of last evening."

Hands up in apology, Reed says, "I'm not really up for any more personal questions."

Mrs. Milos gestures that no apology is necessary. "But you are here for answers. Clearly, Kyle is doing his part to help you get them. His are good hands."

"Though..." Mr. Milos tucks away his pocket square.

"Yes?"

"Be careful of that short fuse."

***

Kyle's return and the Miloses' exit brings Reed relief.

Reed says, "Did you find anyone who can help me?" The way things have been going, he's expecting, 'No,' like a steel door clanged shut and locked.

"Yes. She's on her way here."

In silent appreciation and rising hope, Reed waits with Kyle on the gravel wash.

Finally, at the end of the long driveway, twin beams from headlamps sweep through the darkness, accompanied by a growling engine, the kind heard on a speedway. Reed can hardly believe what pulls up. A low-slung convertible Ferrari. By the look of it, a recent model year. The green two-seater glows in the lamplight, startling Reed to near envy.

As though Tamerlane's valet, Kyle steps to the driver-side door, opens it, and extends a hand. Reed hunches, hands in his back pockets, appreciating the sleek contours, clean lines, wide tires, while wondering how fast the car could slip through the air on a straightaway.

The sound of the car door shutting brings Reed's attention to the driver with her arms around one of Kyle's. Her blonde hair styled, she's dressed in a blouse and skirt. Her heavenly blue jacket complements the earthen color of Kyle's suit.

Kyle looks at Reed, curious. The woman, amused, says, "Like what you see? Perhaps I will let you drive it one night."

"Do not let him near the glove box," Kyle says.

Reed agrees that it's probably not a good idea, having broken the Audi's last night.

After Kyle makes introductions, his companion says to Reed, "A pleasure to meet you, Mr. Williams."

"Everyone's so formal. Reed's fine."

Taking his measure, the woman says, "Formal, yes. Courtesy, deference, and fellowship are foundational to the Society. All the more so here." With a bit of a smile she relents, "But as you are having a trying time, I will accede to your request. Reed. For tonight. However, you will refer to me as Ms. Shipley."

As she parts from Kyle, Ms. Shipley says to him, "Remember your promise..." Like words in a dreamy song, she finishes, "at the masquerade, you are all mine."

Reed follows the woman to the north side of the manor. Strings of cream-colored lights and solar-powered free-standing lamps light their way. A breeze sends dry leaves scuttling by.

"When you were here last night, did you have an opportunity to walk the grounds?" Ms. Shipley waves to each house, "This is Lord Devlin and Sister Catherine's residences."

She informs him that Lady Catherine was the one who conceived of the modern home's construction. Among its many charms, she made sure the house had plumbing and electrical systems sourced on the property, even geothermal heating. Designed for Society functions, the building has space for dancing, music, and games.

"Laborers maintain the groves and gardens year-round. All under Catherine's direction and gifted eye." She gestures for Reed to see sprawling plantings through or around sculptures and structures. According to her, the property does not hook up to the municipal works. The self-sufficiency impresses Reed.

"I've never heard of Tamerlane before."

"Few have. When the original city began expanding, biting westward, it swallowed the estate, none-the-wiser. You won't find it on any maps or in any public records."

They follow a brick path skimming a small pond.

"I thought a stroll might be just the thing. Have you met Catherine? She must be busy with preparations for tomorrow night. I am sure she will introduce herself to you, the talk of the House."

"I am, huh?"

"Certainly. Not flattering talk as it happens. Such is gossip." She shrugs: *What can you do?* "Still, wholly intriguing. To the first, Brother Gideon Thomas reported that you had been less than diplomatic with Devlin last night. That you shared, let us say, your unvarnished honesty and exhibited the quick temper that marks an erif.

"And to the second, the circumstances in which you find yourself. A teething waif without sponsorship."

"Teasing waif?"

"Teething. Pardon my attempt at an euphemism for the newly fanged. Waif is the common term, meaning that you have no standing with any House. That you are young and without a sire or sponsor."

They pass through a short, wooded way that opens near the river bank.

Ms. Shipley continues, "I was informed you are a fireman—a noble vocation."

Reed nods not only to dismiss the praise but to hurry things along. "Kyle said you can help me."

She says, "He may be referring to my facility with dreams. I, and my child, Brother Joseph, assist our fellow members smooth out any vexing personal issues."

Reed almost laughs, "Vampires need therapists?"

"Everyone needs a sympathetic ear. A few need help adjusting no matter how well prepared. Those unable to cope without their former attachments—family, human pastimes, the warmth of the sun—take their own lives within the first few decades. Seldom do we initiate the young and never children."

She continues, "I am not formally trained like Joseph, whose methods tend to the Jungian. But people find that I am easy to speak with and share what troubles them." She turns to him, eyes wide with interest, "Do you dream disturbing dreams?"

"I've been losing my memories. They're stolen. By birds."

Reed describes the nightmares that have plagued him for several nights. How he had begun as a stuffed scarecrow pinned to crossbeams. Crows gathered and stared at him like starved dogs before a thick raw steak. They wanted to pick him apart and gnaw his bones, and had for the most part. He ran and ran. And runs even now. Within himself he had found a white petaled flower. It was, he learned, what the crows wanted most.

Reed says, "It feels like a dream and real at the same time. Even when I'm awake I can feel them, scratching at me. I'm a half-empty bag of clothes. Sometimes I hear one cawing by my ear or I can feel the straw in my body."

He tells her that as he loses straw to the crows, he also loses memories.

"There's not much I can do but run. But they still come, they still try to take all that I have left."

"Would that be so bad?"

"You sound like Kyle."

Ms. Shipley pauses and looks at Reed as though he brought her a chocolate treat, "How so?"

Reed says, "He told me once that he wishes he could forget. I'm beginning to understand why."

Again, Ms. Shipley says, "How so?"

"I drank from him, his ichor. Some of what I saw... I learned something about him that I shouldn't have. His secret. I shouldn't talk about it."

Ms. Shipley doesn't press him, only saying, "I hadn't known. The sharing of ichor is a deeply personal act between two people, partly for the reason you touched on just now. Not something offered lightly. You must have impressed him and earned his trust."

Shaking his head, he says, "Not really. We were in a tight spot without any good options. I was thirsty, and he offered some to get by."

"Go on."

"I don't like knowing this about him. And I certainly don't like that he's got control of me like Marie did."

"You are referring to the bond. Has he abused that control?"

"No. But I can feel him in here." He taps the side of his head.

"That is because you are unused to the effects of the bond and because you are just learning about him. You will adjust.

"Of course, for your sponsor it has its practical side. As I had mentioned, we value our license. Destroying the bond had been one of the chief aims since the founding of the Society. However, we do recognize its utility and the special connection sire and their child share. As young vampires have much to learn, it is considered prudent to leave the bond alone for fifty years. Fifty years marks the half-way point between first and third degree."

Reed's eyes widen for a moment, his mind boggled by the idea of being bonded for fifty years. Remembering Kyle's words in the car, he says nothing.

She looks up into his eyes, "I hope you realize what an extraordinary offer Kyle gave you. I am envious."

He wipes his face, "And I repay him by being an ass."

"Oh, I would rather doubt that."

"I want to trust him. I know he's trying to help me."

For a moment, she says nothing. Then, "Thank you."

"For what?"

She resumes walking, "My admiration for Kyle has deepened by what you just shared with me." Brushing a fallen leaf from her hair, she continues, "I agree with you, however. What you have described to me does not sound like a dream. How often do these crows bedevil you?"

"I'm not sure. They seem to come when my back is turned. So to speak."

"Even while awake."

"Yes."

"And when did you last experience this?"

"Today. Tonight. Just before coming here."

The woman considers, "Have you lost only human memories? That is to say, have you forgotten any of your vampire experiences since leaving Paris?"

"No."

Ms. Shipley says, "And when you saw those crows this evening, was the lily still there?"

"Yes. I still had it. It looked just as fresh as ever; all of its petals were there."

Ms. Shipley falls silent as they draw near a stone bench. She sits, nods for him to do so, and smooths her skirt. After he sits beside her, feeling the solid coolness, she says, "Have you seen the birds *eat* the straw?"

"Yes. Wait." He considers, trying to recall what the birds did with the stolen straw. "No, now that you mention it. I always assumed that they did. Does that mean something?"

"Reed," she pats his knee, then says, "What do birds do with straw and twigs?" like the answer is the most obvious thing in the world.

Finally catching on he says, "Build nests."

"Correct."

"You think they took the straw someplace to build a nest?"

"Perhaps. Worth considering that your memories may not be truly lost, but misplaced and can be recovered."

"How?"

"I cannot say. Have you heard of lucid dreaming? That is when the dreamer is aware that they are dreaming and may thereby direct the course of the dream. It takes practice."

Adjusting her feet beneath the stone bench, she says, "I suggest you learn to guide your scarecrow. Take control. Don't run pell-mell from the birds."

"How do I take control?"

"Our wills are powerful, Reed. It takes will to come back from death. It takes will to survive, endure, stand against time, hone our abilities."

Turning fully to face him she says, "We will exercise your mind to build defenses stronger than you have now. I shall instruct you in some techniques. Shall we begin our session?"

"What, now?"

"Unless you wish to—"

"No, no. Now. Now."

Her tongue plants inside her cheek, seeming amused by his eagerness. "We will begin with breathing. Even though we do not require it, I find focusing on our breath helps ease us into a state of relaxation. Inhale. Exhale. Inhale. Exhale. Yes, good. Slower, slower."

Reed follows Ms. Shipley's guiding voice, "Relax. Breathe with intention. In—slowly-counting-to-ten-then exhale likewise. In and out as you close your eyes and let your mind settle. Do not dwell on anything but your breathing."

Eyes closed, Reed struggles to empty his mind, but he can't clear the room. Thoughts shove one another for his attention. Might he truly find relief from the birds? Is Ms. Shipley right that his memories still exist someplace? How would he find them? What can he do against so many birds?

"Reed," Ms. Shipley says gently, "You're not relaxing. I can see thoughts racing across your face."

"I'm sorry. I've not meditated before."

She chuckles, "That much is obvious. Just continue breathing. Don't let other thoughts intrude."

Patiently, through a number of faltering attempts, Ms. Shipley guides him to calmness, stillness. When he feels his anxiety creeping back or impatience urging him to move, he concentrates more to send them away.

After a time, Ms. Shipley's soft words reach him. "Enough for tonight." When he opens his eyes, he finds her offering an encouraging smile. She says, "A good effort but you will need to practice. Practice until you can reach a relaxed state more quickly and maintain it for a longer period of time."

He rises to his feet. She does the same, "At the masquerade, we can work on lucid dreaming."

"Definitely. Yes. Thank you."

On their way back to the parking area of the estate, Reed says, "Can this training protect me against the bond?"

"The advantage goes to the sire. It's fundamental to our makeup. For the casual exchange, such as the one you share with Kyle, it may be possible."

"Can people do it? I mean, human beings?"

"Anyone can fortify their willpower."

In the final yards to Kyle, who is pocketing his phone, Ms. Shipley says to Reed, "Thank you for entrusting to me what you have shared, which I shall keep between us."

"I hope I didn't make things awkward between you and Kyle."

She clasps his hands in hers before parting, "Not at all. You are dear to be concerned but need not. I wish you good luck with your birds."

seven

Someone Died Behind Driscoll's Diner

Roxy Marchetti loves heights. Few buildings rise above four stories in this part of South Philly rewarding Roxy with a wide view of the night sky where stars throw off their velvet covers and wink back at her.

Here on her rooftop she can clear her mind. On the edge, on one foot, Roxy leans out. Her free foot traces, *rond de jambe*, the emptiness beyond. Should she tip her body farther, shift her center off just a fraction more... She thrills in this suspended moment, muscles taut through her core, senses alert that she's a hair's breadth from plummeting.

She doesn't wish to fall. She needs to fly. So many nights she's certain she *can* fly. One *grand jeté* into space, unbound. After all, fire ascends and so must she. Her bird would catch her, hold her aloft like a dance partner into the twinkling stars. She can feel her true companion stretch its wings, scalding her insides, wanting to burst free.

Since waking this evening, heat sizzles beneath her skin. Actually, when she thinks about it, it's been building for the past couple of nights. Her phoenix wants out.

But soon she draws her foot back, first position, and holds her balance. She will have to fly some other night.

Someone died behind Driscoll's Diner.

She doesn't want to think about that. He's dead. Whoever he is. Nothing can be done for him. And nothing more Roxy can do.

Time to dance.

Roxy hops down, on the safe side, the half-foot drop. Pacing off from the parapet, she glances back at her perch. Still tempted to lean forward, arms back, fingers splayed, bolt for the brick hurdle and launch into space, come what may. Foolish trust that her bird will catch her.

Instead, eyes cast down to a file of candles. A dozen pillars unlit but for the first one.

Slipping in earbuds she then draws out her phone and queues up her songs. Upon the first notes, Roxy, not for the first time, marvels at the technology unimaginable in her tender years of heavy hand-cranked gramophones. Now from a device, mere ounces in her pocket, endless sonic bliss.

Karen had helped her compile this playlist. She's on an electro-swing kick, its strutting pop. The swagger and energy recall the music of her youth, the never-closed clubs with house music she'd peek into, the speak-easies, and later, the desperate dance marathons.

Someone died behind Driscoll's.

Roxy presses play.

For a few minutes she remains in place, feeling the beat, letting it smooth down her body as though she's immersing herself into a warm pool head-first. Her body finds the groove and moves.

"Let's go."

Stirred by air currents the single flame dances too. Warmed up by the first song, Roxy moves to a position down the line from the lit candle. She turns balletic leaping in parallel with the file of candles. The flame brightens and leaps with her. From one wick to the next. At times when she's closer, the flame puffs up and reaches toward her like a fan hoping to touch its idol.

Someone died.

Roxy loses a step. The flame fizzles. Then she stops cold.

Two nights ago, a news app declared: GRUESOME DISCOVERY IN SOUTH PHILLY.

Such a headline is all too common in a city like Philadelphia, like Chicago where she had grown up. A murder in the city results in the shaking of talking heads, but not the raising of their eyebrows. Vendettas, turf battles, injured pride, desperation.

But Driscoll's is where her roommate, Karen, waitresses. In their neighborhood. On Roxy's turf.

Karen shared what she had heard while pouring coffee and listening to her regulars. The body was male and had no ID. Police offer nothing more than boilerplate and that the investigation is ongoing. Officers Tyson and Burke won't give her a hint either.

Karen had said, "Someone told someone, who told me that the heart was missing from the body."

Roxy's eyes darkened, "Do we know who it was?"

"No one's saying. No one thinks it's gang-related. No one's taking credit. But that's not the weird part."

"Missing heart's not enough?"

"Now the body's missing too. Stolen from the morgue. Which doesn't make sense. Who'd kill someone, leave the body, then lift it later?"

Roxy had decided to let the matter go.

Roxy is going to let the matter go.

She is letting her hand go to her pocket. She takes out the digital gramophone again. Time for a different playlist. Something to match the firebird's current vibe. Something frenetic. Something with heat. Something to dissipate her own energy.

Roxy slashes across the rooftop to salsa beats. The candle flame, invigorated, jounces wick to wick leaving a bit of itself behind so that soon the whole file is alight.

She's going to stick to the now.

Last night, she did what she could.

Over a meal of zucchini pasta, her latest food fad, Karen updated Roxy on what she had heard. Not much as it turned out. Just ongoing investigations and the request that anyone with information on the identity of the victim or those who may have knowledge of the murder to call the tip line, where they will remain anonymous and will not be required to testify in court.

The garlic and olive oil in Karen's dish of zoodles, grape tomatoes, organic chicken, and fresh Parmesan smelled of home, of family, of Roxy's mother removing fat garlic bulbs that had been roasting in the oven. Roxy could only savor the pungent odor. Karen got to eat it.

"Probably just a random killing," Roxy said to Karen as the woman drained the last of her single glass of box wine. "Probably just a shotgun blast to the guy's chest. Not much of a heart after that."

Pushing her chair back, Karen stood, collected her wine glass and plate, then carried them to the sink, "Yeah. But…" After a quick rinse, she turned to Roxy, "Why was the body taken?"

A good point that still unsettles Roxy.

So, Roxy had spent the night asking around. Tony at a pizzeria on 9th Street, Joey at a chophouse on Fitzwater, a different Tony at another pizzeria also on 9th Street; the bartenders at the Dumont Bar and Stella's; and where people gathered around barrel fires, sharing stories and songs.

One tidbit, unconfirmed, was this: there was no blood—not in the body, not on the body, not around the body.

This told Roxy it's worth looking into more. Hard to cut out a pound of flesh without letting blood.

She becomes distracted and by the end, the flames return to their natural rhythms.

Or there was never any blood to begin with.

Someone.

Who?

Roxy taps the end of her index finger on her lower lip. Who could take the body from the city morgue? Roxy bets she knows. And if she's right, he'll be paying her a visit.

***

"What the hell are you wearing?" One hand on her cocked hip, Roxy's other hand, fingertips together, shakes the air in sardonic incredulity.

Johnny Vo says, "It's a costume. I'm a pirate." Cargo pants, boots, silk shirt with more ruffles than a flamenco dancer's dress. If she squints just right, he might pass as an extra from a Douglas Fairbanks swashbuckler film.

"You think you look like a pirate?"

Typically, Johnny Vo inhabits a tackle box. Nested compartments and pockets upon pockets, some open wide others buttoned or zippered shut, stitched onto canvas, denim, cotton. Probably a pouch or two in the deep hoods. And always those gloves.

Another vampire in the heart of Philadelphia, the man lives south of Washington Avenue, south of her and Karen's home. Like her, Johnny Vo is unaffiliated. No Society of Brandywine membership card, secret handshakes, or commemorative enamel plates for them.

As he tells it, he's an entrepreneur of select recently liberated artifacts. Even has a website. He's the one people see about for a lost or rare item or valuable information.

Fingers like flypaper, he compulsively pockets things. Roxy has made it clear to Johnny Vo should he ever lay a finger on anything of hers she'll burn his ass.

"What's wrong with it?" He flips up the eye patch and reties the red bandanna, briefly exposing his short dark hair.

"First, why are you even dressed like this?"

"It's Halloween."

"It is not Halloween. And the wait-staff at Front Street Shanty look more authentic. In fact, I would think of all people, you could get your hands on something more convincing." She stops herself and takes a breath. "You know what, forget it. Let's get back to the task at hand."

"Fine, lady."

She makes a hurried motion with both hands, "So, get to work."

They stand in the small lot behind Driscoll's Diner. Whatever amount of yellow police tape had once cordoned off the area, only tatters remain stuck to a pole. Nothing else indicates a crime scene. No chalk outline of a body or numbered markers that investigators place beside shoe prints and blood spatters. Just broken beer bottles and crushed beer cans that never made their way to the blue recycling bins.

"Where?"

"Everywhere."

"I have to touch something."

"So, start getting handsy."

"I'm not touching this shit." He sniffs and scowls as though getting a sudden whiff of an outhouse on a hot-as-blazes afternoon. "It may be shit. And piss and worse."

Even so, he works on his gloves. He doesn't like to bare-touch anything casually. His gloves are special-made so that he can peel, banana-like, the fingers. He needs skin-to-target contact to work, so he says.

Roxy puts her hands on her hips and looks about. The delivery truck would have pulled up there. The delivery boys would unload fresh food-stuffs and discover the body. "How about keep to this area," she draws with gestures to indicate roughly a thirty-foot stretch behind the diner.

"It's been, what, two or three nights now? What do you expect to find?"

"I don't know what."

"Truthfully, without the body here there isn't much for me to pick up on."

True, a body would be helpful. At least she'd have a face, and should either of them recognize that face, then they'd have a name.

"Are you sure he was a vampire?"

Roxy looks sharp, "Who said anything about him being a vampire?"

"I just figured."

"Do you already know something?"

"No."

"Vo?"

"I don't. If he was human, you and I wouldn't be having this conversation, would we?" He glances at her sidelong. "Why do you care anyhow?"

Her expression sours, but she covers by adding an edge to her voice, "If I find out you are holding out on me."

"If I knew something, you know what I'd say." Now fully facing her, "I'd say, 'Cash or trade.'"

Roxy mouths his words, shaking her head on each syllable. "Yeah. Yeah. Yeah." Often perishable, information has to be sold quick and to the right person. For Johnny Vo, the right person is the customer right in front of him.

Heads bowed, both step carefully as though a missed eggshell of evidence will be crushed underfoot. His eyes have shifted, taking on a black gleam. She hopes something turns up here—some clue that investigators had overlooked or dismissed as unconnected to the murder. That's why she had thought to call on Johnny Vo. He can glean psychic information imprinted on an object, typically in the form of powerful emotions, like a beloved teddy bear filled with a child's dreams or a weapon filled with the dying man's terror. Sometimes he senses echoes of the object's past or impressions of its owner.

"Wouldn't a violent demise get captured?"

"Captured by what is the question."

Her lips twist in thought.

"If there was a struggle, then fear or anger might have long enough to linger here. But what if it was sudden? Like a literal heart attack. Then he's dead too quickly. It would be better to have something personal. We'd have better luck if you had what he was wearing; or a personal item like a watch or jewelry or a rabbit's foot. And speaking of watches—I have some new inventory."

With a different approach in mind, she says, "Do you know of any of us who's missing?"

"I'm here—that's what matters."

"You, me, Mikhail, Dewey. Bernadette's been quiet."

"Well, she's flighty. Plus, she's a woman and the body was male."

"If he was a Society type, wouldn't they be looking for us?"

"Mr. Alcott Ashton, for certain. You're right, that would be telling in of itself."

As she's heard it, before she arrived in the city, First House had little tolerance for non-members. As in none. But things have gone lax. Perhaps the little war First House had with the Camden vampires changed their tune. Whatever the reason, they fell out of the habit of policing their "territory."

Should Alcott or any of the other Society members get it into their heads to resume cleaning out the town's riffraff, she'll be damned if she goes. They had their chance decades ago. Roxy would have shipped without complaint then. Not going to remain where she's not wanted. But now that she's set down roots here, she's good and tight. Besides, she likes getting under his English skin and sometimes his shirt.

She says to Johnny Vo, "Aren't you curious?"

"Hey, as long as it's not me that's dead. I don't think it's wise to look too deeply into it."

"What if he were a friend of yours?"

"I don't have friends. I have clients."

"We aren't friends?"

"Why is this important to you?

Neither answers the other's question.

Hunched, Roxy plods across the littered asphalt. Oil stains, a drip of tar, a torn hoagie wrapper with a phosphorescent yellow hot pepper still stuck to it.

Johnny Vo shadows her. From the corner of her eye, she can see him going through the motions, which seem half-hearted. He doesn't believe there's anything to find. And he's right. Looks like what the crime scene crew didn't collect was either taken by passers-by or thrown out.

And why *does* she care? It had rankled Roxy that he even asked, even though it was a fair question. Let humans kill one another—not her business. But this area of blocks that comprise Bella Vista, has become home to her. Yes, over the years much has changed; the people, the storefronts, the feeling that something isn't quite as bright as before. Still. It's a city with a nightlife. People are out here having fun. A community.

"Hello." Near shards of a Snapple glass bottle, Vo finds a tube. First glance, she mistakes it for a piece of discarded drug paraphernalia, but closer, she can see it's a test tube.

Roxy presses the glass between thumb and middle finger. A hairline crack three inches from the open end. Next to her now, Johnny Vo tracks her as she rises.

"Alchemical symbols," he says. At the bottom third are etchings.

"You can read them?"

"No. I'm a pirate not a wizard." He cautiously touches the glass. "Not merely decorative. There's something very faint here."

"What?"

"You know what."

"You skinny-ass, piece of—"

"Maybe Mr. Ashton will be interested."

"Fine. Trade. Trade. We'll settle up at my place. And work on getting your Jolly Roger on."

eight

Roommates

"**O**w!!"

Roxy has Johnny Vo by the ear, now skewered with a sewing needle. Twisting, sliding the needle through the lobe, though not completely to keep the new hole plugged for the moment.

She picks up a small gold ring, brings it close, then swaps it with the needle.

"I should have gotten clip-ons," he says.

In her bedroom, selections of Gilbert & Sullivan play out at a quarter of the volume she'd otherwise prefer. Still, inspiring the look she's going for. A better costume was her trade for the information he gleaned from the test tube. He explained it well enough without needing to raise his voice over, "The Major-General's Song."

Seated at the vanity, Johnny Vo wears a pair of aquamarine track pants she found in the 1990s geological strata of garments piled inside her closet. Lower legs snipped off with shears, the baggy pants only come past his knees, tucked into striped stockings. With his own ankle boots, ruffled blouse, bandanna, and now rings, he's on his way to joining the stage.

Roxy flings away the eye patch. "Now the eyebrow…"

Roxy's adorned with the tricolor of the Italian flag. The green, white, and red silk robe had been a gift from Mrs. Buzzi, brought back from one of her trips with her husband to the Old Country. They sell imported food-stuffs from their specialty grocery store.

Vo grouses long after she's done puncturing him. More than once she presses him back into his seat when he appears ready to jump ship.

She dips into Karen's make-up collection used for her film projects. If the man has two whiskers, she can't find them. She'll rough in a five o'clock shadow to go along with the eyeliner.

As she works, she can hear her roommate returning home from class, so she further dials down the music. Keys plunked down in a small porcelain dish on a shelf by the door, sneakers squeaking on the hardwood floor, the tap running and filling a glass (got to keep hydrated), coat put away in the closet.

"Up here," Roxy shouts over Johnny Vo's head.

Roxy applies the last brush strokes to Johnny Vo's smooth jaw line when Karen appears in the bedroom doorway. She's looking at her phone though, tap-taps some text message before she deigns to glance their way, finally. The woman is twenty-four, but sometimes has the attitude of a fifteen-year-old.

"What do you think?"

Johnny Vo springs from his seat. A flourish. A bow.

She says, "Great," offers a thumbs up, then turns back to the stairs. Tap tap tap. Tap. Tap...

Roxy scrutinizes her work. "Maybe I should pencil in a scar."

***

After Johnny Vo leaves the rowhouse, and Roxy comes downstairs, the kettle on the stove whistles. Waving for Karen to keep seated, Roxy moves to the kitchen, turns off the heat and grabs a colorful glazed mug, which really resembles a bowl with a handle.

Roxy pours the hot water and dunks a bag of tea in, "Did you eat?"

In their agreement, Karen had promised never to let anyone into Roxy's bedroom and Roxy promised never to slash Karen's throat. With their boundaries established, Karen moved in and they have been best friends ever since.

Karen does the errands, gets every shelf of the refrigerator, and every shelf of the cupboards, though they're seldom more than a third full, and control of the thermostat. Roxy covers utilities; Karen covers the phone plans.

Roxy repeats, "Did you eat?"

"Yes, mom. I ate with Trudy. We split a pizza and a Coke. She says, 'Yo,' by the way." Karen raises a hand, thumb and pinky out to relay Trudy's salutation.

"How's her mother?"

"Busy not being one."

Since moving to Philadelphia many years ago, Roxy vowed to herself that she'd be the best neighbor by channeling her passion in more constructive ways like dancing, helping the needy, and bouncing out criminals. Yes, she still starts fires. Small ones. Elsewhere. No more than once a week. Controlled. Mostly. Truly, she does her best. She isn't a blessed saint.

Once the tea has steeped, she brings the mug out to the living room, setting it on the coffee table within easy reach.

"Still bad, huh?" Roxy liked that Karen and Trudy were friends. The poor teen lived essentially alone. "She reminds me of me." Well, after her father had died and her mother's baby blues darkened to twilight. And soon the Depression put most everyone in the same boat. All in the same cramped, leaky boat.

Distracted with the phone tapping, Karen says, "So do I. So does every lost girl. You like to collect us strays. You'd make a great cat lady if you ever got old."

"She needs me." Roxy counts off duple meter then spins away. She still has energy from the clue she discovered and her phoenix delights in the balletic movements.

"No. She needs her mother to get clean."

Roxy springs behind Karen, "I could be her mother."

"No, you can't. Trudy needs someone who can make her breakfast and take her to school, meet with her teachers and doctors. You know— during the day."

Observing Roxy, Karen reaches to untie her cushiony sneakers, then kicks them off. "You're revved to go." Her toes curl and uncurl.

Roxy plunks down on the couch, "I'm hot. How am I going to burn this energy off?" The bird within her struts like the cock of the walk, filling her chest with heat.

Nodding to the front door, Roxy says, "He was able to shed some light our little mystery."

"I thought you were letting it go. Do tell."

"First, promise we'll go out tonight."

"All right, but you've got to help with this scene."

"*Va bene.* Scene, mystery, dancing."

"No. You can't tease me like that. Mystery, scene, dancing."

Roxy tells Karen about recruiting Johnny Vo, meeting him behind Driscoll's, his appalling attempt at a costume—

"You mean, it was worse than what you—. Never mind, continue."

Roxy mock chuckles, then pauses till the moment Karen's about to yell for her to speak. "We were getting nowhere, then the moment we were about to forget the whole thing, we find this…"

She reaches into her bustier and withdraws the slender cracked glass tube with mystical markings.

Karen leans forward, "From a chemistry set?"

"A test tube by the look of it. On the ground I thought it was a pipe. When he touched it, Johnny Vo said he could sense traces of something."

"Traces of what?"

"Vamp blood. Too little and too old for him to get a sense of who it was or anything. But! He also said there was something else there."

To Johnny Vo, Roxy had downplayed his revelation as mildly interesting, less news, more like confirmation of her suspicion. "I figured the guy was a vampire," she had said to him. But inside, Roxy relished the idea that she might have information that the Brandies do not. And if that's so, oh boy, will she have Alcott by his little Ashtons!

More interested now, Karen says, "So our character Dead Guy Behind the Diner is now Undead Guy Behind the Diner. So, what are you thinking now? Killed by another vamp? Oh! Maybe there's a hunter?"

Roxy shakes her head, "Whoever this character was, it's unlikely that I know him. So, hard to say."

By the time Karen finishes her tea, the pair had batted around different scenarios that might have led to Undead Guy Behind the Diner's being found there and who would have smuggled the body out of the city morgue. According to Tyson and Burke, theft of a body from the coroner's office is a big deal, but they wouldn't disclose anything about that or the murder itself that wasn't already publicly known.

For now, Roxy will pocket the clue right back into her brassiere. The fact that the body certainly was a vamp motivates Roxy to learn more. Also, that Alcott will pay her a visit, and that need to get to a club soon before Roxy burns their couch.

Karen reminds Roxy of the scene run-through.

"You read with me. You can even get into character. But first, can you get me a glass of water?"

Karen's phone dings, wanting attention while Roxy heads back to the kitchen. No doubt it's Oliver texting her.

"Is that what's-his-name?" Roxy teases. She rinses the mug under the faucet then fills it, hearing Karen tap-type her messages. Her back resting against the kitchen counter, she watches Karen smile and laugh and type and repeat.

That would be, yes.

From the few times she has met Oliver, Roxy has been... unimpressed. Handsome, sure. Enough that he should be in front of the camera in some supporting role, instead of working on sets for Karen and her fellow students. But could the man deliver lines? He sounded street, but not too bright. He sounded like a hustler—too full of himself. More than once, she's caught him gazing her way, imagining God-knows-what. If he wasn't dating Karen, and if he dialed back the crude compliments, she might be flattered.

Oliver volunteered his manpower to the set design, for which Karen has paid him unlimited fries at the diner. Then, what pays for his high-dollar clothing, watches, and the gifts he provides Karen? Roxy has no idea.

With the phone now back on the table, Roxy returns with the mug of water, reminding herself that she's not Karen's mother and it's not her business whom she dates. Karen likes him and that will have to be good enough.

After a gulp of water in preparation for reciting lines, Karen pulls out a screenplay from the binder, snaps off the clamp holding the pages together then splits the pages, handing one set to Roxy.

"Just read with me. Something's not right, but I can't pin it down. Stupid assignment. I hate sci-fi."

"You like *Metropolis*."

"I do."

She does. She likes silent films and early talkies just as Roxy does. A period of wonderful experimentation, art, and lax codes.

Roxy remembers her child-self seated with her parents in a rowdy Chicago theater, filled with live musical accompaniment, lost popcorn below her dangling feet, her mouth struck open as wide as her eyes, enraptured by the screen and all the wonders that played on it.

After a few read-throughs, Roxy taps the point of her finger into the sheets, "You know what this is. It's similar to the plot of *Mission to Venus*.

Why don't you refocus the story on Astra instead? Have it from her point of view. Then you can cut out the recruitment scene."

"Not bad. Yeah." With a red pencil Karen puts down notes on the pad. Karen wants to be behind the camera full time, but as a student she needs to round out her experience. And being a starving artist, she has to wear many berets to get her short films together—actor, writer, costumer, location scout, editor, sound engineer… Exhausting. A wonder she has the energy to also wait tables at Driscoll's.

"Okay, okay," Karen says by way of apology to Roxy. "Let me type up the revisions and we'll go over it again." Fresh pages roll out of the printer set on a bookcase shelf. Handing Roxy her new copy, Karen says, "This time with feeling."

chapter

nine

The Jolt

K aren taps her knuckles on Roxy's bedroom door. "Almost ready?"
"Yeah." Roxy primps in front of her vanity mirror, catching sight
of her friend, who appears quite the coquette. She has woven her hair into
two golden brown braids. Roxy has always envied her friend's long locks
which mock her own permanent bob. So, she pins it back with bright
colored barrettes.

Karen says, "Is that my dress?"

Roxy wears a slinky silver dress.

Roxy nods, "Your sole qualification for living here is our shared dress
size." They also appear the same age. Roxy passes herself off as Karen's
slightly older sister.

Actually, Karen's sole qualification has been that Roxy trusts the
young woman. Trust is crucial.

After the pair met, they discovered their shared interests in cinema
and music. And when Karen heard that Roxy distributes needed items to
homeless folks living in the area, she insisted on helping. Surprised, Roxy
hadn't known how to react, having done the errands alone for years. No
sensible reason came to Roxy's mind to refuse the help, so she agreed.

Soon Karen would collect donated goods or purchase the items after her shift on the way home, saving Roxy time. Partners, they'd make their rounds and Karen became familiar with neighbors she'd otherwise never meet.

As their trust grew, Roxy confided to her that she had been homeless once upon a time. The experience taught her much about desperation and resilience. She had claimed not to remember a lot of specific moments. For a time, no one looked after her, and she had to learn to be an adult real quick.

Karen listened without judgment, giving Roxy a glimpse of what life was like to have a true friend. She hadn't had one for a long time, and not one here in the city.

Drawn by the woman's energy, Roxy found herself looking forward to their evenings together, at least those not consumed by Karen's double shifts or school work.

Roxy isn't infatuated with Karen, though the woman has many attractive qualities. Karen is a sister Roxy has never had, which makes things simpler.

No, another woman fascinates Roxy. A painter framed by the window Roxy would gaze through on occasion. Perched on a rooftop across the way, Roxy was always thankful the woman finished well before sunup. Otherwise, captivated, Roxy would miss the sky pass from dark to light.

Karen says, "What do you think?" She twirls to show off her green dress and low-heeled shoes.

"Hmm. Add some bangles."

Karen's phone beeps.

"Is it Oscar?"

"You know, if you keep joking, you're going to end up calling him that," Karen says. Tapping. Then her mouth twists. "Shoot."

"What?"

"He says he'll be late, but save him a dance."

***

No sign adorns the grey steel door of the underground nightclub, The Jolt. Past it, down the dark red hallway, off on the left, another steel door thumps in its frame. The porthole of the door permits a view of dancing patrons and mobbed bartenders.

Karen and Roxy dance amongst the kinetic crowd. Every person here does their own thing, sometimes with their eyes closed as though letting the music caress them, possess them, transport them. Others are wide-eyed, performing courtship displays for their partners and friends, their moves acrobatic.

Men saunter up, dancing before one or both of them. Roxy doesn't mind at all, allowing them to try to impress her. But she keeps an eye on Karen. If the guy slides too close, touches her funny, Roxy twitches, ready to seize the man and throw him. But Karen shows no distress tonight, enjoying the men's attention. Hand beside her mouth she'd shout that she has a boyfriend leaving it to each to walk away, or stay, unconcerned or perhaps not believing her, an unspoken: *Why isn't he here?*

Winded, Karen grabs Roxy to take a time-out at the bar. Roxy orders for her. A cosmopolitan arrives and Roxy slides it over to her friend. Over the amped-up music, they shout in conversation, half-hearing what the other says.

Karen doesn't need reminding, but Roxy tells her again to never accept a drink from a man in this place. Drugs won't work on Roxy, but she remembers the times when she was low and reckless and human, she'd down almost anything. Bathtub gin could be lethal.

Roxy chides herself for mothering. She'd rather just be an awesome sister partying with her best friend without a care. It's a balance she's still figuring out.

While Karen checks her phone between raising herself up on her stool like a periscope, searching for Oliver, Roxy wonders if she might see her anonymous girl. Once Roxy had spotted her here, but could not catch her before she left. Thoughts of the woman make Roxy feel what Karen feels—young, excited, vulnerable, in the moment, delighted by romance.

Karen says, "There he is!"

Roxy doesn't see him and turns to say so, but Karen is already off her stool. Roxy watches her friend skim the edge of the dance floor to the far side of the room.

Perched on her butt on the bar's edge, Roxy spots him. He's wearing a flashy shirt and a white brim cap, looking stupid. He's just spoken with a guy, they slap hands and the man walks away.

Karen has crossed her arms. It's hard to see, but she doesn't look pleased. Oh, poor Oliver. Karen is sweet, but she's no shrinking violet. If he's done her wrong, she'll let him know.

He smiles, but it flinches away. Now she's demanding to know something by the way she gestures with her arms. He steps back, put on his back foot by her reprimand. He shakes his hands, smiling again, like: *No, no, baby. You have me all wrong.*

He explains to her why she's mistaken, dropping one hand into the palm of the other to emphasize each point. His posture's patronizing, leaning over like he's talking to a girl, not a woman.

Her arm shoots straight up ending with a twirl of her hand, then one of her body, her back now to him. "We're done here."

Oliver grabs Karen before she can finish storming off, drawing her back to him. She slaps away his hands then shoves his chest. He doesn't budge. He gives her a look of pleading.

Back and forth. Jerk. Baby, I'm sorry. We're through. Don't be like that.

She walks away again and this time, Oliver makes a mistake. He cuffs her by her upper arm, hauling her back that she nearly topples. Karen spits at him. He glares and slaps her across the face.

Roxy's off, leaping her way over to her friend who's doubled over, holding her hot face. Roxy's hot too, the bird stretching out her wings, singeing Roxy's chest.

She can see Oliver stammer. He appears torn between reaching for Karen and slinking away.

Roxy pulls Karen to her and checks her face, which is red and wet with tears. "Are you okay?"

Karen nods, takes a moment, then snags Roxy with her gaze, mouthing a firm, "Don't."

Don't?

Karen grips Roxy tight, pulling her closer, not wanting Roxy to leave her. Oliver must have knocked out Karen's capacity for sound judgment. He's talking, but keeping his distance. Roxy pins him with a human glare instead of a vampire one.

"Don't vamp out." Karen tries to push Roxy back toward the bar. "I told him we're so over. He's not worth it."

Roxy allows Karen to guide her back to their seats, but at the last minute, she whirls away and stalks after Oliver, who skulks for the exit.

"Hey!"

Just as Oliver turns to see who shouted, she shoves him. He smacks against the wall. She presses up against him, her face turned up into a sneer, "You hit my friend."

"Whoa. Easy, girl." He's not looking at her, instead he's checking around himself, to see who may be watching. Does the man have street cred on the line? She grabs his face by the chin, "Karen wants me to behave. I don't want to. So do both of you a favor: Apologize."

"Sorry," he says, swatting her hand away and turning to go for the steel door.

She blocks his way, surprising him that she's fast on her feet. "Not to me, *coglione*. To Karen. Now."

He barely glances Karen's way, "Whatever. Sorry." Smug, he looks at Roxy as though to say: *Satisfied?*

She steps aside and motions for him to continue on his way.

Oliver straightens, his swagger returning. He pushes through the steel door into the red hall. Before he knows it, Roxy is behind him, her hand capturing his right one, the other hand grabbing the shoulder of his jacket.

In the hall, she flattens him against the wall as though she was a police officer subduing a suspect. Her hands warm up, but she holds back her fangs. Music swells and subsides with people going through the swinging door. The two of them must look the sight—the slight-bodied Roxy pinning the larger man against the wall.

"Get off me!" Oliver tries for leverage so he can get free of her, but she squeezes his hand and smacks him against the wall again. "Stupid bitch!"

"Hey, I'm not stupid." She spins him in place, shoves him again, and captures his right hand with both of hers. Before he can recover, she snaps his little finger. He screams.

"I'm going to break every bone in your hand one by one."

"Ms. Roxy Marchetti," a familiar voice calls out from behind them. "I have need to speak with you."

It's a man's firm voice and she relishes Oliver's frightened expression turn to one of hope that he's being rescued. Playing it up, she says, "Uh-oh, I'm in trouble: The vice-principal's here." Keeping her gaze on Oliver, she calls out to Alcott Ashton, "Teaching a lesson, here. See me after class."

"Now." His voice has the edge that's all business. Like a dare.

She breaks Oliver's ring finger. Its popping sound overtaken by his scream. Sweating now, Oliver gives another satisfying cry, "Get her off me!"

She can hear Alcott step closer, perhaps to actually intervene. She peers up at Oliver, saying sweetly, "If I ever hear of you laying a hand on any girl in my neighborhood…" She skips to his index finger, snapping it, "I won't be so gentle next time." She springs away from him. He cradles his injured hand, but doesn't move. When she feigns a strike, he sputters off.

She watches him go, pointedly not looking at Alcott and heads for the porthole door. Alcott steps in between. He passes for handsome, a minus for his thin brown hair, a plus for the thin English accent. But then he pops into her life whenever he wants something and thinks it's charming. He has some mental radar that can find their kind, her especially, it seems. A big minus. Still the banter and flirting can be fun. Plus, again.

Roxy says, "What do you want? It'd better be good."

"You didn't happen to kill a man two nights ago, did you?"

"No. Not two nights ago." She had been right all along!

They move farther down the hall, out of the way of the club-goers. With the violence passed, the humans won't notice them.

"There's been a murder. We don't yet know who is culpable. Everyone is a suspect till I'm certain I have the person responsible."

"I did not kill anyone two nights ago."

"You appeared willing to kill that man."

"Ha. He's not worth killing. Just scaring him so he lays off my friend and thinks twice before hurting other women."

"The point is that I do not know who committed the murder and if the killer intends to harm others."

"How do you know it wasn't suicide?"

"The man's heart was missing."

"That's definitive."

From his jacket, he removes a notepad. He turns its cover over the spiral binding, scans the page, then flips through a few more.

Pen in hand, he reads, "His body was found by Driscoll's Diner. It was left outside for anyone to find."

"Can't help you or your Society buddies, Al."

"Mr. Ashton. Members of the Society of Brandywine are not the only ones in danger. All of us are at risk while a murderer roams free."

"I can handle myself. I've done it all my life." Then looking down the hall, "Where's your sidekick?"

"Pardon?"

"Dark, handsome, and breathing. All the things you're not."

"You are referring to Leonard Webb. He has today to himself, having earned a well-deserved rest. I will share your regards."

"When are you going to turn him?"

"He will be initiated in due course. He is still young, and as such, valuable."

"I'm sure he's charmed."

"Can you prove your whereabouts two nights ago?"

"How's that?"

Pen poised to paper. "Do you have an alibi? Can others vouch that you were never at the diner two nights ago?"

"Around when?" She steps closer to him.

His attention lifts from the notepad to regard her. Their eyes meet and do not waver.

"All night. From the moment you woke up in your cotton nightie, to the moment you got back into it before sunup."

Another step.

"I don't wear cotton nighties."

"For the record, what do you wear?"

Closer. Almost touching. "For the record. Nothing." Batting her eyelashes, she offers a come-hither smile, "That you will get to see."

Her hands encircle his wrists, gently parting and lowering his arms to his sides. She moves into the now open space, picking up the scent of his usual layered cologne that holds notes of mint and lemon over vetiver and sandalwood. Suits him well.

When he leans down, her lips close on his. A fresh mint on his breath this time. Still has a passable technique, though a bit rushed.

As they kiss more deeply, she hears his pen hit the floor, having slipped from his grasp. He wants to move his hands, perhaps to encircle her waist and draw her in closer. But her grip on them remains and he relents, though with a mild grunt of reluctant compliance.

Soon, she leaves off with the kissing, giving him another flirtatious eye. Then, releasing his pen hand, she shoves him smartly, his back hitting the wall behind him.

A rare English smile appears on his face. A flash of handsome. She rewards him with a few more kisses before spinning away, her back to him, his notebook in her hand.

Now she'll know what he knows about this murder.

The page contains a few names, some familiar, but the rest... gibberish. "Oh, crap!" She flips back a page, and another, and another. Just scratches of incomprehensible shorthand.

Straightening, and wearing a now insufferable smile, Alcott says, "I take it our interlude has concluded?"

She stuffs the notebook back into his hands. "You're no fun."

"You wound me." Pen retrieved, he turns to detective-mode. "Have you had contact with the Rotters recently?"

"You people call them that."

"Yes, we do."

"Why would I have? You and the rest of the House made some deal with them—they stick to Camden and you stay out of it."

"You must know Troy Dawson, goes by Blade. Or Tommy Dutton, correct?"

"Only their reps. So, which one's dead?"

"Roxy–I need you to remember any detail. The murder could lead to further conflict."

"I don't keep a diary."

"It was quite recent, surely you can remember."

"The typical stuff. Hang out with friends."

"Where?"

"On my block. Then there's here, South Wave Vibe, the Speakeasy."

"I have not heard of that one."

"A members-only club."

"Where?"

"The location changes."

"Where was it that night?"

"Behind a laundromat on Christian Street."

"Were you with anyone?"

"My friends."

"Human friends."

"They have pulses, yeah."

"Did you feed that evening?"

"Yes, in fact."

"On whom?"

"None of your business who my food is."

"You're my business when you violate House rules."

"That I never agreed to. Your rules. Not mine."

"They apply whether you agree or not. You're free to leave Philadelphia. Camden is more libertine."

"But then you'd have no one to lecture and harass."

"I have enough to do without you here."

"So, you won't miss me?"

"I didn't say that."

"Touching. That it?"

"No. I would appreciate if you would keep an ear out for any leads on this. It's important as I said. I have Wade, Mason, and Ridge rotating shifts here. They will not interfere without cause.

"As you said—important for you—or the Society?"

"Both."

"Well, I don't owe either an ounce of effort. What will you give me?"

"My undying gratitude."

"Ha. You can start by no longer dropping in on me whenever you want something. Call first."

"I don't have your number."

"No, you don't. And I'm not part of your ghoul club. I do what I want, how I want, when I want. To who I want."

"Whom," he corrects. "What do you want for the information?"

"You the know the shelter on... Of course you don't. For Christmas, I want the Mercy Shelter to receive a very generous donation from an anonymous donor. *Generous*, Al."

"A solid tip, Roxy. Something I can use to find the killer."

"You ever think about quitting?"

"How's that?"

"You know, becoming a free agent like me? Maybe I'd respect you more."

"You don't respect me at all."

"Got me there. Think about it, Al."

"Maybe you should think about quitting the rebellious act for father's attention, put down that chip on your shoulder, and grow up. The Society is for adults. Try it."

"Good night, daddy."

ten

A Problem or Three

With Reed in Emma's care, Kyle turns to another matter. At the top of the driveway loop, he adjusts his tie before getting the phone out of his suit jacket pocket. Bars on its screen confirm he's clear of the cell reception dead zone. Kyle calls Alcott Ashton, but catches only his voicemail. He doesn't leave a message.

His brother must be canvassing the city, interviewing everyone he can find who may hold the key that unlocks the Troy Dawson murder mystery. What a relief that would be. Not only for First House, but for Kyle especially. A prolonged investigation will mean violence with Kyle thrust into the midst of it.

A short time later, the phone rings. "Good evening, Brother Kyle. Your call had better not be another matter involving Mr. Williams that requires my strained attention." Mr. Ashton's end of the line sounds as though he's moving through a public space. Voices and music in the background fail to cover his agitated tone.

"No. I would like an update—"

"He still is bonded to you, correct?" The street noise fades several decibels.

"Yes, for a few nights more I would think."

"Renew it before that time."

"I'll take that under advisement."

"Do so. For both your sakes."

Now Kyle makes a noise of skepticism. "I have Reed's trust. That's worth more." For a prolonged moment, Kyle hears nothing from Mr. Ashton. "Hello?"

Then there's the electronic beeps of a car door opening, then the mechanical sound of it closing, shutting out all the street noise.

"You are his sponsor. You are responsible. His trust in you will reflect how you treat the bond. The same as though you were his sire. We keep the bond as a failsafe, for when-I must emphasize when-Mr. Williams behaves rashly."

Kyle takes a moment for himself, switching the phone from one hand to the other. "I want an update on your investigation."

"The update is that I am investigating. I am interviewing. Heretofore a fruitless endeavor."

"Members, but not the sorcerers, I take it."

"No. That will be left to others."

"What about other non-members?"

"I recently spoke with Roxy Marchetti as she resides near where Blade had died—or more accurately, the location where his body had been found."

"Nothing so far then."

"Nothing so far."

"What about beneath the city."

"You have lost me."

"I saw a rat earlier. Maybe two. I saw one last night as well. Seemed interested in me. I saw it tailing Reed too. It may have been my imagination."

"How do you even know about them? Did I discuss them with you and have forgotten?"

"It is not a leap to think of them. Blade was found behind Driscoll's Diner. Food. Trash. Rats. Maybe they saw something."

"Dear Brother Kyle, should the situation become so dire that I must consider plunging into the depths of the city's sewers and seek an audience with whomever may call such mire home, then I fear for us all. And truly that is the only way I can conceive of following your lead, such as it is."

The car engine starts.

"Let us turn to other unpleasant business. You will need to meet Tommy Dutton soon."

Kyle says, "I know. But I want to do that with the information we don't yet have."

"Agreed. I am working on that."

"Do you have any sense of what had happened?"

The two trade theories. To the surprise of neither, they find they share the same ideas. Without further evidence, all is pure speculation. Either Troy had come to meet someone; or he had been lured by someone. Either he was murdered in that lot; or he had been killed elsewhere and his body placed there to be found. Who would have motive? Why would they strike now? What would be gained other than restarting a war between them and the Rotters?

Mr. Alcott says, "I have no reason to believe our House had anything to do with his demise."

"The only possible motive is that someone has an interest in ending the truce. Who and why?"

"The first will answer the second."

"I'm surprised we had not heard from Tommy or the others."

"Yes. Perhaps they do not yet know. But surely, they would have noticed that Mr. Troy Dawson is no longer reachable."

"Maybe they expected Troy to cross the bridge. If he were meeting someone. It might have been for more than one night."

"Let us assume that they at least suspect something amiss. They may do something ill-advised, even hostile, tonight. I have Mason and Ridge keeping tabs on the wards. Wade is with me as we try a few more interviews. I have requested that the wards be reexamined to ensure they're working properly."

***

Kyle greets Emma after she emerges from the eastern end of Tamerlane. Along with her, Reed appears in a lighter mood. Not dancing a jig, but not pensive and downcast as he was earlier.

Nodding to Kyle, Reed moves on toward the manor.

"You were with him a while. I see that he's calmer. Care to tell me what you had said so that I know what to say when he becomes agitated again?"

Emma's attention lingers on the back of Reed, who observes workers tending to their tasks. "All I did was listen."

"I've done that. Must not have your ears."

Smiling now to Kyle, she says, "I will lend them to you, if you would like."

Despite himself, Kyle smiles.

She says, "I must say that it was awful good of you to bring him to me. He thinks well of you which gladdens my heart. He reminds me of you. A man without airs who is refreshingly direct." She brushes at the shoulder of his jacket, "And a touch haunted."

"Haunted by birds. What do you make of them?"

"The matter is perplexing. They have dream-like qualities, but they affect him in a way that dreams cannot account for."

Kyle says, "This has been going on since his time in Paris. His sire suffered something similar. Do you think you can help him?"

A pair of servants have folded up ladders and are taking them to a storage shed.

Reed has gone, but as Kyle knows, not far.

"He had not mentioned that salient detail. It reframes the issue, does it not?"

"I had thought if it happened to both of them, there might be some history of it happening to others."

"On that I do not know. But allow me to speculate. If his sire has this, shall we call it, 'psychic eccentricity?', and he has it as well, then I would surmise that it is a condition he inherited. Therefore, it is a condition of their ichor. And you know where that lands you?"

"In New Hope."

"Will you consult with the ichorists?"

"The sorcerers? Just like that?"

Self-sequestered in New Hope, a town upriver from the city, the ichorists research vampire blood. Kyle has never visited their laboratory. Few have. Which suits him fine, content to stay clear of their work.

Emma says, "I can speak with Brother Trevor, if you would like. Perhaps he could arrange for you and Reed to meet with them."

Like some classified government program, what they toil on remains a mystery. Such secrecy has, unsurprisingly, bred mistrust. A mistrust earned when a scandal escaped their compound by the name of Samuel Lemon and talk of the appalling experiments performed and worse besides.

Not even recent history when, some twenty years ago, Alcott had recruited Kyle, who was tasked to help deal with the ongoing fallout. Unresolved contention brewed into conflict, then broke into all-out hostilities between the ichorists, defended by First House, and Lemon and his children, the Rotters.

"I don't trust them, given their torture of Lemon."

"Given Marbury's torture of Lemon. Marbury's distasteful excesses. And Marbury had been dealt with."

Not willing to dwell on that, he moves on. "I'll consider it." Long after everything else. "I'm also weighing what to do about him being an erif." Kyle can't shake what Michael had said earlier. Reed was not in control. He was just lucky.

Emma turns to give Kyle a serious look. "Watch him carefully. He *is* an erif. Sooner or later, they combust."

eleven

Instigator

Kyle says, "I'm considering doing something foolish." His hand hovers over the gear shifter.

"What's that?" Reed says.

"Losing your memories isn't our only concern. You're an erif. The only other one Alcott knows of in the city is Roxy Marchetti, whom I have no reason to trust."

Seldom has Kyle been uncertain, indecisive. He can scope the heart of a challenge quickly, take aim at the problem, adjust for contingencies, and pull the trigger with pure resolve.

Will Roxy play nice? The alternative is to let Reed figure out his ability himself, gambling that he'll get a handle on his power before it hurts innocent people. And Reed doesn't have years, much less decades, to do so. It's Kyle's responsibility to prepare Reed for initiation into the Society of Brandywine and that means stipulating that the man can fulfill his obligations. If not, blame and sanction falls to Kyle. Devlin would withdraw his promise of the Rite of Ascension sooner than is customary. Knowing Devlin, his sire would push it further out, adding on decades instead of subtracting them. Kyle is not sure his conscience will last that long.

Reed says, "I remember that name from last night. Sounded like she was not Lord Devlin's favorite person."

"She's not a member of the Society."

"How can that be?"

"Reed, I'm only considering asking for her assistance for your sake. You have an ability that's destructive. Consider what you did to Eddie."

Kyle sheds no tears over the death of Marie's British toady. But it has shaken Michael. Kyle has never witnessed an erif using their ability before. He has no idea how it works and could only guess that somehow Reed burned up Eddie's ichor from within the man's body; his blackened skin split open like an overcooked bratwurst. Reed needs to get a handle on that.

Kyle says, "Some night, it could be an innocent person. But since Roxy's not a member, and from what Alcott's told me, she is unpredictable, obstinate. An instigator. You know, like a child who tests her parents' limits to see what she can get away with before being grounded. Then leaps beyond that."

Nodding, Reed says, "The child that your parents warn you not to hang out with? Bad influence? Think she'd rub off on me? That I might get the wrong ideas from her?"

"Exactly. Ideas like not joining the Society. Ignore them. So, here's what I'm going to do. Assuming she's even interested in helping you, I'm going to give you two an hour to get to know each other. If it works out, then we'll arrange for more play time after the masquerade. After I pick you up, we'll finish up the evening with hunting up a meal and getting you back to Lily."

***

Kyle crosses the city and winds his way to the Bella Vista neighborhood.

Reed says, "How do you expect to find her?" He leans up on the passenger door, head on the window peering sidelong at people walking, talking, greeting, departing.

Kyle says, "I know she lives around here. I'll get a better idea in a moment." He parks in the next available spot, then pushes the button that lowers Reed's window.

Startled, annoyed, Reed sits up. "What are you doing?"

"Give me your phone." Kyle holds out his hand. "I'll need it for a moment."

Reed hands it to him, "Why?"

Kyle taps his way to sideloading an app. "I'm installing a panic button. Mr. Webb designed it for the Society."

Reed looks at the app on his screen then Kyle, "Mr. Webb makes apps for the Society?"

Mr. Webb does many things for the Society. As Alcott's human counterpart, Mr. Webb assists in investigations and security. Skilled in technology, he knows a lot of vowel-less acronyms that computers understand. And what Mr. Webb can do with computers impresses Kyle, who pretends to follow what the man is talking about when he explains networks, firewalls, block-chains.

Handing Reed the phone back, Kyle says, "Push it in an emergency. The right people will be dispatched to the phone's location. Until you can take care of yourself, keep that on your phone. You better not use it, though."

Now on his phone, Kyle sends a text. When the response comes, he relays it to Reed, "She's nearby. Alcott had seen her earlier. She wore a beaded silver dress." Reaching back into his own memory of having met her, he informs Reed that the Italian woman has black hair with a bob cut; and that she is about five-four in height, seven feet in attitude.

Circling the intersection Alcott had mentioned, they drive on, taking it slow. Reed scans his side of the one-way street. "Is that her? She's wearing a leather jacket though."

"Good eye." Kyle sees her now. No silvery dress. Just an open black leather jacket with numerous buckles, a halter top, and jeans.

Kyle finds a spot two blocks ahead and smoothly parallel parks the car. Shutting off the engine, Kyle pops out. When Reed does the same, he taps the roof between them, "Stay right here. We'll be back in a few minutes.'"

Taking a moment to check his hair in the sideview, Kyle comes down Roxy's way, jaywalking the cross streets with measured steps. He'd prefer a brisker pace to catch Roxy before she disappears, but the fast clips of his hard-soled shoes on the pavement might alert her into doing so anyway.

On the way, he considers his strategy to hook her interest. Appeals to money, her vanity, her enmity for the Society? Does she possess a maternal instinct?

He slows as he approaches the entrance of the alley. He peers in. Her back to him, she's squatting between two large tote bags. Her extended right arm holds something, and she makes soft noises like she's trying to coax a stray cat out of its hidey-hole. He doesn't see a hole or a cat, but a sewer grating.

With her attention elsewhere, Kyle moves to the other side of the alley's mouth.

With a flick, she tosses cubes of beef like dice. Soon a rat emerges from the grating. It dashes toward the morsels, grabbing one in its front paws to chew.

Roxy says something Kyle doesn't hear well.

The rat doesn't come closer and once it's had the last bite, it dives into the grating.

She waits.

Kyle waits.

She shifts her balance several times and waits some more.

The rat doesn't return.

Having realized this herself, Roxy bounces to her feet. "Come out, you big meatball!"

No one comes out. Kyle can sympathize.

"Fine! See if I care."

She snaps up the tote bags, one in each hand, and heads back.

Roxy raises a brow when she spots Kyle, but does not stop, nor even slow down. She veers to the opposite side, where he originally stationed himself; she's heading in Reed's direction as he anticipated.

Puzzling that another vampire has interest in the city's rodent population. But he won't get sidetracked. Another time.

"Chasing rats, Ms. Marchetti?"

She ignores the remark.

"An erif needs your help, Ms. Marchetti," he says to her back.

He doesn't follow her. Remaining in place, he watches her pace slow just a touch. She heard him.

Casually, he says, "I would be grateful if you could help him."

"My nights are full enough without you Brandies dropping in on me. And that's twice tonight."

"I apologize, Ms. Marchetti. You are in the position to help me a great deal."

She pivots on the spot and returns his gaze. Kyle takes it as good sign that she has remained here. Perhaps he was right to guess she might have sympathy for a child.

He catches a smile rise in the right corner of her mouth before it's chucked away. She says, "A shame what happened to one of your Brothers. Alcott had told me his name... Let's see... Wade was it?"

This causes Kyle to twitch, putting him on his back foot. Not expecting this tack, he takes a moment to consider, then grasps her purpose. She's fishing. "I don't know what you're referring to."

"Bull. Brother Wade or Whoever died the other night. Here. In my neighborhood. That makes it my business to know. I won't have some vendetta that will put the people I care about at risk."

"I have no comment on that. Only to say we will do all we can to prevent more people from being hurt."

Roxy sniffs, "Have it your way." As before she spins on a heel, swinging the capacious totes, and huffs away.

"He needs you," Kyle says evenly. "He lost his wife while on their honeymoon earlier—"

She says over her shoulder, "I'm not grandma—you can't expect to drop off your kid because you have better things to do."

Thinking on what she has said, Kyle re-calibrates, "If he doesn't learn, he'll hurt people. You know how much damage someone with your power can do when *in* control. Think what kind of damage he could do *here* without that control."

Her back to him, she stops at the curb. When the crosswalk signals it's safe to cross, she doesn't. She's still listening.

Stepping up, Kyle says, "Look. He's actually a decent man. He didn't want any of this. I promised to help him, but I can't teach him what you know."

"He's your problem. Not mine," she says, stepping into the street.

"I agree. Just meet with him. I'll make it worth your while."

In a tone of irritation, she says, "I'll burn your ass right now if you don't leave me alone."

He follows her into the street, "You're right." She glances back at him, slowing her pace.

Kyle says, "I can understand wanting to prevent people from getting hurt. I don't want anyone to die either."

She stops and offers her profile. She alternately pumps the tote bags.

Kyle says, "I can't identify who it was, Ms. Marchetti. Things have to be sorted out first. It was murder. Quite unnatural even for us."

Roxy looks insulted, "That's it? I know that much already. You're useless. No deal." She's off again, breezing down the block.

He can't bluff with her, certain as she is that he knows more than he'll say. Of course he does, and of course he can't divulge this. She took a guess as to who was murdered and that he had been a member of the Society. Kyle can't correct her without putting Alcott's efforts at risk. Who knows what Roxy will do with the information and who she'll share it with.

While searching for a satisfying but inconsequential tidbit he could share, he pursues her to the end of the block and onto the next where he parked. "Look, you don't know me very well. This may have been the most we've spoken. Reed is a good man. I know, because compared to everyone else we know in this life, he's a Boy Scout. Just meet him. That's all I'm asking."

All at once she stops. Stock-still. Tote bags slip from her fingers and crash by her feet.

Reaching her side, Kyle notes her gob-smacked expression. Then he glances ahead. Reed stands by the Audi and appears equally stunned.

After a silent moment, Roxy clasps her hands to her heart and says, "Ok."

twelve

Fire Feeds Fire

Absently, Roxy dismisses Kyle from their presence. Eyes stuck on this man, she's still struck by the spark of their meeting. This is new ground.

Within her, the bird becomes alert. A fluttering warmth spreads through her right to her fingers, to their tips.

It's curious being drawn to something, excited for something. As though beckoned, a tugging attraction that strengthens with each step.

He appears as stunned as she. Mirroring her, his hand goes to his heart. He must feel it—his bird reaching for her own. Hers reaching back. Like dancers.

There's definitely something between them. Something more than the heat of her blood kicking up, her bird looping acrobatically.

She doesn't know how long they have been staring at one another, but at some point, she clears her throat. "So, you're the new guy."

He blinks, recovering himself. "I am the new guy." He straightens and offers a tight smile. "Reed." He looks downward. The tote bags dropped at her feet nearly forgotten. "May I help you with those?"

His guileless tone catches her, as does his unexpected gallantry.

"Kyle did say you were a Boy Scout."

He stoops to take the straps of the bags and glances inside. He says, "Been doing some shopping?" Gathering the straps in one hand he swings the totes over his shoulder.

And his warm self-assured voice, flecked with a cigarette habit, pairs nicely with his sturdy body that must have lifted many totes.

"Unshopping, actually."

She circles him, getting all his angles. He must have cut his hair before being turned—it's brown and tidy, though some stubble shades his set jaw. Six-foot, broad in the shoulders and chest. If there is any flab he hides it well.

Her hand flies at his ass. Firm.

"Hey!" Reed scowls, but she grins impishly. Whatever this new territory is, this promises to be a lot of fun.

Her fingers drag across the denim, then the leather belt around to the buckle in front, up the soft weave of his flannel shirt over his taut stomach and chest. And a heat that may soon singe the fabric.

Her own blood sizzles just by being near him. She has to take a breath at the flare of pain. She's tolerated it well all her unlife, even finding it comforting. The bitter with the sweet, like her childhood hours of muscle strain and blisters so that she can glide on air. But now fiery talons prickle her ichor. She's never had such a response to another vampire. But he's not just another vampire, he's someone who understands the Fire. Someone who knows its exquisite pain and its sublime power.

She smiles under a light bulb of understanding. The unnamed feeling is kinship. What they share, they share with no one else. Dancers alone. She wonders what this all means, and she's thrilled to find out.

"You feel it too." Her eyes cast up.

"I feel really uncomfortable." His free hand moves to brush hers off him, but she's quick and captures the hand instead. The increasing warmth of her fingers envelope his own calloused ones. There's a gold band on one finger of his left hand.

Reed shakes her hand loose and takes a step away from her. His eyes narrow, striking flint.

"My, my. Touchy." She spreads out her hands to show she'll behave. For now.

She turns on her heel and walks down 9th Street. As expected, Reed follows, toting her totes.

"Where are we going?"

"Well, Boy Scout, we're going to earn some merit badges."

On the way, she explains to him that they'll be distributing the bags' contents to her friends in the neighborhood.

"You know what a phoenix is?"

"A bird. From myth, right?"

"A beautiful bird feathered with flames rising from its own ashes. That's what lives in here," she points to her heart. "I ignite. I burn. I fall to pieces. Then I rise."

"Are you saying that's what I have?"

"What you have is the Fire. Capital F." She traces the letter over her heart, "What shape it takes is up to you. You've got to learn to nurture it. To listen to it." Seeing the uncertainty in his face, she says, "Think about it."

Reed rubs at his temple. "I think I've already missed a lesson."

She says, "No one gave me any lessons. You're the first erif I've met."

Now they turn deeper into the Italian Market neighborhood. Ahead is a familiar face. Raising her hands to her mouth to project her voice, she yells, "Hey, Howdy!"

A man in a worn coat and corduroy slacks in need of mending, turns and smiles as Roxy approaches. After an exchange of pleasantries, she claps his shoulder, saying, "As promised."

She motions for Reed to present the tote bags, which he does. She hands Howdy the pillow that had been on top, "New, hypoallergenic like you like." From the tote she tosses him a package containing a pair of navy-colored pillow cases to go along with it. "Zippered and stain-resistant."

The man says, "How's our filmmaker doing?"

Roxy would love to know herself. Karen hasn't returned Roxy's half-dozen texts. After her encounter with Alcott, she had gone to look for Karen in the club. She was gone and has been incommunicado since, icing out her friend. Clearly upset with Roxy. Why? Oliver had it coming. Got off easy, in fact. But somehow, Roxy's the one who crossed a line?

Thinking she went home to cool off, Roxy didn't find her there either. The totes were there, already packed. Usually, the pair of them walk the neighborhood giving out the packages together. So, after changing clothes, Roxy grabbed them, along with some vittles for the rats. Maybe she'd run into her roommate on the street.

"She's on the next project. She'll be a Hollywood star before you know it."

"I want an invite to the premiere," Howdy says.

Continuing on, Roxy says to Reed, "Like I said, give your Fire some shape and name it. Like an animal, like a pet, no, like a companion. Took me a while to figure that out myself, so I'm saving you a lot of grief."

Many things had burned before she understood this, though the lessons were deeply satisfying. But she keeps that to herself.

"And yours is a bird? That's been my luck. I'm really hating birds lately."

"Ostriches, I understand. They're mean. Ugly too. But they sure know how to strut. They remind me of Sally Rand. I had seen her perform her fan dances at the Paramount Theater."

He only shrugs.

"Chicago. Before your time." She shrugs too. "You know I'm a dancer? My parents had sent me to dance school. Took it seriously. Trained hard." Not getting anywhere, she says, "I call my bird, Millie, after my sire. Tell me about your Fire."

"Feels like a furnace to me."

"How about a crematorium? You could call it Urn."

"That's very dark," he says without humor.

"It's stupid is what it is. Pick something else."

"I'm not very creative."

"Hmm. Well, there are the fire signs of the Zodiac." She ticks them off on her fingers, "Ares, the ram, Leo, the lion, and Sagittarius, the archer. What's yours?"

"I'm a Sagittarius."

"See?"

"See what?"

"I'm an Aries. I don't think it's a coincidence that we're both fire signs. We'll need to find a Leo to complete our collection. We can start a band."

Though she wants to say more, she checks his reaction. He doesn't crack a smile. She gives him a expectant look.

Reed says, "What?"

"Why aren't you more excited?" She seizes his arm, "This is great. Us meeting. Two erifs. Erifs: Is that the plural form? See, I don't know. We'll have so much fun together. We can do anything," She thinks back on happier times when she was a little girl. A playmate and co-conspirator had moved into the neighborhood. They bonded instantly, finding in one another equal parts bravery and foolishness—love of adventure and the solemnity of secrets.

"I think being an erif comes from who you are. Like it's been there all along inside you. Maybe it was dormant, maybe it was caged, but after you're turned, it's awake, it's free. You're free. Free to do what you want."

She turns quiet as he seems to be taking in her theory.

He says, "Can you help me or not?"

Disappointed, she says, "One track mind with you." But she drops the subject for now. "Okay. Sure." She steps close, enjoying the greater warmth in her nearness to him. "Maybe we can help each other." She lifts onto her toes to kiss his lips.

Fast, Reed's hand puts her back flat on her feet. "I'm married."

Now she regards him strangely, "Still?" The ring glints in the light. Kyle had led her to believe that the woman was dead. "I thought it was 'Till death do us part.'"

Before he says anything, she adds, "You can't deny what you just felt when we first saw each other. What you still are feeling. I saw you."

"Yeah, I feel worse. The fire is worse. Feels like oxygen's rushed in. Obviously, it's because of you. So, you explain it."

She stops and waves at the totes over his shoulder. "Put them down."

He hesitates a moment then sets the bags down between them.

"You're a smoker."

"Used to be."

"But you still have a lighter."

"Actually, I do." He sounds surprised with himself as he pulls one out from his jeans' pocket. The lighter fluid sloshes within the translucent blue body.

"Always keep one on you. Never know when you want to start something."

"Is it possible for us to make a fire ourselves?"

"Yes, but that's too advanced for you."

Reed holds the lighter near himself then squicks the spark wheel while opening the valve in a smooth practiced motion. Instead of straight up, the flame instantly splits. The larger portion bends toward him, the smaller portion toward Roxy.

Roxy had expected to see a flame duly bow to its master. But not two. Look at them, dancing above their blue plastic stage. Gorgeous little creatures. In the deepest part of the flame, she sees the silhouette of a bird, its long neck throwing its head back over itself. Millie.

"Why does it do that?" he says. He adds that he saw something similar with lit matches, their flames drawn to him.

"Fire knows fire."

Roxy takes a single step back. They watch the flames diminish. Her flame stretches and thins. Another step back. It shrinks further. Another step. Disappears into the remaining portion, which points at Reed.

As Roxy steps closer, they witness the reverse. A small flame buds off once again and grows to greet her.

Roxy smiles, "Swell!"

He releases the lighter's button, extinguishing the flame.

She takes the offered lighter and they try again. The serpent tongue flicks at each of them. When Reed moves away, the phenomenon repeats as before.

"We're hot stuff, Reed." She smiles slyly and tosses back the lighter. "Fire feeds fire." Smacking her hands together she adds, "We're stronger together."

Catching the lighter, he says, "We're nothing until I learn to control it."

***

As the tote bags lighten, Reed's impatience grows. Roxy doles out items—undies, socks, travel-size toiletries sealed in bundles—to each person she stops to greet. It's as though she's mayor of the neighborhood glad-handing her constituency. When she hollers their name, they cheer, "Roxy!"

He doesn't know what to make of her. Like Devlin she's from another era. Brash, loud, dazzling. A firecracker.

They must have covered ten blocks by now.

At a corner store a man holds a coffee cup in one hand, and with the other opens the door for shoppers. Given the worn lip of the cup, he guesses it holds loose change rather than joe.

"Well look what the cat hacked up," the man says.

"Hey, Early," Roxy says, "Win the lotto yet?" From the second tote, she presents a sleeping bag, compressed inside a translucent package.

He frowns, "Flowers?"

"It's a garden print. The flowers are gardenias."

"Pink?" He leaves the doorway to take hold of it.

"Pink is just as warm as blue or any other color. There's thermal socks tucked inside."

"Not true. Darker colors absorb more heat."

Reed nods in agreement, but the man pays him no mind.

She takes the cup while he considers the sleeping bag's qualities as though, if unsatisfied, he might return it to her.

She says, "You're welcome by the way."

Ignoring Reed also, Roxy sidles next to Early to ask him conspiratorially, "Have you heard anything about a man murdered near Driscoll's the other night?"

While the two talk, Reed reviews what Roxy has told him. Like Ms. Shipley, Roxy gives him hope that he can get control back in his life—at least hold the line till he's human again. But as he's already told her, he's not creative. How should he picture his Fire? Giving it shape does make sense. Picturing it, naming it, might help relate to it better. But the hour must be coming up, and what does he have to show for it?

He returns to Roxy, "Let's go." He gives her friend a vague shrug of apology.

Roxy says, "You don't really like being out here, do you?" Not waiting for a response, she goes on, "Well, what do you expect to learn in one night?"

He turns to leave, "Forget it."

Roxy says, "Wait! Jeez! We'll start again and head back. Give me your number."

With numbers exchanged, she says. "What have you come up with?"

"I picked a lion." *Mon lion*, Marie had called him. Reed doesn't want to think of his sire and the pet names she purred into his ear. But he won't let her decide for him any longer. Rather, with a lion, he chooses to think of strength, courage, and protection.

"Does it have a name?" Roxy says.

Feeling ridiculous, he doesn't answer, but the woman seems prepared to wait for one. He says, "Florian, the patron saint of fire-fighters."

"Naturally," she shakes her head, "you're a fire-fighter. Talk about being a Boy Scout." She shrugs, "Another point in my favor. What's your earliest memory of fire?"

"My memory hasn't been reliable. I do remember the stone fireplace in the house I grew up in. I can still hear the firewood snapping. I liked poking the iron into the logs and watch them throw sparks. Sometimes I'd let a fire reduce to embers then revive it again."

Maybe there is something to Roxy's theory, that becoming a vampire unlocked whatever has been inside him all along. But theory wastes time. He needs solutions.

"Besides cigarettes and logs, what else do you like to burn?"

"Nothing. Why would I burn things?"

"I do. Fire is…" Roxy clasps her arms to herself, closes her eyes for a moment, then releases a blissful breath. "Nothing like it. Fire can destroy and create. You can't hold it in your hand but it burns its mark into you. The smell, elemental, and peppery. The heat on your face." She caresses her arms sensually, "In your skin. In the very heart of you."

Reed recalls sweltering under his shirt and bunker jacket, his feet sloshing in his sweat-logged boots. "Okay. Okay."

Roxy chucks his arm, "Told you: We'll make a great team. I'll start them and you can put them out."

Not amused, Reed says, "We're not committing arson." He starts the lighter again, "Now help me."

The gap between what she says is possible and what he fails to do seems unbridgeable. Over the next however many minutes Roxy tries to guide him in shaping the flame. Patience, apparently, is not Roxy's strong suit any more than it is his. They take turns being frustrated. She curses in Italian at his shoulder and he mutters his own English ones.

"See? You're thinking wrong."

"How do you know what I'm thinking?"

"I can see it in your face. You think it's just something you can use brute force on. It's a partnership. You have to dance with it."

She concentrates and a void appears in the flame's center. The flame forms a ring. Then the top of the ring forms a pair of arcs while the bottom narrows. Soon it's a burning heart. The heart separates from the lighter and floats up in the air. Then it bursts into tiny winged things that fly apart and soon are consumed.

"Feel its connection to you—to your heart. You share that heat, that pain. That pain is part of the price we pay. It never goes away, but you can release it, as you will learn."

"Are we vulnerable to fire? Can we burn too?"

"Fire destroys everything. But we're more resistant. And since we can control it, it's not much of a threat. And in case you've not learned by now, the more we use the gift the sooner we'll need to feed again. Blood is its fuel and if you're not careful, you'll run empty too soon. That's the other price we pay."

Reed lets out a long noise of realization. That was why he had been ravenous for blood after his fight with Eddie. He had released the Fire and it had to be replenished.

Roxy tilts her head, "Yeah?"

"Nothing."

"Tell me."

"Let's just say the Fire got free. I was really thirsty after that."

"And what did you do?"

Reed doesn't elaborate on the circumstances. Only to say that he was in a bad way and out of options for blood besides his wife. So, Kyle offered his own ichor.

"Well, he is your sire, after all."

"No. He's not."

"Is Devlin your sire?"

"No."

"It's not Al. He would have told me."

"You wouldn't know her. Her name was Marie."

"Was… Did you kill her? Turn her into a Florian flambé?"

"Let's just drop it."

"Well wait… If Kyle's not your sire… he's your sponsor? Are you not in the Society yet?"

"I'm learning."

"So you're not. You know how it usually works, right? Marie would have prepared you to join while you were still human then during initiation you're turned. But that didn't happen. What's in it for Kyle? No wonder he's over his head. Ohhhh. I bet Devlin put him up to it. Because you're an erif. Of course. They couldn't have me, so you're their shiny new toy."

"Apparently."

"And you're okay with this? Being used?"

"We're using each other."

"You don't need them, Reed. I'll teach you what you need to know."

"Your lessons will be fine."

"You're naive. Do you know what the initiation is?"

"A ceremony. Like joining the Masons or something."

The phone in Reed's back pocket chimes with a text message.

"That's true. And during said ceremony you pledge to support the House. It's binding. They have a favorite toy, a Boy Scout action figure. Use it, abuse it, melt it with fire, till they've had all their fun. Where will that leave you? You better think on what you're getting yourself into. Long and hard."

A second chime.

Pulling out the phone, he says, "That's why you've not joined?"

"I'm not a joiner. Prefer my independence. Isn't that the point?"

Reed isn't listening. He's in motion. Where's Kyle? "I gotta go."

The texts are from Lily.

SPOTTED A SHADOW

Then:

FOLLOWING HIM

thirteen

The Stake in Both Our Hearts

A t her apartment, Lily picks up Aleron, never having expected a man other than Reed to spend the night here. Lily has considered giving him the apartment for the remainder of the lease so that he has a place to grieve. But this isn't his home and he will return to Paris tomorrow, which is suddenly too soon.

Continuing the arrangement they had in a Paris hotel suite, Aleron sleeps on the sofa, a cushier spot than across the back seats of his Peugeot, which has been his home for a year or more.

Though he has accepted joining her for dinner, he still appears forlorn and defeated. He shuffles his feet, stooped over by grief, and his voice strains to greet her. His beard and mane of grey hair need a trim and a brush. He shrugs on his trench coat over the fresh shirt and khakis she had purchased for him back in Paris.

It pains her heart to see him so, and all the more painful that she's at a loss to help him. For all the man has done for her, she feels any help she can offer to be woefully inadequate.

The cab lets them off on South Street. They stroll east in the cool air that stirs up now and then. Appearing lost in his grief, Aleron raises his head briefly to note the landmarks and murals Lily points out.

In French, he says, "I'm afraid I am not a good companion."

The man doesn't speak English, which suits Lily fine. Fluent herself, she enjoys the opportunity to *parlez Français* with him. The roots of her family run deep and firm here. Her mother's English side goes back before America's independence from Great Britain, and her father's French side shortly afterward.

"You have nothing to apologize for. And I appreciate your company."

They reach a corner restaurant with a window on the kitchen. Lily holds the door open for her friend. Inside, it's a narrow way to queue up and place an order. While explaining the menu options, she assures Aleron that these are not-to-be-missed, genuine Philadelphia cheesesteaks.

She orders in English for the counter man and French for Aleron's benefit. A large with peppers, onions, and sharp cheddar on an Amoroso roll for him; hers without the onions on a sesame roll.

Backs to the customers, the cooks tend to the piles of meat and vegetables on the flat top grill. Their spatulas slap the metal surface while slicing up the beef and corralling them to make room for raw cousins. When a batch has lost enough pinkness it's scooped up with peppers and onions and laid out on a cheese-slathered roll.

The pair take their seat.

They eat in silence, though Aleron barely touches his meal. His hoagie lays open like an autopsy—the meat oozing with melty strings of veggies and cheese sauce.

Lily says, "What will you do when you get back to Paris?"

Aleron probes his food with a plastic fork, shrugging.

She's struck by how, only a few nights ago, they had been sharing a meal at a little restaurant where she was the one who couldn't eat. She was too preoccupied with finding her husband. Every moment spent sitting was another minute Reed was getting farther away, another minute not knowing if he was safe or if he was hurt.

After chasing shadows from Paris to Philadelphia to find Reed and confront Marie and her gang, Lily and Aleron now face new uncertainties. Though Lily has Reed, Aleron will return to Paris with no one waiting for him but Marie's paralyzed body.

"Please eat, Aleron."

He saws off a corner of spongy bread with a dollop of cheese and peppery steak to chew.

"When I was in your place you had told me to eat, that I needed my strength." She prods him to take another bite, "Remember? You took care of me; I will take care of you."

He sips his Sprite.

"Aleron, look at me." His grey tired eyes, more aged than before, regard her. "We trust each other. I know I didn't when we first met. But with all that we've been through together, I consider you a dear friend. You know you can trust me. I worry for you. What are you thinking? Tell me."

He scrubs his whiskered jowls with both hands then smooths his beard, "The difference is there was much ahead for both of us. Now, for me, this is the end."

He crumples napkins into his tightening fist. "This is no resolution. No resolution at all. Marie is not dead. And she is not alive. I cannot mourn her, and we cannot build a life together as we had promised to do. There's a stake in both our hearts. Neither of us can move.

"You tell me, Mrs. Williams—what do I do? Should I tear out that piece of wood from her heart?" He leans forward over his food tray. "Hope that she will return to her senses and remember me? That she will smile— the same smile she had worn when I proposed to her? Or maybe she's already at peace. Or maybe she has not changed, and when she opens her eyes, she will only see the man who put that stake in her heart and stopped her from taking your husband back to Paris. Back to destroy the one who damned us all."

Lily says, "St. Croix." The one who had stolen Marie away from him and made her a vampire.

"Yes. That was Marie's purpose in making Eddie, Ron, Clarice, and Jean-Paul, and your husband into shadows. If I take the stake out, she may kill me." He spreads his hands, leaning back, "Should it please her, let it be so. But now she's free. Free to ruin the lives of more Alerons and more Lilys and more Reeds. And even if she can muster a force of numbers will she prevail over St. Croix? This I doubt. And even if she does succeed, what will that accomplish? Will she be at peace then?

He spikes the waded napkin onto the red plastic tray. "Perhaps. Still, as she is, perhaps she is already at peace."

Lily nods, understanding as well. Last night, seeing the madness in Marie's eyes as she demanded Reed kill his wife chilled her; and seeing her prone body on the floor of the hotel moments later yielded no sympathy from Lily. Though her grandmother would chide her to forgive Marie, she could not. Hearing Aleron just now, her heart has softened somewhat. 'Never' yields to 'maybe one day,' but not 'now.' And now, what is most pressing is finding a cure for Reed.

What would happen if Reed forgets her completely, and she has to put him down? She couldn't possibly bury him knowing that he was still "alive." But what could she do? Arrange him on his bed, pull the covers up, and tuck him in? Treat him as a coma patient?

"Well then, do I leave the stake where it is? Do I bury her? Would that be cruel? Or is it more merciful that I destroy her? Perhaps take her near the water she loved so. Sit beside her until morning comes and let the sunlight cleanse her. Will her soul return to God? And will mine be damned to Hell?"

Lily has nothing to say. All of these questions leave her bewildered. Nothing in Catholic school touched on the finer points of dealing with a lover turned vampire.

Aleron continues, "I know you blame Marie for this. I understand, truly. But I cannot condemn her or turn my back on her. I love her still. So, I do not know what I shall do when I return to Paris. I will not know what I will do with her until the moment I see her again. God help me."

***

The Delaware waterfront has gone through several improvement projects. Docked on the river, ships dip and rise. One has been converted into a restaurant, popular as a venue for weddings and corporate events. On deck, people dressed in evening wear chat in clusters or lean over the rails, peering back at the city or at Camden across the water.

In French, Lily informs Aleron that there's a marina up the way. "My brother, Charles, has a sailboat. We've gone out on it a number of times. But I have yet to convince Reed to get aboard. He doesn't like boats. Have you sailed?"

"I have been hired for shoots on private vessels. But I've not sailed for leisure. Marie loves the water. I thought we would honeymoon on the Seine. Take a voyage all the way to the sea. Like being on a moving island, just the two of us, champagne and dinner under the starlight."

They both smile. Lily thinks it's romantic—a different kind of honeymoon than the one she had planned for Reed and herself. Reed had never been to France, so Lily wanted her groom to see the country where the Martin-half of her family hails from. But they never got to finish theirs and Aleron and Marie never got to even marry.

Gently, she says, "You are wrong about one thing, Aleron. This is not the end for you or Marie."

Aleron turns to her, eyes open with interest.

"I will find a cure for Reed. A way to undo what was done to him and make him human again. And what can be done for Reed can be done for Marie."

Aleron nods, though in his expression, she senses that he does so more as a wish than a certainty.

"Keep faith, Aleron. It has gotten us this far." She says confidently, "And think on this: with God's help, when Marie is herself again, you will have your wedding. A lovely wedding followed by the best, most well-deserved honeymoon."

Aleron smiles.

She knocks her hip into his. "Think of the toast I would give. How do you think your guests will react when I tell them how we met?"

His smile cracks wider till laughter escapes. She joins him and soon they're both doubled-over.

After she recovers, she says in a tone that's meant to encourage him, "When you get back to Paris, find the priest you had met. Your confessor, correct?"

"Father Lambert. I do not know if he ever believed me."

"In any case, go to him. If he doesn't know himself, he must be able to point you in the right direction. I will research on my end."

Aleron warms to the idea. "I will do it. Whatever I learn I shall share it with you. As you say, with God's help, we will prevail."

***

They continue on. Several paces behind Lily, Aleron now observes the storefronts and landmarks. Lily hopes her words have lifted some of his gloom. By giving him an objective, a practical goal, he will have something to occupy his mind.

They move west on the north side of South Street. Coming up to a camera and electronics store Aleron stops to peer into the display window. Beyond the security gate and glass are several models of camera, kits, and accessories.

"A Leica was my first camera. It was my mother's and her mother's." She notes his French carries a wistful tone.

Aleron is a fashion photographer—just as Marie had been a fashion model. Though much older than Marie, he pursued her. They dated and he proposed to her at the Musee de l'Orangerie.

Lily says, "You need to work again. I've seen your portfolio. You are talented. Marie would want you to be happy and pursue your passion. Let it bring you to life again. It's not too late."

They move on.

Ahead, on the next block, a commotion brews. Cries and laughter ring out at South Wave Vibe Lounge, locally famous for its risque Thirsty Thursday radio ads. Women huddle together, wrapping themselves with their arms, little prepared for the gusts of colder temperatures of the late evening.

Lily can't remember the last time she had been to a nightclub. Grad school, maybe. With her best friend, Margot. She has not been comfortable at such places compared to the cocktail parties and galas her family attended, where she doesn't need to raise her voice when chatting, or dance with strangers. Much of the focus was on Charles being groomed for law and politics; Lily didn't hold such aspirations, having repeatedly made that known to her parents who insisted that she at least marry one in such circles.

The crowd simmers as its mood shifts. Shouts of surprise turn to anger. Its shape balloons, forcing a few people past the curb onto the front fender of a stopped SUV, others into the street.

Someone's drunk and mean.

Approaching the intersection, Lily tells Aleron they'll cross to the other side of South Street.

The brouhaha bubbles over. Patrons hurriedly backstep, making a hole. A costumed man emerges. The instigator? Hands shove him along his way. He's dressed like a pirate. A bandanna covers his hair, a ruffled shirt, cut-off pants tucked into striped leggings. Gold hoops in eyebrow and ear glint in the neon above.

Deaf to their jeering, he's preoccupied with something in his hands, holding whatever it is at eye-level while he ambles toward the intersection. He pauses under the light of a streetlamp. A bracelet. No, a lady's wristwatch. The man's got a cartoonish five o'clock shadow daubed in by makeup, flat black along his jaw. He's talking to himself, his lips smeared red.

Lily stops walking. Instinctively, her right hand reaches for Aleron's arm and pulls him close to her.

Fresh shouts draw hers and the pirate's attention. From the Lounge crowd, two men charge down the block toward him. He turns in place after fastening the lady's watch on his right wrist. It happens quickly now. The pair of men, one in a varsity jacket, the other in flashy jeans, gets right into his personal space. Sharp words, then sharper jabs. The pirate dodges. They circle around one another this way till finally the pirate sweeps a leg, getting one off balance then knocking him into his friend so that they both go down.

Pirate walks quicker now, arriving at the intersection, not appearing to notice Lily or Aleron opposite him. Instead, he turns the corner of his block, up 4th Street.

But Lily has noticed him and the red smear. And she noticed that under the streetlamp, three men cast onto the pavement two shadows.

"Aleron, do you see?" she asks in French.

"I had hoped you hadn't."

A vampire. A shadow.

Now in motion, she says, "Come on." They move in parallel with the vampire on their side of 4th Street.

The shadow is not hurrying, seeming to have forgotten the two men he left sprawled on the pavement. His red lips move while his hands seek out the belongings of the pedestrians approaching him. Talking amongst themselves, they don't notice him until he's feeling up their coats, scarves, and purses as though inspecting for contraband.

The pirate vampire appears delighted, even as they yell and shake him off. He relents, bowing away, hands behind his back, showng them he means no offense. More guarded, they hurry away only to be replaced with the two men scrambling for a rematch.

Catching up, one attempts to grab their target, but the vampire dodges. The other tries too, only to grab air. Each time the vampire springs ahead, keeping just out of reach. They shout in frustration, cursing him.

Lily quickens her step, waving for Aleron to keep up. What is she even doing? She's reacting, just as she had back in Paris, in Aleron's Peugeot. Parked along the Seine, they had witnessed two vampires drag a hands-tied human being to an awaiting boat. She didn't know what to do, she had no plan, but she had to do something to save that man.

Here, Mr. Varsity has height over the vampire; his buddy has the advantage of weight. Won't be enough. By trying to land a hand on him they're poking a bear.

One last time, the vampire leaps without looking and falls upon a bundled-up person pushing a loaded shopping cart. Now the taller guy seizes the opportunity to seize the vampire and slam him into the brick wall.

As though jarred herself, Lily winces at the bony impact.

She gets her phone to text Reed. She has difficulty typing, her hands shake so.

First, she taps:

SPOTTED A SHADOW.

Then:

FOLLOWING HIM.

Mercifully, the vampire isn't fighting back. But why?

No response from Reed. Wherever he is, he's in no position to do anything, but still, she'd like to hear from him.

Whether the vampire is playing with them or not, this won't end well. She then texts:

CALLING 911

Then she does so.

Then she ends the call.

Kyle's words come back to her. If she involves the authorities, that would violate Reed's probation, their agreement. Reed is her collateral. What would happen to him? Though Kyle's threat was vague on consequences, she believes it was sincere and certain.

Both men have the vampire pinned to the wall. The shorter, wider one, wearing a new pair of jeans, stone-washed denim stiff and bright, jabs the air with his finger, while the other yells down at the shadow's bandanna-wrapped head.

Lily keeps the phone out. In French, she says to Aleron, "We have to do something." She steps off the curb.

Aleron says, "I do not like when you say that."

"Aleron, he may kill them."

"Or me. Or you. Or me."

They hurry across the one-way street when the way is clear of oncoming cars. Closer, she can hear Mr. Varsity. The man flips the vampire around and gets into his face. "How do you know that?"

His stubby friend, Mr. Jeans, says, "My friend asked you a question," fingers gunning the air.

From a safe distance—she hopes—at one end of a parked car, Lily says, "Leave him alone. He's—"

Mr. Jeans looks over his shoulder, annoyance on his face. "Who are you? His momma? Get the hell out of here. We're having a private conversation."

Trying to replace nerves with confidence, she says firmly, "He's dangerous."

The second man takes a couple of steps toward her.

She holds up the phone, bluffing, "Police are on their way."

The vampire hasn't stopped talking. Sounds like he's repeating a word. "Honest." But that doesn't sound quite right.

Mr. Varsity throws the vampire to the ground and holds him there. Again, the force startles Lily.

In the distance, Lily hears sirens. The phone nearly slips from her hand as she listens. Yes, sirens. She didn't make the call. What is going on?

Frowning around unpleasant mutterings, the short man digs out his phone from a shiny pocket and makes a call.

Prone, the vampire says, "So many stories!"

Mr. Varsity says, "Tell him to hurry," to his friend, who's speaking in Spanish, his free hand chopping the air.

Someone from the Lounge must have called 911. Lily surmises that the vampire had hurt someone back there and now these two are here to settle things.

"Honest," the shadow repeats. Then, the shadow bucks the man off him, getting to his feet. It appears effortless.

Lily's heart kicks up and she steps back, Aleron right along with her. "Stay away from him. Please listen. You're going to get hurt."

The second man looks back in time to get caught by the vampire. In one smooth action, the vampire throws Mr. Jeans clear over the car she and Aleron stand by. He smashes gracelessly onto the street.

"*Mon Dieu*," Aleron says. He races after the fallen man.

The vampire looks astonished at what he just did. "Honest," he says again then laughs with disbelief. Disbelief, yes, for Mr. Jeans must weigh 250 pounds, if not more.

Lily glances back at Aleron who's waving his arms at approaching vehicles, pleading for them to halt. Brakes shriek. One vehicle comes narrowly short of hitting him and the guy moaning on the ground.

She gives a quick prayer of gratitude.

Mr. Varsity says takes a big swing at the vampire. The vampire catches the arm and pulls the man in, then bites the man's hand.

Lily moves in, holding her crucifix out at the end of its chain. A glow emanates from the gold icon.

The vampire squints then shoves the man into her with such force they both go down. Her shoulder, then her head, hit the car and her butt hits the pavement. The tossed man's impact to her chest takes the wind out of her.

Snapped from her hand, her phone clatters to the asphalt beneath the car.

She grunts, feeling deep bruises already forming. Lumps will surely follow. She wriggles under Mr. Varsity who has fallen across her. He's got to weigh two of her and then some.

Her eyes flick up to the shadow, looming over them. She wonders if he can hear her heart pounding.

The vampire says, "Honest."

The throb of a headache begins.

Not 'honest.' He's pronouncing the last syllable strange. "Agnes Martin gave that to you as a Confirmation present."

She doesn't understand. His eyes are on her chest. She looks down to the chain and icon there. The one her grandmother had indeed gifted her. She says, catching her breath, "How do you know that?"

"Honest."

No. Not honest. Onyx? Is he saying, 'onyx'? That makes less sense.

The man rolls off Lily and attempts to crawl away.

From beneath the car, her phone rings. Of course. It's Reed. His ring tone is the first bars of one of their shared songs. Reed is out of reach.

The vampire says, "I see her. She saw us." He sounds astounded. Eyes black as sin, appear even larger. "Ore. Gold. Melted. Sculpted. Blessed. An order of nuns. Will you sell it to me?"

Lily is very confused.

Sirens close in.

"Thirsty." He grabs the man's ankle with one gloved hand. With a sharp yank, he pulls the man back with the same delighted laugh as before.

"Let him go," Lily says. "Please."

"I'm thirsty. It's Onyx and I feel so good," he says exaggerating the words.

Strobing lights flash across the masonry.

While the man struggles to kick himself free of the vampire, Lily folds her legs beneath her. Forming an idea, she says, "I like your watch. Will you tell me about it?"

As she had hoped, he remembers the stolen wristwatch and releases the man in order to look at it. She pulls her knees up just before he hunches down by her, his fingers touching the pavement as he looks to her.

Free, Mr. Varsity scrambles away, gets to his feet, and shambles back the way he came.

Unfortunately, still well within reach of the vampire, Lily struggles not to panic. He is clearly touched in the head and thirsty for blood.

Holding out his arm so that she can see the watch, he says, "This belonged to Athena Joy Roberts. I don't think I'd get even ten bucks for it. Maybe not even five."

Within a ring of rhinestones, the second hand sweeps by. Though in good condition, she wordlessly agrees with him that it wouldn't fetch much money.

Lily presses back against the car. "You need to return it to her. It's the right thing to do. And it may have sentimental value."

Holding the watch up at eye level, he frowns. Disappointment in his voice, he says, "It doesn't. She got it with a five-finger discount. Her friends dared her." He then says, "She's the one with the Onyx."

He looks to the South Street intersection when an ambulance wails toward South Wave Vibe Lounge. "I should go back to her for more."

The shadow looks back at her. "But I'm thirsty now." His eyes are black. She swallows, afraid she'll fall into them. But there's no room to maneuver. He's too close.

One of his hands takes her knee possessively. He coils to strike her. A breath tanged with rust rolls out of his widening mouth sprouting fangs.

Her wrists itch and her heart pounds. Instantly she's back in the penthouse, back in the chair, back in Jean-Paul's grip. She feels that grip with its vampiric strength, smells his bad cologne and worse breath. *She pays for Ron's life with her own*, Jean-Paul had snarled in French.

Despite her heart racing, Lily also remembers her prayers. She remembers what her grandmother Agnes would sing with her. Lily says, "How did you know about my grandmother?"

A sudden rattling noise steals their attention.

Too late to dodge, the vampire takes a shopping cart to his face and is flung onto his back. Lily looks up to see Aleron, his hands gripping the handles at the other end of the cart. For good measure, he rolls the cart back then thrusts it once more when the vampire attempts to pull himself up.

Helping her to stand, Aleron smiles wanly, "It is no Peugeot."

Now they both have their crucifixes at the ready. Aleron's is larger and without a chain.

The vampire spins up to his feet, looking at her. Less in anger and more like he's confused by the turn of events. In the crosses' glow, he blinks and turns aside.

Lily spares a look around them. Pedestrians gawk from a safe distance.

The vampire falls upon the cart's contents. He looks ecstatic. A big smile on his face, his hands touching the shabby blanket and the tied-up plastic bags. Forgetting Lily and Aleron, he talks to himself. Rummaging. He laughs. "I hear you. I hear you. I see you!"

The cart's owner, a bearded man with a wool cap, smacks the vampire's hands, "Don't touch my belongings. They are my belongings. They belong to me. I didn't say you can touch them."

"You have so many stories in here." A kid at a toy chest, the pirate dives in searching for the biggest or noisiest or most intricate prize.

Turning to Lily, Aleron wonders what to do now. She wishes to know herself. Neither one has a stake to use to subdue the vampire. He's already demonstrated himself to be strong enough to causally throw a grown man.

The cart's frantic owner simultaneously tries to restore order, repack his belongings, and chase the vampire away.

"How much for this?" In his hand is a wooden doll, the size of an infant. The yellow of the thin fabric of its dress has faded in spots.

Suddenly Lily feels Aleron's protective arm around her, drawing her backward. He had seen what she hasn't till just now. Two more men have come for the vampire with Mr. Varsity cowering behind them.

So engrossed with futile haggling, the shadow isn't even aware of the new players until a knife is close enough to his throat for a shave. Its wielder is a bull-necked, bald-headed man with tattoos near his threatening eyes.

Lily feels Aleron communicating through his tightening grip on her upper arm that she's to stay out of this. He's right of course. None of this is their business. Just because a vampire is involved should not mean that she involves herself.

The vampire's enthusiasm hasn't lost its edge. Still with a delirious smile. And distracted this way, he doesn't notice the doll's owner grabbing what's his, then quickly carting everything away.

Knife Man isn't smiling. "You touch my things, you touch my woman, you gotta pay."

"That blade was used to carve your initials on Carla Esteban's right thigh."

Pressing the knife, the man says, "Who told you that?"

Safely behind Knife Man, Mr. Varsity says, "He's always saying things like that. He knows, man."

The ringtone calls her again. She had forgotten. Reed must be frantic. But she doesn't dare take her eyes away, to turn her back to these men, to stoop beside the car and grasp for the phone.

With a single nod toward 4th Street, he says, "Go check on Louis."

Eager to do so, Mr. Varsity hurries to where several people have gathered around Louis, some stooped beside his prone form, others using their phones.

The threat of being sliced up hasn't caused the shadow's happy record to skip. He babbles on about the knife, where it was made, its composition, that it had been used to wound or kill several people, his fangs and dark eyes evident, but perhaps, considered part of his costume.

Lily sees it. Keen as the blade. Something has shifted. The shadow's smile curdles into something cruel. "Their blood full of pleas, full of screams. Blood. Blood. Blood."

"Leave him alone. Please, just go." Lily's words sound pathetic, even to hear own ears.

She's ignored.

"I'm thirsty."

The vampire lunges up for the man's throat. At the same time, the bald man counters, slashing. The knife gashes the vampire's throat. Skin opens, bloodless. Undeterred the vampire bites. Desperate Baldy swipes again. Again ineffectual. Then he plunges the knife deep into the shadow's upper back.

Inexplicably, all of Lily's hesitation, doubt, fear are walled away, replaced with resolve that she can't account for. The resolve coats her body, strengthens her heart, rises from her throat, "Leave him alone!" She's not bluffing confidence now. Panic has fled her.

With nothing to back up an unspoken threat, she is calm and singularly determined. She parts from Aleron, leaves the relative safety of their distance from the fighting men. She steps toward them with an authority that she absolutely does not possess.

As though possessed herself, she moves to the vampire, her gaze steady on his demonic eyes. "Leave. Now." She says the words fully expecting the shadow to comply, though he has demonstrated that he could overpower her even easier than he already has with these men. But he doesn't. Doesn't move a hand toward her. Makes no threats. He does exactly as she commanded him. He lets Knife Man go, turns, and runs off.

She watches him go, racing up 4th Street and out of view. Once he's gone, she trembles, then breaks. All the fear she somehow banished returns at once, crashing into her.

At her gasping, Aleron takes her side, holding her, holding her up.

She says, "What just happened?"

"Something miraculous."

fourteen

A New Place

L ily's texts spin Reed into motion and he runs to find Kyle.

Once in the Audi, he tries to raise Lily, but gets no answer. No answer from Lily means the worst, that she is hurt, bleeding, needing medical attention.

After minutes of tense silence, she finally texts back. She's safe and not all that far.

Reaching Lombard Street, Reed leaps from the car just as it comes to a stop at the corner. Lily paces outside a community center while Aleron watches from where he's seated on a concrete structure.

Hearing his shouts, Lily breaks from her pacing. He reaches to hug her, but she crosses her arms and shies from his touch. "I'm fine. I'm fine. Just bruises." Lily unfurls a hand in Aleron's direction, "He did warn me not to get involved."

"Well, someone has sense," Reed says.

Reed hadn't even glanced Aleron's way till now. The man drifts closer to them, posture and expression hang-dog. Reed won't say so, but the man looks defeated. Marie's quasi-death has turned him into a ghost.

Abashed, Lily says that her plan had only been to follow the vampire. "I couldn't just watch."

"Then don't. You could have gone anywhere else, kept your head down. You didn't have to stalk a vampire." What could possess her to do that?

"I wasn't intending to do anything at first. Just see what he was up to. Then there's a fight and I tried to warn the two guys to back off. Of course, they didn't listen."

With an accusing finger pointed at Reed, she adds, "And don't tell me you would have walked away. That you wouldn't have helped."

"I would have left it to the police. Vampire or not, you could have gotten hurt. Any one of them might have had a weapon."

He's relieved that she's okay, but he realizes that there's something wrong. The feeling of being apart touches him now, even with Lily. It's like she's fuzzy, blurred at the edges. Details are missing. It's like he hasn't seen her for months instead of hours. She's different. No, Reed is the one who's different.

"Reed?" Lily says.

"Let's go home."

Kyle cuts in, "First, I have questions, Lily, Mr. Aleron."

Reed shakes his head. "They can wait. She's tired and shaken up."

"She either talks to me now, or she talks to Mr. Ashton later." Kyle adds, "None of us want that."

"It's okay," Lily says, giving Reed a look meant to reassure, but fails to do so. He doesn't like any of this. But no sense in making this an issue, to argue when it can wrap up in a few minutes.

She turns to Kyle and explains what she and Aleron have been up to while interpreting for her friend. Kyle listens attentively and Reed bites his tongue at turns of her story. Wasn't a man dressed as a pirate enough of a warning not to get involved? Or that he was handsy with just about everyone he passed? Or that he was undead and dangerous?

At the point where she says the vampire pitched a man into oncoming traffic, he says, exasperated, "You should just have left it to the police and been done with it, Lil'. You said you were going to call them."

"I was." Back to Kyle, "Then, I thought about what you had told us." To both, "All I did was try to warn others to keep away from the man." Making a point to Kyle, she says, "And I said nothing about him being a vampire."

Kyle says, "Apart from what he was wearing, can you give a description of the man? Height, weight, race, distinguishing marks like a scar or tattoo?"

She provides Kyle a physical description as best she can. In the excitement she mostly recollects his clothes and make-up.

"He'd repeat himself. He'd say what I thought was the word, 'honest,' but then when I was closer to him, it sounded more like 'onyx.' Do you know what he meant?"

"No."

"He might have been on drugs."

"We cannot become intoxicated. Drugs have no effect on us."

"Well, his behavior was strange. Don't you think? He didn't seem to understand his own strength. He appeared surprised by what he could do. What he did do."

Kyle gives a small shrug, noncommittal. "I will say that I agree with your husband. Don't do this again, Lily. It may turn out differently."

"This wasn't what I had in mind for a night out."

"And thank you for your discretion and leaving before the police arrived to question you. I won't mention this to Mr. Ashton."

Reed says, "Who is this guy?"

"Doesn't fit anyone I know."

"What will you do? He's gotten away. He's going to harm other people."

"It's like you said, he was antagonized by a gang. He was defending himself."

"But he wanted blood."

"We all do."

Lily looks to Reed, who ducks his head, not wanting to know what she's thinking.

Kyle says, "I'm genuinely glad you're both all right. But if I had not been clear to you before, stay out of our affairs."

Folding her arms, her face sets in an expression, Reed recognizes. "As you say." Meaning the matter has been tabled, but not concluded.

***

In a cab, Lily tries to catch Reed's glances. He's tense, and he must still be stewing on her heedless pursuit of a shadow. She's not. She hadn't meant to worry him, but she doesn't regret following the vampire. Maybe she could have handled it better, but on the whole, it was right.

Along with Aleron, they ride in silence. Slouched, Aleron absently paws his beard, eyes half-closed. Reed sits knees apart, one hand atop hers in the space between them. In the fabric of his flannel, she can smell beer, leather, and a trace of feminine perfume.

In fact, she feels charged. Like being over-caffeinated. Tinged with the excitement of having done something illicit, naughty.

She puts her other hand over his, stroking the large knuckles. Her nails are unpainted. She hasn't kept up on her appearance since that morning in the Parisian hotel, sobbing into the bed sheet, not knowing if her groom was hurt or dead.

Vampires have given her other priorities.

Reed raises a silent question when his eyes finally meet hers. She gives him a sly smile. He doesn't smile back.

The cab rolls to a stop before her apartment building. Reed reaches past Lily offering his hand to Aleron. The men shake firm, eyes meeting, holding for a moment. A handshake that says more than can be said in English or French. Lily's pleased to see it.

Lily follows Aleron up to the door to see him inside, remind him of when to be ready by in the morning, and wish him *bonne nuit*.

She hurries back to the cab. "You're right. You're right. I know I worried you."

He's listening. Encouraged, she takes his hand and seals it with a tender kiss. The tenseness in his expression softens. A little bit.

She says, "Look at it this way: Now I have more experience dealing with…," she eyes the front of the cab, checking the driver, "shadows."

"Let's not make this a thing, Lil'."

She means to make light of it, but clearly, he's not won over yet.

"He said something strange. The shadow, that is."

"He spoke to you? What did he say?"

"He knew about my necklace." She brushes her fingers over it. "He knew that my grandmother had given it to me. He knew her name."

"That's… something. How would he know that?"

"I have no idea how he would know such a personal detail."

"Well, I'm glad you have it. See? I was right. Never take it off."

The vampire had been so off. She doesn't care how dismissive Kyle had been when she said the vamp was high on something. He was. Either that or otherwise unbalanced.

She says, "You were right."

"Why didn't you tell Kyle?"

"I don't know. Maybe I felt it wasn't something to share. It felt personal."

"We can't give Kyle any more grief. I feel like I'm hanging by a thread as it is. I'm sure nothing this evening has gone as he planned."

"What does that mean? Where did Kyle take you? What had you done tonight?"

He doesn't answer. He has a far-away stare, and she will give him the time he needs. All the while, she pets Reed's shoulder with her free hand or nuzzles against it.

Breaking the silence, he says, "I did meet some people who are trying to help me. Oh, Lil', she's got this gorgeous Ferrari"

"That's what you want to talk about? Her car? Who is she?"

"Her name's Shipley. She interprets dreams. So, I told her about the crows and losing my memories. She helped me figure out something and told me that I might be able to fight back. Get my memories back."

"How?"

"This whole time, I thought the crows ate the straw. But I don't believe they did. They're out there somewhere. If I can find them."

"What do you have to do?"

"She gave me exercises to help strengthen my mind. Put up a barricade to protect myself. She said psychics do it, but really anyone can."

Psychics now, Lily silently wows. "Have you practiced what she taught you?"

"A little, while Kyle drove me around."

He continues to tell her about Emma Shipley's theory that if he learns to control the dream-not-a-dream, he could defend himself from the birds' attack and learn what they did with his straw.

Lily says, "I thought they were eating the straw."

"I did too," he says almost in a laugh. "But when I thought about it, I realized I didn't really know. I just assumed."

***

Inside their new apartment, the lights are off. With bare floors and the lack of furniture, nothing softens the hollow quietness. They shuffle in, Lily ahead of Reed, who gropes for a light switch.

When the lights spring on, so does Lily. Illuminated, she drops her purse and gazes at him with a look he's slow to recognize. She leaps into his arms, throwing hers around him, her lips to his for a long, ardent kiss.

Astonished, Reed falls back a step but holds his wife aloft. His surprise melts into shared passion. He has wanted her touch all evening, but only now, enveloped in her warmth, her scent, her caresses, does he realize the depths of his longing. His earlier concerns about feeding, forgotten; the crows, caged; Lily's misadventure, well, she's obviously more than all right.

Her touch is magic. The press of her lips, her fingers at the nape of his neck, the sound and feel of her breath.

Moments like this are of the kind they should be sharing while on their honeymoon. Present, carefree, delirious, thousands of miles from their everyday world, tasting every food simply prepared, yet zesty, to see the sights and heights of the French cities and countrysides, being charmed by the locals, who in turn are charmed by Lily and by extension, Reed, treating them as their own, a young couple happy and hopeful, looking forward to a bright future.

When she comes up for air, her beautiful brown eyes shine at him. Even with normal human vision she appears haloed with life, beautifully aglow.

Grinning, he says, "Well, all right."

"Are you okay?" She means her being suspended.

"I can hold you forever."

Her laugh lightens his heart and broadens his smile. She dives back into more kisses.

His boots clap the hardwood as he weaves between stacks of gift boxes from their wedding registry. Linens, cookware, small appliances promise a normal wedded life in this spacious home. One that anticipates a crop of children. At least three kids, maybe five, darting underfoot, trailed by bubbles and giggles.

He finds their bedroom down the hallway and carries his bride across its threshold into the semi-darkness.

***

In the room's half-light Lily laughs, hanging onto Reed more tightly when he spins her around till she's hovering over the bed, an air mattress set atop a fold-out aluminum frame, the best she could manage today.

Silly with excitement, she's been wired since the fight, even after the spent adrenaline. She needs Reed to ground her and help dissipate this energy.

Hungry kisses along his rough jaw then to his ear where she snatches at the lobe between her teeth, nibbling the fleshy morsel.

He gooses her hip, and she whoops in laughter, releasing his ear. When they fall atop the covers, Lily gives a gasp. Pain flashes across her upper back, surprising herself and startling Reed, who instantly pulls back.

The mattress squishes beneath her shifting weight when she sits up. "I'm all right. I'm all right." Her arms guide him back to her, showing him that he can, and that he must, continue.

Reed eyes her with a skeptical tilt of his head. Then, to her delight, he smiles slyly, "I'm going to have to see for myself."

He helps her out of her navy top, lifting her arms and gently sliding the fabric up till it's over her head and discarded. Concern returns to those eyes. Her head drops and they both take in the damage. A swath of deepening purple across her chest and a splotch on her stomach toward her right side. That's what she gets when a grown man's body slams into her.

He peers over her shoulder. Going by the tenderness she suspects worse purpling. She meets his eyes after he's done inspecting, hoping their intimacy hasn't already come to an end.

"How does it look?"

"Like the car won."

He sits beside her, the mattress wheezing, and takes her by the hips to draw her into his lap. Brushing aside her hair, he kisses the back of her neck. She shivers despite the warmth.

He nuzzles into her, and speaks softly by ear, "I think you'll live. You'll be smarting for a few days."

The tenor and care in his voice carries tremors to her ear and quickens her pulse.

"I'm glad you're safe," he says in a more serious tone.

His large, warm hands caress the rounds of her shoulders rousing goosebumps. Then his fingertips whisper over the skin of her upper back, skimming near the edge of the bruising, she winces, but also finds it's a good kick of discomfort.

He murmurs, "I've wanted you all night." His hands circle to her front. They gently cup her bra-clad breasts, his thumbs teasing at the material.

She wets her lips, flushing with heady heat that demands that she get out of the rest of her clothes and he out of his. With great reluctance, she parts from him.

On her feet, she backs toward the bathroom, "I'm going to freshen up. You better be here when I return. And looking more comfortable."

***

After the door to the *en suite* closes, Reed hurries out of his flannel and under shirts, kicks off his work boots, stomps out of his jeans. Does a breath check, then sniffs his armpits.

Iffy.

Maybe Lily has some mints in her purse.

He already misses her, the physical connection he just shared with her. He knows she'll return in a minute, but in her absence, he feels an emptiness, the distance he's felt all his short vampire existence.

Reed turns a lamp on. The bed had been made with a sheet set, blanket, coverlet and a pair of pillows. From one end of the mattress, he follows the cord to its control wand. He presses a button, activating a whirring vacuum noise. Not adding air, he realizes, expelling it, deflating the mattress more.

All at once, several thoughts grip him. The device slips from his hand. Does he remember how to make love to Lily? What excites her? Where are her favorite spots and positions? What is their policy on protection now that they're married? What had they done in Paris? What if he goes too far? What if he loses control and his eyes turn black like they had earlier with Eleanor? What if he bites her? What if he burns her?

His mood sinks as he looks to the bed where his insecurities now lie.

***

Still tingled by her husband's touches, Lily's body hums before the mirror. Though tender, the bruised spots reflected on her front and the splash of mottled purple across her back don't dampen her mood. She's still giddy, more than she has a right to be. Who could have predicted such an encounter as earlier tonight? Her, raised to be a proper lady of society, chasing after vampires?

Thrilling, in retrospect. Is that the right word?

Reed would chastise her. Had actually. And in the mirror, she can picture mother certainly doing so. Anne would remind Lily, again, of her being as willful as she's always been, insisting on going her own way.

Maybe they're right. But for the grace of God, things could have turned out differently tonight with bystanders seriously injured or killed.

Chastened a touch, she takes comfort in what has followed and what promises to continue outside this door.

Surveying the double vanity, Lily finds no more than the essentials she had left here from prior visits. This should have been their home by now, but apartment hunting took longer than either expected. A week before their wedding, they signed the paperwork for this place. Once back from their honeymoon, they had planned to pack Reed's belongings and send them here. Then, it'd be her turn next month.

Having neatly folded the rest of what she wore tonight, she attends to hygienic things, finishes brushing her teeth with travel-size spearmint toothpaste, applies scented soap to her hands, face, and underarms. She finishes with a brush and makes the best of her hair that had been abused by wind and sweat, careful of the fresh bumps on her scalp.

A momentary pout for not thinking ahead. Discreetly she had bought Parisian lingerie to make Reed say "ooh-la-la" one lucky night. But it is also not at hand. Her dun-colored bra and panties will have to do.

***

Lily steps back into the bedroom, pleased to see Reed down to his briefs.

When he turns to look at her, she catches the shadow of something in his expression. Pensive? Gloomy? But then it's gone. Whisked away, if it had been there at all.

Smile returning, he saunters her way, getting an equal eyeful of her as she has of him. Maybe she would have once demurred under his gaze. But just as she had on their first night as Mr. and Mrs. Williams, she feels like the bride she is, loved, adored by her man, safe in his arms, in their new apartment.

Now, bare and open, she hopes to recapture their newlywed glow. She can share anything and everything with him, whom she trusts like no one else.

His lips to hers. They kiss as before, his hands toasty warm, their touch pats of butter melting into her skin, heightening her energy, bring her to her toes, arching, reaching for him to be closer to him to melt into him in return, to be the one flesh they had vowed to one another.

Then. Then…

Reed has stopped, his head down, contemplative. A moment happens, and in that moment, she feels the energy of the room shift. She looks down herself. His left hand holds her right forearm, his thumb grazing the raised scarring there.

"Reed? Are you all right?"

"I was thinking of this earlier tonight. I know it's important, that it means something, but I can't…"

A scowl of irritation crosses his face. His free hand rubbing at his temple as though trying to coax something out of it.

To soothe his agitation, she insists she's all right. "It doesn't hurt. Sometimes it's sensitive."

He lets her go, takes a step back, turns aside. "The crows came back. They took more of me."

"Oh, Reed." Her hand briefly covers her mouth. "Just now?"

He simply shakes his head.

"When you were with Kyle? What happened?"

"I really don't want to talk about it. Didn't go well."

"Reed, talk to me."

She reaches for him, but he shies away. He sounds so vulnerable. Her heart squeezes in shared pain but then is dashed to pieces with what he says next.

"I feel the man you married is slipping away. I'm on this downward slope; every step gets easier but I'm heading in the wrong direction. To a cliff or a pit. Then I'll be like Marie."

An anguished sound escapes her as tears come. This has all gone wrong. She thinks of her discussions with Aleron in Paris and here at home—how he lost Marie piece by piece till they didn't recognize each other.

"*I* scare myself." He tightens up, not saying anything more.

Lily flings her arms around him, bringing him to stop. "I am *not* afraid of you. And I wasn't last night. Not of you, but of what's become of all of us. And you're right." Head back, her wet eyes look up. "You're right to be concerned and torn and frustrated and angry. And scared. I am too."

Head bowed, he's listening, but doesn't appear convinced.

"You're not alone. I'm here. Kyle's looking out for you. Michael and the professor. They helped you last night. With all that was against you, Marie, Eddie, the crows, you pulled through. You can do it again."

Touching his shoulders, her hands seek to reassure. "And the fact that you are struggling with this shows that you *are* still human. You're still a good man."

"Don't say that," he says, tone blade sharp as he cleaves from Lily and paces away. "I killed Eddie, didn't I?"

"Yes." She blows out a breath. "You did. And if you hadn't, he would have killed me and Aleron. You had your back to the wall. Marie put you in that position. She put us all in that hotel room. You didn't see what they had done before you all arrived. I saw. They were depraved and cruel. I watched them drink from that poor woman. Like a horror movie. Like a satanic ritual."

Helpless, Lily had witnessed the woman die. She vomited at the horrid sight. Even recalling it now, she wants to retch. "Jean-Paul wanted to kill me next. He was right in my face and I could smell her death on his breath. See her blood around his mouth."

Trying to convince him, she says, "You are not them. That will never be you."

"You don't know that. You don't understand."

To his back, she says, "Help me understand. Tell me how I can help you."

"I didn't drink tonight. I couldn't do it. I..." He shakes his head, wrestling with what he must be wanting to say. "We didn't go to a store or a clinic." Then softer, as though with shame, he wrings the words out, "It... it has to be fresh. It has to be from a person."

He would have to drink from someone. Their blood.

By what she has read, she's not surprised, yet she had hoped it would be different for Reed somehow. That maybe he could avoid needing blood at all.

After a moment he says, "We've just got to find a way to bring me back. Before I do worse. Before I forget who I am."

"Look at me." Closer to him, "Please look at me."

Sullen, he turns, and draws his eyes up.

She points to the burn on her arm. "This is when we met. You rescued me. Just like you had last night. That's what you do. You and Chuck and Diego and Downey and so many others who go into danger to help perfect strangers. If you forget again, I will remind you again."

Closer still, her finger circles his heart. "I'm here. Now and forever." She casts her eyes up to his, "Do you want to drink from me?"

"Absolutely not, Lil'."

"Why not?"

"I have to explain?" Again, he breaks from her.

"I know it's not..." She reaches for a proper word. "Ideal? But it would be a lot easier with me."

He turns away, "I am not considering this."

"Listen." She reaches for him, softening her tone, "It's not so different than when we kiss, you know, a little too passionately. Love bites. Hickeys. Couples do it all the time. We've done it."

"Not the same."

"I don't agree." Now she turns away, frustrated with his stubbornness. A yawn escapes her. She turns back on her heel.

"Promise to think about it. The shadow we saw tonight wasn't... all there in the head. I guess? Maybe he was high, maybe he wasn't. But clearly, he wanted blood. I don't want you to let yourself get like that. Promise me that you won't."

"If it comes to it, I will come to you."

He returns to her, arms open. She presses into the shelter of his body.

He says, "I can't believe you ran after a vampire."

"Impressed?"

"Are you really all right?"

She yawns, "Yes."

"How did he know about your grandmother?"

"He seemed to know a lot, not just about my necklace, but other people's stuff. He said they spoke to him. Maybe he's psychic?"

He kisses the top of her head and guides her to the bed. She gets comfy in the crook of his muscled shoulder. He absently strokes her arm. "I'm sorry this didn't turn out like we had wanted."

"You'll have to make it up to me."

part
II

chapter
fifteen

Refuge

A grey pall clings to Philadelphia this late morning.
Expecting rain, pedestrians tuck umbrellas under their arms, top their heads with caps, and take the bite out of the October chill with steaming coffee and tea.

Lily's heart feels overcast by all that has transpired. A shapeless, cloying shroud. She would lose her way in this fog, but for knowing where to turn. Here, even under murky despair, church offers an undimmed light.

Still, Lily must be cautious. A silk scarf wraps her hair and frames her face. Along with over-sized sunglasses, she hopes the accessories allow her to pass incognito. For added measure, she has avoided her family's church by coming here to St. Patrick's. Being recognized by a clergy member or parishioner of her church would prompt questions she's unprepared to answer. And if word of her sighting got back to her family, everything would come undone.

As he had yesterday, Aleron accompanies Lily. In a way, Aleron is also part of her disguise as she may be mistaken as his daughter, given their age gap of more than twenty years.

Both bruised in battle and sustained by their shared faith, she has leaned on him as he has leaned on her. An abiding friendship despite having only met less than a week ago. Even in his grief, he has been a listening

133

ear, and mindful of that grief, she has tried to comfort and give space in
the right measures.

When Aleron had rescued Lily from a brutal fate promised by her
tormentors, she had no idea how immeasurably trusting of him she would
become given her initial contemptuous disbelief. She dismissed his hinting at
creatures of the night as delusions. For goodness' sake, she actually saw their
inhuman features and refused to believe her own eyes. She was sorely wrong.

Over breakfast earlier, she updated Aleron on what Reed told her
about Ms. Shipley and her idea to help him turn the tables on the crows. If
she's correct, Reed may be able to recover his memories. And on that point,
she asked Aleron how soon Marie had lost her memories of him.

In his baritone French, Aleron said, "You still have time. Marie had
remembered me even after months apart."

And there it was, Lily realized. All that Aleron and Marie experienced
were markers on the same road she and Reed travel on. A shared destination.
Will there come a day when Reed will no longer know her, that he too will
destroy lives for some mad scheme, that Lily must put a stake into his heart?

So, to church she's come to pray for a different course.

Once through the vestibule and into the sanctuary, the gloomy weather
is forgotten. Candlelight and their reflections thrown by polished marble
and wood illuminates the space offering respite. The score of worshipers
huddle in the walnut pews or wait their turn at the confessional booths.

Lily and Aleron dip their fingers in the basin of holy water, bless themselves, then proceed to a nearby pew, where they genuflect toward the cross
before taking their seats.

Seated, Lily removes her rosary from her purse. Turning it over in her
hands she takes a moment to reframe, and bring herself into a spiritual
space. Her fingertips worry the circle of wooden beads.

Between her and the aisle, Aleron bows his head, his brow nearly
touching the pew before him. He has the attitude of prayer, quiet and still
but for his lips shaping unvoiced sentiments.

She turns to her personal prayers, beginning with gratitude, thankful
for God's blessings—health, family, friends and her students, Reed's love.
Then she petitions for the healing of the sick, which now includes Reed
first on the list.

Close to her heart are memories of the Sunday mornings she and her
grandmother had spent together in church. As a girl, she absorbed her
grandmother's evident love for service. Lily recalls the sweet tenderness of
her voice, her knotty fingers, and her sky-blue eyes.

She wonders how the vampire pirate knew so much about her grandmother's necklace. Slipping it out from beneath her blouse she holds it by the tips of her fingers just as Reed had last night. The thought that Reed could, even for a moment, believe that God has forsaken him anguishes Lily.

Though… had Reed's concern been unreasonable? Given how Aleron, and even herself, used their icons to hold back the vampires that were ready to bite and kill.

When she first saw Aleron's crucifix glow, she assumed the effect was due to a trick of the light heightened by fear and adrenaline. No, she had seen it right.

Why did it glow before the vampires that night in a Parisian park, but not before Reed in his apartment? Is it because the others had meant her harm and Reed does not? Or her fear of them and her trust in Reed?

Chanting to himself, voice subdued, Aleron broods still. Since their clash at the Whitpain Hotel, his eyes have turned from weary to defeated.

She grips his hand and leans by him, "I am sorry." She reminds him what Kyle had told them both that night. Marie's body will be transported in a casket to a mortuary in Paris, where Aleron would receive it upon his return.

How will the man return home now that Marie is in a coma of sorts? Will Aleron be able to find new purpose, return to professional photography, and gain back some of what he lost?

Outside, by a waiting taxi, Lily embraces Aleron in a tender hug. This is goodbye. She tries to impart to him the solace she received from her prayers. Despite a tear or two reaching his beard, a lightness has come over him and she hopes it will accompany him home.

Once he's away, Lily returns to the church and seeks out one of the priests here. She has already considered what she will ask in a way that's more casual than suspicious.

When one is free, she steps right up. Careful with her words when speaking with a man of God, she implies that she is researching a book. More truthfully, she says she's interested in Catholic Church lore on the subject of supernatural beings and how the Church dealt with them, perhaps even cured them.

The young priest offers to schedule a time to meet and discuss her questions. In the meantime, he tells her she may browse the library and suggests also inquiring at other churches in the area.

She promises that she will and thanks him.

That's one avenue of attack. Lily will try another.

sixteen

Penny Sedgwick

A long the Schuylkill River, flows the Manayunk neighborhood, once a mill and factory town, now a popular enclave within the city. Often Lily comes here to shop the charming boutiques and grab a bite with friends.

She's less familiar with this particular block of Main Street businesses, their backs to the canal, their fronts resplendent with colorful facades and autumnal ornaments. The single picture window of Penny's Arcane showcases seasonal decorations. Taped to it, a flyer welcomes all to attend an upcoming book signing.

The sun penetrates the cloud cover, throwing dazzling beams.

From the copper door handle, aged green, grows a stalk topped with a pinwheel, which spins when Lily pulls the door open.

Past the chime of the door, Lily is surprised twice. The shop is larger than she would have guessed from outside. Racks, shelves, and stands of merchandise extend well past the off-center checkout counter.

Also, there are more customers than she expected.

College girls in twos and threes, orbited by boyfriends, peruse fabrics and jewelry with their fingers. One pair snickers while voguing with glamorous wigs before a mirror. A woman, older than the girls, considers the books a man holds in each hand, debating which to purchase. Near the checkout counter, girls examine baubles in a tray.

Wooden steps creak as a couple descends the staircase from the second floor. A sign by the lower landing indicates more books and specialty items may be found upstairs.

The place appears as any Halloween shop might. Large spiders dangle before lacy webs, skeletons drape over tombstones, ravens peer at dolls resembling witches.

With the register abandoned, Lily wonders if this Penny Sedgwick is even here. Perhaps one of the chatty girls assists with running the store? Lily should have called ahead, but she hadn't expected a bustling shop.

Near the entrance, packets of colorful powders, incense sticks, resins, herbs, and roots offer tranquility and healing.

Lily heads over to a collection of masks. May as well shop for Reed while she's here. In the meantime, Sedgwick may show up. Many of the masks are based on familiar horror characters and classic movie monsters. Rubbery faces with holes for eyes and mouths, fake hair, blisters, warts, green skin. Though harmless in her hands she can imagine when worn with matching cloaks and cowls they would frighten. A spindle rack holds accessories. Fake blood capsules, makeup palettes, silicone noses and ears, wolf claws, vampire fangs, demon contact lenses, temporary tattoos, latex wounds.

Her own students get excited this time of year, telling her again and again what princesses or superheroes they'll dress as, what candies they hope will fill their sacks. Often, she will get caught up in their delight, thinking of when she will take her own children-to-be to the doors of neighbors, holding their tiny hands, helping them climb the stoops, reminding them to say, "Thank you," when receiving their treats.

She puts back a gaudy Mardi Gras mask in favor of a simple domino mask made of black leather with satin ribbon ties. Reed will look dashing wearing this. Too bad she won't get to spend the evening with him while he wears it with his only suit. He does not like dressing up.

From the checkout counter, a phone rattles loud enough to be heard from any corner of the shop. A woman wearing a pointed witch's hat excuses herself from a customer to answer it. The sleeves of her white blouse billow with her quick steps.

"Penny's Arcane. We're open till six o'clock. Yes…" After finishing with the caller and setting the phone down, she peers at Lily, noticing her looking her way, "Yes? May I help you?" She approaches Lily.

"I certainly hope so. Are you're Penny Sedgwick?"

"Yes. I don't believe I've seen you in my shop before. First time in the Arcane? Welcome. Welcome. What are you seeking? Interested in some decorations for Halloween? We have many items that enhance the ambiance of any gathering, or seance, or haunting." She says the last word as though channeling a ghost. "Items on that table are discounted. Readings are by appointment only."

Lily says, "No. Thank you." She needs to warm up, "I will need to purchase a mask for my husband."

Up close, Lily sees a comma of white hair escape from the hat, which is pulled down tight. Her blouse is embroidered with green leaves and purple insects. Pinned to the fabric is a pinwheel brooch made of bright copper.

Looking up now she notes the painted ceiling depicting a gorgeous sunny sky, windswept clouds, and brilliantly feathered birds.

Then something in her peripheral vision dashes by, just above eye-level. The animal's sudden movement startles Lily. She twists around and finds a habitat trail. The clear plastic tube worms through the shelving along the walls. Lily tracks its length till it disappears to the second floor.

Larger than a mouse and sleeker than a guinea pig, the animal has scurried down the tube to another area of the shop.

The woman says, "That was Cincinnati on her patrol."

Lily turns her attention back to Ms. Sedgwick, who appears to be in her forties. Spots of glitter in her makeup.

Lily says, "A ferret?"

"A mink, actually. She has quite the social media following." Ms. Sedgwick adds, "A cat would be too cliche." Her hands flutter over the witch hat, bangles rattling.

"I don't know how to put what I'm asking into words."

"Well, gather your thoughts. When you're ready, I'll be here. You'll have to excuse me, this is a very busy—"

Again, the phone rings. Sedgwick waves a hand over it: *See?*

She answers it. "Yes. Till six. Want to make an appointment? Let me see. I'm afraid that's too soon. You should have called in August. Anything I have will be after the 31st."

To Lily holding the mask, she says, holding the phone away, "Care to purchase that?"

"I need your help."

"Appointments only. I can see what's avail—"

"No—"

Sedgwick holds up her forefinger: *Quiet.*

When the woman finishes the call, Lily says, "This can't wait. You see, my husband and I..." She leans closer, "We were attacked."

"Do you need a healing spell? I have the standard sundries."

Lily lowers her voice, "My husband—he's not human."

"What is he? A dog? I'm difficult to shock. Out with it."

Lily considers not saying more. She doesn't want to endanger this woman. But if this Sedgwick is the real deal, she'd already know of the supernatural, and if not, she'd won't believe Lily and that will be the end of that.

She clears her throat, "A vampire."

Ms. Sedgwick says, "Perhaps you'd do better to visit Mr. Sandusky, the therapist a few doors down."

"Excuse me?" Lily says. Then she picks up on the woman's meaning. "I thought owning a shop like this you'd be more open-minded."

"Open-minded, yes. Foolish, no."

Before Sedgwick leaves the register, Lily quickly intercepts.

"I'm telling you the truth. Why would I make this up?"

"You'd be surprised the types that come to my shop or call. Some sincere, most juvenile. Happens more than you'd think." Ms. Sedgwick examines Lily, who won't budge, "You can try to convince me."

Lily says, "He can't be out in the sunlight."

Sedgwick says, "Porphyria."

"He has fangs."

"Recessed gums."

"Needs blood."

"He's anemic."

"He doesn't cast a shadow." *Pin that on a medical condition.*

Sedgwick's demeanor changes to one willing to listen. "What is it you want from me?"

"Anything that can help me make him human again."

Sedgwick shakes her head, "I don't like vampires. Negative energy. And the way they can sneak up on you." She wraps her hands about her shoulders as though chilled.

Lily nods, knowing the feeling too well.

Sedgwick steps back to the register. "Come back tonight." Then she pushes keys on the machine, "The mask will be $47.50. No returns."

chapter

seventeen

Arcane

M ain Street remains busy, even after hours. Orange lights string along shop windows where painted pumpkins gaze out. Posters invite passersby to visit the old haunted mill for a spooky good time.

Lily passes these as she returns to Penny's Arcane. According to the placard stuck to its display window, closing time had been 6:00 PM. Ms. Sedgwick may have used the hours between then and now to close the books, neaten the shop, have a meal, and freshen up before receiving Lily.

Gripping the pinwheel handle, Lily pauses for a quick prayer that somewhere in this shop exists a cure for Reed.

"Hello?"

Lily closes the door behind her. About to call again, she can hear the ceiling creak with footsteps. Soon Ms. Sedgwick's face appears over the upstairs banister. She waves, bidding Lily to come up.

The woman has washed her face clean of the festive makeup and wears whirling clothing and scarves.

Floor to ceiling bookshelves line the walls of the second floor. Display cases, more orderly than on the first level, form neat columns. Following Ms. Sedgwick past their ends, Lily gets glimpses of goblets, daggers, fantastic sculptures and many things she doesn't recognize.

Above a curtained doorway a sign reads: STAFF ONLY. And above that, the plastic tubing for the mink tunnels through to the other side. Through the open curtain and accordion metal gate, Lily finds herself in a quasi-office.

"Would you like herbal tea?" Ms. Sedgwick holds a ceramic teapot.

Lily seats herself at a small round table. A lacy purple cloth drapes over it. Wishing to be gracious, Lily accepts the tea and locally-sourced wildflower honey, but no on the local dairy milk. "Thank you for seeing me. I know that you must be busy."

Lily eyes the course of the tubing which finally comes to an end where it joins a cage set on the floor. Though the cage door is open, the creature seems content to remain there, curled up, its nose and ears twitching.

"Did you say its name was Cincinnati?"

Ms. Sedgwick glances back at her pet, "Yes. Not very imaginative I'm afraid. It's where we found each other. Ever been there? She may introduce herself later once she's comfortable. She's awfully curious and may wonder whom I've allowed back here. Don't be startled—she won't bite you."

"I didn't know minks could be pets."

"Goodness, no. They are not domesticated animals like ferrets." Lily notes the woman retired her hat, revealing stark white hair cut short on the sides and left longer on top where it's swept up by a phantom breeze. A lock above the temple has been dyed, looking like a bolt of blue streaking across a cloud. "And Cinci is not a pet. She owns the store and permits me run it."

Lily blinks.

"I'm kidding you, dear. Got you," Ms. Sedgwick says, returning the teapot to its set on a side table.

Cincinnati chirps from inside her hutch while regarding Ms. Sedgwick and her guest.

The room, part office and part... tornado disaster, draws Lily's interest. Atop the desk sits a computer and printer. Behind the desk and the wooden chair are filing cabinets. Strewn atop heaps of papers, small clay pots bud with flowers, cacti, even Venus flytraps. Tolerant of some disorder herself, she wonders how this woman can find anything. God-forbid that some slip of paper in this morass has what Reed needs. They'd spend a week sifting through it all.

One final thing strikes Lily. Daylight pours in through the window facing the street. But the sun has already set.

Lily asks about this.

Ms. Sedgwick says, "I prefer natural lighting. Don't you?"

"But how?"

"Well, if it helps, think of the window like a solar panel—absorbs during the day and releases at night."

No, it doesn't help, but Lily drops it.

"Now through the end of the year is my busy season. People at all hours, from all sorts of places, from all walks of life, seeking something precious, personal, unique. If I have it or if I can get it, I do."

"Then perhaps I've come to right woman." She crosses her fingers.

Down to business, Ms. Sedgwick says, "Please share with me your husband's circumstance."

"I don't wish to tell you too much that would put you in danger."

"I do appreciate that consideration." She stirs the tea and asks, "Has someone threatened you?"

"It was made clear to me that they, that is…," she pauses.

Before Lily can say 'vampires', Ms. Sedgwick does. "They know of me and I of them." Ms. Sedgwick motions with her hands toward herself: *Lay it on me.*

Lily does, summarizing for Ms. Sedgwick what happened over the past few days. Hers and Reed's honeymoon cut short by a gang of vampires determined to kill her and use Reed in some plot of revenge. She covers her initial disbelief that such creatures could exist, though she could not deny the blood, the fangs, the protection of her crucifix and God above.

The panic she felt then in her frantic search for Reed that led her back to Philadelphia. She omits the fight in the Whitpain Hotel and the murdered couple there. Only to say that vampires here helped rescue her and Reed.

While she takes a moment, Ms. Sedgwick's white brows rise to nearly join her hairline. "Extraordinary." Only now does she set the spoon with a decorative handle onto the saucer.

"Not the word I would use," Lily says. She looks away when tears threaten to spill. The events catch up with her now, stealing her breath.

She looks back to find Ms. Sedgwick cover Lily's hand with her own. Ms. Sedgwick's touch is blessedly warm and reassuring.

"You're safe here, Mrs. Williams." She takes an embroidered napkin from the tray, holding it out for Lily.

Dabbing her eyes, Lily says, "He's not the same, my husband. I'm afraid he'll slip away if nothing is done. He says the right things, but I see that he's holding back for my sake. And he must do things that neither of us would ever imagine doing. I fear for his soul. And mine. I know he's a good man. A good man who's ill. That's what I must believe and that there must be a way to make him well again."

Nodding, Ms. Sedgwick says, "I must say, I'm surprised that there were vampires willing to aid you and your husband. The few I've met have been the creepy sociopaths you see in the movies."

"How have you come to know about them?"

"Personally, I would rather have not ever come to know them."

"I don't blame you. I'd rather have continued being ignorant for the rest of my life."

"Life in ignorance certainly may be easier, safer. With knowledge comes a responsibility that can be difficult to bear. But it also comes with power. Power tempered with wisdom can do a lot of good." The last she says with a tone that Lily can't make out. Disappointment? The woman's hand goes to her white hair which moves even when left alone. "But without wisdom, power can do a great deal of wrong."

Ms. Sedgwick sips before going on, "It's the nature of my business to come in contact with the unusual. Now and then, one will come to the shop during winter time when the sun sets earlier. I suspect they send humans the rest of the year."

"Aren't they hard to spot? A friend, the one who rescued me, referred to them as shadows. Always with us, but never noticed."

Ms. Sedgwick brightens, "I must say I like that. It is true that they can go undetected. Like camouflage. Magic is that way as well. The miraculous dismissed as mundane, and so, unnoticed, unrecognized. It would do us all well to pay attention more. But no, the bell at the door gets my attention.

"That reminds me!" Suddenly in motion, startling Lily, and nearly spilling both their cups of tea, Sedgwick hunts around the room. Looking. Looking. Does she have a system at all?

"Ah!" Farther back, she opens a small lacquered box and takes something from it. The box lid falls back into place with a single clap. Whatever is in her hand is small, but Lily sees a glint of something.

Sitting once more, Ms. Sedgwick says, "Please hold out your left wrist." In her hand is a slim woven bracelet.

Curious, Lily extends her left hand. The woman circles Lily's wrist with the bracelet, tying off the ends, loose, but not so loose that it will slip off. The color is jet with one thread of silver in the center.

"There. This will help with that. You'll know when you're in the presence of vampires."

"It will do that?"

Ms. Sedgwick nods. "It will impart a chill. Though it won't harm you, it may be a nuisance when you're around your husband, I'm afraid."

Lily touches it gingerly.

Ms. Sedgwick says, "Now with that and your cross, I'd say you're a bit more protected."

Her hand goes to the necklace, "Thank you." Perhaps reading her mind, Ms. Sedgwick tells her that the bracelet is a gift.

Then she says, "Do not remove it, otherwise it becomes an ordinary bracelet. But black goes with everything," she says with a laugh.

"Can you perform magic? Is there such a thing as real magic?"

"I do very little now, and only in very circumscribed moments. I don't trust myself, otherwise. What I do now is simple crafts, blessings for good health, fair weather…"

"Winning lottery numbers."

"That would be cheating, Mrs. Williams. What you put out to the universe you get back threefold. Invoking true magic is like pulling a rubber band, eventually it will snap back with a wicked sting."

Lily says, "So, the safe kind of magic is altruistic?"

"Magic or not, doing good deeds are their own reward."

Lily nods. "We agree on that."

Ms. Sedgwick blows out a breath, "I'm afraid I cannot help you, Mrs. Williams."

Lily says, "Please don't say that." Her heart sinks to her feet. "If it's payment you need—"

Ms. Sedgwick shakes her head. Not money then. "Were he not your husband, I would tell you stay far away from him. Don't involve yourself in their affairs."

She regards her tea cup, stirring her spoon gently. "And frankly, I only have a very superficial understanding of their… their… how would you say… their physiology."

"Please. There must be something." The room becomes stifling warm and small. She must appear nauseated as Ms. Sedgwick urges her to drink the tea.

It does help.

What will she do now? She draws in a breath, trying to hold her composure.

Ms. Sedgwick closes her eyes, considering something. She opens them again, saying with reluctance. "There is one person. He *might* help. But then again, he might not."

"Please. I will meet with him."

She raises a finger in warning, "I don't trust him and neither should you. If you have no other course, then try contacting him. He's a former customer. I banished him when he attempted to steal from me. His name is Horton."

eighteen

The Fire Reaches Back

Not wasting time, Reed uses the car ride to get started strengthening his willpower. He convinces Kyle to help him.

Actually, he does not need much convincing.

Kyle pulls on the bond while Reed attempts to resist his command to slap himself.

Reed's right hand flies up as though it's Kyle's.

"Slap your other cheek."

"Give me—" Reed's own hand strikes the words from his mouth. Kyle's voice inside his mind, its volume pushing out his own thoughts, not permitting Reed to concentrate long enough to mount a defense.

Kyle repeats this a half dozen times. Reed's hand acts as though ashamed to be attached to his body, slapping Reed's face for the indignity, the wedding band especially stinging.

With mounting irritation, Reed says, "Stop it."

"You stop it."

Another barrage of slaps follows. Half of Reed's face turns numb. His lion, Florian, reflects his growing ire with a low threatening growl.

"Strike harder."

Reed grunts, jarred jaw set, determined to cut through the noise. His left hand quavers, moving with less conviction than before.

A headache comes on. "Enough already. Damn."

Kyle says, "That was unexpectedly satisfying."

***

Reed double-knots the satin ties of the domino mask when he and Kyle arrive at Tamerlane. Feeling ridiculous, he adjusts the mask to sit more comfortably on his face.

No comfort in this suit either. No matter the fit, dressing up always feels confining. May as well wear an all-body girdle. Collar too snug, jacket too stiff, his body too warm. So seldom worn, his dress shoes are polished steel clogs.

He itches.

Normally, Lily helps him with his tie, but not tonight. She was not in their apartment when he awoke and not at his Fishtown home. She had left a message to say that she'd be out in Manayunk following a lead, so she'd likely miss him, but wanted to wish him good luck at the party. He only just finished dressing before Kyle arrived at his apartment door to pick him up like a prom date.

Ahead, people in bunches chat on the pathways leading toward the old manor, the new house to its right, or under the hickory boughs.

Before they get too far, Kyle stops him. "Reed. Listen to me," Kyle says, his voice firm, eyes on Reed's own. "You may not care for your hide, but think of Lily. Whether there's a cure or not, you have to play ball, and even make some friends. And if you don't care enough to do it for her, then you'll do it for me. I vouched for you. Everything you say here, every person you displease, will be noted by those for whom gossip is their stock and store. And that reflects on me as your sponsor. And don't take getting initiated for granted. You're on probation. Fail that, then you're on your own."

The sounds of laughter and music swell each time the doors of the new house open.

As far as Reed sees it, Tamerlane is another country club with its own exclusive membership and elite airs. Just missing zooming golf carts.

Reed says, "I don't fit in here. I'm not someone who likes to dress up, wear masks, and pretend."

Kyle softens, "I get it. Lots of strangers here." He sweeps an arm out to the gathering guests, "But look at it this way, they don't have to be for long."

Unlikely.

What passes for small talk, anyhow? *Catch the ballgame last night? Some weather we're having? I had the most delicious blood?*

Masked men greet Kyle, each one shaking his hand or clapping his back like fraternity brothers reuniting and reminiscing.

Reed doesn't want to shake their cold hands, meet their cold eyes peering out through their masks, or even learn their names. For all he knows, he's among killers. Why would he join this club?

But heeding Kyle's warning, he tolerates several introductions and a few handshakes while pulling on a polite smile.

He feels stifled, closed-in, under pressure. His mask itches.

Time for a smoke break. To a distracted Kyle, he says, "I'm going to look around."

He finds himself inside the manor. Back in the same parlor in which he had waited with Leonard Webb, Alcott Ashton's human partner. A decent, perceptive man, who was the first in all this to treat Reed as a person.

Thinking on it now, Reed wonders why Webb chooses to work with vampires. Does he want to be one himself?

Fire burns in the hearth casting light onto the many oil portraits hanging on the walls, imparting an eerie aliveness to the posed subjects. Among the tight crowd of wigged men with severe expressions there's a woman in a yellow dress looking more serene, lounging on a settee. Webb had told him that the portrait was of Lady Catherine, who lives here but Reed has not met. Has she lived here all this time with Lord Devlin? Centuries? To think what they have they witnessed! Who they knew, who they called friends. After inspecting each portrait again none look familiar.

The fire snaps in the hearth, its belly full of hickory logs. Colorful leaves, collected from where they had fallen outside, and unlit candles atop brass candlesticks, decorate the mantelpiece.

Sharp laughter, dress shoes and heels, and the groans of couches, and scrapes of chair legs come from the back rooms off the central hall.

He inhales the wood smoke and the memories of hayrides and campfires, marshmallows, and spooky stories. And he thinks of the fireplace and irons of his childhood. Lost in thought of better times he only realizes now the fire before him reaches out a hand to greet him. Its fingers flicker at the trifold screen.

He sets the screen beside the stand of irons, each with a 'D' sculpted in the handle. A pop of heated air escapes to the flue. His lion stirs. Woodsy smoke thickens the air. Reed holds out his right hand as though warming it from a deep chill. Orange-red fingers reach back.

***

Kyle frowns when Reed ditches him before he can say anything. The strong current of guests sweeps Kyle toward the new house. With each turn of the conversation, people peel away to go their own way, replaced with more arrivals.

Lukewarm banter inevitably turns to two hot subjects. Who is Mr. Reed Williams? Is it true that he killed five vampires? You're his sponsor? When will he be initiated? Are we sure he isn't the one who killed that dreadful Rotter?

Troy Dawson is the other subject. If Reed hadn't killed him, then who had? Has Brother Alcott arrived yet? Here is the perfect place to find someone who may have information on the Rotter's death. Is New Hope at risk? Was it a reprisal killing—a cold revenge after all this time?

They enjoy the speculation—the who and why of the crime—without showing concern for their own safety or the implications for First House and the Society of Brandywine. Troy Dawson was a Rotter after all, so his death to them was more a service rendered than a warning delivered.

No one here, including Kyle, can name a member who had a personal grievance. Not one with a motive to commit murder.

He glances a third time in the direction of the old manor. Once more relieved not to see Reed tossed out or the structure set ablaze.

Kyle says, "I wish you all a pleasant evening."

Inside the new house, sounds of conversation greet Kyle. The Miloses attend to last minute details while musicians tune their instruments. Cliques of guests chat.

"Good evening, Brother Kyle." Elias Devlin, his sire, approaches, predictably wearing the clothing of an 18th century gentleman—silk breeches, stockings, buckle shoes, frock and waist coats. For a crown, he wears a white wig tied in the back with a black ribbon. A faithful recreation, as the man had long since worn the original items to rags.

He claps a hand on Kyle's shoulder—strong, assertive. He holds his mask in his other hand. "I trust you are well this night."

Kyle bows his head, "Sir." Devlin's presence also lurks in Kyle's mind due to the natural bond of sire and child. Strong as ever, putting Kyle reflexively into a attitude of deference.

"And where, dear Kyle, is your charge? You have not lost him so early, have you?"

"He will be along soon."

"Good. Am I correct to assume that all is well with him?"

"Yes, sir. He has much to learn, and we're still getting to know each other."

Despite Devlin's lighter mood, Kyle can't help feeling he's a boy in front of a stern father. He adds, "He has his misgivings as you can imagine. But I have made it clear to him what is expected of him. I have things in order."

"I wonder…" He pauses, looking at Kyle.

"Yes, sir?"

"Brother Alcott informed me that Mr. Williams supped from you on the night you and he met."

"Yes."

"But you had done so only after the occurrence of his calamitous actions at the hotel. Actions which have brought such vexatious exposure that Alcott has had to redress." Leonard Webb has been the one to do the redressing, but Devlin will not appreciate the correction, and certainly will not give the man credit. "Allowances have been made owing to that he is a neophyte and your assurance such things will not be repeated."

"No, they will not."

"Good. Continue to maintain the bond."

"I will consider that. But sir, trust must go both ways."

nineteen

Masquerade

B efore the fireplace, Reed's right hand brushes the warm air with long, slow strokes. Flames wave back.

The lion paces in his chest, its head fixed on the flames. Reed pictures golden eyes reflecting the firelight, curious and wary. Reed still doesn't see his way for making the lion control the fire. The Fire, capital F. F for another four-letter word. He cannot think of a word that sums up how unreal all of this still is. How he feels half-mad sometimes, delusional, disconnected from people around him, even Lily, and even more so, himself.

Despite the heat, he doesn't perspire. But his mask itches all the same. He whips it off.

Fool. There's a four-letter word. He feels like a fool. A fool to think he could stop Kyle from making him slap his own face. A fool to think he can grasp what both Ms. Shipley and Roxy have been trying to teach him. A fool to believe he can control the Fire.

The leather mask balls up in his hand.

This self-pity talk isn't going to solve anything.

He will try again. Because, as Lily would surely agree, Reed does not give up easily.

He must relax. Let go of expectations, as Michael had said.

Gazing unfocused upon the fire before him, Reed opens himself up to it, opens his senses, meditating, being present. Trying to not control things, not get ahead of himself, be patient.

The incense of slow charring wood, the crackle of the fire, and flashing heat on his face remind him of nights by a campfire. He had always appreciated that wood smell, the crackle, embers shooting up like flares. He savors the memory.

He sees the lion's golden fur and its mane bright as a halo. It paces in the cage of his heart peering through the ribs at the fireplace and the numerous fingertips caressing the air between them. How does he get across?

Reed considers what Roxy had said. To think of the Fire as a partner, someone to dance with, not attempt to control. He's not a terrible dancer, but what does he remember? No music here-just the finger-snapping from the hearth. Undaunted, he holds out his arms as though holding Lily, one arm at her waist, the other clasping her hand. Like so. The first few steps are awkward but soon his dress shoes tap out a decent box-step on the hardwood floor.

Soon he realizes the fire settling into a waltzing pattern. He hasn't forced it. Just let it be. He can feel something. A touch. The lion's posture shifts. All at once he can feel that connection. He sways. The fire sways.

The heat within Reed fans out from his chest as it has many times before. *See the lion*, Reed tells himself. *Mon lion*, Marie says.

"Shut up," he sneers. Mentally he chases Marie away.

He sighs, gathering himself back on track till the lion returns. Its forelegs extend through his arms as though they were shirt sleeves. Reed's arms warm up more.

Now there's a synergy, like the two fires find a shared frequency. Like what he had felt with Roxy. Heat and hearth.

The fire hand reaches a bit farther. The lion's paw swipes for it. A surge channels through Reed's arm, then hand, then pain. In mimicry, the fire hand swipes back.

Snapping his hand back, Reed discovers the sleeve of his jacket caught fire. Now staggering away, he slaps at the flames. Not good enough. He hurries to get the jacket off himself then balls it up to snuff them out.

Grimacing, Reed inspects the damage. Not too bad—the dark fabric hides the singe marks.

He pauses having the sudden feeling he isn't alone. Turning his head, Reed sees several figures at the parlor's entrance. Exposed mouths smile amused, others astounded having seen more than just the finale but his entire performance.

Stung, he throws on his jacket, picks up the dropped mask, and hustles through his audience and out of the manor.

***

Inside, the ample space of the house appears specifically made for events like the masquerade. The spacious open floor plan flows to Reed's right and to his left. Twin staircases sweep up to a second level gallery, where balconies bump out in several places. Enormous crystal chandeliers illuminate and dazzle. Tall windows opposite the main entrance continue to each of the wings, cupping a garden beyond.

Colorfully dressed women and men swirl across the rosewood flooring while the sounds of strings, woodwinds, and harpsichord fill the air. Reed spots Lord Devlin adjusting the pegs of his violin before joining in the performance. He's wearing a wig and clothing like the men in the paintings. Reed wonders if the man lives in that time, unaware that the world has moved on.

Near one of the staircases, a woman breaks from a group of guests, with whom she had been chatting. She's dressed in the kind of ball gown Reed would expect from a children's story. A circus-tent-sized skirt, corseted waist, poofy shoulders, and lots of sparkly detail. Near her face, she holds a mask by its handle like opera glasses.

All smiles, she greets several other newcomers on her way to him. To Reed she extends her gloved hand, "I am Lady Catherine, this evening's hostess. Am I correct, that you are Mr. Reed Williams?"

Ah—the woman he had seen in the yellow dress. Mr. Webb had mentioned her being kind. He shakes her hand hoping Webb is right. "Pleased to meet you."

She takes her measure of him before saying, "Brother Kyle had neglected to introduce us earlier. How are the two of you getting along?"

"All right." He feels he should say something witty but nothing comes to mind. "I like your picture. Ah, the painting of you in the other house. It's well done."

"Do you think so? Most kind of you to say." Her eyes look up a moment, "I do believe Mr. Copley accomplished a fair likeness, though perhaps the nose a touch too broad." She tilts her head, "Sitting for one's portrait was most tedious, I recall." Returning her attention to him, "How much simpler it is with a camera. Why in a second it can capture what had once had taken days."

She considers her mask, turning its handle so that it slowly rotates in her hand. "A painting, like a photograph, gestures at the moment observed. Both are an interpretation of the subject. One may be more realistic, but is it any more true? A camera can tell a subtle lie as well as a brush." She places the mask on her face, saying, "Which captures best? How we wish to be seen, or what we truly are? Is there a difference? Do we even know?" Lowering her mask once more, "Which to trust?"

He nods with vague agreement, though not really understanding, nor wishing to. "When was it painted?"

"My, my, Mr. Williams—are you hoping that I will reveal my age?"

"No. No." By being genuinely curious he's blundered already.

She tsk-tsks, thankfully, good-naturedly. "Do not be troubled. It is a masquerade after all. No one is here to harm you. Tamerlane is neutral ground. Neither violence nor the threat of violence is permitted here. Nor are members permitted to use their sympathies on fellow members without their permission. You will take care to keep a cool head here."

"I will," he says appreciating her graciousness.

"We will chat again before long. Enjoy your evening. And don't give Brother Kyle too much trouble, will you?"

As she floats away in her skirt, Reed turns to see Mr. Alcott Ashton stride through the entrance past him. He doesn't have a mask, nor is he wearing a costume. Just a drab colored three-piece suit similar to the one Reed had seen him wear the other night. He pauses, spreading his hands out on his waist and scanning the room. Without a glance in Reed's direction, the man heads toward gathered guests.

***

Before Reed can rejoin Kyle, a fresh cluster of guests gather about him. Foremost among them are the Miloses. Even masked, he recognizes the close pair—the short, solid Sebastian Milos and the tall willowy Vanessa Milos.

And just as Reed hadn't been surprised by Lord Devlin's costume choice, he isn't all that surprised by their attire. Both clad in reptile leather. Snakeskin, if he has to guess. His graphite jacket and trousers, red tie and scaly boots. Constrictive, hers is an oxblood red from ankles to throat; the material winds around her form, exposing parts of her thigh, hip, stomach, back, missing her left shoulder and arm completely, and clasping at her neck. Her mask is part of an elaborate headpiece meant to resemble the serpents of Medusa. Though perfectly still, they look ready to bite.

Mr. Milos holds a scepter of polished ebony and silver detail, which he wags at Reed, while his wife introduces Reed to the others as though the couple had discovered him, a wondrous marvel that they unearthed, and have brought him here to impress. Look, a real erif, well-preserved. A handsome fledgling nursed to life by Brother Kyle.

Even in normal circumstances, Reed does not like such attention. He hopes by his terse, but polite returns of the guests' greetings and questions they'll disperse.

Then to his shock, Mrs. Milos says, "The poor man has been having such distressing dreams. Has Sister Emma been helpful in soothing your anxieties?"

The heat in his chest kicks up. The lion growling. Flexing. Wanting to swipe at the woman. Who is she to share that? Why is that anyone else's business? Reed bites the inside of his cheek. Through his teeth, he says, "Yes. Well, I need to find Kyle. Excuse me."

The guests melt away. Except the Miloses. Mrs. Milos takes his arm in hers, leading him along. It's all he can do to not shake her off and leave the party altogether.

"Has Brother Kyle told you about the casks that will be set out tonight?"

"No."

"Casks are earthenware vessels. They're among the earliest practical devices from New Hope. You have heard of New Hope?"

"The town? Yes." The night Reed had returned to Philadelphia, Alcott had taken a sample of Reed's ichor and sent it to New Hope to determine if he was in fact an erif.

With delight, Mrs. Milos's fingers writhe. "Ooh, such a remarkable piece of our history."

Mr. Milos adds, "Before our time, alas."

She nods, sharing his disappointment. "With the stirrings of rebellion in the colonies, the idea of the Society was coming to fruition. Its founders sought a way to liberate themselves from the bond. Select men pursued this goal and scouted a suitable location for their work. New Hope was found to be the ideal spot."

Mr. Milos grins up at his wife, "A wonderful period of experimentation."

"What I would give to have been a part of it, my sweet one." Then to Reed, she says, "The men conducted research into our blood, what they would call ichor. Naturally, such work required volunteers, sacrifice, pain."

She says the last with relish. "Knives in flesh. All manner of instruments prodding their bodies, testing their resilience, prying secrets from their ichor."

Though disturbed by what the pair share with him, his interest grows. Research into what make vampires tick. Their ichor. Perhaps those men know something Reed can use. Could he meet with one of them? Maybe Kyle can introduce him, or at least tell Reed where to find them in that town.

"Imagine it, Mr. Williams. A new frontier of knowledge. They didn't even have all the tools necessary. They had to be invented. Such as a method to store blood. That's what casks are for."

"I thought blood has to be fresh."

"Yes indeed. It is fresh when it goes in. Once sealed the blood does not age."

"So, people cut their veins into bottles?"

She says nothing.

"Who does that?"

"Countless have. Over centuries, many have contributed one way or another," she says, teeth sharp.

"What are you saying? There are kegs of blood being brought here?"

She smiles, "We would like for you to assist passing the cups to fellow guests. It's an honor for you to serve in this way. Will you do that for us?" she asks, though it's not really a question.

Just ladle out blood from a punch bowl. He didn't think tonight could get creepier.

The snakes practically hiss at him while Mrs. Milos awaits his answer. What can he do?

"Uh, sure." He hopes he'll be conveniently elsewhere when the time comes.

"*Polí kalá.* Sebastian will summon you."

***

Kyle is speaking to a pair of men when Reed catches up with him. Eager to share what he has learned from Mrs. Milos, he hasn't given the men more than a glance. Until one of them plays a few notes on a harmonica.

Instead of masks, the men wear sunglasses and matching dark suits, fedoras, and skinny ties rolling down the front of their white dress shirts.

Reed hadn't thought of Michael and Malcolm much this evening. Now he is suddenly grateful for their company. Their stoic expressions change when Malcolm brings his palmed harmonica to his lips.

Surprising Reed, Michael sings, "We came to party…"

Malcolm plays some blues notes, though not well. More like screeching.

Michael continues, "but found Tamer… lame."

Malcolm blows, *dah-dah-dah-dah-dum*.

"No booze to be drunk, no ladies game.

"Just pals Kyle and Reed, oh what a shame."

Michael takes out his own harmonica and plays on, far more expertly than Malcolm.

Few passersby smile appreciatively; more wrinkle in annoyance.

Reed says, "That was very horrible."

Malcolm tucks his shades and presses his fingertips along the long sideburns. They've been pasted on, askew.

Reed nods for Kyle to follow him to a less occupied portion of the room. The other two follow.

"Mrs. Milos told me about what goes on in New Hope," Reed says. Leaning in, "Maybe their research can help me. Do you think one of them will show up here? Tonight?"

Kyle says, "They aren't members, though they have a standing invitation to attend these parties." He shrugs, "I've never seen one here. I've been told they rarely leave their compound, especially the older ones. Maybe a junior one will show up."

Michael's expression turns skeptical. "Why are you interested in talking to a sorcerer?"

Reed says, "To help me. You know…"

"Don't trust them. I heard they're into dark rituals and demon-dealing. Bad mojo."

Kyle says to Michael, "Where did you hear that?" Then to Reed, "They don't share details of their research—it's sensitive work. They keep to themselves, and don't go out all that much. So, in the absence of facts, people make up nonsense and," Kyle looks pointedly at Michael, "*others* believe them."

Michael shrugs not offended. To Reed he says, "Be careful, is all I'm saying. You want something, believe me, they'll make you pay for it."

Malcolm picks at one of his fake sideburns, "Their reputation has been tarnished as of late, Brother Kyle."

Reed asks, "What are you talking about?"

Kyle says, "It's in the past."

"How far back are you talking?"

"Before our time here in Philly," Michael says, then pivots to Kyle, "but not his."

Reed says, "Tell me now."

Malcolm says, "Some experiments require subjects willing to undergo vivisection without ether or anesthetic."

Michael adds, "Or not so willing."

Kyle says, "It was an unfortunate incident. A man greatly suffered. Those responsible were dealt with. Satisfied?"

"Great," Reed says.

Michael repeats, "Bad mojo. Watch yourself."

Kyle puts himself between Michael and Reed, "Measures have been put in place since then to ensure there's not a repeat of abuse. Quality control. Don't get worked up about it."

"And now they have my ichor," Reed says. Unconscious at the time, Reed was in no position to object to Alcott Ashton taking some of it.

"Yes. Routine. It was used to confirm that you were an erif. That's all."

"But maybe they know something. Have some idea. If it means—"

A wolf-whistle rises from Michael's harmonica. They all turn to look. Ms. Shipley comes round smiling radiantly to the four men. Jeweled in turquoise, green, and blue, she resembles a peacock in her beautiful gown and feathered mask.

"Hello gentlemen. My pleasure to be in the company of such handsome rogues."

"Hello, Sister Emma," Michael and Malcolm say in unison.

"It is especially good to see you here tonight, Mr. Williams. Have you been practicing?"

"Yes, thank you."

Twining her arms around one of Kyle's, she says, "Enjoy your evening. I must steal Brother Kyle. He may not survive the night, so give him your blessings and farewells."

While allowing Emma to lead him away, Kyle says to the men, "Behave."

***

Kyle leads Emma in a Viennese waltz. One hand clasps hers while the other braces her waist. She's a touch chill but her floral and bright perfume warms him.

She glides with him across the wood floor under the chandelier lights and enchanting music. She says, "At last, I have you to myself. And you are handsome."

She fondles the material of his jacket. "You do surprise me sometimes." She marvels at his shantung silk suit—sky-blue. The sun-orange color of the stitching around the flower hole matches the four-pointed folded handkerchief rising out of the breast pocket.

"Tell me, do you own a pair of dungarees and a leather jacket with buckles?"

"I do not. I wear only suits. Even to bed and in the shower."

"You need to improve your humor."

"Noted, Emma."

"Will you not compliment me?"

"You're the most beautiful woman in the room."

"Merely the room?"

"It is a large room."

"You do need to improve your humor."

Kyle leads her though several twirls.

She says, "It's pity you cannot grow out your hair. I recall a Mr. Bertram who has hair red as yours that reached his shoulders. Quite becoming." Her eyes shine at his, looking delighted. "But you are no slouch here on the dance floor. I had no idea you were so adept."

"I am a gentleman."

She laughs, "That you are."

"When I was his initiate, Lord Devlin had suggested that I learn to dance." Repeating the man's words, Kyle says, "A true gentleman must be able to entertain a lady of society; to lead her firmly, gaily, in step with the music."

"Credit to Master Devlin," she says, then lets out a laugh of surprise when he dips her.

He says, "It feels... nice to put it to good use." In fact, dancing with Emma feels more than nice. Being part of the many pairs of bodies floating on the music brings a genuine smile to his face. They drift about the main room near the windows where the illuminated garden and pond beyond can be seen.

"Now, tell me about yourself. Any disturbing dreams?"

"Emma."

"Kyle. Why suffer needlessly? Let me help you."

"They are my demons. I will deal with them."

"I wonder if you prefer their company."

"Rest assured, I prefer yours."

"Yet you brood. You wall yourself off. You've done so for nearly as long as I've known you. When you were human, you weren't so aloof, so burdened. Now you're a miser with your smiles. What's changed? This is the life you had wanted, what you trained for, and yet you are all the more despondent."

All true.

A quiet murmur draws their attention. Whispering goes around from couple to couple as they catch sight of a newcomer having entered the house, costumed and masked.

"Well, such a wonder," Emma says.

"You know who that is?" Kyle says.

"It has been a while since I've seen him."

"Who?"

"Magus Jonas Oakes."

"From New Hope?"

She nods, "Impolite to stare, Brother Kyle."

He had heard of the magus, one of the most senior of the ichorists in New Hope. The rare sighting explains the hushed chatter, the instant gossip. What could possibly have brought him out to a party?

Kyle and Emma course through several more pieces, which change tempo, style, and step.

Emma says, "Come to a show of mine. Till then, a night of tea and chat? You've not been to my home and I've redecorated. A vision I assure you."

"If it's only tea and chat I would be delighted."

"Excellent. Just a hint: Bring flowers. I suggest orchids."

As they circle the floor, Kyle notes Reed leaving through French doors to the garden. He is following Oakes. Now what is that about?

Kyle says, "Thank you for speaking with Reed last night. From what he told me, you've been very helpful."

"My pleasure." She loops her arm in his, "He's quite a project for you." Kyle says nothing. "Though he has lost some memories, he still thinks of himself as human and wishes to be one again."

Alert, Kyle looks out at the dancers swirling around them. Had any of them overheard? In an even, quiet tone, he says, "Reed has told you this?"

Emma shakes her head, then speaks by his ear. "I merely surmised, but by your reaction..."

He understands. He should have let her comment pass unremarked.

She's enjoying his consternation. Then she draws her fingers across her lips. "I will not betray your trust, Brother Kyle."

He nods, appreciative. "He will come around. He really doesn't have a choice."

"Of course he does. There's also the wrinkle that he's an erif and he certainly has the fire in him. If he's not careful he will burn others if he doesn't immolate himself first. And you have no natural bond with him to curb waywardness."

Again, with the bond. He has respected Reed's autonomy and Reed has given no reason to take that back. He will let the bond run to its natural end.

"He will do fine. He's got discipline and a wife who anchors him."

"If, as he fears, he loses his ties to her, what then? You can't be too indulgent of him. If you were his sire, you wouldn't hesitate to use the bond. You must remember: Your senses are different, your once human rhythm changes, sense of who and what you are. Like having to become left-handed after injuring the right hand."

Shaking her head in thought she adds, "You have never sired. It isn't easy at times. No matter how much I had prepared Joseph, he still resisted me and tried my patience. One by one we had snipped his ties to the human world but it holds him still. That is why he is not here, but at some psychiatry conference."

Kyle leads her near the garden windows.

Emma says, "Perhaps it was a mistake for you to have saved his bride. No doubt it has occurred to you to use her to ensure Mr. Williams's cooperation. But she could become a liability by not cooperating herself. As well as bring unwanted exposure. How will you handle that?"

"The way we usually do. Once Brother Alcott has finished with this mess with Blade, he'll follow protocol to finalize Reed's human affairs."

"What do you make of that falderal? The Rotters, the scions of Lemon? What can you tell me about the investigation?"

"I'm certain I don't know more than you. Alcott's interviewing everyone to see who may know what happened."

"What is your speculation? Are we in danger? Do we have another crusader to contend with?"

"I am sure the matter will be resolved quickly. Brother Alcott is up... to... the... task." Kyle turns dumbstruck by what he sees past Emma's shoulder, through the windows, and the garden beyond.

An erif.

Immolating.

twenty

Horton

L ily wastes no time getting here, this residential street in Bella Vista. Ms. Sedgwick had produced a phone number and this Warnock Street address. The phone number had turned out to be no longer in service. That left showing up.

She asks the cabbie to keep the meter going, circle around, if need be, but not to leave until he hears from her. Who knows if this is the correct address? And if it is, what kind of man is this Horton?

Given what just happened off South Street, she is wary and can hear Reed admonishing her: *Don't get involved.*

She dashes across the sidewalk and up the three cement steps to the door of the rowhouse in the middle of the pack. She double-checks the street numbers fastened to the masonry.

Phone in her hands, she texts her location to Reed. Just in case. Not expecting a response, she's disappointed nonetheless that he doesn't text back. He must be enjoying himself at the party.

Gathering up her courage, she rings the bell. "Hello?" She raps on the navy-colored door, then yells at it, "I'm looking for Mr. Horton."

Stamping her feet to keep the evening chill out of her body, she chides herself for not bringing gloves.

"What's up, gorgeous?"

Lily looks down at the doorbell cam. "Hello? I'm looking for Mr. Horton. Does he live here?"

"Wrong house, lady."

No. No. First no phone number, now no address. It's much too soon to smack into a dead end.

"Would you know where I can find him? Please. It's very important that I speak with him." Glancing about she leans in and decides to go for it. "I was told he is an expert on the supernatural. On vampires... Hello?"

She shivers while waiting. "Hello?" More waiting. Taking the hint, she turns to leave.

The door opens a crack and a young man's face appears. "Comin' in, or what?"

Relieved, she hurries in as though he might slam the door in her face. She shakes as she steps through the vestibule, toward the living room area. One hand grips the phone, ready. The other hand is in the pocket of her coat curled around a small can of pepper spray, ready.

Typical of rowhomes here, the main floor is open from one end to the other. Staircases along one wall go up to the second floor and down to the basement.

Closing the front door, the man hangs near the inner door, eying her as she does him. In his twenties, he'd be nice looking if he wasn't leering. This is the man? Much younger than she had expected. Younger than her.

"Mr. Horton, thank you for seeing me," she says, shrugging in her own coat as she thaws. About to say more, she can hear footsteps. Someone taking the stairs from the basement. They both look down the way. The door opens. Another man.

"I'm Horton." With a bad comb-over, he appears close to Aleron's age, wearing dark jeans and denim shirt stained on the sleeves and cuffs.

Lily squares her shoulders, "Hello. I'm Lily Williams." She positions herself by an armchair to give herself the vantage of seeing both men and feels relief that they cast shadows.

Horton doesn't break her way, but walks over to the younger man and slips something into his right hand, a hand with pairs of fingers taped together, the kind used to splint an injury.

Mr. Horton says, "Hit all the clubs this time. And I need good notes. Got it?"

"No problem." Without a glance at whatever the item is, the man transfers it to his good hand, then pockets it.

"Good. Get out of here."

Mr. Horton shuts the door after him and turns back to Lily. Instinctively, she takes a step back.

He smiles, which doesn't put her at ease. She says, "I was told you can help me."

Looking her up and down as though she came here to be propositioned. "You are a lily."

"Yes, well, thank you."

He moves, not toward her, but toward the kitchen area, "You'll have to excuse my manners. I don't regularly receive strangers, especially beautiful ones. Can I get you a drink?"

"No. No, thank you."

He inspects a metal tea pot, runs the water out of it into a sink and refills from the tap. Bowls encrusted with cereal bits pile in the dish rack. The electric burner reddens. He puts the tea pot on it.

"I don't want to take up much of your time. I have someone waiting for me."

Poking into the cupboards, Mr. Horton finds a box of tea packets. He fingers them one by one. When he decides on a packet, he sets it down on the counter. "No tea then?" he asks while hunting for a cup and saucer. "You caught me at a good time," he says. "I just took a break from my work." He crosses his arms, looking at her from across the room.

The visible space here has utility not style. Masculine like Reed's apartment. Minimal furniture, no plants. Above the credenza hangs a Vincent van Gogh print, perhaps from the Philadelphia Museum of Art gift shop. Nothing hints at magic. Nothing like Sedgwick's shop nor props from a Vegas act.

"That is fortunate. I had tried to call you, but I had the wrong number, evidently."

An arm waves to the fabric sofa, "Why don't you sit?"

"That's kind of you," she says, taking a small step.

"You had said something that caught my ear. A word. That is why I let you into my home, beautiful stranger. Lily. What was that word?"

Her hand grips her phone to reassure herself. "Vampires, I believe."

"That is the word. Yes," he says. "Why does someone young and pretty as yourself know such a word, come to a stranger's home, and inquire about it? It can be a very dangerous word. You know this?"

Lily swallows, "I'm beginning to. You see, I know one."

"I assumed as much. I would very much like to know, Lily, who gave you this address."

"I'd prefer *Mrs.* Williams. And I understand, but does it matter who?"

He raises a hand to his heart, "Married. Of course. I neglected to note your ring."

The water simmers behind him.

"It matters a great deal, Mrs. Lily Williams," he says her name pointedly. "Secrets are my work, and I am careful whom I trust with them. Not only for my own sake, but the sake of my clients. What has this person told you about me?"

"I was told you know magic."

He nods, "Magic. What else?"

"I was told not to trust you."

"I am hurt. And yet, here you are. Desperate?"

"Determined."

He smiles at this, "She told you to see me? Come now."

"She told me *not* to see you."

"That witch. That witchy Wyck of the West." He looks to her to confirm his guess.

Lily looks away. Ms. Sedgwick never asked for confidentiality, but all the same, Lily would rather not involve her any further.

The tea pot whistles and Mr. Horton turns off the stove. He pours himself a cup of the steaming water and dunks the bag of tea.

While the man sips his tea, she says, "You've seen vampires, yourself?"

"Certainly."

"They don't unnerve you?"

"To the contrary, I find them endlessly fascinating."

"Why, do you think, they need blood if they have blood themselves?"

"You're mistaken. They have an altogether different substance in their bodies."

"Huh," she says, allowing him to look impressed with himself that he corrected her. "Well, what spooks me the most is their shadows—they move on their own. Have you seen that?"

Mr. Horton pauses in his sipping, "They don't cast any shad—" He smiles more, "Testing me, are you? And right you are to do so."

She smirks. Good to put one over him. Meeting his eyes, she says, "The vampire friend I mentioned: Can you cure him?"

Mr. Horton's demeanor changes instantly. "Mrs. Williams—you're in luck. That has been my work." He turns, putting the tea cup and saucer down on the kitchen counter.

To his back, she says, "Please tell me you're not joking."

The air shifts instantly. Suspicion turns to eager openness.

"I am not," he says, sounding giddy. Finally, he turns back, "Mrs. Lily Williams," a smile spreading over his face, "it seems this is kismet. You've come to the right man. You and I can help one another."

The tea forgotten, he approaches her, "I am in need of a vampire to prove my cure a success."

"I can hardly believe it." She truly can't. Her guard goes up once more. "You will help him?"

"Of course. I will need him."

"My husband, Reed. What do you need?"

He grimaces apologetically, "There is a fee."

She nods. She didn't expect this to be a favor, and if it means having Reed whole once more, the money will be well spent.

"Ten thousand. In cash."

She repeats the figure to him. She has the money, but its loss will make Reed urge her to look for a better bargain. So, she will not tell him.

Mr. Horton says, "Magic is expensive, I'm afraid, as is insurance."

She nods, understanding, kind of. "I will get it tomorrow. What time do you want me to bring him here?"

"After sundown, of course."

"And what exactly will you be doing?"

"Trade secret. Magicians never tell." She hears a sour note there, "Suffice to say that we'll begin by taking a sample from him. Then I'll need you both to wait while I synthesize the formula. Once done, he can drink a small amount to ensure no adverse reaction, and assuming none, he can down the whole thing."

Lily beams, "Oh. This is wonderful. You can do it?"

Mr. Horton says, "Yes, well, besides the fee, I will need one more thing."

chapter

twenty-one

Mingle

M ichael says to Reed, "You're new blood. Go mingle."
         "I don't know what to say."
   "Some guests here are visiting from other Houses and may not know anyone. You can start with them." He directs Reed's attention across the room. "Take that woman. I had heard she's a Goth. The ones who sacked Rome. Right, Malcolm?"

Reed says, "Really? You're kidding me." He wonders about the historic upheavals the woman must have experienced. Where had she traveled, who had she met, what artifacts might she still have? His mind reels with questions.

"Only one way to find out."

Reed says, "What do I say?"

Malcolm says, "You can ask her about the Battle of Adrianople."

Michael shakes his head. "You've got a great story, man. Your wife was kidnapped by French mercenaries." He bucks Reed's shoulder, holding out his other arm, a gesture to some imaginary tableau before them. "You came up with a cunning and daring plan and traveled across the ocean to get her back into your arms. You faced and defeated powerful foes and saved your wife's life!"

Not quite true, and not something Reed feels particularly inclined to repeat to anyone, much less boast about. But he takes their point that he should meet those here, overriding his earlier misgivings. He'll try. And who knows, maybe one of them may know about a cure, or at least share more information as Mrs. Milos had. And talking to someone who has lived for nearly two thousand years is an unmissable opportunity.

He catches the woman's eye, then makes his way through the spinning couples and introduces himself.

"The erif," she says to her friend. Both wear uniforms of military officers from bygone armies. One in Continental blue, the other in British red.

"Yeah. That's me." By habit he offers his hand to shake. "I was told you're a Goth who fought against Rome."

"Excuse me?" she says, perhaps not having heard him correctly. "Who told you that?" she speaks with an accent far from the lands of a dead empire. Closer to here, like Jersey. As in New.

Reed's eyes widen at his mistake. He turns back, cutting his eyes over his shoulder. Michael gives him a thumb up, and Malcolm smiles to his ears.

Reed wipes the embarrassment off his face, "Just a joke. An ice breaker, you know?"

They toss him a pity laugh.

Tipping back her tricorn hat, she says, "I'm Bethany, and this is Charlotte."

They all fall into a comfortable conversation, the small talk of new acquaintances. Both women are visiting from Windsor House, which covers a swath of the Garden State.

As it turns out, they fence. The swords on their hips are not props.

"You fight with those?"

Charlotte adds, "We will demonstrate later tonight."

"We could teach you, if you'd like."

"Want to hold one?" Charlotte draws hers from its scabbard, ready to hand it to him, but then doesn't.

Their expressions change, looking no longer at Reed, but past his shoulder.

From behind him, a man's voice says, "Mr. Williams. I am Jonas Oakes, a magus of New Hope."

***

Dressed like an over-achieving Eagle Scout, Jonas Oakes wears a quilted dinner jacket resplendent with badges. Like a shield over his face lies a wooden mask, painted with leagues of ocean dotted with marine life and a whale nosing downward along the right cheek.

Excusing himself from the two women he has been speaking with, Reed follows the shorter man through the French doors into the garden. Night song overtakes the chatter and music inside.

Smooth, small colorful rocks, arranged in geometric patterns, form the brick-bordered path they walk. The scent of fresh mulch and flowers lingers over the beds between the path and the house among intervals of ornamental bushes such as viburnum and crape myrtle.

Reed waits for Oakes to start talking, cautiously optimistic that the sorcerer will be helpful. You wish to become human once more? Of course, we do that all the time in New Hope. After the party we'll head there, wave a wand, chant some words, and you'll be back to normal with Lily before sunup.

Through the slot in his mask, Oakes says, "I understand this is all very new to you, Mr. Williams." Reed nods several times. "It is uncommon for members from the manse, such as myself, to speak with non-officers of the Society."

Their course loops around the above-ground koi pond.

Reed says, "Thank you all the same. Actually, I've been hoping to see you—not you specifically—anyone from New Hope, really."

Oakes regards Reed, "As it happens, we wished to speak with you—specifically you. Is it correct that your sponsor is Kyle Dowd?"

"Yeah."

"Has he told you about us, what we do?"

"Something to do with ichor."

Oakes says, "In fact, it has everything to do with ichor. We research the substance and have found its nature to be as opaque as its hue, yet mercurial and surprising in its properties. Endlessly fascinating. Uncovering each of its secrets has been hard won."

Koi break the surface then dash below becoming ghostly streaks of orange in the green water.

"Our history coincides with the founding of the Society. Our earliest members were given the audacious mandate to sever the bond. To accomplish this meant learning about ichor itself."

Spreading his hands, Oakes says, "Nothing was known just three centuries ago. Our European brethren were worse than ignorant. Incurious, they failed to the ask questions we ourselves were asking and continue to ask. Foolishly, they dismissed ichor simply as a humor unique to our kind."

Here Oakes removes his mask. Strands of brown hair fall over his eyes. He brushes them back then sets the mask in a planter. His pale face is fuller than Reed had expected.

"I trust you are aware we had received a sample of your ichor from Mr. Alcott."

"Without my knowledge or consent." He says this more sharply than he should have. It hadn't bothered him before but now it seems what Alcott Ashton had done crossed a line. Like something very personal had been stolen and its value Reed is only now understanding.

"Nonetheless, we performed our preliminary examination, following standard protocols." All Oakes is missing is a stethoscope and a medical chart. "Think of it as similar to a human medical lab performing blood diagnostics to determine indications of illnesses. And so, we did of yours. We're here to discuss those results with you."

Reed unties the mask and stuffs it into the inner pocket of his suit jacket. "I'm an erif, right?"

"Correct."

"Did you happen to see a lion in the sample?"

"I'm afraid I don't catch your meaning."

"Nothing. I was told to think of the Fire," he touches his sternum, "as a lion as a way to focus."

"Has that been helpful?"

"Not sure yet."

Oakes says, "Your affinity with fire is what we refer to as one of the low sympathies, like the four classical elements: Fire, earth, water, and air. Most of our kind possess one of the higher sympathies. Ethereal gifts, if you will. Aura-reading, telepathy, clairvoyance. Along those lines. Philosophically speaking, some consider these aspects superior to the elemental ones."

"Not that I care, but I've heard fire is in demand."

"The Society may think so."

"What does this mean for me?"

"As it does for each of us, you will need to learn to master your gift."

"I already know that." From a pocket, Reed gets out his blue lighter. "May I?" Held in his right hand, he flicks the lighter's spark wheel, bringing a jet to life. He'll try to repeat what he had done by the fireplace. With more control. Well, any control.

The pair come to a stop. Oakes notes Reed's singed sleeve, "Are you sure this is wise?"

Reed can feel Florian rouse from his nap, then stretch to his feet. His amber eyes watch the flame.

Wow. Is he starting to get this?

As he has come to expect, the flame bows to Reed.

Oakes says, "Most remarkable."

Now what? He hadn't been humble when he told Roxy that he isn't very creative. He decides to keep it simple.

Florian chuffs in preparation, then lets out a single roar. A blast of heat fills Reed's chest and the flame, as though bowled over, curls, then unfurls, and now points toward Jonas.

"Well, I'll be damned," Reed laughs, both surprised and proud. He does it again. The flame obeys its king. Clumsy the first few tries, it soon does somersaults, squashing itself into a wobbly ball, and spiraling up to its full length. Though not a smooth, easy performance, Reed smiles with satisfaction to having been able to do it at all.

He releases the button and juggles the lighter in his hand.

Oakes says, "A modest but admirable beginning. But that is not why I am here and not what I wish to discuss. Your ichor has anomalous properties. Or so it seems."

"What are you saying?" Reed flicks the lighter on and off, on and off. The lion bats a paw, landing most of the time, causing the flame to puff up then relax.

Oakes says, "It could be an error in the testing or it may be something. Whichever the case, we request of you another sample to confirm our suspicion."

Reed's smile falters, "Am I dying?"

"Nothing indicates that at this time. We don't know if or how this anomaly affects you."

Reminded of what Michael had said, Reed's hackles of mistrust rise, "So what will you do with my ichor? How much of it do you need?"

"For now, double the amount taken before. Do you experience unusual symptoms?"

Like no heartbeat? No blood? No shadows? Wait—the crows?

From his jacket, Jonas produces something like a single cigar holder, but instead of metal or leather, it's made of hardened clay stamped with markings that do not mean anything to Reed.

"I have nightmares." Reed decides not to say more. Don't give him anything. But could there be a connection? They've all told Reed they don't know what to make of the crows. Kyle, Emma, Alcott—they are all stumped. Maybe he has mutant ichor and that causes memory loss? Marie lost all her memories. So did Eddie, and Ron, and the other two—Jean-Paul and Clarice.

"Nightmares? They can be caused by anything. Perhaps they're related to what we have observed. We'll know more as soon as you donate your sample."

"Well… I'll think about it."

From the opened end of the clay case, something like a pencil with markings slides out onto Oakes's palm.

"What's to consider? Though painful, the procedure will be quick, then you'll be fine."

Noting the sharpened end, Reed says, "You have to stick that in my heart, don't you?"

"Yes, in fact." Oakes gestures toward the grounds beyond the perimeter of the house. Several concrete benches dot the turf. "It's better that you sit. Or perhaps lie yourself down."

Remaining where he is by the house, he says, "I've been staked before. I didn't like it," Reed says.

Kyle had taken Reed by surprise and staked him in his own home. Immediately immobile, blind, and dimly aware of what was happening to him, the feeling of vulnerability and helplessness was almost too difficult to bear. He shudders with the memory.

Suddenly warmer, he feels confined in his suit once again. "I was told not to trust you."

"That is wise, and understandable. The nature of our work is dangerous and secrecy is a must. That is why we sequester ourselves. But secrets invite wild speculations. It is unfortunate that others think the worst, but there is little we can do."

Some of the symbols on his jacket match the tube and mini-stake. Reed doubts they're only decorative. Magic symbols.

His eyes narrow as he looks directly at Oakes, "I was told some guy was made a guinea pig. You or your friends up there tortured him. Is that true?"

Oakes' lips draw tight for a moment. "An overstatement of what had occurred." He adjusts his shoulders, then swallows, "However, much as I desire to, I cannot deny that there was a breach in our safeguards. Such a breach will not be repeated."

"Cut him open, I take it. See what makes him tick. Would you do that to me?"

"Not without your express consent, Mr. Williams. You may have been told this already, but we have had to rely on willing participants for advancing our understanding of our own anatomy. Discovery requires sacrifice."

"I understand nothing is free." Reed rubs the back of his neck, "When do you need to know by?"

"We are immortal, Mr. Williams—we have time. But do you? We cannot be certain if the anomaly is benign or will harm you."

Returning to flicking the lighter, Reed says, "It has harmed me."

Curious, Oakes says, "What do you mean?"

Going for broke, Reed says, "Tell me how I can be human again and I'll give you what you want."

Oakes says nothing.

"There's got to be a way back."

"Our inquiries are scoped to the nature of ichor, its properties and applications."

Roxy's words come to him.

If there's a way back to being human, if they truly know a way, do you think they'd tell you?

"Tell me how. What do you care? What does anyone care?" Reed's voice takes on an edge. "It's no loss to you or anyone here if I'm human again. Before Wednesday, none of you ever heard of me. So just give me what I'm asking for and you can have whatever the hell you want."

"I am in no position to offer you anything other than to recommend to my colleagues that we take up this inquiry. But candidly, I will tell you that it will likely fall quite low in the primus's priorities."

Reed steps closer to Oakes, "How long? Weeks? Months?"

Jonas laughs dryly, "Hard to say, with little to go on. Decades, optimistically. Our methods are deliberate and methodical. Tasks must be prioritized—"

"I don't have decades or even years, or even months. I need answers now."

Reaching for Reed's shoulder to guide Reed toward one of the benches, Oakes says, "A sample of your ichor, if you please. That will at least allow us to further test your ichor's peculiarity."

Reed throws off the man's hand. He's not going anywhere. He flicks the lighter while glaring down at Oakes and pressing him back. "I'm sick of the games. The runaround. The secrets. I'm fed up." In the leonine fire-light, Reed roars, "You're not getting a drop more until I have some real fucking answers!"

***

Kyle can't believe the scene that sparks before his eyes.

His initial distracted glances through the windows to check on Reed had become an attentive stare when Reed's body language turned tense and the distance between his face and Oakes's narrowed. Then the ordinary flame atop his lighter blazed and streaked into the air.

"Reed!"

Having hurried from Emma's side, he now comes to the garden, yards short of his charge and the ichorist. From behind, he can hear the shuffling and talk of others gathered at the French doors. And he can feel their stares on his back as much as they must be on the confrontation before them all.

Keeping his distance, Kyle commands in a crisp, authoritative voice, "Reed. Put the lighter down. Stand away." His words tug on the cords that bind Reed's will to his own.

Has it worked? Is Reed's silence owed to the bond or to his shock by Kyle going back on his word to never use it?

For his part, Oakes appears surprised, not alarmed by Reed's ill-con-sidered and heated words. Then the man's composure returns.

At his limit with Reed's outbursts, Kyle exercises his own control. Tamerlane is not a place for conflict. Of all places, here, and with his peers peering at them, Reed has chosen to lose his cool. Kyle is close to losing his own.

But then Reed's shoulders slump as he steps away from Oakes. The red-orange lion that curled between them snuffs out.

Kyle nearly regrets having used the bond, but now that he has, he may as well keep going. So young, so emotional, Reed needs the bond as much, if not more, than any neophyte. Emma, Alcott, and Devlin had been right.

Still on the reins, Kyle says, "Apologize to Magus Oakes."

Reed clears more distance, returning to the sorcerer his personal space. "I'm sorry." He then turns, raking Kyle with his glare as he runs off to the end of garden and disappears around the corner of the house.

Instantly Kyle considers that he made an irreparable mistake. Reed's baleful look may as well have been a solid jab to the nose. He hates this business.

When Kyle moves to follow him, a firm hand holds him back.

Brother Alcott says, "Let him go. We need to talk."

As Alcott regards him, Kyle sees Emma, Catherine, and Malcolm behind him, just inside the wing. Do they stare at him with reproach? Disbelief? What will the gossip harpies take from this?

Emerging from the group, Michael jostles past them all and says to Kyle, "I'll talk to him."

Alcott leads Kyle, not back into the house, but through the garden, casually following where Reed had gone.

Kyle cuts Alcott off before he says a word, "I will take care of this."

With a slow nod, Alcott accepts this, "You will need to take care of something else as well."

They wind up by Kyle's Audi parked in the front.

Alcott says, "The time has come for you to contact Tommy."

"Do you have an update?"

"Little more than what little we already discovered."

"And no idea why Blade was in Philly in the first place? Why he'd violate the truce? Why now?"

"Naught. Naught. And naught. Tommy must suspect something. I don't know how frequently he was in contact with his brother. We cannot rely on them being estranged. If he gets the notion that Blade is missing and that we are to blame, he may come here with an entourage. Truce or not, it will only exacerbate the situation, muddy the investigation, and put more of us at risk."

Kyle leans in to see himself in the Audi's sideview mirror. He fixes his tie as he considers his flashy blue suit. He had only thought to wear it to impress Emma, but now seems garish for what's to come.

"Meet Tommy. Now. Convey to him only the facts. Don't speculate. Assure him that we are continuing the investigation and will report what we discover to him as soon as possible. If he has any relevant information to share, all to the good."

"Do you think his death was meant to convey a message?"

"Speak with Tommy. Make sure he understands the truce is still in effect. Violators will be dealt with."

"I don't know how well Tommy will be able to keep the Rotters in hand. Especially now with their leader dead."

"For everyone's sake, his hand better be firmer than yours."

twenty-two

chapter

Sundae

J ohnny Vo hasn't texted or called.

Reed hasn't texted or called.

And Karen hasn't texted or called.

And Ratu, well, he doesn't have a phone. But why hasn't he showed up, or at least, sent her some rats with a message?

The first two she lets slide. They don't owe her anything. Though basic courtesy would be nice for what she has done for them. But what the hell, Karen? Is she still angry? Over what? Oliver has some broken bones. He deserved that. He'll heal. Nothing permanent.

Maybe during Roxy's walk, Karen will turn up. Or Reed. Or Johnny. Maybe Ratu will gift her with his presence. She had left enough treats around sewer grates and garbage bins for all the rats, hoping to entice them to show up and answer her damn questions.

Maybe he doesn't know anything. Maybe, like Johnny, he thinks she should drop her investigation, such as it is. The anonymous vampire's death doesn't matter. Let him go.

Oh no! What if Karen doesn't let Oliver go? What if he had apologized for his behavior, and she decided to forgive him and take him back?

Be strong, Karen, is what she'd tell her friend and roommate if she would answer Roxy's damn messages!

Her phone rings.

Karen!

Before Roxy can say a word, Karen cuts to it, "You didn't listen to me last night."

Excited, Roxy says, "I know, but I couldn't let—"

"No. I'm talking. You're not my mother, and I can take care of myself."

Though smiling, Roxy tries to keep to a tone of contrition, "I know. I know you can."

"It wasn't even for my sake, was it? You let yourself fly off the handle to make yourself feel good. I needed my best friend, not a rage monster."

"I'm just so glad to hear from you."

Karen takes a breath. "You never liked Oliver, did you?"

"No. Not really. I didn't say anything but I wanted to…"

Karen's voice sounds like that she's nearly done being mad. "I'm glad you didn't, though. I wouldn't have listened or have said something I'd regret. It must have been hard to keep your tongue still."

"It was. You deserve better."

"I do."

"So… what did you two even argue about?"

"Oh…" Roxy can picture Karen sweeping her hair as she winds up, "Get this: He's a drug dealer. Something new and exclusive. He tells me this all casual, like it's no big deal. All this time he's been selling drugs at The Jolt and other places around here. Onyx, I think it's called. He just sold some of it to a guy just as I showed up. I saw him put the cash away and I asked him about it. He showed me a sample. Black crystals. Oliver said it's better than Molly. It's going to be the next big club drug."

Intoxicated humans make for easy snacks. Roxy only says, "Unbelievable. Well, I'm glad it's over."

Karen agrees. Turns out she has been with Trudy all this time. While they chomped on a shared hoagie, she told Trudy what had happened at the club, though sanitized to leave out the vampy parts. Trudy urged Karen to call Roxy back and tell how she felt and make up.

All's well that ends well.

*   *   *

Nothing like a decadent sundae to cure the blues. With a cherry on top, no less.

With satisfaction, Roxy watches Karen excavate the bowl of black-and-white ice cream, leaving much of the airy dollops of whipped cream untouched. She saves that for later—a dessert to the dessert.

Even off-shift, Karen often comes to Driscoll's to eat patty melts or cheesesteaks. She gets discounts. Close to midnight, bursts of customers come and go, city workers taking a break, couples on a late-night date, college kids craving munchies.

She's sworn off Oliver, so she says. She's clearly still hung up on him. With each chime of the phone, she leaps upon it. He's already offered apologies for his behavior and wants to see her again. Some texts were from Trudy, but she's since gone to bed.

In his last text, Oliver reported that he'd be around the clubs and hopes to talk to her there. Probably pushing his Onyx crap.

Seeing Karen conflicted, Roxy had told her not to engage. And if he lacks all sense and shows up on set, Karen is not to be alone with him and tell him—in front of the cast and crew—that it's over.

With that, talk of Oliver ended before the ice cream arrived.

And talk of Reed Williams began. A new vamp on the block—well Fishtown—who's in a big jam and needs help.

Karen cuts in, "I thought you went unshopping after the club. Didn't see the packages when I got home."

"I did. Went fine. Howdy asked about you. But while I was handing them out, I met this guy. He's got the Fire, like me."

Over the years, Roxy hasn't shared with Karen a whole lot of the particulars of being undead. But she's too excited by the new kinship.

"It's like I found my long-lost twin. Drawn together because of our shared make-up. Like we have a secret language and we fill in what the other lacks. You should have seen us practicing. The Fire burned bigger and brighter. Only a matter of time till we can fly or something else awesome."

Licking her spoon before another dive, Karen says, "So, when are you seeing him again?"

Roxy turns glum. "I don't think he wants to see me again."

"What? Why not?"

"He ran off. He's a mess. And he's new. And I don't think he likes my methods."

"What does that mean?"

Roxy looks away, then back, abashed. "Well… you know how I like to provoke. See… he's a stubborn clam, uptight, won't open. Too focused on learning, while being too impatient. I was trying to shake him up. So maybe, I got a little too…" She makes squeezing motions with both hands.

"Grabby?" Karen says.

A phone chimes. Both women turn their phones over. Roxy wins. The text reads:

WHERE ARE YOU?

"The Lion." She sends him her location.

Intrigued, Karen says, "He's coming here?"

"Wait till you see him. More yummy than a sundae."

"What happened to the painter?"

"She's a long-term project. I plan to wear her down."

"By not ever introducing yourself? Just stalk her while she's blissfully unaware you exist? Good plan."

"Recently, I saw her someplace other than her studio."

Karen straightens, intrigued.

"Saw her while I was shopping at the market. So, I followed her down the aisles. Among other things, she uses an amber and honey shampoo.

"Well, that explains the new bottle in the shower." Karen brings out her I-have-news-and-I-need-to-tell-you-now grin. "I can do you better."

Roxy adopts a royal posture and tone, "Is that so?"

"I know her name."

"What?!" Roxy gasps. Leaning over the table, she says, "How? What is it?"

"I accidentally-on-purpose bumped into her when she was about to enter her place. Figured it was her. She matched your description. My age, pixie-cut dark hair, which she's growing out by the way, starving artist thin. Plus, her tote bag had art supplies. Asked if she's the painter a friend told me about. When she confirmed it, I said that I can probably hire her on for the sci-fi project. Then we exchanged info."

Roxy's torn. She likes the mystery, that anything is possible. In her imagination, she can't be disappointed. But, she's too curious. "What is it? Tell me!"

"I don't know…" Karen sits back, arms crossed, considering Roxy's case. "You actually *spoke* to this Reed guy."

twenty-three

Playing with Fire

F ists pulse. Skin seethes. Reed glowers as he stalks away from the garden on his way to... well, he's not sure to where. His only desire to put
miles between himself and that charlatan Oakes, Kyle, and the gulping
sharks staring at him as though he unzipped his fly and whizzed into the
koi pond.

But Kyle was his ride... Well, if he has to wear out the soles of his dress
shoes walking back to Fishtown, so be it.

The noises of guests and music fade. Soon replaced by footfalls
approaching. When near enough Reed twists around, fist raised, ready to
bring the hammer down.

"Hey, man! Easy." Michael skids short, flinching, hands up in an I'm-
unarmed gesture.

Reed glares, then eases off a degree. He huffs, returning to his course.

"Hey man, are you all right?"

Reed considers an acid response, but by Michael's tone of concern
without the hum of humor, he merely says, "No."

A ride would be better... "Get me out of here."

Michael looks around, "Are you sure?"

"To hell with them."

***

In no mood to talk, Reed slumps on the rear bench of Celestine dwelling on what just happened. Part of him feels humiliated by Kyle who had used the bond to make Reed apologize to Oakes. Like he's a kid told to remember his manners. Reed didn't need to be told to apologize. He would have. Eventually.

And he was dressed down in front of everyone. Malcolm, Michael, Mrs. Shipley, and half the party stared at him where they gathered behind Kyle. Look! Come see the idiot.

But more than that, Kyle betrayed Reed. He went back on his word to never use the bond. Marie all over again. Controlling him, making him her puppet, making him nearly kill Lily that night in the Whitpain Hotel.

He stews, hands rubbing his brow. Damn. Did he screw it all up?

Pulling out his phone, Reed checks on any pending messages. Several from Lily. Thinking-of-yous. A lead from a woman in Manayunk, who gave Lily an address in South Philly. He bolts up, alarmed. She didn't go there at night alone, did she? She did. He cringes. Then sighs with relief. She's safe. Back at her own apartment with good news. Going to bed. Talk tomorrow.

A text from Roxy:

LET YOUR LION ROAR!

And several more, asking what he was up to.

The woman had been right. The Society won't help until they have what they want from him. And they're in no hurry. They can wait.

Decades!

Reed says to himself, "It's all a game to them."

Michael says, "I forgot we picked up a sad sack of suck."

Reed speaks up, "You said not to trust them."

"Who, the sorcerer? I did. What I did not say was for you to burn off his face."

"I didn't burn anyone and I wasn't going to."

"If you say so. What did that guy want anyhow?"

"More of my ichor."

"So, of course you said no."

"Yeah. Right?"

"Right. You could have turned him down with a simple no. Or even a polite, 'No thank you.' Masquerades are supposed to be fun.

Leave-your-worries-at-the-door kind of thing." Michael turns off the expressway back into Center City. "Reed, you have to relax. Frankly, you scare me."

"I scare you?" Reed sits up. Had he heard right? He tries to catch Michael in the rearview mirror.

Michael says, "What you did back at the hotel. To Eddie. He was a righteous asshole, don't get me wrong, but how you toasted that English muffin."

Reed slides into the middle of the bench and tips his head back. "He didn't give me a choice. And I don't have control of this power. I've never been an erif before."

"I hear you, man. But that's my point. You go off again—who knows who gets burned next. Kyle has to look after you till you can take care of yourself. But you have to do your part by being chill. Understand?"

To Malcolm, Reed says, "What about you?"

"A comparison might be observing a meteor on a destructive course, appearing to crawl across the sky, then streak, then cinders."

"Great."

"A force of nature."

"Got it."

"Thrilling in its potential danger."

"I said, I got it."

Glancing at Reed, Michael says in a mollifying tone, "Straighten up. Don't let anything get you down." He smiles wide, "Learn to go with it. There are no setbacks, just different streams to the same destination. You'll get there when you're meant to."

Reed knows. He should have taken a breath, counted to ten, like Lily has always told him.

Michael says, "If you need to learn control, shouldn't you see that erif, the Roxy woman?"

"I met with her already."

"Meet with her again."

***

Driscoll's is a diner like every one Reed's eaten in—a checkered floor, a counter with swiveling stools and rotating cakes, booths with

188 *J.P. Cane*

coin-operated jukeboxes. The memorabilia on the walls consists of slices of Philadelphia life and candid photos of Philadelphians.

Cooled by the time Malcolm and Michael have dropped him off here, Reed is only a few steps through the door when the lion is up again. Like a Labrador retriever hearing the approach of mommy's car, he's at first still, then alert, then springing to the front door, nails clacking, tail lashing.

Having sensed him as well, Roxy looks up. With a wave and spreading smile she invites him over.

Reaching the booth, he finds a college-aged girl. "I didn't know you had company."

Roxy introduces her roommate, Karen, who waggles her eyebrows in his direction, then gives Roxy a coded expression.

"Nice suit."

Reed nods. He should have thought to change on the way here.

Karen, the roommate, says, "Married, I see." Then with weird emphasis, "I did not know that." Followed by that coded expression. They must have been talking about him.

"Yes." He looks at Roxy, "Happily. And you're not going to pull any crap again. I'm here to learn. That's it. Got it?"

Looking at Roxy, Karen says, "Oh, not to worry. She's promised to behave from now on."

Roxy grumbles agreement.

"Damn right. I've had a terrible night. But," Reed takes in and releases a breath, "I'm going to go with the flow." Then he does relax. "Besides, I've got nothing else to do before sun up."

***

They escort Karen back to their home. At the door, she says she would love to film their practice session. Big pleading eyes accompany, "Please?"

Roxy pinches Karen's cheek, wishing her sweet dreams.

As they walk, Roxy throws her arms skyward. "Beautiful night. Look at that moon."

Reed looks up. Unclouded, the brightness of the fat moon shines silver. "Shouldn't moonlight burn us too? It's reflected sunlight."

Roxy says, "Because the moon cheese absorbs the sun's zeta rays. *Idiota.*"

Reed chuckles, "Okay."

She grins, "Got you. You *can* smile."

They turn onto Bainbridge Street. "Have you eaten yet?"

"No."

"We'll do that first. Send you home on a fully belly."

"I don't want to hurt anyone."

"Better than killing them, Reed."

"Have you killed anyone?"

"Not recently. But don't worry. We'll be good little vampires."

She suggests going to one of the clubs. They are reliable locations for feeding. She offers a tip: The intoxicated make for good meals because they're often happy for company, pliable, and tend not feel the pain of the bite or even remember it. Show them a good time and you're home free. And no need to worry about contracting anything. Drugs, viruses, bacteria have no effect.

"You will only need a little blood at a time if you do it often enough. That's the trick between hurting people and killing them."

Even if the evening hasn't already been a disaster, Reed is no mood for clubbing, or dancing, or even mingling. "I'm overdressed anyway." He's tempted to burn this suit.

"Fine. You won't have to go in. Just wait for me outside."

On their way, he says, "Thank you for helping me."

She waves his words away. "Stick with us. We look after each other." She tells him of some vampires like Johnny, Mikhail, Dewey, Bernadette, who live in the area, and like her, do not belong to the Society. "Maybe you'll meet them."

Indifferent, he says, "I'd rather not think this is long-term for me. If there's a cure right now, I'd take it. And I'd be happy to never see Kyle, or Alcott, or Devlin again. And you." He shrugs: *Sorry.*

She waves again, not offended. "You know, if you stayed a vampire, think how much easier fighting fires would be. You'd be a phenom. Well, once you get a handle on your power."

He concedes with a small smile. "I guess that's true."

Under awnings and lamp light, they weave through the late-night crowds.

"When I lived in Chicago, I had considered joining the Society. That House was a corrupt boys club, as far as I could tell. More so than here. You know, for all the jazz I give Al, he's actually pretty decent."

"But you won't join."

"Can you picture me at that party tonight?"

Reed chuckles now, "I couldn't even picture me there. And they won't have me back. I went off on one of them."

"Really? Good for you." She puffs herself up and deepens her voice, "Bet *Lord* Devlin was pissed."

Less amused, he says, "I made things worse for myself."

"Doubt it. You're still alive and they need their firebug. Rules. What's the point of all this if you're just trading one set of rules for another? They love their control. All they've done was replace the bond with the Compact. I refuse to be a pawn. I'm my own queen—I move where and how I like. You should do the same."

She tells him that she had grown up fairly well off until it was all gone. Before the Depression, she lost her father, then her mother couldn't cope with losing a husband and their changing financial situation. Her mother wasn't a cheerful person even when papa was around—so she quickly went from bad to morose.

Roxy was soon on her own. People she had thought were family friends shut their doors—like her new impoverished state was contagious. "I learned quickly not to lean on anyone. They'll disappoint you when you need them the most."

Reed says, "I'm sorry that you lost your parents so young."

She shrugs. "In the long run, it's better with no attachments. We're going to be around an awfully long time. You need to let Lily go, Reed. Best for both of you."

"I told you already, I'm not playing. You and I are not getting together."

"I'm not talking about me. You're both stuck on the past—an old life. Break free of it so you can know what you really want. And if you go back to her, then you'll know it's right."

"I love Lily—she's not my past, she's my partner."

"But she doesn't know you anymore. She wouldn't understand this. She can't. She sees the old Reed, human Reed. Have you told her everything? What it's really like, your real feelings? Have you craved blood yet? Like an addict craves a hit? That you'd take it from anyone, even her, if you needed to? And you're such a mess that you don't even realize what you're doing. Do you know what I'm talking about?"

"Yes," he says slapped by the memory. Back in the hotel room, Reed was fixated. He sorely contemplated sucking the blood out of the sheets in the hotel room where dead bodies had been tucked into the king bed as a morbid joke.

"Think she'll understand that?"

At first, he doesn't answer.

With a shake of his head he says, "No, you're right. She doesn't understand. And I don't know what to tell her. I can't talk to her. Not without scaring her. Because I scare myself. I'm ashamed of how she must see me."

Eyes wide as her smile, Roxy says, "You know, you could turn her. Make her a vampire, then you'd have one another forever."

"No. What the hell's wrong with you?"

"It's not the worst idea."

"It is the worst idea. The worst."

***

Reed watches Roxy lead her puppy into the shadows of the alley. All she's missing is a leash. The man looks plastered—wide eyed and yipping with giggles. His shuffling feet knock an empty glass bottle rolling into the brick.

Watchful for bystanders and police, Reed keeps to the door frame the pair had exited through. Out of the pool of light from the floods above, Roxy lets the intoxicated man paw at her. He's wearing a white bucket hat and a teal warm-up suit. His hands slide over her hips, butt, and up the sides of her breasts. He hunches over her as she kisses along his jaw to an ear then down his throat.

He can hear them panting. Any moment, he expects the man to scream. But so far, the man is liking his chances tonight, whistling approval when Roxy shows some cleavage.

A third wheel, Reed turns away. Below a drain pipe, the sheen of water captures the moonlight. What is he doing here? Well past midnight, out behind a nightclub, dodging cops, he's a junkie waiting for his dealer.

Roxy teases, "Easy baby. We'll get there."

Reed glances back. Roxy presses into the man, his back against the brick wall. Behind, at her waist, Roxy awkwardly waves her hand. Reed realizes she has been signaling him.

Come here.

He doesn't want to, but this is what he's here for.

Roxy waves again, now in sharp halting motions. *Come. Here. Now.*

With a grimace, Reed steps carefully toward them. The man doesn't notice him and won't as long as he doesn't call attention to himself. Just a shadow on the wall.

Roxy's signaling hand now covers the man's crotch groping there. She makes a sound of delight. The man shudders while laughing as though he heard the best joke ever.

Closer now, Reed can see his eyes are dilated and spots of his shirt dampen with sweat. He looks stupid in that Gilligan hat. He's half-tempted to play Skipper, grab it off his head and smack him with it.

"Thirsty," the man says, swallowing.

"Me too," Roxy coos by his ear. "Would you roll up your sleeve for me?"

She gives him the space to fold the sleeve past his right elbow. Rewarding him with another flash of her cleavage he becomes a grinning fool and leans in to kiss her there. Turning her head, Roxy mouths to Reed, "Ready?"

She laughs as though enjoying herself. Turning around, she snuggles her back into his front. He smells her bob of dark hair while she takes hold of his arm. She bites by the elbow but the man doesn't scream or even flinch with pain.

Twin tracks of red slip down, bead up, and, about to jump to the ground, before being caught by Roxy's tongue.

After a minute she stops and holds the arm out to Reed like she's passing a bottle of liquor. All the while distracting the man by guiding his other hand to her bosom.

"Who're you," the man asks mildly when Reed relieves Roxy of the bleeding arm.

Roxy cups the man's face, turning it back to her, "No one baby. Relax. I'll take care of you."

The inner elbow, smeared with red, captures Reed's attention. Two neat wounds. They don't appear deep. Blood oozes out. He can smell the iron. His fangs sharpen eager to bite. But he doesn't need to. He can just taste what is already there. He'd better hurry. Drops splash onto his dress shoe.

Go with the flow. Do it. Do it. He huffs as though about to plunge his face into icy water. Reed bends his head and seals his mouth over the man's skin.

The blood. It tastes as blood should—salty, rusty. Warm and runny.

And more than nourishing. More than taste or smell. Colors and sensations. Reed has tapped a line. All the lights come on, bright and humming. That zip of life surges through him, filling him over capacity. An aliveness.

Troubled too by this intimacy, as though walking in on someone undressing or overhearing a private conversation. But the flood overwhelms such cares.

He feels substantial. Filled out, meat on bones. Present. Real.

Reed feels connection.

"Enough," Roxy cuts in. When he doesn't yield, she twists his ear.

He lets go, letting the arm drop to the man's side.

She shoves him away, "Go. And fix your eyes."

Staggering a few steps, Reed realizes his eyes have shifted. He raises his hands to his face, peeking back at the pair. Vivid blue auras flare around both Bucket Hat and Roxy. They ripple; and, Reed notices, they ripple synchronously.

As when he had fed from Kyle, impressions of this man, Alexi, tumble through. Melon oranges and bashful blues. A club. Dancing. Alexi is large, but weightless, bulletproof, silly, content. A sun orbited by men and women, celestial bodies, who share his vibe. No strife or grudges, all their concerns lost in some distant nebulae.

***

After several blocks, Roxy catches up to him. "Come on! Let's loosen you up and grab some fun!"

She howls a long note, then motions for him to do the same.

Despite himself, he grins before giving a quick whoop.

Hands to her hips, back arched, she lets out a bigger howl, while waving for him to go again.

Less self-conscious, he yells louder. She claps for another. He mimics her, fully arched, chest out, letting a howl ring the night. While he does so, her fingers fly at his taut stomach, attempting to tickle. Though not ticklish, he breaks into laughter.

She nods approvingly. "Finally. I was beginning to think you were permanently gloomy."

After a breath, he lets out another and another. They stretch out their yowls in an unspoken competition of who is alpha wolf.

She wins. "My father sang opera."

***

Giddy, Reed continues to feel good. What had he been worried about? Feeding was easy and Alexi the Bucket Hat was no worse for it. His blood was satisfying.

Now, he feels lighter than air, an orange balloon loose in the sky, filled with the innocent joy of a child. His cares and concerns abandoned on the ground, while he's up in the air untethered. Just fluff free to drift. Maybe he'll pop right up into space, up to the zeta-ray-absorbing moon.

He wishes Lily could be here with him. Inseparable once again. No edges between them. One flesh. They could float together. Breeze back to Paris.

Would Lily want to be a vampire? Would that be so bad? Wouldn't it be easier to stop struggling and just give in to it? Could Roxy be right?

"Of course, I'm right."

Stunned to a stop, Reed says, "Have I been talking this whole time?"

"Yeah. You're been babbling for three blocks now."

He wipes his face.

"Forget about it," Roxy grins. "You know, if both of you were vampires, you'd cut down on a lot of expenses. Food, medicine, doctor visits, insurance."

"True..."

"And... what if Lily turned out to be an erif too? We'd be awesome. Unstoppable. Is she a Sagittarius too? Or an Aries or a Leo?"

"She'd never go for it."

Roxy perks up, "You would ask her?"

"I don't want this for her. I don't want it for me. I can't even talk to her about it. How I feel. What I've been doing the past two nights. How the blood I need has to be from a person, not a pet or a juice box. That I went to some woman's apartment for her blood. What would I have done if I had gone inside? What kind of man would I have been? What kind of man am I now? Not her man. Not her husband. She'd be horrified."

He feels so open. He checks his feet. Yes, they are touching the ground. He is walking. "Is it normal to feel like this after, you know, drinking? I feel all weird. Don't you feel it?"

"I do. It is screwy. I feel I'm on my way to the moon too. Ever wish you could fly? Sometimes I think I can. That I can take a step off the edge and keep on going, higher and higher. Fly anywhere I want."

"That would be cool. Skip over all the traffic. How would it work? Do you just think of a direction and go there or do you have to point? And how much can you carry? Only what you're wearing, or can you carry another person?"

"Reed?"

"Yes?"

"I want to start some fires."

***

At some point, each finds a lighter in their hand. "One, two, three... shoot!"

Flames burst into gorgeousness, wiggling before their eyes, bowing to their masters like genies released from their bottles ready to grant wishes.

Roxy's flame takes wing, parting from a smaller flame of the lighter. The bird, her Millie, loops and glides through the air. In response, Reed shapes his own fire into a stout lion silently roaring. He's beautiful—tawny coat with a majestic mane, like fiery sheaves. A tail flails behind Florian, heating the air near Reed's face.

Unlike before, Reed now intuitively grasps the Fire. His pain is Florian's impatience. Cooped up, the lion wants to pounce on something, tear into it, relish in his power.

After some final tricks, the creations melt into the air.

They turn off the jets. Reed exults in his progress, whooping. Roxy cheers. "You're a quick learner, Boy Scout."

***

The fire in a metal trash can begins as a heap of kindling—newsprint, cardboard, used napkins, rising upward, quicker than should be possible. Burning plastic and paper turns the air acrid and curls of black smoke thicken and rise.

Something feels wrong. A dark premonition passes through him. Then it's gone. He's feeling too good to care. Especially with the sight before him. It's really cool. Now ten feet tall, the fire takes the shape of a bird with massive wings. Shadows flicker across the brick wall. With the smoldering trash at its bird feet, it looks like the phoenix Roxy had described earlier.

Millie is alive.

She's so pretty.

Reed falls back from the heat of the fiery thing.

"You try," Roxy smiles, like: *Can-you-do-better?*

In awe, Reed doesn't dare try. How could he possibly compete with this beautiful blaze?

Her words come out sing-song, "Come on. You gotta practice, right?"

Nodding, he tries out what she had taught him so far. He raises his arms as though about to conduct an orchestra, encompassing the phoenix in his gaze. The twisting reds and oranges shimmer gold. Feathers loosen and sail on the currents of the heat.

He concentrates. The wings change again. Now they're arms of a Goliath. They lift, making giant fists.

"I'm the champ!" Reed says, thinking of Goliath as a boxer who just won by a decisive knockout. It mimics Reed's pose, arms pumping triumphantly.

Whatever is wrong catches Reed again. He quiets as though listening, as though someone will whisper to him what it is.

Roxy hollers and claps, "Go, champ!"

Its gloves graze an awning, which instantly catches fire. Then so does an air-conditioning unit stuck half-out of a window and soon the casement. Reed wonders how the flames will be put out. Then he remembers he's a firefighter. Fire. Fighter. Knockout. So funny.

Roxy says she's thirsty. Or did he say that? Is he thirsty? That can't be good.

The champ crackles with fiery brawn. Farther and farther, its gorgeous flames spread ahead of avian screams, which turn Reed instantly sober. How does Millie do that? How is Roxy doing that? His balloon pops. The wrongness has returned.

And so have the blackbirds.

Bursting through the flames, black shapes arrow toward Reed. Falling back, Reed shouts and covers his face with his arms. He can feel gusts of air beat on his ears and whip his hair.

Reed falls on his ass. Sunlight streams between his X-crossed arms stinging his eyes. Shadows flit over his shaky body.

He's a scarecrow. The sky fills with the damn birds. He's never seen so many before. They're as numerous as locusts—winged and ravenous, they'll descend on him like a plague and strip every last piece of him till he's empty rags and a battered hat. He doesn't stand a chance. The sun and sky are gone—just a curtain of darkness thrown over this world.

The lily! He still has it. But for how long? It's what they're after. He collects himself. Startled that's all. He can control this, if Ms. Shipley's right. He's still strong. He won't yield. He'll fight to protect the lily with everything he has.

But the crows—it's as though they brought their friends, who then called up reinforcements.

Mr. Oakes had said his ichor has an anomaly—these nightmares and filched memories. With Alexi's blood, Reed feels stronger. Maybe the anomaly is too?

The sheet of black contracts, swirls, expands and plummets. It's as though Reed's watching a great funnel in the sky—a tornado of wings and feathers and beaks converging. On him.

Just the weight of the birds would obliterate Reed.

Then all at once Reed has a thought. Florian should be here. If the anomaly's power can appear here—so can Reed's. As the crows come, Reed rises to his boots, planting them firmly in the earth. He's calm. He's resolute. His arms lift high. Beneath his feet the earth turns hot.

The birds scream, diving at him, wings tucked close to their bodies for speed, angled straight for him, a vast bomb falling toward the bullseye.

His scarecrow form doesn't flinch. His hands stretch to their utmost. A whip of flame snaps from the ground. Florian bulks up quickly and leaps past Reed. He roars defiantly—shaking the whole scene. Like a fireball launched from a catapult, the lion arcs through the sky on a trajectory to demolish infantry ranks.

Reed can feel heat lash his face. So close that he's singed. Not from Florian. From where?

The birds break formation, peel away, pulling back up into the heavens.

Hot, stifling air carries crackling, snapping, whooshing noises. Feels like a wall of heat has fallen on him. Wisps of smoke curl up his sleeves like morning fog, bringing pain. His hands pat his arms.

He's back on the street. A fire appears before him. What had been Goliath the Champ has returned to its natural destructive shape.

Where's Roxy?

He doesn't feel good. All of this has been too much. He's spent. He needs to call someone. He's hyper focused on the fire. The flames are beautiful.

Shaking his head he tries to remember he's got to call someone. Tell someone. Fixation is bad. Fixation means he's very thirsty.

The fire sizzles as it bends to embrace Reed.

Reed fumbles to find and get his phone out of his pockets.

His champ is gone. So is Millie. Just a natural blaze and roasting heat.

Isn't there an app?

Find the app.

Activate the app.

Push the button.

Has he pushed the button?

The fire.

So lovely.

twenty-four

Bridge Under Water

W ind ripples through Kyle's short red hair and tugs at the lapels of his jacket. Otherwise motionless, he stands just about dead center of the span of the Ben Franklin Bridge, erected nearly a century ago. Dead center of the evening too, so traffic is minimal. He's on the pedestrian path suspended over one hundred feet above the cold water of the Delaware River.

From the east end Kyle spots a figure in jeans and a sweatshirt trudging toward him. Even with a grey hood hiked over his head and down to the brim of a baseball cap, Kyle recognizes Tommy's shuffling frame. Like a beak, his brim flicks side to side as though expecting someone to flank him, despite the lack of cover for an ambush.

In the closing yards, Tommy pulls off the hood and focuses on Kyle. The wiry black man has changed little—a young man's face with older eyes.

"Tommy."

The man's high-top sneakers halt at an invisible line just ten feet short of Kyle. Tommy's level gaze is all business, "Been a long time."

Kyle nods, "Perhaps more for me than you."

Because Tommy had more sense than Troy, a zealot for the cause, Kyle knew Tommy was the one he could convince. And once Tommy agreed to the idea of the truce, Tommy could talk Troy and their children to agree as well.

Tommy crosses his arms over his chest and takes a wide stance.

He has had the past few nights to think of what he will say. A "cat-on-the-roof" approach—revealing the truth little by little—may ease Tommy into his grief. But direct is best and more respectful.

"I have to be the one to tell you, Tommy: Troy is dead."

Kyle wants to rush through the rest, get out the details now, but he lets Tommy have a moment. Though the man doesn't say a word, his body expresses his thoughts all the same. It tenses and his lips draw closed as though he pulled the string of his hood taut, sealing off his face.

"It's true, though I wish it wasn't—"

"How the hell do you know that he's dead? What did you do? Where is he?"

"We believe it happened Tuesday night or Wednesday morning."

"Three nights ago?!"

"It took time for us to recover the body from the morgue. Philly PD had been called when it was discovered by delivery men behind a diner called Driscoll's. And we wanted to have some answers before we reached out to you."

"And?!"

"Unfortunately, we don't have much. No motive and no suspects."

Tommy turns and paces in a tight circle. "I want Troy's body. Tonight. He's our problem now. We'll deal with it."

"I can't give it to you yet. I can't hand *him* over yet." Kyle holds up a hand to explain. "We're still trying to determine what happened. Once we're done, we'll give it to you. Give *him* to you."

"How did he die?"

"His heart was removed. I have pictures of the wound on the phone here." Kyle takes out the smartphone, flicks to the photos Webb had shared and holds up the screen.

"Yeah. Fine." Tommy steps over quickly and looks down at the picture of Troy's body laid out on a table. He cries, looking away, "I wish I could be sick. You know?"

"I understand."

"You don't understand! You're telling me Troy's been murdered and I'm supposed to believe you had nothing to do with it?"

"Yes. We have no reason to kill him."

"You sure about that? You don't think, maybe, the New Hope monsters were involved? Back to their old tricks?"

"Alcott Ashton is investigating. He's good. We're working on figuring this out—"

Tommy steps closer to Kyle once more, "You mean covering it up. I know it wasn't any of my people. We're tight. Someone in your House figured Troy had to go." He paces away again.

"Nonsense, Tommy. It's me—okay? We worked together, to make the peace. I'm asking you to trust me again. The House and New Hope do not have any cause to hurt or kill Troy. If—*if*—it was a member of the Society, it must have been a personal matter. We'll find out who and deal with him."

"A rogue. Like those before. Like I just got done telling you. You're having sorcerers look at him now, aren't you?"

"Yes."

"So, they get to defile him? Like a final insult to him? To us?"

"Tommy—"

"No—you sit on this for three nights and allow those sadists—have their way with his body."

Kyle says, "It's not like that. There's no conspiracy. Cool down. We're on the same side here."

Tommy throws out his arms, east toward Camden, west toward Philadelphia. "We've not been on the same side for twenty years! Let's not forget who did what—who's responsible for all of this."

"I have not forgotten."

"Those sick ghouls, Kyle! Who knows what demon crap they're doing to him now. Hell, removing a heart sounds like a ritual, doesn't it? Of all of us, who does that? They do. I see you know what I'm talking about. They don't answer to you or to Devlin or to any House."

"We fixed that Tommy. They wouldn't do something like this again."

"I believed you. We believed you. We bet on you and took the deal. But we were fools to think any of us could change. No one does." He looks in the direction of the steel railing and river flow.

"I did. You know that."

Tommy's gaze returns to Kyle. "Did you? Maybe you're back to type."

"I promise we'll find who killed your brother."

Tommy says, "And when you do, we'll deal with him. Our way."

"We'll figure that part out then. Let's find him first."

"Do you know who Troy was to me?"

"He was your brother."

"More than that. Brothers because our father was Lemon, but also because we've been in the foxhole together, like soldiers. You don't know what he means to all of us here." He looks like he wants to say more but cuts himself off.

"What can you tell me, Tommy? Any information you have might help Alcott find who did this? Did Troy know someone there? Was he meeting someone? Did he need something?"

Tommy looks away, "No, he didn't tell me."

Kyle wonders if this is true.

"Where and when did you last see him?"

"We last spoke, I don't know. Last Saturday I think."

"No contact the night he died or since? Did you think something was wrong?"

"Yeah. But he's gone silent before."

"Did you try calling him? Or visiting his home?"

"Look I'm still in shock here. And I'm not sure I trust any of you."

"I'm trying to help. If we did this, why would I be here? Okay? Let's work together again, Tommy."

Tommy retreats several steps, "I'll think about it. I've gotta tell my people."

Kyle says, "Make sure they don't take this matter into their own hands."

"We have a right to do our own investigation."

"Not in Philly. It will just put us at cross-purposes. And that might get more people killed."

Tommy bounces back toward Kyle. "Maybe that was the point? Whoever did this wants to restart our feud?"

"Alcott considered that. All possibilities are on the table right now."

"If it is, they may have succeeded."

"Tommy, don't."

"Your fucking Society, Kyle. You think you get to tell everyone what to do, even those on the outside. We don't recognize your rules. And we've seen what you do to those who don't obey. There shouldn't be clubs. We should all be a family—looking out for each other, teaching each other, sharing. You all keep it to yourselves. Those ghouls worst of all."

"Believe what you want, Tommy. I'm trying to keep this truce and prevent any more deaths. We're willing to work with you. And once we discover who did this, we'll deal with it together. I understand Troy meant a lot to you."

"He meant a great deal more than you'll ever know," Tommy says, heading away again.

"Accepted. Again, I'm sorry."

After a sorrowful shake of his head, Tommy pulls up the hood. "You don't know yet how sorry. You don't know how sorry you'll be, how sorry we'll all be soon."

part
III

chapter

twenty-five

Initiative

*T*he roof of a parked car buckles under the weight of the beast that drops on top of it. Curls of vapor puff from the beast's nostrils when it lets out a tight breath, then it straightens up to its full height of over seven feet. Under the grey fur, muscles ripple, straining against the many gold bands around its arms, wrists, and ankles that adorn its body. Saliva drips from its muzzle, full of teeth like knives.

Gripped in one clawed hand is a carved wooden staff. Bones, held together by leather thongs, rattle from where they are tied to it. Then the beast thumps the end of the staff on the roof as it turns its four-hundred-plus pound bulk. Aglow in the moonlight, its amber eyes, set in a wolf's head, fix on their target.

You.

"Roll for initiative." Eric peers over the tri-fold screen set before him at his end of the gaming table.

His players toss their multi-colored, vary-sided acrylic dice onto the red baize table covering.

"Yes!" Jared says, pleased with his result of seventeen.

Eric rolls as well, then reports the lineup, "Jared, Amity, Chris, then the pack."

Jared says, "I pull out Owain's Fang," and does so, plucking up the short sword from its place beside his chair. Inlaid with the finest gemstones, it is a relic from the mists of Welsh legend. In reality, the nameless, unremarkable sword in Jared's hands had been purchased on sale for $259.99, plus shipping. After its unboxing, it had to be sharpened.

To his left, he holds it out toward Eric. "And I point it in its direction, and I say, 'We're going to send you back to the pound, Fifi.'"

Eyes of the other players roll like dice.

Chris snorts, "That was weak."

"Shut up," Jared says.

Next to Chris, on the love seat they share, Amity says to them both, "Keep in character." Then she says to Eric, "I prepare a spell..." She takes out a small leatherette pouch and from it a piece of folded paper. "Blindness."

Eric nods, "You have practice with this one, so just roll to see how many turns it takes to cast."

While Amity's dice roll, Chris says, "I aim my crossbow at the beast's heart, and I say 'That was lame, Gareth, the Unbowed.' Then I fire the silver bolt."

The basement-slash-game room has served the group for many years. The bookshelves are a shrine to role-playing games, from first edition source books, to hand-painted figurines, to practical props.

More rolls of the dice. Eric says, "Your bolt wings him. No apparent damage. Seeing him up there, you swear there appears to be a smile in that muzzle." Eric then affects a guttural sound and says to Amity, "With your Animal Ken skill you understand it to mean, 'With pack, never alone.' Then it lets out a howl that chills you all. Soon its howl is joined by another. Then another. Then another. In addition to these, you can hear movement, panting, and rustling gear. All of these sounds surround you."

Perched atop a stool, Eric swivels to consult some papers on a smaller table behind him. Then he brings out painted pewter figurines. On the tableau before them, he arranges three creatures in rampant poses on a play mat. They encircle other figures representing the players. Lines drawn in wet-erase marker outline the area, filled in with die-cast cars and cardboard structures.

Amity sighs against Chris who scratches at his wiry goatee. She has dressed as her character, Annalee the Blessed. She wears a long white dress trimmed with purple and deep sleeves. Her velvet cape has many symbols stitched on in silver thread.

Amity makes her own wardrobe and accessories. She sells her crafts online and at the Camden fantasy convention, where she models her creations each January.

In countless campaigns, in dozens of game systems, popular and obscure, she's been properly attired for each one. Occasionally the others will as well. Except for Jared, who reliably wears camouflage-printed cargo shorts and one of his ratty t-shirts over a midsection that had been shaped by the snack food diet of his human days.

They all share a very pale and hollow complexion. They do not heal as rapidly as other vampires. Along with the room temperature skin, they could be mistaken for the wrong kind of undead—zombie instead of vampire, though their small permanent fangs would clinch which.

Chris absently strokes her back with the knuckles of his hand. He does the production work of her photo and video shoots, posting them all on her website and social media.

From the top of the staircase, they hear the door slam open and feet hurry down wooden risers. By custom and the pace of the footfalls, they all know Henry has finally decided to join them. They don't bother looking his way, even though he sounds to be in an uncommon rush. He shouts for their attention when reaching the landing where he turns ninety degrees to take the final four steps onto the basement floor.

They barely mutter their acknowledgment. He's the oldest of those here and whose seniority and intelligence they respect. But that's no reason to be late again.

Slightly stooped beneath the low ceiling, he pushes back his round spectacles, "Gentlemen! Lady!"

Eric calls for an initiative roll.

"Players!" Henry leans over the bespoke table, hands flat on its surface. He had designed this table. Longer than he is tall, the spacious table features felt-lined drawers for dice, memo pads and pencils, glass beads, tokens. Leaves can be removed for a more versatile play area. The stout carved legs depict a fantasy motif. And as a considerate touch, the table has cup holders for when human guests play with them, unaware of the true nature of their campaign companions.

Jared says, "Where the hell have you been, Henry? We started without you. We left your sorry ass back in the motel."

Rapping his knuckles, Henry says, "This is important."

Chris says, "We do need him right now. We're surrounded."

Nodding, Amity says, "We could say he came with us, but was held in reserve."

"Fine."

Conceding for the moment, Henry says, "I check for traps."

Chris laughs, "You mean apart from us already being ambushed? We're in the middle of a parking lot in the middle of the night in the middle of Pontiac, Michigan. What other traps are you expecting to find?"

"Won't know till I find them. Guys, forget the game. I have news."

Eric says, "We already know."

"Really?"

Jared points to Henry's usual seat, "Sit your ass down."

"The bootleg was released. We'll watch after we're done here."

"Why bother? We know it'll end in a mess. They screwed up another franchise." Jared shouts to the heavens, "More villains do not equal better story!"

Henry declines to take a seat, "No. None of that matters right now." Looking to each of them he says, "You have to come with me."

"What, Henry?" Eric asks, annoyed.

"Tommy told me to get you all. We have to meet him at the Dreary. Now. The whole family."

***

Murmuring fills the first floor of the Dreary. A house, but not one lived in, though a few members will occasionally crash in its basement.

Area rugs cover most of the floor. Below valences, heavy curtains are swooshed aside to let in the evening and a view of Erie Street in this Camden neighborhood, a short walk from the Delaware River.

Amity's grandmother had a place like this where she was busy knitting or crocheting. From her comfy easy chair, she was an old spider spooling out clothing and cozies. She had bowls of candies—a cloying smell of wintergreen spread over the home.

Folding chairs surround Tommy who watches the front door or whispers to those who approach him with questions.

While they search for seats, Amity notes just about everyone has shown up except Tommy's brother, Troy. His crew is here. A few straddle their chairs and others stand loosely nearby, glancing at the door, waiting for their father to arrive through it. Many are clad in leather with studs. They're more of a gang unto themselves that keep to themselves. In fact, Amity can't remember when she last saw them, nor remember most of their names.

Perhaps by being older and having seen more action, Troy's children are more aggressive. They act like survivalists sometimes. If they were human, they'd have hoarded cans and jars of food, water bottles, and guns in a bunker.

They haven't accepted that the war's over. The family lost. Amity's not one to judge, but Henry, Jared, Chris, even Tommy have moved on—why can't they?

"We're all here, yeah?" Tommy says. Under a dusty brass chandelier, he paces before dozens of souls seated in chairs, hanging along the staircase, or leaning on a wall. Most chat among themselves.

One dude, legs spread, leans back with his hands clasped behind his head and says, "Everyone, but Troy." Amity recognizes him as Alfonso, a child of Troy. One of his oldest.

Amity notices how they've all self-segregated. Troy's progeny up front, Tommy's own farther back, and the rest of Lemon's descendants sprinkled in. It's seldom that they're all in the same room.

"Has anyone heard from him?"

Tommy fingers his scalp while looking at his scuffed boots. Then he looks up, his eyes tired. His voice falters and an attempt to smile fails, "It's good to see you all."

"Where's Troy?" someone else says. Others echo the question.

She looks back to Tommy, who hides shaking hands by pressing them on his jeans. His face looks pained. It says everything.

Oh no.

Tommy says, "Quiet while I get through this. Seeing you all here. I want to say so much… but another time. I'll just get to it." He heaves out the next three words, "Troy is dead."

Everyone's quiet as though what they heard cannot be, must not be. Troy is late. Troy is feeding. Or even Troy is hurt. Amity knows she heard it right and that Tommy isn't joking. He's in pain. Though she hasn't known Troy as well, she adores Tommy and her heart goes out to him.

Henry opens and closes and opens again a pocket watch; Jared shrugs with unconcern as though: *Troy, who?*; Chris pulls Amity into a comforting hug; Eric mouths their way: *What the hell?*

And Tommy hasn't stopped. He's still talking, "… Dowd of First House. His body—"

Then the shouting starts. Many erupt from their chairs aiming fingers at Tommy.

"Shut up," Tommy says, "Let me get this out. Troy was killed three nights ago."

Cries of disbelief war with hisses for silence.

Lucia, one of Emerson's, bawls into her hands.

Tommy's voice barely carries, "Let me finish. They don't know who killed him. Kyle Dowd says it wasn't any of his people."

Shouting, many in the room express their disbelief.

Though some two decades have past, what Amity remembers of Kyle Dowd makes her doubt the man had some hand in Troy's death, but given the mood of the room, she does not share this.

Others ask, "Where's the body?"

Tommy says, "They have it. They're holding it—holding Troy—for another night before they return him to us."

"What's the proof?"

"Why would they make it up?"

Tommy raises his hands in a gesture that everyone should settle down. "I saw the proof—he showed me pictures."

"He took pictures? Sick!"

"Maybe he's not dead. You only saw a picture. It could have been manipulated." Those around him ridicule the stupid idea.

Tommy says, "Quiet! He doesn't know what happened. They're trying to determine that."

"We're supposed to believe him?"

"I say we grab Dowd till we have Troy's body back."

"And answers!"

Making a face, Tommy says, "We're not taking hostages. We're all upset, but we can't lose our heads."

"How was he killed?"

"His heart was removed."

"What? How? Who does that?"

Tommy says, "There weren't any other signs of injury in the pictures. Just—just a hole in his chest."

Gasps of horror bound around. Amity's own hands fly to her mouth.

Henry lifts his eyes from his watch, "Was it surgical?"

"Surgical?"

"Did the 'hole' appear neat and symmetrical or more rough and jagged like a tear?"

"I didn't look that closely. Torn, I think."

Lucia asks, "What does that mean?"

Henry answers, "Surgical would imply he was first subdued so he couldn't fight. The killer had time to do his work."

"He was found in South Philly."

"He'd never go there."

Ideas of how Troy ended up on a street in South Philly pings around the room.

"They're lying."

Tommy says, "We don't know what happened. That's what Kyle Dowd is trying to find out."

"Their first call should have been to you."

"So what? We're to believe Troy was killed by some random asshole—had his heart ripped out or whatever?"

"Hell with that. Definitely someone from Philly or New Hope."

"Yeah, they did it. Probably kidnapped him and did their experiments, like they did with Lemon. They ran out of volunteers again."

"Tommy, if they did do this, then you could be next. Any one of us could be next."

With a firm voice, Tommy says, "All the more reason to cooperate with them to learn the truth. If we don't, then they may take the initiative, expecting a fight with us."

"We should just leave Camden. We shouldn't have to stay here to get picked off."

"To where? There are Houses all around us."

"I got a good job here."

Tommy says, "No one's going anywhere. We'll play along till we have the advantage."

Alfonso all but spits, "No way. Troy's dead—truce is over."

Tommy shakes his head.

Rising from his seat, Alfonso says, "You're going to bend over and take whatever Kyle Dowd gives you? Not us."

Tommy says more calmly, "Now's not the time for this. You go in, you'll get slaughtered. We play along till we know more and make a smart move."

"You've gone soft Tommy. We lost too many already. Troy's the last straw!"

Tommy's face hardens, his eyes taking a sharp edge, "We all lost. I lost more than Troy did, and now I've lost him too! Don't talk to me about going soft. I paid! His death means it's just me now and I'm responsible for each and every one of you. We're not losing anyone anymore. Troy was my brother—we didn't agree on a lot, but we trusted each other."

Someone next to Alfonso says, "All the good that did him."

Tommy shouts, "You're out of line. I tried—" Then he catches himself as though reconsidering his next words. Calmer, he says, "He was trying to fix us, fix our ichor, make us stronger, so we don't lose loved ones anymore. He took risks for all of us."

"So, we honor him by being cowards? Sitting here doing nothing? Hoping Dowd doesn't come for you or any of us next?"

Before she knows what she's doing, Amity springs to her feet, her mouth spouting what's in her heart, "I believe in Tommy. I don't know much about these Society creeps. I would think Dowd's okay, but we don't owe any of them anything. But I believe in Tommy. Not because he's my father, or because he's next in line, but because he's always put us first. If he says to give Mr. Dowd time, then we do it."

"Sit down, Princess." There's some laughter. "You all play dress up. Let the real men and women handle this."

She's suddenly aware of her appearance as a caped spellcaster of a mythical game. Not the most inspiring wardrobe given the circumstances.

Jared jumps to his feet, "If anyone's pretending, it's you, you G. I. Jokes."

More people launch to their feet; fingers point every which way as accusations hurtle across the room.

After a sharp whistle, Tommy says, "I'm in charge now. Only me. Troy cared a great deal for each of you. We're not going to fall apart. We'll get through this as we always do-together. Like the family we are."

At his direction, Amity and Jared take their seats. A few more do as well.

"And no, we are not going to sit around doing nothing. Lucia, Cyrus, and Sugar, get me recruits to interview."

"On it."

"We'll prepare. Once we have Troy back, we'll honor him and celebrate his memory. Properly. Then I will tell you what our play will be."

Leaning Alfonso's way, Tommy says, "You're right. This is the last straw. But we'll do this smart, and we'll do it at a time of our choosing. So, all of you: Fall in line. No more discussion. No more of this sniping at each other. We're family."

Amity beams with pride. Tommy sounds like a leader.

Meeting over, people break into groups of commiseration, then pass their condolences on to Tommy before heading out the door.

Tommy splits Amity off from the others on their way out. "I need to talk to you."

Chris says, "We'll wait in the car."

While pretending to examine her cape, she listens to Tommy speak to Alfonso, who says little but a few angry words. But Tommy keeps a sympathetic tone and is actually sweet. By the end, he pulls Alfonso into a hug with back slaps.

When he returns, Amity offers a hug of her own, "Tommy, I'm so sorry about your brother."

"Thank you."

"How are you doing?"

"I'm still—well, I can't believe it even though I'm not altogether surprised."

"Why?" She had heard Troy and his children kept vigilant as though an attack would come any night. They'd spar and drill to keep in fighting form. But as far as she's aware, everything is status quo.

"Look, Amity, I need you to do something for me."

Eager, she says, "Of course. How can I help?"

"This has to remain between us, okay? Think of it as a secret mission. I need you to go to South Philly and look up someone there."

"What? You just got done saying we're not to do that. We're not allowed over there." They weren't allowed anywhere, really.

"I know. That's the secret part. Can you do it? Can you go there, find him, and come back without getting caught?"

Looking to the door and back, she says, "I've got to tell Chris, probably Henry, and the others too."

"You're to do this alone. The more of you out there, the more likely Alcott Ashton will find you. He's good at that." She has the vaguest recollection that Mr. Ashton is a Society detective type.

"We can do it; we're experienced."

Frowning over her costume, he says, "Amity, this isn't one your fantasy campaigns."

"Will Mr. Ashton kill me if he does catch me?"

"I don't know that. Likely, they would hold you till I bailed you out."

"I've never been to jail."

"You don't have to do this. I'd do it myself, but there's too much going on right now. It's just me." He gasps at the end.

She rubs his shoulder, "I know. I'll do it."

"Are you sure?"

"Yes." She kisses his cheek and heads out.

"Amity...?"

"Yeah?"

"You need to know who you're looking for."

"Oh, yeah. That would help. Who is it?"

"A man named, Horton."

chapter

twenty-six

Courage Check

W hen they return to their house, Amity doffs her silly cape on her way to the living room full of comfy couches and enveloping easy chairs, entertainment center, and large flat screen TV.

Jared says, "Where did we leave off?"

Instead of joining her in the living room, the others follow him back to the basement, back to the table, back to the game.

Eric says, "Miracle of miracles: Henry's orc cleric has conveniently appeared to help even the odds."

Amity scowls at their backs, "Hey! We're not going down there. We have to talk about this. Was I alone back there? Did you not hear that Troy had his heart ripped out? That Tommy has to do this all alone?"

Before he disappears down the stairs, Jared says, "We can roll dice and talk about our feelings at the same time."

She snags Chris's sleeve, giving him a reprimanding look. He shrugs, like: *What can I do, the men have spoken?* Resigned, she trudges down and takes her usual spot, her hands pressing into the cape folded across her lap while the others continue conferring about the game.

Eric says to Henry, "Monk Balduhr, your intuition that a trap had been set proved correct. Your compatriots find themselves surrounded by large furry demons that offend your gods by their presence in down-town… Pontiac."

Chris glances at Amity, who gives him the look of pleading topped with exasperation. "Guys, all right, come on. Someone say something."

Amity relaxes a bit, thanking Chris with an appreciative smile.

"Troy was a bad ass. Too bad about going out like that," Jared says while examining his sword.

Henry adds, "Troy was a good uncle. A nearly absent one after the truce, but, as Tommy eloquently put it, he looked out for us."

Eric says, "It doesn't make sense to me. With the fighting over, I thought we'd all be around for a long time."

Chris says, "Who would have killed him?"

Many of the questions voiced at the meeting echo here. The who, the why, the how. And the why now?

Brushing his beard, Henry says, "I doubt the experiments have resumed. And even if they have, and the necromancers somehow got hold of Troy and killed him, why would they dispose of his body in such a manner?"

Heads nod to this solid point.

Running his index finger along the length of Owain's Fang, Jared says, "For all we know Tommy killed Troy."

Along with the others' groans, Eric says, "Shut down that talk right now, Jared."

"Just saying—could have been anyone."

Chris almost laughs, "Like you?"

"Yes. I could have." The others howl at the idea, preposterous. "I didn't. I don't know the exploding heart trick."

Amity directs a bolt of reprimand at each of them, "None of us here killed him. But that's not the point right now. Troy is dead. Can you pretend to care? I didn't know him for as long as any of you. I remember he was there when Tommy turned me. When I first woke up, he was there, and he actually smiled. How many times have any of you seen him do that? It was a like a shooting star-there and gone. He was sweeter than he let on. He checked in on me, made sure I was drinking enough, adjusting well, and all of that. And he gave me that Elsbeth statuette."

Jared says, "Sweet, my ass. I saw him fight. He was a mean, undead machine, who could brawl with the best of them. I had always imagined he'd go out fighting a pack of them and taking them all with him. He'd have a bandoleer of grenades and let one go off when they got close enough."

Nodding, Henry says, "He was fearless too. He was out in front with Lemon—human or vampire, he didn't care—he put himself in danger before any of us."

Jared says, "Tommy, not so much."

Henry says, "More of the brains than brawn type."

"Like you," the others say.

Amity nods, "He knows when to fight and when not to."

Jared says, "You mean a coward."

Amity sits up more, rebuking Jared with a glare, "Tommy is no coward."

Eric snipes at him, "You always think the worst of everyone."

Making a dismissive gesture at them both, Jared asks rhetorically, "You think Alfonso and his crew will fall in line behind Tommy?" His tone answers: *Not-a-chance.*

Amity says, "We're family. We'll get through this together. They'll see we need Tommy-now more than ever." She looks around for confirmation. Assurance that it will be all right.

Jared says, "They're probably plotting right now on who will take over."

Henry shrugs, "Tommy has been good for us. But Troy's progeny have not liked him, or us, as evidenced earlier tonight. They think Tommy capitulated to the Society. And will again."

Chris says, "I'm with Amity. We *are* family, and we have Tommy's back. We owe him more than that."

Eric says, "Troy disappeared a lot. I assumed it was business nearby. But do you think all this time he was sneaking over to Philadelphia?"

Chris tugs at his goatee, "Why would he go there?"

Amity says, "That's what Tommy wants me to find out."

Chris tilts his head as though to gauge whether she's joking. "You?"

"He spoke to me after the meeting."

Jared snorts with naked skepticism, "Why you?"

"Because I'm his favorite."

"You are not."

Chris smiles to her, "You're my favorite."

The others gag.

Chris says, "What does he expect you to do?"

With a more confident posture, Amity says, "To go to Philly and find some guy named, Dean Horton."

"Who's he?"

"Never heard of him."

"Well, Tommy thinks he might know something about Troy's death."

"Like what?"

"If we knew, I wouldn't have to ask now, would I?" Looking to each of them, "I had asked if you can come with. He didn't like the idea. But... he didn't say no."

Eric says, "Thanks for thinking of us."

Henry speaks up, "You will need to be quite careful."

Shaking his head, Jared laughs, "I'm going to stick with getting my ass kicked by the wolf demons."

Chris turns to Amity, "Where would you even start?"

"Where Troy was killed."

Jared picks up several dice, rolling them in his palm, "Sounds like a set up for failure."

"Where's this attitude coming from?"

Henry says, "You've not lost before."

"What?"

"We've been through the war."

"The slaughter, you mean. They call us Rotters for a reason. We're fodder."

Indignant, Amity shoots to her feet, "I *have* lost. I lost Cole, you insensitive assholes!" She dares any of them to tell her otherwise.

Henry begins, "Yes, you lost Cole. But his is a different case. He wasn't murdered like—"

Amity ends Henry's point with her death-stare. Then to each of them, "Pathetic! You play at this table every night pretending to be heroes. Now you have a chance to do one small thing and you chicken out. Unbelievable!"

On to the game table, she throws the cape, smothering pewter warriors and monsters.

"Not every night."

Henry says, "Perhaps that is why Tommy chose you. You're not weary of war."

"Yeah, you're naive."

"*Et, tu*, Chris?"

"Babe, I support you. But..." Chris shrugs.

"Cowards." She stomps for the stairs, "Fine. I'll go myself."

twenty-seven

Cole

A mity led her boyfriend into a room of vampires.

She wanted to be sure Cole's last evening as a human being was a celebration. The balloons proclaimed Happy Birthday and Get Well Soon— the closest sentiments available for choosing to die and return undead.

There were streamers and candles and other festive items. Lemon cake with butter cream icing and champagne. The cheery atmosphere did not banish Amity's qualms however. Despite all their preparations and excitement, there was still a chance, more like a certainty, that once Cole's blood left him, and his heart stopped, and his lungs took their final gasp, Cole would never wake. And despite ample precedent, Troy believed Amity would succeed where the others of her generation failed. That Amity would be the one to beat the curse.

If Cole suspected her doubts, or had his own, he never let on. He was as sweet as butter cream. The night before, he had his favorite meal—a heap of spaghetti and monster meatballs in a lake of gravy.

Cole gulped a glass of bubbly while Amity watched. Others chatted among themselves or with the two of them. After licking up some icing, he smiled to her, "I'm going to miss this."

***

They had met in theater class and went on to perform together in Shakespeare's *The Tragedy of Romeo and Juliet*. By curtain call they had been dating a full semester.

One day Cole shared with her a secret: he had a terminal illness. The survival rate was quite low.

The news was a tank, flattening her. She didn't know how to react, especially since he seemed so calm. Maybe he had absorbed the shock already or maybe he was pretending to be calm for her sake.

This turn of events hadn't fit into any picture of the future they had planned together. They stashed money so that instead of going straight to college, they would travel abroad. Live like Bohemians—hell go to Bohemia—which was in Europe someplace. Be buskers, backpack, hitch-hike. The experience would be better than any college, plus how much they'd save by not having student loans. He was all in with her. But now he wasn't—he couldn't be. She would live and he wouldn't.

She pulled herself together enough to hug him tight and promise to be by his side. She wanted to learn everything. As they embraced, she tried to impart positivity. People beat the odds and what do doctors know, anyhow?

Parent-and-child pairs filled the waiting room on her first appointment with him. A few flipped through colorful magazines, some whispered to one another, often they held each other for mutual comfort. One kid appeared as healthy as any their age, the others not so much. There was a girl with a scarf over a bare scalp, her head tucked into her mother's shoulder. A boy missing a portion of his left leg—whether that was due to his illness or an accident, she couldn't guess. Maybe it was her nervousness but the room was hushed and solemn.

Beyond the pain or fear or anxiety, she saw cruelty. A promise was broken. A fundamental law violated. Kids shouldn't be here. How did Cole end up here? How did they end up here? How do any children end up here? This was a cosmic mistake. The deal was that kids get to grow up first, then screw up their lives.

When the nurse called for Cole, Amity jumped out of her skin. He stood by his mother and headed to follow the nurse down the hall beyond the door. Looking back, he gave Amity a wan smile.

The moment the door closed, the temperature of the room dropped, or the lights dimmed, or the odor of something spoiled arose. All at once

Amity felt ill, alone, and overwhelmed. A premonition. The word entered her head. She felt an ill omen. Before she knew it, she was on her feet, which turned and ran, taking the rest of her body with them out of the doctor's office, into the hallway to the elevators, down to the main floor of the building and outside. Cole's mom had driven them here. She ran down the street till she stopped and stooped over, hands on knees, feeling the worst. The reality was too great to bear and she felt scared and ashamed. She was the worst girlfriend.

The days following, Amity barely ate and nearly gagged on what she did manage to push down her throat. She didn't dare return Cole's calls to the house. By what right did she have to react the way she did? Why was he handling it better than her? She couldn't face him.

She told her mom to say she wasn't well which was true. Mom urged her to tell him how she feels—he deserves to know. He did deserve that and more, but she couldn't work up the nerve yet. She figured she was dumped, but even so, she would like to be a better friend. She only wanted to take away his disease, for him to be well again, grant his life back so that he could be happy and find his Juliet, even if it wasn't her.

If only there was a way.

And then she found it.

***

Since 9th grade, she had played role-playing games. The kind where friends gathered at a table and participated in a story where they were its central characters destined for fantastic adventures; their success determined by the players' decisions and rolls of the dice. Plus, plenty of chips, pretzels, candy, pizza, and liters of orange and cola soft drinks.

During recess and sleepovers, they portrayed their characters in store-bought or homemade costumes and props. Humans, creatures of myth, or from other dimensions; brawny fighters, clever charmers, wondrous spell-casters. She liked playing scrappy underdogs who had better luck than she did.

It was engrossing escapism that her parents preferred over her partying or joyriding all night.

When she got a bit older, she met Chris who held game sessions in a basement with older kids, even college age ones. She felt adult among them. One of the few girls who played with any regularity and who took it as seriously as the guys.

But after betraying Cole, she quit without notice.

Chris tried calling her. Her mom had answered, explaining in a too-loud voice that Amity wasn't available.

Eventually, Chris visited on the pretext that he was Amity's classmate and was concerned that she was falling behind at school. Amity dragged herself downstairs and whispered to Chris that he was going to get them both in trouble.

He was telling her mom the truth, that he was there to help with studying and getting her grades up. But also, he could tell how she was upset with something and he wanted to help with that too.

When she explained her self-imposed exile, he responded, "That's all?"

"What? I was horrible."

"He'll be dead soon, and it won't matter to him anymore."

"Now you're horrible. How can you say that?"

"It's also true. Everyone goes sometime. You won't, if you don't want to."

"What do you mean by that?"

"You don't ever have to die. Stay young forever like me."

"Yeah right. You have some magic potion like from the Cave of Iverson?"

"I do have a potion as a matter of fact."

And one night he showed it to her. Vampire blood, which wasn't red. It looked like black molasses veined with crimson. And it came out of his veins.

***

When she came to know that vampires existed, she wanted in. Wanted in bad. Like now. But Chris told her that she'd have to wait until she was a bit older. Besides, things were tense and uncertain in the vampire world, or at least this part of it. In the meantime, they would prepare for her immortal life.

When that night came, she remembered Cole. He was still alive. Well, in fact. She went to him, apprehensive, bracing for the worst he could give. A verbal thrashing, real punches, or worse, icy silence. "I'm sorry to have run from you." She continued apologizing, tearing at herself.

He spared her any further self-flagellation. "S'okay. I don't blame you."

This wasn't what she expected. He was far more mature than most people she knew. She had been surprised that he'd even hear her out, much less meet with her. She was grateful for his decency even as undeserved she believed it was.

"It was an awful thing to do. I was freaked out, and I couldn't deal with it. Look, I was a terrible girlfriend."

"You were a really terrible girlfriend."

"I'm sorry, Cole. You deserve a wonderful woman."

"I know, but I'll settle for you."

"Ha. I deserve that."

"I don't know how much longer I have, but I want to spend a lot of it with you."

"Me too. I promise I'll make it up to you. When you're ready, I'll share something I've never shared with anyone."

In retrospect, that was probably interpreted by Cole differently than she intended.

When the disease took a turn for the worse, she said, "I'm ready to share now."

"Oh wow. Right now? Here?" He began to take off his shirt.

"Yes. What if I told you there's a way for you to live as long as you want? With me, if that's something you want."

"Sure. Sign me up."

"When I tell you how, you might not like it."

"I trust you."

"You do?"

"I know I have every reason not to given what you did before. But since then, you're a different person. You're better. You're an awesome young woman. And I know you care for me. I feel the same."

Turns out he needed more convincing than either expected. Getting him to believe vampires existed and that she was one was a task in of itself. Then proposing the idea that he become one as a way to beat the disease nearly sent him away. He had already made peace with death—he was prepared—his family was prepared. He had ideas for the funeral, who'd attend, eulogies, burial, legacy.

Amity hadn't considered that.

"Well, we'll have our own funeral, a better one—believe me. I can't wait. We're going to do a whole initiation. Champagne and sugar cookies."

"I thought you can't eat food."

"Before, Cole." She smiles, "Before. You'll have something light. Don't want to do this on a full stomach."

They gathered in the Dreary. A half dozen others circled them, including Henry who came despite his grief. Amity wouldn't let herself worry about that and she certainly wouldn't tell Cole.

All preparations were made. Amity led Cole to the center of the gathering and handed him a glass of champagne.

"Something sweet."

"The last sweetness I want on my lips is yours."

People around them mingled and chatted with one another till the ceremony began.

Amity says, "Repeat after me: I—say your name."

"I—say your name."

Amity laughs, "Dork."

"Dork."

"Enough! Be serious."

"I thought I should be Cole."

"Do solemnly swear."

"Do solemnly swear to pledge my undying loyalty to the family, to be a righteous creature of the night, to have and to cherish my fellows and to have lots of fun. I swear."

Cheers and applause. Cole drank the champagne.

"Come with me."

They disappeared behind the curtained area and settle on the deep leather couch draped with soft towels.

They smooched.

"I can't wait to have fangs. So cool. You look sexy."

"Are you scared?"

"I was. At first it was hard to believe."

"You freaked."

"I did. But I remembered you're still Amity—the Amity I've known since 9th grade. The Amity I fell in love with. I've always wanted to be with you. Now I get to do that. Now I'm excited. So, let's do this."

"All right. Relax." Her words were for herself as much as for Cole. Desperate to believe Troy's prophecy that she'd be the one who could break the curse.

"Just relax. You'll feel like you're falling into a deep tranquil sleep. And when you wake up, I'll be here. I'll be the first person you see in your new life."

"'Thus with a kiss I die.'"

And died he did. Three hours had gone by and Cole's body had grown cold, pale, slack. Amity was vigilant and only when Chris peeked in, did she look up. She shook her head. He was not coming back.

Troy had been wrong.

chapter

twenty-eight

Leveling Up

U p in her room, Amity tears through a deep closet of clothing. In her pajamas, she tosses blouses, skirts, dresses, pants, tees, unsure what she's looking for.

Exhausted by Tommy's devastating news, then seeing him nearly dethroned, and her so-called friends unconcerned with both, she's thrown herself into finding the right outfit for tomorrow night.

Foolish. She was so certain they'd join her across the river to find this Horton guy.

She steps over piles of clothing, holding out a tunic for consideration before one her many mirrors. Wrong. What is she thinking? She recrosses the hills of fabric and hangs the tunic once more.

Turning back to the room, the largest upstairs, her eyes hunt for inspiration. She can't very well head into danger without proper attire.

Atop one bureau, foam heads display wigs—short hair, long hair, natural, synthetic, blond, red, pink, green. Trays for latex and silicone prosthetics and pots, powders, and tubes of makeup, most of which she uses on the guys more than herself.

Her work area, her favorite spot, holds an antique Singer sewing machine mounted to its stand festooned with bobbins and thread. Beside the stand, a wicker sewing kit contains patches, ribbons, swatches, rhinestones, glitter, shears.

An adjacent table has soldering implements, spools of wire, a 3D printer, and plastic beads.

Over the years she has become a skillful seamstress and fashion expert. She has spent countless nights sketching ideas and collecting material, then spinning and sewing both into fantastic and realistic costumes.

She models her wardrobe for an online audience, one that has grown into quintuple digits and may reach six by the end of the year. Requests for her work have more than paid for the materials. Not bad for a dead girl.

But, to her great sadness, she has had to turn down appearances. Leaving Camden wasn't possible. Well. Now, yes. But not before now.

If she does this. If she dares cross the river into Society territory and survives to cross back then why not take the Jersey turnpike to any place in the Garden State, or, hell, New York City? The conventions, the fashion shows, the musicals.

She sighs, wistful. When she accepted Tommy's offer to become a vampire, she didn't think of this, being stuck in Camden. She only thought of saving Cole.

It's ridiculous. Why should any of them be under house arrest? Why hadn't Troy and Tommy gotten a better deal from the Society?

And Troy's dead. Found in Philly—a no-go zone. That's why they don't leave Camden or else they'll end up dead. Does Tommy really accept the Society's version—that Blade's murder wasn't punishment for trespassing?

Troy was strong, so if he couldn't survive being over there, what chance does Amity have?

Maybe she is foolish. What can they expect to find in Philly that will be of any use? Is it worth the risk? If she gets caught, will they kill her immediately? Or will they take her to New Hope and be experimented on like they had done to Lemon? From what she had heard they put him through hell and changed his ichor. Tainted it. Cursed it.

Unwittingly, Lemon passed it on when he made his own children, including Troy and Tommy. And in turn, they passed it on to their children, like her and the guys. And as they can't make their own, they're dead ends. They look it too, with their moonlight tan.

Bunch of sickos, those ghoulish sorcerers.

A knock at the door. Chris enters, hands in his pockets, "Can I come in?"

"Yeah."

"Look, Amity, I'm sorry. Don't be mad."

"I'm disappointed. In you especially. I thought you'd have my back."

"Look, I want to help, but it's crazy. We're no match for what they've got over there. But I am sorry. I should have heard you out and not let everyone gang up on you."

She looks at the statuette standing by the Singer. Pride of place. Amity is taken by the beautiful figure, its feminine, strong, noble bearing, ready for anything. Wishing to have those qualities herself, she based her Elsbeth character on her. In the game, Elsbeth is of royal blood, but had not known this for much of her life. Courageous, she couriers information through dangerous tunnels as a way to support the dissatisfied factions in their effort to overthrow the system.

Now, it's all she has left of Troy. How can she let him down?

Then. She turns to Chris, "I'm not going."

"You're not? Oh, that's a relief."

"No. Elsbeth is. She's quiet, quick, and deadly when cornered."

"Your character from the Diezel Realms campaigns?"

Excited as the idea blooms in her imagination, she says, "Don't you see? None of us have to go. We go as our characters. Make it a side-adventure. We have a mission. Find the mysterious Dean Horton, learn what he knows, then report back to our employer, Sir Thomas of Camden." She grins, "Say a thousand experience points each."

"This isn't a game, Amity," he says, an echo of what Tommy had told her.

"It is. I'm leveling up, and so are you."

"Hmm. A thou each? Seems light."

"And a two hundred bonus to the one who finds Horton first."

Chris laughs impressed, "Brilliant. You are brilliant."

"Just because we don't have super powers doesn't mean we are helpless. Besides, now we have what none of you did back then: Me."

part
IV

chapter

twenty-nine

Familiar

"Absolutely not." Penny Sedgwick hands change to a customer standing beside Lily. The man thanks her and heads out with his purchase. "You wasted no time going to Horton. I thought I made it clear that he was to be your last resort."

Before Lily can respond, a delivery woman has taken the customer's place, where she parks her hand truck stacked with its cargo.

Delighted, Sedgwick claps her hands then raises them, thanking her goddess before rounding the counter. Evidently, she knows the woman, Felicia, as they engage in small talk while Sedgwick accounts for the sealed cardboard boxes, and signs the electronic slate Felicia holds out to her.

Lily considers returning after closing when Sedgwick may be in a better frame of mind and hopefully more receptive to Lily's request. But she can't wait and she doesn't know if she'll have time then herself.

She doesn't even know where Reed is right now. She has not heard from him since he had sent a paltry text from the masquerade last night. He hadn't responded to any of her voice mail and text messages. So much has happened.

Without a word from her husband, she peeked into his apartment in Fishtown. No sign. His bed empty. Then, on her way to Manayunk, she stopped at their new place. Again, no Reed. He had to have been sleeping somewhere. Even knowing he wouldn't answer during the day, she called and left Reed a message.

He must meet her at Horton's tonight. A cure is at hand! If only she can convince Sedgwick to agree to Horton's condition. Then she and Reed can either get back to their honeymoon, or pick it up another time, like on their first anniversary.

Not finished with Felicia, Sedgwick leads the woman to where her outgoing packages are. More chatter while the packages are scanned in and loaded onto the hand truck.

Once Felicia has left, Lily says to Sedgwick, "He said he had been working on a cure."

Sedgwick hands a sealed cardboard box to Lily. "Help me carry these."

Heavy in her hands and stamped FRAGILE, she holds it close. "Can you believe it?"

"Not really. Neither should you."

Hugging the box, Lily follows Sedgwick up the stairs. Customers descending veer aside as they pass. "I already got the money he's asked for."

At the landing, Sedgwick frowns, "Do not give him anything."

Lily says, "I believe you. But I have to try."

She had considered deceit on Horton's part. She's no fool. But it would be foolish to pass on this opportunity with nothing more than vague suspicions. Either the man can cure Reed or he can't. Still, Sedgwick's own mistrust may cheat them of finding out which.

Sedgwick chuckles.

"Is that so funny?"

"Not at all." They cross the room and into the little office. "I know he's had his eyes on Cincinnati for years."

Setting the box down where she's told, Lily says, "Horton said he would need Cincinnati for his ritual. He assured me it won't harm her." She had made that condition clear to him, to which he had responded, "A dead mink is a small price to pay for the cure."

She could not argue with that.

Picking up on Lily's squeamishness, Horton had said, "Don't worry. The animal's no good to me injured or dead, so you won't need to call the ASPCA."

Horton had not elaborated on what he would do tonight. Part of her still rebels at the idea of vampires and magic. With a skeptic's eye, she surveyed the past week. What she observed could be mostly explained, but not everything. Not what she felt as much as seen. Yet—magic? She hopes that all Horton needs from the animal is a whisker, or a snip of her fur, or a swab of her saliva—some catalyst for the serum or whatever he's concocting.

From a drawer of her desk, Sedgwick finds a box cutter. "I will not give up Cincinnati to anyone, much less that charlatan."

In her cage, the mink grooms her white fur, unaware of her importance to the discussion.

Slicing through the packing tape of one of the delivered boxes, she says, "Do you know what a familiar is?"

"No. I am willing to pay you."

"Before you offer anything, know that Cincinnati is no mere mink. She's also a spirit, a familiar. Familiars, mundane and exceptional, are creatures that aid a witch in her spellcasting. Do you remember what I had said about the rubber band?"

"Yes. That what you put out returns threefold."

"Just so. Among other things, a familiar helps keep the snap from being too severe."

"Like a shock absorber."

"Crudely put-yes. I did not have Cincinnati when I was younger and more naive. It cost someone I cared about dearly. The little magic I still do is carefully considered and with Cincinnati by my side."

"I'm truly sorry, Ms. Sedgwick. Clearly, to help him do—whatever it is he'll do—Horton needs Cincinnati. That should keep everyone safe."

"Nonsense. She's my familiar—not because she happens to be in my company, but that we're connected. Cincinnati would have to accept Horton. That is not a simple matter. He wants Cincinnati so I'd no longer have her."

"I'm having difficulty believing any of this and I won't pretend to understand. She's important to you, that I get. And I'm sorry to put you in this position."

"Then don't." Styrofoam peanuts boil out of the box as Sedgwick lifts something out of it. The object is further wrapped in paper. "He tried to steal her before."

Peeling off layers of paper, Sedgwick is left holding a small item compared to the box it had shipped in. "Cinci's good at finding things as well." By the way the woman holds the pottery, it looks heavy. It also appears ancient, like something freshly dug up by an archaeologist.

Cincinnati chirps, then noses open the small gate of her cozy hutch.

Lily says, "I'm willing to put up a substantial amount of money to have him try though. Please don't let him fail because of this."

"Horton is a hedge witch who has..." her hands search for the words, "he would phrase it as ambitions while I prefer the term delusions—of becoming something greater. A true witch."

"Let me ask you this, Ms. Sedgwick. In all honesty, do you think Horton can help my husband?"

"I have no earthly idea. For me there's light and dark magic. The former works with the universe's will, while dark magic subverts it. It is natural for life to begin, to age, to die. I don't know if what he plans for Reed can be considered restoring your husband to the natural course of life or not."

She scrutinizes the piece in her hands, turning it over, peering at its bottom. She seems to have forgotten Lily.

With a few more chirps, the mink slinks their way. Surprising them both, she scampers up the chair leg and nestles into Lily's lap. No match for the animal's adorableness, Lily awws and gently scritches behind her ears.

Less impressed, Ms. Sedgwick gives Lily and her new friend the same look Lily's mother often gives her: *I know what you're up to and it won't work.*

But, of course, time tells otherwise.

Coming around to the idea, Ms. Sedgwick finally huffs, "Goddess, help me... fine. We'll all go together."

Lily brightens, "Really?"

She relents more with a smile, "I will relish Horton's reaction when I breeze in."

thirty

Live-Action Role Play

Once the sun sets, the house rouses from eerie stillness to ebullient frenzy. Henry witnesses Amity dash room to room putting out wardrobe fires. Suddenly the men are as helpless as boys dressing for prom. She helps them with clothing choices, fixes their hair, and applies their makeup.

One by one they assemble in the family room as their characters. Amity sweeps by each of them. "This is going to be so awesome! You all look perfect."

The men compliment one another's fashion choices. Henry even catches Jared smile.

She checks the camouflage paint on his face. The streaks of ocher, green, puke yellow blend with his shadowy jaw. In the many pockets of his trench coat, he has stashed knives and other weapons. Dog tags hang from his neck. He actually wears pants, albeit just a longer version of his cargo camo shorts. The cuffs disappear into tight-laced steel-toed work boots, ready to stomp on some danger.

Chris likes costumes as little as Jared does. Many of his characters conveniently are average Joes who happen to wear what he'd himself would wear. In other worlds, he's a skater or a hacker or an engineer. Tonight, he's a saboteur and all Amity could add to his usual attire was a toolbelt with wire cutters, a universal solvent (toothpaste), utility knife, and a big-ass wrench. Using stencils, she wrote MAINTENANCE DRONE #432 in black marker on duct tape and smacked the strip onto his shirt.

Eric is going as an avenging spirit from a popular comic book. He once had a crush on the actor who starred in the movie version; and with his lean, toned physique, he closely resembles the performer as well. Already corpse pale, all Eric had to do was smear on some black makeup around his eyes and across his lips, then throw on black clothing: Flattering tight pants, long-sleeved tee, and leather jacket.

Skoog, Henry's steampunk detective alter-ego from the Diezel Realms, is dressed in layers of brown leather, from boots to gauntlets to duster. Strapped over his eyes are those welder's goggles with brass fittings.

Amity herself wears a riding hood style cloak with a deep hood. Simple blouse and loose pantaloons and boots.

Henry runs down the inventory list he has written on graph paper. Always bring torches (flashlights), flint and tinder (cheap lighters), spyglasses (binoculars), gold pieces (cash, in case information must be obtained with legal tender) and armor (ordinary chain mail hauberks they had purchased years ago from a local blacksmith who specializes in replicating period arms and armor. Maybe they'll be good against pointy wooden sticks; Amity declines this as it's not in keeping with her aesthetic).

On the same pad, he drafted maps of their approach to Philadelphia, rendezvous points in case of a hasty retreat, and the area where Blade's body was supposedly discovered along with an inset that magnified the block and the blocks adjacent to it. Arrows swoop in, indicating where they might ask people who may have witnessed the man's death.

Henry advises everyone to charge up their phones and be ready to record clues. "While on the mission, refer to each other by our characters' names."

"Okay, Skoogy."

***

For the first challenge, they must formulate a plan for entry into the city. Henry, like many members of the family, has suspected mystical tripwires exist around Camden and at entrances to Philadelphia, namely the bridges: Betsy Ross, Benjamin Franklin, Walt Whitman, and Commodore Barry.

Thus, experience points to the one who comes up with a foolproof way to cross the Delaware River without being detected.

Taxis? Ride-sharing?

Amity had said, "That puts other people in danger. If we're in the back of a civilian's car, he might get killed. And if we do make it in, do we want to have to rely on someone else's getaway car?"

Chris suggested, "We could go by foot."

"Good thinking. Then we'd get our asses run down."

Going by boat would require one, which they don't have nor know where'd they get one readily. Likely, they'd have to steal several. Then they'd have to chart a course and decide where to land and tie up the boats. How swift are the river currents? If the vessels capsized, would they sink too? They'd need life jackets and once in the drink will they want to proceed while sopping wet?

Ultimately, they awarded Jared one hundred points. Simple is best. They'd split up, taking two vehicles across the Ben Franklin Bridge and wait at the other end. If after ten minutes no hulking SUVs with blacked-out windows, menacing grills, and high-powered headlamps barreled their way, like in so many movies, they're likely in the clear. But if they spot trouble, they'll retreat to Camden.

Henry says, "We cannot rule out conventional means of detection—perhaps there are cameras atop buildings aimed at the approach or surveillance drones above."

Chris says, "Those would require someone monitoring and knowing what to look for."

Eric says, "We have no idea either way. If Troy crossed by way of one of the bridges, that might have been all that was needed to alert them. Then they killed him."

"The Society?"

"Well, who else?"

"Assuming his outings were to Philly, then how'd he slip by the previous times?"

***

After rechecking the inventory list, fuel tanks, and smartphone apps, they start their engines. Henry drives Jared in the Mystery Machine-inspired conversion van while Chris drives Amity and Eric in her hatchback.

Traveling at the tail-end of rush hour, they scrutinize tailgating cars and watchful for those notorious villain SUVs.

The next phase of the plan is simple: Wait while parked (illegally as it happens) on 4th Street, with the bridge to their rear. Three pairs of eyes peer out the windows. Any sign of danger, imposing vehicles or a phalanx of men, converging on their spot, then they will haul ass, taking right turns back onto the eastbound lanes over the bridge.

Seated behind Amity, Eric says, "I don't think I want to run campaigns anymore." Over and over, he pulls and releases the safety belt strap.

Chris glances at his friend in the rearview mirror, checking that he has heard him correctly. Give up writing and running their table-top adventures?

"I think I'm burned out."

Amity says, "You're great at it. I love your campaigns-wonderful details that bring me into the story."

"I know. I am talented that way," he says unable to deny the truth. He attributes his skill to being well-prepared, good pacing, and detail. "But I think after this 'campaign' you've created," he actually makes quotation marks with his fingers, "I'm quitting."

"Okay," Chris says, disappointed. "Henry will take over. Guess his orc never did reach Pontiac after all."

"Fine. But I'm done with it all."

Not believing her ears, Amity turns in her seat. "No more dungeon master? No more gaming? Costumes? All of it? What are you going to do?"

"I don't know. Something real. Something that matters. Find a man to love. I'm realizing how small Camden is. It's even smaller when you're in a basement all night."

Amity looks to him with concern. She can understand, a little. Disappointed, but she keeps this to herself. She loves the worlds he has created for them, ones where she has more control of her life, where she's beautiful and brave and needed. Even a leader once in a while.

Nodding solemnly Eric says, "What are we even fighting for anyway? It's like I know we're stuck, but it wasn't till tonight that I realized the reason was myself. I'm not judging. I'm not judging the games and I'm not judging any of you. You're awesome. But for me, however this goes down, I'm not going back to the basement."

***

Once Henry and Amity text the go-ahead after the appointed ten minutes, each team drives their respective routes toward South Philly, then find suitable parking spots in the pre-designated areas.

Three characters, a spirit, a rogue, a saboteur, jump out of their wagon and explore the town. Three blocks up and one over they come to the diner. According to the reporting Jared had found online, delivery men discovered Troy's body behind it. Crime scene tape and a chalk outline have long ago been pulled down and erased away, leaving no evidence anyone had died here.

Amity wonders what the forensics team thought of a heart missing without so much as a a drop of blood. Not in the chest cavity, not on the victim's shirt, not on the ground where he lay. Maybe they thought they had an obsessively clean serial killer on their hands.

Would there have been traces of ichor? Did swabbing with cotton-tipped sticks pick up some black oily residue? If so, that wasn't mentioned in the press. Perhaps intentionally, so that the police can screen legitimate leads.

Chris says, "But did he actually die here? Or was he moved here?"

Squatting, Eric looks around. "Well, none of us have forensic expertise or equipment. Unless we find an envelope containing cards saying it was Colonel Vlad with a shotgun in the parking lot, I don't know what we're doing here."

Amity says, "According to Tommy, Troy was in contact with Horton. He must work or live around here."

Chris says, "He may have just come from seeing Horton. Do you think Kyle was telling the truth? That they didn't kill him?"

Amity says, "I don't believe what anyone in their stuck-up club says."

***

The three move on to canvassing their assigned blocks. Henry and Jared do the same on a parallel street. Each one pops into businesses, mostly eateries and bars, and works down the street.

Amity chats with the employees and customers. To her delight, she receives compliments on her outfit and gear. So much so, that she nearly forgets to ask about Horton and the dead body that had turned up a few nights ago. No one can add anything to what has already been reported and all hope that the bizarre death does not portend further horror.

About to leave her third restaurant, her phone pings with a text from Jared. Reading the single-word nearly stops her cold.

RUN!

Run, yes. Rather than sink, somehow she's able to body surf the wave of panic that swells within her. She needs to get to the car, so she runs.

On her way out, she collides with a man on his way in. He grabs her and before she knows what's happening, she's face down, nose in the tiled floor. She barely gets out a weak, "...help!" before the man drops onto her back. She feels him securing her arms.

"Shouldn't be over here, girlie."

She struggles to get her hands free so she can lever herself up and away, but the man has her good. An insult really. He's able to hold both of her wrists with one hand. There's the jingle of metal as he gets the cuffs ready.

"Amity!"

Chris?

Just then, a single groan escapes her attacker as he slumps to the floor beside her.

It is Chris, or rather Maintenance Drone #432. With his heavy wrench, he knocked the guy out.

Chris gets her up and she hugs him her thanks.

"Hurry," he shoves her out the door.

Where's Eric? Did he get Jared's message?

Outside, she spins in her cloak. Where is he? Just then Eric charges out of the shop he was surveying.

"Eric!" She jumps up and down, waving her arms.

Her friend sprints over and all three hurry across the street, nearly sideswiped by a taxi. Long-legged Eric is already half a block ahead. Chris lags with Amity not leaving her side, which she appreciates, as she's beyond scared. Her adopted family remains weak, helpless mice in the cats' paws of the Society. Nothing has changed. She's such a fool to think she could possibly succeed when Lemon, Troy, Tommy, and others have failed.

A movie SUV thumps over the curb, landing a glancing strike on Eric who bounces off its steel-reinforced grill. A man wearing sunglasses pops out and lunges for him. Eric reels out of the man's grasp and runs as all get out. Chris grabs Amity by the arm and urges her up a side street.

They almost succeeded. Even if they never did find Horton, they could at least boast to Tommy that they crossed into Philadelphia without incident. Proving that it could be done and that it was all a bluff. Instead, they're going to die right here. Right near where Troy had.

Fitting. And maybe intentional. Maybe Kyle Dowd lied and the Society had murdered him.

Both she and Chris dare to look back when they reach the end. The man in sunglasses pursues. What has he done with Eric? Did he kill him?

"Get off me!" Chris yells. Torn from her side, Chris is being pulled back by a second man. A kidney punch sends Chris to his knees.

"No," she screams, pained at seeing him hurt.

"Who's this one," Goon One says, catching up to the one holding Chris. They both look her way. Their lips curl, revealing fangs.

Goon Two clocks Chris on the jaw.

"Stop it!" Amity cries. While Chris groans, the goon cuffs his hands.

"Come here, little girl. Surrender and we'll be gentle."

"Go! Go!" Chris says before getting punched again.

Goon One steps toward her as though approaching a deer, not wanting to startle her away. She doesn't want to run. She can't leave Chris, or Eric for that matter. This was a stupid, childish idea. They're in this because of her. She thought they could do this. What does it matter to the Society if they're in the city? They're not hurting anyone.

The second one pulls Chris to his feet and moves back the way they came, while the first continues slowly toward her.

"Don't hurt him," she says. She's less scared than incensed with the whole situation. They've done nothing wrong. These are bullies shoving them around because they can.

And they can. She's got nothing. She yells for Chris one last time before he's pulled out of sight and taken to join Eric's fate.

The first presses forward once more, "Do your yourself a favor and surrender."

She hears something high-pitched, distant, but coming closer. It's not a single sound, but many. The goon must hear it too because he looks around for the source.

Louder now, it sounds like lots of squeaking. Then she sees... what is she seeing? Small dark bodies suddenly emerge, fountaining out from unseen geysers. Streams of eyes and teeth converge. The rats rush past Amity toward the goon swamping his legs. Alarmed, the man stomps his feet and crouches to brush the rodents off. Outnumbered, his legs fester with dozens of brown and black rodents with more on the way.

Horrified, she turns aside. Can vampires be bitten to death by rats? Not wanting to find out she whips around to escape and call Tommy once she's found a place to hide.

After about five steps, she halts. A reserve phalanx of rats line up before her. Her immediate thought is that some gruesome trap has sprung on her. That she too will be a feast. She had heard that they go for the eyes first and she whimpers at the thought of being blinded then chewed up.

But the rats are not moving. And then, under the sheen of panic she recognizes another astonishing thing. They've lined up in formation, like a marching band. Bodies aligned in the shape of a single quivering arrow.

thirty-one

Low

R oxy wakes in blood. Its smell rouses her, old as it is. Decayed on her lips and smeared on her chin. Sitting up in her bed, she's still wearing last night's clothing stained with reddish-brown streaks that may never come out.

She feels good though. She must have taken more from that Alexi guy than she had realized. After Reed was done with him, Alexi seemed fine when she put him back into circulation at the club.

But that blood was heady and delicious. Bliss infused Alexi and Roxy was right there with him. As time passed, the feeling ballooned. Like she was coated in a slipperiness that worry could not grasp; a soap bubble that lifted her high above her cares. Nothing could touch her.

And Reed, the same. He was more relaxed, more open. In fact, he gushed like a fire hydrant—all that angsty turmoil that had been building inside him busted out.

She liked that: The sharing, the listening, the kinship. She even tolerated Reed's going on about his wife, Lily. She will never understand what's happened to her man; what being a vampire is like, an erif even less.

Reed's problem is he's clinging to his old life. Is that for Lily's sake or his own? Eventually, they'll both have to learn to accept what he is now and move on.

Last night was a good first step. With his first taste out of the way, Reed will find hunting easier, and soon he will come around to Roxy's way of thinking. Oh, the fun they'll have then. A swell time.

Not tonight, though. She hasn't forgotten her promise to Karen. Tonight, she'll find something appropriate to wear and seek out the painter for a proper introduction.

She reaches to touch her hair gummy with blood. "Ugh." Unlike her to go to bed without washing up or undressing, she must have crashed hard. *What a night.*

A sudden impish smile rises with a thought. What would the Brandies do if they have two erifs to contend with? They'd be sore for sure. Maybe they'd back off for good.

More likely they'd be a greater pain. Al, maybe Kyle, and whoever else they've got, will harass her till she joins or leaves.

She frowns.

She will leave, eventually. Karen certainly will. They can't live in this apartment forever. Karen will finish school, head to the other coast, and before Roxy blinks an eye, share the red carpet with the biggest talents at the premiere of her film. Roxy will miss her to pieces.

Opening the unlocked bedroom door, Roxy pads down the hall to the bathroom. In the mirror is a creature out of a campy vampire film. Blood caked on her face, her throat, halter top. She frowns thinking of what must be on the pillow cases and sheets. More laundry.

Under the warm water of the shower, honey-and-amber-scented suds cleanse her hair. As Roxy scrubs herself fresh, Alexi's dried blood melts off her fingers. She hadn't taken that much, had she? No. This can't be his blood.

Peering at the pinkish water sluicing between her toes and down the drain, she knows her recollection is not quite right, because she would have exchanged the soiled clothes for fresh ones. Instead, she and Reed went to play right away. Dancing with Millie had been so effortless. And Reed was a natural. Impressive with his lion.

She towels herself dry, brushes her teeth, and fixes her hair in the mirror. A more agreeable sight. She makes faces, tugs on her ears, tilts up her head. All clean.

After snatching the tricolor robe off its hook, she leaves for the hall. Approaching her bedroom door, she notes blood on the knob. Stepping back her attention drops to the floor where spots of blood, like muddy paw prints, track between her legs. She pivots to look behind her, then follows their lead through the half-open door, into the semi-darkness of the second bedroom.

Was someone in there? Karen's on her shift. Trudy? But the girl wouldn't be here without her pal.

The half-light reveals larger spots of blood have dried on the floor. A sickly-sweet stench smacks away Roxy's jaunty brightness.

Overtaken by a leaden feeling, she turns on the light with a reluctant hand. Reddish brown spatters lead to the bed that looks tossed with the blanket half-off and a pillow on the floor.

And a body. Skin pallid, but for purpling in the fingers. The neck plastered with blood-matted hair. Eyes staring, but sightless. Their once bright promise clouded over.

Roxy's breath leaves her. She staggers forward then collapses to her knees before a dangling arm. Holding that arm near her face, she rolls her thumbs up the cold flesh as though she can knead life back into it.

Dried blood flakes away.

No-no-no. Karen should be waitressing, or at school, or directing a scene. Her body should not be stiff and lifeless.

A surge of anguish threatens to suck her under, but she won't let it. Roxy has defied so much in her life, and she refuses to accept this. Fangs emerge and Roxy gouges her own forearm, directing the ichor to well up from the wound and letting the oozy fluid drip onto Karen's unmoving lips and into her mouth.

That mouth, which slurped ice cream last night. That mouth, which smiled with Roxy's own in silent conspiracy when Reed came to their booth. That mouth, which spouted lines of her own dialogue that may one day be recited by a movie star.

Desperately, Roxy's trembling fingers prod, trying to slip more ichor in, but the locked jaw refuses to widen. The more Roxy works, the more Roxy's body heaves, a creaky streetcar hitching up-up-up, till finally, a tremulous wail tears from Roxy's heart. She pulls her friend into a tight embrace, rocking with deepest sorrow.

Karen is gone and the ichor won't bring her back.

***

After leaving Karen positioned in her bed with as much dignity as possible, Roxy's feet slap the hardwood floors on her way out into the hall.

She would never harm Karen, her sister, her confidante.

Had she done this?

Turning on bare toes over and over, she knits together memories of last night. She and Reed fed from Alexi. They talked, practiced, then played with Millie and Florian. All the while feeling increasingly good. Great. Awesome. Blissed-out. Like Alexi had...

Her pace slows.

The man had been high on something.

Onyx.

The word bursts to mind. Alexi was high on Onyx. And she must have been too. Roxy drank from countless men and women, who had injected, snorted, imbibed all kinds of chemicals with no effect on her. Why had this one? Shouldn't have.

Yet it had. Somehow... somehow... it got her. Played with her emotions and her Fire, cranking up its intensity.

And it made her thirsty.

She must have left Reed at some point and returned home. Returned right here to Karen's door. Knew Karen must have been sleeping. An easy meal.

Roxy's eyes snap shut, refusing to see what she had done last night. Her hands form fists, one knocking her forehead, trying to hold back the churning grief. She needs to be clear-headed.

Focus on the Onyx. Onyx did this. Made her senseless. Made her crave blood. Made her turn on her friend.

Alexi took Onyx. He bought Onyx. Someone sold him the Onyx.

Roxy stomps into her bedroom and flings off the robe. As she hunts for some basic clothes, Karen's words at Driscoll's return to her. Oliver dealt Onyx. That it would be the next big thing. *Better than Molly.*

This stops Roxy cold.

Yes, she had said that. Oliver sells Onyx. That *stronzo*!

Roxy holds a crop top to her middle, her grief yielding to boiling anger. She should have never let Oliver go. Damn Alcott Ashton for interfering. Damn herself. She should have busted Oliver into a heap of kindling, one that had to be hauled out in a wheelbarrow.

She had a chance!

The fabric twists in her hands till its seams strain and sizzle. Before it can ignite, Roxy balls up the garment and chucks it.

Pain crackles within her as her anger rises for letting that man get away. She grits her teeth as she recalls Oliver's hand smacking Karen. Sweet Karen. Talented Karen. Ready to take on the world. Like a proud mother,

Roxy had looked forward to seeing her thrive in the years ahead. Decades. She deserved that.

Grief and guilt tear at her insides while her fists pummel her outsides. Not her fault. Not really.

This all started with that little worm. She'll wring his neck. No. Needs to be slow and scorching hot. Burn him one square inch at a time.

But she needs to find him first. He could be distributing at the The Jolt again or another club.

Dressed, she puts on one of her sneakers as an idea comes to her. Ratu could find him quicker. She sours at the thought of the rancid stew she'll have to wade through to talk to her friend. Steamy, stinky, and dark. Her nose crinkles with disgust.

Almost enough to not want to go down there. She had already tried coaxing Ratu out with meat treats for his rats. No bites.

Pain in her chest flares again. Millie's anguished and angry too.

Fine. Fine. Roxy will go below.

Kicking off the sneaker, she jams on Army surplus boots instead, and laces them tight. Then she throws on her leather jacket.

She'll just have to add this trip to Oliver's bill of sins. Once she gets hold of him, he will pay.

chapter
thirty-two

Double

K yle feels it all coming again—the feeling of an inevitable disaster. A diesel train barreling down the track toward the Society freighted with needless violence. He feels caught in a space too narrow to dodge the locomotive. Penned in by his responsibilities, his vow, his bond to Devlin.

He had thought he had been clever with his truce idea, escaping by selling it to his fellow members, then the Rotters. He wouldn't need to take another life. And it had worked. Peace. But, really just a cease-fire. Buying his future. Now it has arrived.

Tommy will tell his people, share their anger and anguish, acknowledge their demands for retribution. Tommy has Kyle's sympathies. The man will have to cool their tempers, convince them to let the investigation play out, to hold the truce.

It's difficult for Kyle to see ahead—so many years have passed and he hadn't known many of their members back then and so he cannot guess their disposition. Though he hopes they take the wiser course, Kyle expects the Rotters will get right to planning and recruiting. If that's the case, Kyle will need to find new terms for a continued cold peace, sound it out with Alcott, then propose it to Devlin, who will take it from there.

"Keep your head, Tommy," In the mirror Kyle does up his silk tie while making a four-in-hand knot.

The tie is one of his flashier ones—a bold pattern—a reminder to himself of Emma and their time together dancing. He's glad she had insisted he keep his promise to her. He did enjoy her company. The woman had been a refreshing change to his decades-long rut. Just for her, he had worn the bespoke sky-blue suit. Her reaction did not disappoint.

A vivacious dance partner also.

No doubt she will check in on him in a night or two and invite him over to her place. Before last night, he would have respectfully declined. Tonight, he's not sure. He does have concern that she will pry into his demons. He will have to be clear once again for her not to look there.

Kyle lives in an armpit of the Schuylkill River east side. Once an Irish community—many working-class families, markets, bars. A boxing ring. Much of it unrecognizable today.

He visits his mice on the first floor. Three now, he's reminded. Over the years he has tried to keep the rotating rodent roster entertained and well fed.

Why is Kyle responsible for keeping the peace? Why does he feel the burden on his shoulders? Why does he feel that he's the only one who sees the danger chugging their way and the need to derail it before it's too late?

He doesn't have time for this. Reed will need all his attention.

And with this, Kyle's mood sours.

At the kitchen sink, he turns on the tap, refills their water dispenser, and returns it. He notes to himself to find them new toys. Without their play, the house will be dead quiet.

He will take his time getting over to Reed's apartment. Is the man stewing in his anger? What had the man done last night after threatening Magus Oakes and storming off?

In Reed's petulant wake, Emma had said nothing—only looked at Kyle with empathy, concern. Michael had come back to get Malcolm and off the two went as well.

Kyle returns, securing the bottle upended. "I'm in over my head." The trio noses around their cage. Feeling indulgent, Kyle reaches in and tickles their small bodies. They seem to like it.

The phone rings. A call from Alcott. Has Tommy already done something foolish? Is it do much to hope that Alcott will report that he has the responsible party in custody and a confession?

After closing the cage, he answers. Alcott gets right to it, "Do you know where Mr. Williams is?" *Trick question?* The man would certainly know as he can locate their kind anywhere in the city.

"I assume he's at his apartment. I was heading there shortly."

"I will spare you a guessing game and tell you directly. He is at the Logan safehouse, brought there by Mr. Webb last night. Fortunate that you provided Mr. Williams the distress call service. He had used it. When Mr. Webb located him, there was quite a conflagration, one he or Ms. Marchetti started. Perhaps both. She had gone by then."

"I had no idea."

"That much is obvious. According to Mr. Webb, your initiate was— once again—out of sorts and now this time, parched for blood."

Kyle shuts his eyes for a moment. His grip on the phone tightens as a flash of anger passes through him. Then he says, "Is Mr. Webb all right?"

"Certainly. He is a very capable man. He cracked open a cask. As he tells it, Mr. Williams all but plunged his head into it and licked it clean till he regained himself."

"I will reimburse you." Kyle hadn't expected Reed's boorish performance at Tamerlane to have an encore.

And to have cracked open a cask. What had he done to need all that blood? A whole cask? And now Kyle will need to pay for it.

"Yes, you will. Double I should say."

Double?

"I don't know what to say."

"Best not to say anything. I lack the time and interest to do your job. You chose to ignore my recommendation to strengthen your bond. The Rotters remain an open question now that they know Blade is dead. I do not believe I am any closer to solving the murder than the night before. As House Monitor this is my focus. I only spared Mr. Webb to intercede for the sake of First House not any feeling for Mr. Williams."

"What did you mean when you had said he was out of sorts?"

"Mr. Webb said that Mr. Williams appeared to be quite ebullient when he first encountered him. The man seemed taken by the fire he caused, not at all mindful of its destruction."

Kyle echoes Lily's words, "Like he was high."

"I rather doubt that. In any case his behavior these past few nights are really too much. End it now."

Despite the man's dispassionate tone, the words are scathing. A solid rebuke, "What will happen to Reed?"

"You will collect him at the safehouse immediately. You will have him drink from you tonight and on an ongoing basis. Beyond that will be a matter decided upon at Tamerlane. Fortunate for you both, you have an advocate in Sister Emma."

thirty-three

Safehouse

I n the safehouse again. Reed recognizes the efficiency apartment the moment he wakes upon the narrow cot. The lack of decor, the spare kitchen area, its appliances looking untouched since they were installed circa 1980.

Without a glance, he knows that behind him are drapes, and behind the drapes are blinds, and behind them is a window sash that won't budge. Just as the front door of the apartment had not opened for him the last time he was here. Mr. Ashton and Mr. Webb have some trick for the turning the knob.

Of the two men, Reed prefers the human one. And here he is, seated in the kitchen, absorbed by his phone.

Through the thin mattress, Reed's body suffered the unyielding cot and he rubs and stretches away the mild soreness. Despite this, he feels refreshed, good energy, and less burdened.

The crows! They seem to be gone. He recalls Florian gobbling them up in his fiery jaws. Gone for good? He prays so.

"What the hell happened?"

"That is my question for you," Mr. Webb rises to his ramrod posture, back straight, shoulders square, head at twelve o'clock and not a second off. He looks good in his wine-colored suit.

"I was drugged."

"You were drugged." Mr. Webb says, skeptical. "That's a new one. Gotta say, you seem to have a specialty for getting yourself into unprecedented shit." Footfalls echo as he approaches. He lowers his eyes, not his chin, to the seated Reed. "And I'm still mopping up after what had happened at the hotel."

"I'm sorry?" Reed says, his facetious tone meant to add that he doesn't even understand why that should be his fault or his problem.

No sooner is Reed on his feet than Mr. Webb comes ready with questions and his phone to take down Reed's answers. Reed has his own questions and in their exchange, they piece together last night.

Since feeding from a guy wearing a bucket hat outside a nightclub to starting a fire with Roxy that got out of control, Reed had been high on something. Really high.

This draws more skepticism from Mr. Webb, who had responded to the emergency call and found Reed showing the signs of thirst. Reed was fixated on the fire and talking nonstop, first to himself then to Mr. Webb.

"What did I say?"

"That you were thirsty, something about sending the crows away." He checks his notes. "Onyx. You said Onyx a few times."

"Right. I think that was the drug Mr. Bucket Hat was on."

Mr. Webb taps this into his phone. "Had this drug, Onyx, affected Ms. Marchetti as well?"

"I believe so. Where'd she go?"

"Home, I presume."

"I'm not thirsty now." Had he hurt someone?

"We keep casks on hand for emergencies. You'll have to reimburse us."

"How much?" He pats the pockets of his slacks.

"Six liters."

"Liters? What are you saying?"

"You took in blood, you return in blood."

"You want six liters of blood? I *drank* six liters of blood?"

Mr. Webb shakes his head and explains that a cask holds about three liters. An opened cask can't be resealed. Not by him anyway. Like opening a can of soda that goes flat, the blood's nourishing properties evanesce. So, it must be drunk or it goes to waste.

Fresh and human.

"You owe a second cask so that you learn this lesson well. I'm not picking up any more bodies for you."

Where the hell is he going to get that much blood?

Answering the unspoken question, Mr. Webb says, "Mr. Dowd will help you. Since he's your sponsor, the debt's on him."

Feeling his chest, Reed asks, "Did you take another sample?"

"Of your ichor? No. I saw no need to."

"Good. I don't consent. I want it on record that I don't want any of my ichor taken."

Mr. Webb grins, white teeth flashing beneath his black mustache with a patch of white, "I will add your name to our Does-Not-Consent-to-Ichor-Draws list." He laughs, "'I don't consent,'" as he takes out a device from inside his jacket.

It's Reed's phone that Mr. Webb hands over, "It's been beeping. Text messages."

The texts are from Lily:

GOOD "MORNING"!

WHERE ARE YOU?

MEET ME AT THIS ADDRESS.

CALL ME! THERE'S A CURE!

Reed can't believe what's he's just read. A cure? Lil found a cure? Is his wife amazing or what?

Reed jumps to his feet, "I need to go."

"You'll leave with Mr. Dowd. Till then, what else can you tell me?"

Reed adds that Roxy was having him practice controlling his power. And when things got out of hand, he pressed the emergency button.

"Kyle had told me you came up with that app."

Mr. Webb nods.

"Did you serve? Army?"

"I'm a sailor, not a soldier."

"Lot of call for seafaring in the Society?"

Mr. Webb doesn't say.

"Why do you help them?"

After further silence from Mr. Webb, Reed lets it go. If the man wants to help the undead, that's his business. He's feeling too good to argue. And soon enough, none of it will matter.

He senses Kyle returning to his head. With a subdued hum in his mind, Reed isn't surprised to hear knocking on the door. Mr. Webb lets Kyle in. They exchange greetings.

Smiling wide, Reed holds up the screen to show Kyle Lily's texts.

Kyle ignores it. Looking none-too-pleased, his eyes cut to Reed's.

"Lily found a cure!"

Kyle's fist smashes Reed's nose. Reed winces, losing the phone. Kyle barks, "Are you trying to get yourself and your wife killed?"

Holding his nose tenderly, Reed blinks several times. "I didn't kill anyone."

"I'm not talking about that. I'm talking about how you made a scene at the masquerade. And now you end up here. Again."

"What?"

"Shut up. You're out of free passes with me. I tried to give you room to find your own way but that's over."

The sting of the initial pain subsides, but Reed laughs, still giddy. "Get out of my way. Lily says there's a cure!"

"Stay where you are." Kyle's words compel Reed to remain rooted to this spot.

"You're going to drink from me right now, and for the foreseeable future, till you learn to stop cannonballing into a pool of shit and splashing us all."

Reed laughs more, "I don't care. You're going to take me to South Philly, then I'll be done with all of this."

"What are you talking about?"

thirty-four

Beneath

A mity wonders how she fell into the Diezel Realms game. The sewer system could be the steam tunnels Elsbeth travels, station to station, valuable secrets or crucial intelligence rolled into her courier bag.

Having heeded the arrow of rats at the mouth of the alley, she soon came upon another group of them sitting up on their hind legs, balanced by their tails. Forepaws signaled to her like the ground crew at an airport directing a returning plane.

Mind blown.

Any other time, she'd pause over how adorable their synchronization is, but the goon's terrified screams are still fresh in her ears and she expects reinforcements to jump out any moment. She must move.

An open manhole. An escape. With relief, she wishes she had some cheese to share as a reward for their help.

With a quick look over her shoulder—no goons in sight—she descends into the dark using the handholds. Down, down, down. At the bottom, the temperature has turned up along with the humidity. She can hardly see, so she takes out the compact flashlight and clicks it on.

Under layers of odors and vapor, she feels like brined meat. Ahead, several rats have waited for her to arrive, now turn tail and lead her farther into the gloom.

Luckily, Elsbeth is ready in her soft leather boots, her cloak, her torch, navigating unchartered territory.

Who else might be down here? *What* else might be down here? Are there also turtles or gators or other pets that have been flushed down into the sewers, once young and now grown and sentient? Maybe there's some menagerie kingdom—a society of outcasts working together, helping each other like a family. Like her family.

Do these intelligent rats have a king or queen? Is she being led to their leader? Or some welcome committee? Or maybe a trap, but then why would they help her escape?

She stops with that thought. Why would they save her at all? Who is she to them? And is she the only one? Did they help Chris and Eric get away too? And what about Henry and Jared? Several times she asks these questions, but none of the rats pause to answer.

Maybe they all escaped down here the same way she has. Several times, she shouts their names. Nothing returns. Nothing.

The eeriness unsettles her more.

Down the tunnels, they lead and she follows, whispering commentary along the way. Not all game sessions take place at the basement table. They also play out their adventures on the university campus, in abandoned buildings, or in parks. But it's one thing to pretend to be in a dungeon, or a castle, or a swamp, quite another to actually be in real darkness and danger.

She moves again. She should get points for this detour—skill points in subterranean orienteering, or animal kinship, or rodent empathy, if that's a thing.

She's lost track of how far and for how long they've traveled with so many turns. Ahead, long stretches of darkness, slashed by the meager light in her hand, revealing brackish water passing through old brick structures.

She's lost for sure. Though not claustrophobic, her unease grows.

Deeper now, her boots catch on a random rock or piece of concrete. Each lurch forward nearly throws her face down in filth. How long has she been going? The stillness and thickening darkness unnerves. She wonders if she should turn around. But could she get back?

The number of rats dwindle. She counts three now.

"That is close enough, child."

Amity shrieks. So startled, she nearly falls backward. Her hands draw to her chest as though to protect her heart and massage it back to rhythm, not that it has one to begin with. Her reaction whisks the light onto her herself. Blind, her head snaps left and right. Where had the voices come from?

"Who's there?" she dares to ask.

She turns the torch out, bringing light once more. Like a searchlight, its beam tracks high and low over a shadowy placid ocean.

There. About fifty feet out. The fingers of light barely touch a brick arch which partially conceals a trembling shadow about the height of a man.

While she scrutinizes the figure, the rats go about their business. Are they under the voice's control? Is he or she their leader? Maybe he's disfigured like Erik from the *Phantom of the Opera* and has secluded himself down here. Are they below a theater? Or maybe he's an eccentric vampire cast out of the Society. Or something altogether different. Not human—not undead, a spirit? A real phantom?

She looks about herself and sees nothing indicating this is a special spot in the sewers—no chairs, table, shelves, cages, shackles. Why bring her to this spot?

"Who are you? Are you a rat king?"

"I am no king." The eerie voices are hard to understand, pitched high. "Merely someone who will help you find who you seek."

"Why? Not to sound ungrateful—I am—I mean thank you for helping me get away. I mean, that was your doing, right? But why?"

"For the sake of my benefactor. Your aims align with his."

"Did you save my friends? Are they here too?"

"They are not seriously harmed."

"How do you know?"

"Many eyes. Many ears. You need to go."

"Where?"

"To the man you seek."

"But I don't know where he is."

"Above you."

***

So, this is Horton's rowhouse. The rat king, or whatever he was, had told Amity it was the third house north of where she would emerge from the sewer. Mission accomplished. Lots of experience points.

Wait. She's getting ahead of herself. He may not be inside.

She notes the door camera which prompts her to text her location to the others. Risky, considering the goons might read her message and head over. Henry insisted on devising a counter-sign. If the reply was anything other than "Natural 20" then communication was compromised.

She simply texts that she's near the target.

She rings the bell and straightens up. No answer. She tries again. No answer. She presses the button a dozen successive times.

"You're early for Halloween," a voice from the intercom says. "No candy for you. Go away, girl."

"I'm here about Blade," she says, trying to bring authority to her voice. With all that's happened, that's difficult. "If you're Horton, then you'll let me in."

"One moment."

A minute passes until she hears the door being unlatched.

Check for traps. Henry's words spring up. Past the vestibule, the open area appears harmless. Not much here. Basic uninspired furniture likely from kits put together with Phillips head screwdrivers and hex keys. Like he took the house as-is and added nothing. Maybe even subtracted any taste it might once have had. Over the front windows are drawn oatmeal-colored vinyl shades, the kind that rolls up on itself with a sharp tug.

He's human and old, like in his forties. She has no idea if this guy is friend or foe. Here's to hoping he has something valuable to share about Troy that she can take back to Tommy. Something that can help the family.

Pulling back her hood, Amity glides after the man to the rear kitchen. He takes a can of flavored seltzer from the counter then looks her up and down. He doesn't offer her anything. Likely because he notes her lack of shadow. Or maybe he's rude.

"What's with the costume? You look like a druid zombie."

"It's for my mission. Which was to find you."

"I'm touched that you dressed up for me," he says not meaning it.

"When did you last see Blade?"

"I don't know you. You obviously know about me and where I live. That'll have to do till I know more about you, sweetness."

"My name is Elsbeth. Blade's my maker's brother."

"A Camden kid? What did you mean when you said you're on a mission to find me? And talk fast. I am expecting company." He sips while glancing between her and the front door.

"Just that. To find you and find out about your connection with him. How do you know him? When did you last see him?"

He checks the social calendar in his head, "A few nights ago. Did the last batch work? Did he like it? He never gave me a report. How did it go?"

"I don't understand. Blade didn't tell me anything."

"Then why are you here?"

"You don't know?"

"We're going in circles and I'm getting a touch dizzy. Show me your cards or get out. I've got customers."

"Blade's dead."

Horton blinks, suddenly attentive. He leaves the can to fizz on the counter. "Dead? Are you sure?"

"Yes." Sudden hurt choking her voice. So occupied with the mission, she has scarcely thought of her uncle and the reality of his death.

His eyes cast about searching for something. Then he sighs, "Damn." Absorbing the news, he's quiet for a time. "It's over now."

"You really didn't know that he died?" Which was fair considering she hadn't known right away either.

He gives an irritated, "No." A heaviness settles on the man as he slumps against the counter. "How did he die?"

"We were told his heart exploded out of his chest."

"Damn," he whispers.

"What is 'over'? What were you the two of you working on? Horton? Why did he sneak out of Camden to see you? How long has that been going on?"

"Doesn't matter now." He crosses back to the front windows and parts a shade wide enough to peek, then lets it sway back.

He sighs again.

"I'm not leaving without answers."

He lifts his head, regards her, considers what she says, then his demeanor shifts. A sly smile comes to his lips. "You want answers? Maybe we can help each other."

"Help with what?"

She follows him to the basement, which definitely sets off Henry alarms. Stooped as she goes, she peers into the open space as it rises into view. No torture racks, or shackles, or iron maidens. Looks like a laboratory, one for sober, serious, straight business.

There are open shelves and long metal tables, cabinets, stools, and one leather easy chair. There are pipes and beakers, test tubes, a portable stove, clamps, boxes, sheeting and tarp. She wanders between the tables, touching glass flasks, graduated cylinders, and notebooks with alchemy-like symbols on the covers.

A monitor displays the doorbell camera feeds of the front and back entrances.

"What is all this?"

"A bit of this and a bit of that. Experiments. Trials and too many errors to count. But the work keeps improving. I swear we were nearly there."

"Nearly where?"

Past rows of steel lab tables Horton comes to the last one. Each has equipment of one kind or another. He unlocks a cabinet, opens the door, and withdraws a small jug. He beckons her to join him where he sets the jug down. It appears to be baked clay with marks or glyphs inscribed around it and on its sealed cap.

She sweeps between the final two tables, standing across from him, but not taking a seat.

Years ago, Horton explains, he had been introduced to Blade. This was after the truce began. Blade had taken stock of their situation, their future under the new rules. And it was a bleak one. He wanted Horton to help change that.

"He provided me samples of his ichor. Do you know what ichor is?"

"Of course. It's our blood."

"It's more than that. So much more. It's black gold. It's money. It's power. Except, well except for Lemon, and his children down to you. You know all about that."

Yes, her and her sterile generation. If ichor was power, it was stolen from Lemon's lineage.

"Blade had told me that Lemon had been experimented on, affecting the properties of his blood. But why? To what end? Blade didn't know or care. He just wanted to know if it could be undone. Could the disease be cleansed from his ichor? His and yours. We worked together to figure that out."

"How would you do that?"

"Elsbeth, my dear girl, I know a bit of magic. First, we analyzed Blade's ichor to isolate the contaminate, then see what could be done to remove it."

Amity considers how determined Troy had been that he was willing to share his ichor with this man. That was a big leap of faith. She wonders if Troy had misjudged, though.

"Each time was a risk, but I did all I could to reduce the chances of serious harm. As the treatments improved, the focus turned to making it permanent."

Amity can't believe what she is hearing.

"Are you willing to give a sample and see what we can do?" He takes a small rectangular box from a shelf. The top face of the box has a stylized 'M' with a playing card diamond set above it, like a ring setting and its jewel.

When he opens it, she smirks. "What is that?" Once he has it in his hand, it appears to be a wooden fountain pen. Looks like symbols from a spellbook adorn its length.

"A special syringe for ichor. I will need two draws to start with."

"You came up with all this?" She indicates the pen and jug.

"Not all of it. I have, let's say, a patron, whose resources are considerable, and who will remain anonymous. You may consider this a research grant. In exchange for what I'm provided, I report my findings."

He asks for her to pull up her shirt.

"What?"

"Ichor... from your heart."

Suddenly she doesn't feel well. She grimaces as he guides her to the armchair, which she sinks into. "Really? Won't it stun me?"

"It won't. It won't tickle, either, but I'll be quick. But if you don't want to do this..."

No, she doesn't. But... she's here. Considering what she, what all of them, had gone through to get here, she doesn't want to go back saying she chickened out.

He waits.

Can she trust him? He could be lying and then she'd be completely at his mercy. Troy had trusted him. But he could have killed Troy and made all this up.

"Be quicker." She untucks her blouse, drawing it up her stomach. When the hem reaches her diaphragm, he says that's far enough.

Eyes closed and braced for the worst, she nods that she's ready, too tense to say anything.

Without ceremony, he stabs the pen right in. Worse than any needle she ever got from the pediatrician's office. Her jaws grind and a fang punctures her lip. Still, being able to move means that the stick doesn't stun and Horton had spoken true.

The moment passes in seconds as does the pain. All the held tension suddenly releases and she lets the soft leather of the chair hug her.

Horton takes the magic pen, streaked with her black blood, to the jug, putting the nib into a corresponding socket on the cap. When that's done, he moves back to her.

Her weak ichor means slow healing, which for once, is a small blessing as it means the second draw won't hurt as much. It doesn't, but there's a weird sensation of being probed all the same.

"Now let's see what we got." This time he takes the pen with him. She turns around, following him with her eyes as he gathers several items off the shelves or in bins, placing them next to a contraption on another table.

Then, a spiral notebook in hand, he flips several pages. "This'll take a few minutes. You're one generation down the line, so I'll factor that in when making adjustments to the formula."

She straightens her clothes as the wound heals. "He kept coming back here? How? Without being caught?"

"No idea."

"And what did you both do? What came from all of this?"

"Like clinical trials, we set a baseline and tested dose after dose. We made progress. He was stronger, he healed quicker. Then later his powers improved."

"Troy had powers?"

"Along the lines of precognition. He claimed to see things that will happen."

She had thought when Troy spoke of the future it was more as hopeful predictions rather known outcomes. He had been wrong about her and what she could do for Cole.

"And? And?"

"Oh, well he said that his visions were very vivid. They were real to him. He was certain the cure would work. He spoke of Tommy—"

"My maker."

"He shared of some of what he claimed to have seen. I wrote it down." Here he breaks to get out another notebook and flips it open. "An Alfonse, Lance, Amity…"

"That's me. I'm Amity."

"You said your name is Elsbeth. Oh. A cover. Good instinct, girl."

"What did he say about me?"

"He was certain that you would be able to make your own vampires."

"He was wrong."

Horton shrugs, "That's what he told me."

"Did he know he would die?"

"He never spoke of that. He knew there were risks here. Just coming to the city to meet with me. We're doing pioneering work. And it's not like we can test on rabbits or guinea pigs. It was an iterative process. In the early days we took small steps, then bolder ones as time went on. I kept notes, as you can see. More recently I was surprised the cure didn't last longer than it had. I kept making tweaks. The last time…" He looks to her, "he must have died after taking the dose. I'm sorry."

Amity watches the man mix some liquids together, then add pinches of powders, puts the whole concoction into the contraption that looks part blender, part centrifuge. He reviews his notes some more, nods to himself, then goes to find another ingredient. Finally he slots the pen end into its socket. Here she can see her own ichor trickle down the glass of the blender.

An obnoxious noise, like that of school bell, buzzes around the basement. Not the contraption. Horton looks to the monitor. Filling the entire front door camera is the torso of a woman.

chapter

thirty-five

Oliver

S pitting mad, Roxy Marchetti drops into the muck of the sewer. Down into the confining, wet, smelly, dark, rotting sewer. Into the insufferable, insulting depths of the sewer.

She moves careful not to come in contact with one particle of this subterranean stew. But in seconds she feels slathered with a funk that will never rinse away.

She wants to die. She deserves to die. But not yet.

Karen's death is not only her fault. She needs to find Oliver. Find him and let Millicent out of her cage. Let her fly at him and do many wicked things to him. Let the bird flay his skin till it blisters, blackens, and splits open.

Ratu can find him faster. This unappealing option means crawling under the crust of the city. And so, she had heaved a manhole cover aside and descended into the dark. And dark it is, as she presses through the city's lower colon. The farther she goes, the more her frustration replaces her disgust. Where is he? Over the splashing, she hears rats chitter. Soon she can see a few of them amble over narrow shelves of concrete, their fat tails waggling behind them. Filthy things.

"Ratu!"

Her friend has to be here somewhere. The phone's flashlight sweeps back and forth. Once she finds him, he will lead the way to her quarry.

"I need you!" Her voice sounds weak here. Does it carry? She won't get his attention at this rate.

A rat squeaks nearby, alarmed by her shouting and splashing. Roxy hurries after it, seizing its tail before it can escape into a crevice. She yanks it up like a caught fish. By size, it's a football in her hand. Its head and legs wriggle futilely. Her grip won't let it slip away.

She glares down at it. Her black eyes meeting its beady ones, contemptuous of its pitiable struggle.

"I'm in a mood to burn some shit," she says, glaring down at the triangular rat face. "If you don't get your saggy, soggy, reeking ass out here right now, I'm going to lose it!"

The rat tosses its head back and forth, bearing its yellow teeth. She holds the rodent so it can't bite her skin while she trudges farther down a corridor, feeling saggy, soggy, and reeking herself. She's angry. She's grieving. She's ashamed.

Millie stretches her wings. The Fire in Roxy's chest spreads through her shoulders and down her arms till her fingers sizzle. Her hands feel like they may ignite.

"Ratu! You hear me?!"

As her grip tightens on the rat, the smell of singed fur reaches her nose and the pained squeals reach her ears.

Then she hears a familiar stream of voices coalescing into one. More or less. "Though I appreciate your visit to our home, you will not singe your host as a way to ring the doorbell."

"Then consider getting a bell. And a door."

There. A shadow just a touch lighter than the surrounding dark. A separate quivering mass. From that direction, the voice says, "You appear perturbed."

"I am perturbed. Yes." She drops the rat, "I am wet, and I stink, and I'm red-hot fucking angry!" Her voice echoes through the tunnel. "You're going to tell me where to find a piece of garbage named Oliver Mills. Just point me to the club he's at and I'll be on my way."

When she doesn't hear anything, she adds, "He's a white skinny-ass guy. Average height. Has broken fingers on his right hand." She holds up her hand, waggling her fingers. "Deals drugs."

"I have many eyes, but they do not see all. For instance, I have never seen you so… combustible."

"I need to find him now!"

"I am not clairvoyant. I cannot simply conjure his location. My senses, while extensive, are still limited."

"Send your rat minions scurrying and the moment their beady eyes spot Oliver, you let me know where." She turns to leave.

"Your friendship is dear, Roxanna Marchetti. As a friend, I must caution you to not pursue this."

"What the hell does that mean?"

"This Oliver Mills must have pained you dearly. But take care not to act rashly. Unless you take time to cool, you are more likely to burn yourself far more than him. Revenge seldom serves the wronged person well. As a friend, I will not help you. You will be worse for it. I am truly sorry."

"Fuck your sorry."

***

Grief, rage, guilt ping around in Roxy's heart, making her want to tear herself apart. But she must find Oliver first.

Without Ratu's help—the useless sewer troll—she wracks her brain on how to find him. Stalking the neighborhood streets, she scans for signs of Karen's former love. How Karen had trusted him, opened her heart to him, texted him…. Of course! Roxy has it.

Roxy's feet fly home and bound up the stairs. She skids to a halt at Karen's bedroom door. Before entering, she gathers herself and pinches her face, eyes shut, and charges in. At the nightstand, her hands feel around till fingertips touch the glass screen of Karen's phone. She grabs it and hauls out of there.

She texts Oliver:

I MISS YOU

By the time she's back on Bainbridge Street, he has texted back.

ME TOO.

MEET ME?

She taps:

DRISCOLLS

Roxy spots Oliver a half block from the diner where she and Karen had talked over her last ice cream sundae. He appears too pleased with himself. Maybe he expects Karen to forgive him. More likely, he's thinking she just overreacted and will apologize for breaking off their relationship and that Roxy had been wrong to hurt him. She'll beg Oliver to take her back.

Oliver must have gotten Onyx from someone. He doesn't strike Roxy as the chemist type, making the drug himself. No, that's someone else.

Roxy paces him, knowing he won't see her till it's too late. Then she pounces, letting momentum carry them both to the ground. Atop him, she gets in his face. "*Pezzo di merda!*"

"I didn't touch her! I haven't even seen her, I swear!"

"You're going to tell me what is in that Onyx crap. And you'd better talk fast. You still have so many bones I can break."

"I can't tell you!"

As a start, Roxy squeezes his bandaged fingers. "You know I'm not hearing what I want. You need an incentive. Like if you eat your vegetables, you get cake. Well, if you tell me everything I need to know about Onyx, I will let you die less painfully."

"I don't know, I swear! I don't know how he makes it!"

"He? He who?"

"He'll kill me!"

She leaps off him, pulls him up, and hoists him off of his feet. Her eyes go black and her fangs appear. "Haven't you been paying attention? I'm going to kill you."

chapter
thirty-six

Hedge

L ily rings Horton's bell. After a long moment Horton's voice comes over the intercom. Sedgwick holds the pet carrier in front of the door camera, giving Horton an eye-full of Cincinnati while concealing herself from view.

Horton's all-business voice says, "Got the money?"

Lily says, "I brought the money. Cash like you asked."

"I'll be up in a moment."

After letting Lily inside with her cargo, Horton crosses to the kitchen, perhaps for more tea. Glancing their way, and seeing Sedgwick emerge from the vestibule, he does a double-take. His expression curdles.

Now he turns back, eying Lily with displeasure with her uninvited guest. "I asked for the mink, not the witch."

"I did what we agreed to."

"No, you did not. I'm sure the witch would *agree*," he looks pointedly at Sedgwick, "one cannot be sloppy in magic." He steps to a credenza set midway along the length of the main floor.

"Detail matters. Following directions are essential. We had *agreed* you would bring the money and the mink. That was all."

Handing the carrier to Sedgwick, she says, "And my husband, of course."

"Yes. Yes. I want the mink outright—no strings attached. Not on loan from the Charmed Collection. I wouldn't have cared how you got it, but that it would become mine."

Sedgwick says, "*She* is not for sale. Whom she serves is her choice and she chose me."

Horton picks at a sculpture set on the credenza. "Well good for you. Does nothing for me." He looks to Lily, "We're done." He points to the front door.

Not to be dismissed, Lily steps toward him "If you need Cincinnati to help Reed, Ms. Sedgwick has agreed to have her help as long as she's not harmed."

"You are not listening. It is of no concern of yours the reason I want the mink. Only that I am to have it. The witch's weasel and the cash are payment for my services. Period. Not acceptable? Then get out."

Clasping the carrier to herself, Ms. Sedgwick says, "I told you his word could not be trusted."

"You're one to talk, witch." Horton says icily.

Lily says, "She has a name."

"He knows. And he knows I am a Sedgwick of the Sedgwick line. Our roots go deep here and further back to the lands of the Old North, its soil, its people, with whom for generations we have shared our harvests, our protection, and our wisdom. You are a charlatan, a pretender. Nothing more than a common street cheat doing three-card monte. You couldn't pull a rabbit out of its cage."

His hand grips the statue. Horton narrows his eyes at her. Would he hurl it at her? "Be that as it may, I have another customer."

Sedgwick says, "Oh? Do they also have a familiar?" The woman presses on, "Let me guess. Mrs. Williams pays you, you put on a show to 'cure' her husband, then apologize when it inevitably fails. So sorry, no refunds. Am I right?"

"You're wrong witch. So very wrong. I've learned a great deal since we last met. And I have a benefactor who's accelerated my research. I've been developing something that will change everything for humans and vampires alike."

"Then prove it," Sedgwick says.

Horton considers before saying to Lily, "Bringing the witch here has made this more trouble than it's worth. I have another volunteer to help me anyways. When I told you my price, you didn't bat an eye. So, let's triple it."

Sedgwick says, "You greedy—"

Lily waves her to keep quiet. She's not interested in antagonizing the man further. "Okay. But I can't get it to you now. You'll get it after."

"I know you got the funds. I did my own research on you—Lily Martin Williams. Read your wedding announcement. Daughter of Richard and Anne. Quite the power couple, aren't they? Now where's your husband, Reed?"

A phone chimes. Realizing it's her phone, she digs it out and finds a text from Reed. "My husband's on his way. What do we need to do?"

"Get her out of here. I don't want her stealing my trade secrets."

Sedgwick makes a derisive noise. Strands of her hair flutter. "You have nothing I could ever want, Horton."

"Give me the cash. When he comes, I'll take a sample of his ichor. In the light of a recent development, I'll want to double-check something. You, your husband, can come back tomorrow night with the rest of the cash and we'll finish this up. Even the witch can come, if she must."

"Here. Let's get it done tonight. I promise you to get you the rest. I will give you collateral."

Horton considers this.

Sedgwick asks, "What do you need to double check? Doubting yourself, Horton?

Before he retorts, Lily says to Sedgwick, "Please. Mr. Horton has been gracious to offer his help which we gladly accept."

Suddenly, Lily feels a biting cold around her wrist. Reflexively she rubs by the woven bracelet that Sedgwick gifted her. Glancing at Sedgwick, she must feel it too. A vampire is nearby. Reed? All three look down the hall where a young woman, thin and wearing something out of a Renaissance fair, appears.

"Your lab is so cool," the woman says, moving to join Horton. Then noticing the two women, she smiles, "Oh—hello." Friendly. She has no shadow, confirming that the bracelet works.

She has something in her hands and shows it to Horton, "Can I have this?"

He gingerly takes the object from her hands. A wooden gun with a rubber band stretched over its length. "Careful, little girl. That's protection from your kind. Not lethal. But it'll put you down long enough for a getaway. Can never be too careful when dealing with the unexpected and the undead." He puts it gently down on the credenza.

Sedgwick says, "Is this your customer?"

"I'm Amity. Pleased to meet you." She says, grinning in delight, revealing small fangs. Noticing the pet carrier, she claps her hands, "So cute! Is that a ferret?"

She approaches.

But Sedgwick steps closer to Lily, putting the carrier between them. "You'll forgive me if I ask you not to get too close."

"Fair enough." She turns back to Horton, "How long till it's ready?"

Horton says, "Now, most likely."

"You're seeking a cure too?" asks Lily. The girl looks half-starved and exceedingly pale. She had thought it was make-up, but maybe not.

Amity nods, but a touch wary, she says, "Why would you need it?"

"It's for my husband."

Now more suspicious, Amity says, "Your husband? Who? No one in the family is married to a human."

Lily rubs her chilled wrist. She's tempted to tear the bracelet off, but won't. "Well, he's new."

The doorbell rings.

Lily brightens, "That's him!"

chapter

thirty-seven

Cure

I ncessant bell chiming switches to violent banging on the front door by the time Horton reaches it.

A male voice cries, "Horton! It's me! Open up!"

Not Reed, Lily laments to herself, who alongside Sedgwick, looks to see who the newest addition to the party will be.

Opening the door, Horton says, "Oliver? What are you—"

The young man, Oliver, wild-eyed, stumbles forward. Shoved. Behind him, a woman, arm extended, jolts his shoulder, pushing him farther into the house.

Horton dodges out of their path.

Wearing a leather jacket, hair bobbed, the woman locks the door, then turns to seize Oliver before he escapes her reach.

"Do something. She's crazy!" Oliver holds up a busted bandaged hand.

Lily had seen this Oliver right here last night. Horton had discreetly put something into those wrapped fingers before sending him on his way.

Preferring to keep her own fingers intact, Lily recedes from the busy entryway, drawing Sedgwick and her companion with her.

Amity remains, casual in posture, looking on from her spot by the credenza.

"She made me bring her here," Oliver says, squirming in the shorter woman's one-handed grip.

Looking back at Amity, Horton says, "One of yours?"

"No vampire I know."

"What?" Oliver says, who then shouts in pain. His skin has a sheen of sweat and his restless eyes look everywhere at once.

The woman takes a moment to assess, noting each person in the room with a tilt of her head. She addresses Amity, "You: Get with those two."

Amity slides on over to join Lily, Sedgwick, and Cincinnati, giving an apologetic wave to them.

Horton says to Oliver, "Are you high?"

"Hiiigh," he squeaks. "Hell, yeah! She made me take half a bag. I'm freaking out! Do something!"

"Half?"

"She said she'd kill me. She hates me. Always has. Probably told Karen never to talk to me."

"Shut up. Don't say her name again."

Horton says, "What do you want?"

With rapid delivery Oliver says, "Please, please, please let me go. I'll stay away from you, from Karen. I swear you won't see or hear from me again!"

Roxy scowls, giving Oliver a few shakes. "What did I just tell you? *Stupido!*"

Lily attempts to cool this down, "Please listen to him. Let's all just talk it out."

Ignoring her, Roxy pulls something out from a leather pocket. It's a small plastic sachet. She waggles the pouch, half-filled with dark coarse-grain crystals, holding it up like a special treat for Horton. "I want to know about this."

"Who are you?"

"Roxy. The one with moxie." Her fangs flash and snap the air by Oliver's throat. "Good ol' Ollie here tells me you make this. That true?"

Quivering, Oliver says, "I won't deal any more, either! I promise! I promise!"

"What is it you want?" Horton says while backing toward the credenza.

Roxy says, "Stay where you are." She palms the pouch and makes a quick gesture in Horton's direction. Inches from his nose, a burst of flame appears, casting him in an orange glow for a moment till it's eaten by the air.

Horton flinches, turning aside and shielding himself with a raised arm.

Amity bounces on her toes, "You're Roxy? *The* Roxy, the firestarter? We heard about you. That was so cool!"

Nonplussed, both Lily and Sedgwick turn their heads, to give her a look of disbelief, not seeing this rising tension as praise-worthy.

Subdued, Amity says, "Well, it was."

Firestarter? Like Reed. This is the woman who's been showing him the ropes?

"Nice to have fans. What's with the get-up? It's not Halloween, you know." She mutters something.

Oliver says, "Can I at least have some water? I'm thirsty. Thirsty. Thirsty."

Roxy says, "Good idea. You, fan-girl, get him some water."

Amity quick-steps to the kitchen.

Recovering, Horton says, "It's a drug. I call it Onyx. What good is it to you? Drugs don't work on vampires."

Roxy puts the packet into Oliver's shaking hands, "Open it."

With a sudden realization, Horton says, "You've had it before," but turns puzzled when she confirms his assumption.

"Yes. Last night."

Oliver whimpers as he unseals the packet.

Roxy coaxes, "Good boy," while she pats his back.

"You drank from someone high on Onyx and got high yourself?" Stunned, Horton says, "It never occurred to me that could be possible."

Sedgwick says, "You made a street drug? That's what your magic has to show for itself? All these years and you end up making ecstasy for vampires?"

Horton says, "Shut up. I told you my game has improved since you last saw me. And Onyx works even better than I had imagined." Far from abashed, he looks triumphant.

Roxy says, "The come-down is horrible." She motions for Amity to give the tall glass of tap water to Oliver.

As Amity does so, she says to Roxy, "Love the jacket."

Oliver nearly drops the glass twice before getting it to his lips, then empties it in a few glugs.

Scooting beside Lily, Amity asks Horton, "What's in it? How does it affect us? How is that even possible?"

Lily had been right. Not 'honest.' 'Onyx.'

"Have more, Oliver." Roxy says, taking the glass from him, tossing it.

Feebly, Oliver shakes his head, though his fingers work around the mouth of the sachet.

"What is in it?"

Horton's lips twist, reluctant to speak. But he does so the moment Roxy raises her hand. "Onyx is made from ichor and some other ingredients for the perfect bliss."

Amity's tone changes, "From Troy's blood? You were supposed to use it to make a cure."

"It was a mutual arrangement. He gave me his ichor to experiment with. Progress on the cure came along quite well and Onyx was a happy byproduct. And a lucrative one. A bit of brilliance, if I do say so myself."

Lily says, "But the cure still works, right? You can make vampires human again?"

Amity, Roxy, and Horton look at Lily like she is high herself.

"Human?" Horton says. "What are you talking about?"

A panicky rabbit kicks inside her heart. She swallows, trying to grip herself. Lily says, "The cure for my husband. You said..." But seeing Horton's face, her grip fails. She sinks to a crouch. Disappointment sours her stomach.

"The cure for us," Amity says. "Our family. Our ichor's cursed."

Roxy says, "You're Lily?" She cackles. "Reed told me so much about you. Oh, how he talked and talked. How he can't be himself around you. The shame he feels. I told him, you will never understand what he is now. But I do. We get each other. You need to move on. Better for him. Better for you both. If you love him you will let him go."

Roxy's throaty laugh sharpens the bite of her words, making Lily feel so much worse.

Oliver sniffs, "I feel awful."

Roxy says, "Me too. But don't worry. It'll be over for us soon. We won't suffer much longer."

Roxy opens wide her mouth and clamps onto Oliver's neck. He screams and thrashes, dropping the remaining Onyx which dusts the floor.

At the same time Horton has gotten himself near the rubber band gun which lies on the credenza. He picks it up and levels it at the pair. Roxy releases Oliver, letting him slip to the floor in a gurgling heap. She licks his blood off her lips.

Laughing at Horton she says, "What is that?"

He pulls the trigger. The released blue loop sails across the distance. Roxy waves her hand and the rubber catches fire. For a moment, it becomes a comet streaking silver sparks, then a chary lump that drops nearly straight down.

After a bout of manic laughter, the woman raises her arms, "I ignite. I burn. I fall to pieces. Then I rise."

chapter

thirty-eight

Millie

Despite Kyle's earlier violence, Kyle's demands, and Kyle's put-upon attitude, which has mellowed during the ride from the safehouse to this Bella Vista neighborhood, Reed remains elated. With genuine joy and excitement, he had danced his way into Kyle's car. Now, mere minutes from a true resolution, an end to this week-long nightmare, Reed will be human again. He can nearly feel his heart beat. He and Lily will have their lives back. Soon it will be as though all this trial had truly been a fitful dream that vanishes upon waking.

Looking through the passenger window capturing streaks of light from urban glare, a wistful smile forms at the thought of sunlight overtaking the gloom, feel its warmth on his skin, rather than the heat in his chest. He'd hold Lily close as they watch the sun climb the sky.

They could use the rest of their time off to move his belongings into the new apartment. And while unpacking, they they'd plan a new honeymoon. Somewhere with lots of sand and drinks and food.

Food! Oh, to eat again!

According to the GPS, they were just a few turns away from the address where they're to meet Lily. With rising excitement, Reed's fingers patter on the dash.

Kyle says, "Did she tell you what the cure is? How it's supposed to work? Any details at all?"

Reed shakes his head. "But it won't be long till I'm not your problem anymore."

Kyle says, "I look forward to that. But Reed, be careful. Be sure you know what you're getting into. Could be a scam."

"Don't worry. I'll make sure it's solid."

Turning onto Warnock Street, Kyle says, "I will not apologize for earlier because you deserved it. But you also deserve getting your life back and I hope this is the real thing. It was good knowing you."

Reed nods his thanks.

Out of the car, they approach the house matching the street number Lily had provided. Kyle points to the pair of windows by the door. Reed has already noticed flitting silhouettes drawn across the shades like a shadow play.

Neither know what to make of it.

Then a spot on one of the shades blackens as though it's the hide of a steer being branded. The spot becomes a hole, from which a curl of smoke steams out. More spots appear, more holes, and more smoke suffused with a red-orange glow.

***

Everything seems to fall apart, but Lily pulls herself together, determined to put aside Roxy's taunts for later. She hurries over to the bitten, young man left discarded on the floor. With assistance from Sedgwick and the costumed vampire, they drag Oliver away from the vestibule area already prickling with small fires.

The poor man sobs, clutching his own throat where it leaks blood. A crimson smear trails his prone form. Lily lets out a sob herself, shuddering with the memory of being in that hotel room where Marie and Jean-Paul bled the newlywed to death.

Unconcerned, Roxy waves her hands as though flinging unseen seeds on her way to the basement door. More fires appear and blossom. Blazes surround and confine the central area where they gather.

Lily's hands flutter by her face to calm herself before she gets on the floor beside Oliver. He looks stricken, pale and sweaty, quieter, but breathing. His neck and shirt damp and sticky with blood.

The vampire girl, Amity, kneels opposite Lily, holding Oliver's hand, and appearing stricken herself.

Lily says, "Hold on, Oliver." She needs a compress to staunch the flow.

Busy in Lily's peripheral vision, Sedgwick rummages through her capacious shoulder bag. "When dealing with vampires, you've got to expect bloodletting." From the bag she finds a jar, the kind that once may have held beauty cream. She unscrews the cap and hands it down to Lily. "Slather it on his wounds."

Lily does so as quick as possible. The goop is slippery like moisturizer but with bits of things she doesn't recognize. Oliver's already lost a great deal of blood but the salve does dam the flow. Now all Lily can do is pray.

The heat of the room suddenly increases by ten degrees. Flames multiply, swooping through the air like flocks of sparrows, kindling another memory. The one of Lily having been trapped in a fire, debris falling around her, smoke invading her lungs. So vivid, the memory may smother her before this actual fire does.

She looks to her sleeved forearm. Though unseen, she can feel the sensitive blasted skin there. She would have died had Reed not reached her in time. Where is he now?

The gauzy smoke shrouds the room and the fires edge closer in from all sides. Where can they go?

Sedgwick dives back into her bag and takes out a sack with a drawstring closure. Going in a clockwise direction, Sedgwick dispenses salt crystals onto the floor.

"I'm going to check on Horton." Amity pops up and hurries in the direction both he and Roxy had gone.

The witch has drawn a circle around herself, Lily, Oliver, and the pet carrier containing Cincinnati. Once the last salt crystals fall, the witch says some words and makes some gestures. A light breeze picks up, bringing blessed coolness to the stifling heat.

"The circle will keep out the fire and carbon monoxide but it won't do us any good if the house collapses."

The breeze turns to wind, then faster still, tracking along the circumference. A commotion from the front window draws Lily's attention. Out of the haze, someone makes a clumsy entrance.

***

Outside, Reed watches the fire eat up the rest of the window shades, revealing huddled figures within a churning column of air that repels the smoke.

"Lily!" Reed says, rushing for the front door.

Locked.

Moving to the window, Kyle says, "I'll get her. You need to put this out. Hope you learned enough."

Great.

Kyle dashes about, looking for who knows what. He's found it. In his gloved hand he's got a rock. Up to the window, he smashes the rock against it, cracking the glass. He repeats till the window is battered down enough to give Kyle room. Giant tongues instantly appear to greet him.

Reed needs to know that Lily is safe, but he resists charging after Kyle. The man was right—if not dealt with, the fire will destroy everything and everyone within its brick shell.

***

Fire licks up the walls and dances on the furniture. It's difficult for Lily to see anything beyond the tight vortex, as though she, Ms. Sedgwick, Oliver, and Cincinnati are in the calm eye of a hurricane. Smoke spins around them, fire buffeted away. But how long can they remain here?

Unconscious and very pale, Oliver still breathes—his chest rising in shallow takes. He needs medical attention.

And someone has just vaulted inside the burning house. The landing is terrible but he rolls farther into the room before picking himself up.

It's Kyle! He's saying something, but she can't hear him over the wind.

Reed must be here, but where?

Sedgwick holds out her arms in warning, "Stay back! Don't break the circle." Kyle's dress shoes come short of the arc of salt on the floor.

He says something. He's going to get them out, she thinks he's saying.

Lily points at him. "Kyle!" He looks to see flames caught a ride on his jacket when he had tumbled in. He scrambles out of the jacket, tossing it, then looks around himself. Too much by the vestibule. The window he came through looks worse than ever as though a hundred snakes slither over it.

He rubs where smoke stings his eyes then hurries to the back of the house. There's fire there too, but Kyle pushes aside obstructions in the path to the rear door.

Sedgwick glances around them. "This fire isn't natural. That Roxy woman must be controlling it. We've got to get out."

Above, the fire unzips the ceiling, exposing the joists of the story above. Voracious flames attack the wood, termites chewing it to pulp.

In seconds, the buckling ceiling becomes a widening split and patches of the subfloor are eaten away.

Lily gives a cry and Sedgwick looks up. Directly above their heads, they can see the underside of an unsteady chest of drawers or an armoire pushing through. Farther away, other bedroom pieces sink into the compromised flooring. Fresh flames caress them as though bidding them to complete their fall.

With nowhere to go, Lily will be crushed before she's burned up. Not wishing to see the end, she stoops down and clutches her crucifix.

Beams crack and furniture groans.

In an instant all that was teetering above them comes crashing down. Lily braces herself, making herself as small as possible. She and Sedgwick both shout in terror.

The thunderous crash rattles her teeth. Certain that she's already been crushed, Lily suspects she'll awake in the afterlife.

After a moment, Lily dares open her eyes. She's... she's unharmed. The armoire landed on its back beside her. A hand's breadth closer and she would be flattened like the Wicked Witch of the East. Splintered, charred wood surrounds Sedgwick and the pet carrier.

Unfortunately, the circle itself has been breached. The circulating air ceases, the wind instantly dissipates, and Lily chokes on the sudden intake of smoke.

Visibly shaken, Sedgwick gathers herself and marshals Lily to the other side of Oliver so that she can redraw the circle away from the furniture. Circle reestablished she stoops to open the pet carrier. "No time for preparation." She scoops up the mink and says to Lily, "I'm going to try to expel the air. No oxygen, no fire." She coughs, "I hope."

After allowing the animal to clamber up her front, Sedgwick wipes sweat from her face. "Inside the circle you and Oliver will be fine. But snap back for me, though I hope my friend will help with that."

Before Lily can ask or object or even understand what's happening, Sedgwick gestures with her hands, and from her shoulder, the mink squeaks and bobs its head.

A bomb goes off. A giant thunderclap sends everything outside their circle airborne. Whatever isn't fastened down, flies outward into the walls, through doorways and windows with a great crashing noise.

***

Reed staggers back. He's wrestling a formidable demon and he needs to reassess. Florian growls Reed's frustration. The fire seems an alive thing. As though it has a will all its own.

As though Roxy is here. Why would she be here?

Yes, she is. He sees her signature in the flames. A flock of birds—a thousand Millies commanding the air like a squadron of fighter planes with smoky contrails.

He hears distinct, chilling caws. Flitting amongst their avian sisters, crows fix their golden eyes on Reed who is thrown under their collective shadow.

With instinctive fear, Reed shrinks back as the burning house disappears. "No." Hands rise defensively. Hands in those old leather gloves. Hands at the end of stick-thin arms.

"No," he says again, but with returning resolve. He won't let the crows intimidate him. They won't stop until he stands his ground. He's going to fight Fire with Fire.

He steels himself and mentally calls out to Florian. But their connection is as tenuous as it originally had been. The effortless teamwork he experienced with the lion last night was a fluke, the result of being on that Onyx drug. Without it, his strength and command have softened. Just when he needs his power the most, he feels weak and clumsy.

Small consolation that by equal degree, the crows are fewer in number, but no less threatening, no less frightening. He's still vulnerable.

"Come on, come on, come on!" Like starting an engine, he keeps cranking until he feels a spark. Meanwhile the crows do not cede him any time. They're coming and all he can do is run and dodge. He channels the Fire within himself, feeling the burn through his chest, shoulders, down his arms.

In pain, frustration, fury, he skids to a halt, turns back on the coming crows and screams. He's not going out, not like this, not when Lily's in that burning house.

The crows won't relent and he's desperate to reclaim the power. "Come on! Damn you!"

Florian roars, suddenly beside Reed, then charges into the striking flock. The crows wheel away and scatter. Florian leaps for them, each bound greater than the last, catching some then more of them, crunching bone, severing wings, knocking them from the sky.

He tastes moments of triumph over these birds that for too long, have tormented him, tearing away his memories, his connections to the human beings he loves.

Refocusing, as Florian bounds around him, Reed makes out a structure in the distance. It's broad and low in profile. Not a building—something between a sculpture and a treehouse.

A shelter. Reed speeds toward it.

The crows firm up. Blots of ink flock over his head and sweep in front, attempting to harry him, steer him and Florian away. They want to prevent Reed from reaching it. Why? What is it?

Claws divot the dirt as Florian sprints ahead, doing his best to beat a path. Nearer now, Reed recognizes the structure for what it is. Woven golden straw and bronze sticks throw near-blinding reflected sunlight. A nest. A damned nest.

His memories... Ms. Shipley had been right!

Whooping, Reed pumps his legs harder, his human connections just yards away. He feels like he's caught the football and is determined to make it to the end zone, leaping, swatting, dodging all comers. He needs this win.

He's so close.

Yes! Though astounded when he reaches what resembles a giant wicker bowl, he doesn't hesitate to unweave some of the straw and stuff it into his shirt where it belongs.

Lily's burn mark.

Days after they had properly met at the fire station, Reed visits Lily at her home to pick her up.

"How are you feeling?" He hands her a clear-wrapped gift basket. Delighted, she smiles, her hands going to her heart before accepting it.

The burn on her right forearm is visible now that the dressing has been removed. Still some swelling and redness, but with continued care the wound looks like it will heal with minimal scarring.

"It's got lotions, aromatherapy, protein snacks, and chocolate. My friend, Mina, helped put it together."

He remembers.

Lily's words return. *This is when we met. You rescued me. Just like you had last night. That's what you do.*

He remembers.

If you forget again, I will remind you again.

He remembers and the realization overwhelms him. He staggers a step with disbelief. He had nearly given up hope that he'd ever recover any of these precious moments. More than relief, he has a sense of peace, a feeling that a bit of his soul has been restored.

He craves more of it, more than the crows do. He dodges several of them as he circles the nest. As he scrambles to get more pieces, an explosion blasts him off his feet.

thirty-nine

Onyx

A locked door? Roxy smirks at the interior door Horton had barred behind him when escaping to the basement. Gripping its handle, she gives a resolute jerk starting at her shoulder and down to her hand, tearing the door from its brass hinges and leaving it to fall over.

Such is the gift of Onyx. Steel in her muscles, jet fuel in Millie's engines. Roxy laughs. And to think she had hesitated in drinking the Onyx via Oliver's vein.

She hadn't planned on doing that. She hadn't planned much at all. She had no plan when she arranged to meet Oliver near Driscoll's Diner under the pretense of being Karen. When he squirmed under her grip, a tempting idea occurred to her: Break his wrists, then his ankles, and leave him in disjointed agony within a circle of fire. She'd be deaf to his pleadings as the flames slowly consumed him.

More honestly, for her part, she should be there with him. Maybe so. And maybe soon enough.

But Roxy still had questions and luckily for Oliver, she bent to her curiosity and spared him. What did he know about Onyx? Where did he get it? How was it made?

Then it occurred to her that it would be apt that he take the Onyx. He'd probably be more pliable. Under her fang-revealing sneer and her onyx-dark eyes, he heeded her threat and took out one of the little bags, unsealed it, and snorted up pinches of black flakes.

She almost regretted it, the way he babbled on and on with little to say. He had only been dealing a short while. The drug was intended for the clubs, raves, concerts. Places with lots of repeat business. None of the clients seemed worse for it. It's harmless. Maybe even legal.

While she listened, her grief warred with her rage. She wanted to scream at him. She wanted to tell him that Karen was dead, and he was to blame. How did that make him feel? Was he even capable of even a morsel of remorse?

Sweet Karen. Gone because of Onyx, because of Oliver, because of Roxy. Karen's tenacity, her truth, her spirit gone forever. How terrified she must have felt. Had she put up a fight? Had she screamed? Begged? Cried? Whatever Karen's final thoughts were of Roxy and her betrayal, they were kinder than Roxy deserved.

Dwelling on Karen hurt too much. Grief was sewn into Roxy's heart with a blistering hot needle and blood red thread. She wished she could rip that heart out.

But she got hold of herself, determined not to tell Oliver. Not yet. Instead, she assured him that once they get to their destination, and she meets this Horton fellow, she'd let him go. She'll move on, like Karen had.

But at the end of this, things needed to burn.

So, the Onyx. Let its bliss do the work and slough off her grief. Up and up. Karen's death can't touch her high up here.

Roxy feels powerful once more. The Fire gives so much. A bounteous goddess. A thousand fires as though Millie fledged a brood. They paint a gorgeous tableau on the walls, the furniture, the ceiling. But she cannot linger to admire.

Soon smoke will choke the humans out of the house before their skins crisp. They will not meddle. There's Horton to see. The woman with the white hair and a pet carrier had implied that Horton knows magic. He confirmed as much. She hopes it's true. It'd better be true.

Her boots descend the staircase step by step. When the basement comes into view, she doesn't find any magical things like pentagrams, cauldrons, or tomes.

There he is. Horton. Seems in an awful hurry to pack up and skedaddle. She laughs.

He spares her a glance while he dashes from shelving and back to duffel bags set on a steel table at the far end of the basement. And when they're full, he shoves what he can inside a satchel.

There's a fire extinguisher—a red cylinder and short black hose. But she hasn't brought the fire down here. Yet. She needs something first.

Coming to the first steel table near the landing she brushes her fingers on its surface. "The Onyx works better than you know."

He hesitates, looking expectantly at her though his hands still work on filing papers into the satchel.

"It amps up my power." She grins, gleeful. "You should see Millie-she'll soon be as big as the Spruce Goose. I can't wait to fly with her."

"Can you do that outside?"

"This is where the magic happens." Fingers trace figure-eights. "You said that the ichor came from Blade. Does he know you make drugs with his blood? Seems like something he should license, make a buck or two."

"We worked on a cure. For him, for all those in Camden."

"What's in it?"

"A bit of this and that. I tried XTC, Molly, ketamine, mescaline. Different combinations to see what worked best, then blended with his ichor using an alchemical process."

"And once you had your formula you needed a distributor: Oliver."

"Yeah. This was all some new kind of drug lab to him. He has no idea about our side of things. The really Real."

"One more question, Horton. Answer carefully. Can you raise the dead? Someone who was recently killed?"

"Resurrections? Isn't that what your kind does?"

"Too much blood loss."

"Yes. The answer is yes. But I need my lab." He gestures to take in the whole basement. "Intact."

A clatter of shoes tromping down the first few steps calls their attention. The vampire girl. Fireflies drizzle and hazy smoke billows behind her.

"Please, Ms. Roxy. Don't hurt him. We need him. We need you both."

***

Amity holds Cole's hand, his pulse weakening, his life ebbing. Blinking the illusion away, she reminds herself the man lying on the floor isn't Cole. She releases Oliver's hand. Nothing she can do for him, just like she could do nothing for Cole. She's merely a vampire. A shadow of death.

But these two can. On her knees, Lily acts with confidence and speed, taking a jar from the witch, unsealing it and scooping out a large amount of thick grease. She spreads it into the two deep wounds in Oliver's neck. The seeping blood that has pooled onto the floor slows and soon stops.

If her husband is a vampire, does she do this often?

Back on her feet, Amity looks around. Fires crop up around her, smoke blurs her vision, and the stench of melting materials irritates her nose. Horton must have fled to his lab below. And Roxy must have followed.

The witch pours salt out of a suede bag—the kind Amity and her friends use for holding game dice. In hurried steps, she draws a salt circle to encompass Lily, Oliver, and the ferret in the cage. Amity remains outside of it. Once the final salt crystals fall to the floor and the witch utters some incantations, a draft rises. Quickly, it picks up, becoming a breeze that plays with the ends of Amity's cloak. The breeze turns to wind riding the course of the salt.

Magic. Real magic. How cool is this?! The witch is conjuring a mini cyclone spinning the smoke away. How many countless game sessions had Amity pretended to know magic, and now here she witnesses the real thing.

The guys will be sooo jealous when I tell them.

If she gets out of here. And she needs Horton.

The rising heat and spreading fire urge her to hustle. She rushes toward the stairs leading to Horton's basement lab, grabbing the rubber band gun off the floor, then ducking under the ruined doorframe now alight with small flames that cast orange light and shadows onto the staircase. She fans away smoke and ducks below the flitting fires. Hunching, she peers through the balusters to pinpoint where Horton is.

She spots Roxy first. By the landing, the woman paces the length of one of the lab tables and back. Her fingers strike discordant notes from the metal surface while she watches Horton spin about at the other end of the basement. Two overstuffed duffel bags sit on a table by him. They hadn't been there earlier. Frantic, Horton grabs whatever he can, notebooks and some of those clay tubes, and crams them into a satchel.

Thankfully, the fire hasn't reached down here.

"Don't hurt him, Ms. Roxy," she repeats, coming down the rest of the stairs, hands out to show she's not a threat.

Wide-eyed, Roxy says, "Oh, I won't. I need him." She titters. "The Onyx Maker. Mr. Onyx. See what I can do?" she presents her hands like a magician might. Nothing up the sleeves of her leather jacket. From nothing that Amity can see, twin fires appear above her upturned palms. About the size of softballs, the flames whorl in the air.

Amazed, Amity watches their shapes change into human figures that leap and tumble like gymnasts.

Roxy brightens, "I've never had such control." One of the performers juggles three little fires, then tosses them to its partner.

Amity says, "We need you, too."

The figures shrink to empty air as the woman chuckles bitterly, "I'm the last person you need." Then more subdued, "You live long enough, you learn you can't trust your heart to anyone. They'll let you down. Even me."

Amity shakes her head, "It's true, we do need you. We lost Blade. Troy Dawson. He's dead."

"Dead? Dead how?" She shoots a glare at Horton, who ducks his head.

Orange-red birds with long tails, like phoenixes from myth, swoop over their heads. They dive-bomb, scorching metal and setting wood, upholstery, and books aflame.

Horton cries out at the destruction and Amity stammers, "His heart blew out."

Heat cranks up, but Amity keeps her cloak on.

Roxy turns her head to her, "The man found behind Driscoll's Diner..."

Amity nods, sorrowful. "You see? We need you now more than ever."

"I knew it." Her laugh rings hollow.

As casually as she can, without Roxy seeing, Amity reveals to Horton his wooden gun poking from her courier bag. "We're desperate, Ms. Roxy." She creeps toward the table where she left the bag of rubber bands, its metal surface reflecting the firelight.

Roxy says, "He died from Onyx?"

"No," Horton says. "He never knew about the drug." He pauses in his packing and says with a contrite tone, "It was the cure we'd been working on. I must have missed something."

The wooden shelves beneath the staircase burst into flames. Amity leaps clear, but now she's within reach of the bag. "We'll do whatever you want, Ms. Roxy. Put the fire out, and let Mr. Horton help us. Help all of us."

Sweat beads Horton's face. "I will bring your friend back. I promise."

"I want to believe you." The fires abate and diminish.

"Believe him, please!"

Roxy appears possessed by vying emotions. One moment she seems gripped by anguish, clutching at herself, pacing. The next, well, Amity can't be sure if the woman is racked by laughter or sobs.

Winding down, Roxy gasps one last time as the fires die away once more. She says to Horton, "Do you know what it's like to kill your best friend?"

"I do, Ms. Roxy."

Seeing the pain in Roxy's face and to hear it in her shaky voice nearly moves Amity to put her arms around the woman, to console Roxy in their shared grief.

Surprised, Roxy regards Amity, "If I still feel this disgusted while high, what happens when it wears off?" She looks back at Horton, "And before it wears off, you ought to know—"

A sudden gale turns the basement topsy-turvy. Amity is swept off her feet and sucked up the staircase, as though the bulkhead door of a jet plane has been torn away. Grabbing the railing at the last second, she holds tight. Papers, glass pipettes, metal boxes, fly through the air, smashing into one another and into the walls. A scale just misses her face.

Her ears feel like they need to pop, but working her jaw doesn't relieve the discomfort. Squinting, she sees Roxy has been flung smack into the wall of the landing while being pelted with debris.

Then the wind ceases. Amity falls to the ground with a painful crunch. Nothing broken, but her ears still feel wrong. She can't hear anything and there's pressure and pain in her chest.

Stunned, she stares at what remains of the lab. Most everything is broken or inverted, and several of the tables have slid into one another.

The fire has gone out—not a lick of it left. The witch's spellwork must have expelled all the air to snuff it out.

No air means no breath...

Horton convulses as he clutches his throat, trying to get air that's absent. Eyes straining, skin boiled red, he soon slips from spasms to unconsciousness.

Amity hurts all over and struggles to move. Can she die? Just then, with less of a punch, the displaced air returns, restoring equilibrium.

Roxy leaps to her feet, an angry slash for a mouth and eyes ablaze. The air shimmers around her hands like asphalt on a hot day. Amity feels the waves of heat. Then she gasps. Roxy is not touching the ground. She floats four-or-so inches above the floor.

The gun. Amity still has it. Where are the rubber bands? Crap! They blew who-knows-where. She scrambles, searching.

Meanwhile, Horton revives and turns over wheezing, then hacking. Once recovered enough, he sits back against the wall. Still red-faced, he grips the satchel in his arms. His eyes beckon Amity.

Amity scrambles toward him. A fireball—a freaking fireball!—blasts past her shoulder and explodes into the concrete wall above Horton's head, disintegrating into sparks.

"Holy crap!" Amity dives to the floor. Colorful loops lay scattered nearby. She reaches for one, but a tugging on her cloak convinces her to look back. Horton shows his hand. A vial—a test tube with a cork stopper. With ragged breaths, he says, "I hope Blade was right." The tube rolls of out of his fingers. She snatches it, tucks it away, and gets up.

Feet on the ground, Roxy moseys their way, her face twitching. Her hand rakes the air above her. Fires, like conjured gremlins, appear and sizzle furrows into the ceiling. "Step aside, girl. I'm getting thirsty. You can have whatever is left."

Amity moves between the two. "No, Ms. Roxy, it's the drug. Don't give in to it. He can help us!"

"It's much too late for us. And I don't want to feel anything anymore."

With ease, Roxy shoves Amity back, then crouches before Horton. Her long, sharp teeth plunge into his neck.

chapter
forty

Sanctuary

L ike being bounced hard from a nightclub, a sudden wind tosses Kyle
through the back door of the house. He smashes into the rear wall of
the concrete patio.

Rattled, he picks himself up and looks back. It is as though the house
has become a pair of lungs hacking up foreign bodies—a great wind spews
debris through its windows and doorways.

After its last spasms, he hurries to check on the people he left inside.
He's relieved to see Reed hugging his wife, though the white-haired woman
doesn't look well and the man on the floor looks worse.

"Check downstairs," Lily urges Kyle.

Rising heat and sounds of shouting and struggling greet Kyle on his
way down to the basement. Fire sizzles along the wall and crawls over spots
on the ceiling.

A cloaked woman struggles with another, who's feeding on a man
slumped against the far wall. Her back to him, he still recognizes her as
Roxy. The other woman pleads for her to leave the man alone.

By the time Kyle reaches the landing, the woman has taken out a
wooden gun, aims it, and pulls the trigger. The released rubber band snaps
at Roxy's back, who then instantly slumps against the man.

Kyle races over to help roll Roxy off the man and onto her back, scalding his hands. She's an erif for sure. And with her eyes closed, Kyle cannot determine if she's unconscious or dead.

Desperate, the cloaked woman rips a piece of her blouse off, wads the remnant, and presses it to the man's neck. The greedy fabric soaks up the flowing blood. The man shares her panic, his eyes fluttering, his body fighting death.

Surmising that she's one of the Rotters, he wonders how she ended up in this house with Roxy.

Through the narrow upper window, flashing reds and muffled voices warn Kyle that time is running out.

Near tears, she turns to him, "Can you turn him? I can't do it."

He knows her now. Amity. He hadn't seen her for decades.

Kyle shakes his head, "Ms. Marchetti took too much of his blood."

A guess, but also an excuse. He wouldn't do it anyhow, even if it weren't against House rules, which it is. Initiation is by consent and without duress. But personally, he has no appetite for more responsibility. He's already done a whole lot of awful in just a few nights.

She bends over the man, saying she's sorry, wiping her hand across his brow. Kyle gently puts his hand on her shoulder. He doesn't know what she had meant by not being able to turn the man, but it doesn't matter.

The breathing shallows, the twitching lessens, the eyes draw heavy.

Kyle says, "You're going to get caught, I'm afraid. The House Monitor is on his way, most likely. He will find you."

With a start she's up, adjusting the strap of a satchel over her shoulder. Something is in her hand—a test tube—and she hurries to the stairs, dodging a shower of embers. The fire has relented since Roxy went down, but small comfort. Any moment all will be consumed.

To her back, he says, "Don't resist. He won't hurt you as long as you don't give him reason to."

She's gone.

Just him and Roxy now. He bends down to cradle her head in one arm, then smacks her face with his free hand. No time for niceties. "Wake up!"

On the third strike, her eyes tremble, then all at once she's alert and sits up.

"Goddamn, Brandie. What the hell are you doing here?"

Attempting to help to her feet she instead bats him away. "I'll burn your ass if you touch me again."

"We'll both burn if we don't leave now. Let's go."

"Just go, you ass! Let me die."

Her anger is half-hearted. Something must have gone wrong. Is she punishing herself? "If you're not going, then I won't either."

"Idiot! I need you tell Al something. Tell him I learned who killed Blade."

"You do? Who?"

"No one. Tell him that and make sure he writes that check."

"Tell him yourself."

He sits beside her, his brown eyes roving the ceiling aflame. The heat and smoke increasingly unpleasant and less bearable.

She says, "I mean it. I'm not going anywhere."

Perhaps she's stubborn, committed to a game of chicken. See who gets up and runs first. Though he's not certain if either of them are bluffing. This could be the end for him. And perhaps that's for the best. He hadn't imagined his demise being burnt in someone's basement, but he is content.

He's killed many people and hurt many more. This unlife has turned out very different than he expected. One thing he could count on was time. Time enough to make restitution.

He wiggles a finger in one of the gashes of his shirt and slacks.

Foolish to think he could.

Dying here will get him out of his sponsorship of Reed. And he would no longer be bound to Devlin; likewise, Reed would no longer be bound to him. Win-win. Plus, whatever tonight's fallout will be, he won't have to contend with the Rotters any longer.

But he did enjoy dancing with Emma. He would like to do so again. And he had promised her that he would attend her show. Would not be gentlemanly of him to stand a woman up.

"At least tell me why. You weren't like this last night. And it seems to me—"

"I killed her, okay?" She chokes, "I killed my best friend. She didn't deserve... that." She holds her stomach, "I hate this."

As though in empathy, the fire around them wails and whips the air. Another groan of the house and roar of the fire promise that it'll be over soon.

"Believe me, Ms. Marchetti I've been where you are. One night, I'll tell you about the lives I've taken and what I'd give to bring them back. But we can't, and you know what I learned? I learned that I don't deserve to get out of this hell. You don't either. You don't get to wipe your hands. Your friend deserves her memory honored. You owe it to her to make up for what you did, even though you can't, but you'll try all the same. You deserve your pain for at least one more night. And you owe me a new suit."

Roxy bows her head. Shame, grief, despondency, he doesn't know which. But she's listening.

He brushes his hair. "Have you ever seen someone burn to death?"

She nods.

The fires slacken.

"I'm sure it's painful. Even more horrible for us since we can't succumb to the smoke first."

Her shoulders hitch.

He feels the sizzling room cool to stifling, and soon just balmy.

And despite the erif heat her body gives off, he tolerates the pain and draws her close. She yields and turns into him. Her fingers clench his shirt and she sobs.

***

Amity sprints out of the house through the back door. She slides to an abrupt halt, surprised to see the witch waiting here. Not for her. Oliver lays on the concrete. Alive, she's not sure. The ferret, free of its cage, sniffs by the woman's feet.

Fresh sirens draw closer to the block.

Amity says, "Glad you got out of there. Did the other woman, Lily, make it?"

The witch nods. She's winded as though she just finished a marathon.

Amity wants to comment on the spell the woman had surely cast, which sucked the air out of the house. Awesome, though it perhaps contributed to Horton's death. "Are you okay? Can I do something?"

She shakes her head with a voiceless thank you.

Of course. Amity is useless once again. Her fingers slide along the test tube in her hand. She wonders if she should drink its contents.

Through the gate, Amity steps into the communal area shared by all the homes ringing the block. Around her, in this late hour, lights have turned on and neighbors poke their heads through windows and doorways to see what the commotion has been about. In the sky, streaks of red flash from the fire trucks.

At one end of the courtyard, two mean-looking men in suits come her way. She can't be sure, but they look like the men who grabbed Eric and

Chris, and perhaps Henry and Jared. The Society. How had they known to look for her here?

She turns to go the other way and take one of the corridors that lead out to the street. Another man, this one wearing a brown suit, hair thinning, approaches. He calls to her, calm and casual. Like he is a friend checking on her. He knows her name. Wants her to come along quietly.

She's failed everyone. She's such a screwup. First with Cole when he was alive, then again at his death. She failed her friends on this botched mission. Could do nothing for Oliver or Horton but watch.

And if she gets out of this, she'll have to face Tommy and the others with nothing to show for it. Who knows what this stunt has done for their situation and the truce.

Her grip tightens on the vial. Her ichor, altered. Enhanced? Or poisoned? If she takes it, will her heart burst too? But if she doesn't, what use was any of this?

Troy had died for this. He risked his life for all of them, for their freedom. How could she not honor that?

They're closing in. She's trapped. She trembles. She doesn't want to die. And she doesn't want to let anyone else down ever again.

Her fingers slide up and down the strap of Horton's satchel. She wears it across her body. Horton had stuffed it with whatever he could grab, while trying to figure a way to escape the fire and Ms. Marchetti. It may be holding information Tommy can use.

Don't resist. He won't hurt you as long as you don't give him reason to.

In a quick motion, she breaks the seal of tube, tips it up and lets the dark liquid slide past her lips into her mouth and down her throat. After the last drop, she puts the stopper back and tucks the tube away, adjusts Horton's satchel, then slowly raises her hands in surrender.

***

Whipped off his feet, Reed lands in reality. The crows, the lion, the nest, are all gone. Before him, wind jets out of the front windows of the rowhouse. The hurricane seems to have extinguished the great fire that had been inside.

"Lily!"

He leaps up and bounds through one of the front windows. He lands in a debris field and steps onto a Van Gogh print. Objects of all kinds lay shattered and splintered. Over their heads, Reed can see the floor above, like a gaping wound, and its own ceiling beyond.

Miraculously, Lily, rising to her feet, appears all right. He runs to her side and embraces her tightly. "Thank God!"

She winces. "I'm okay, Reed. Just yesterday's bruises."

He checks her out anyway. She could be in shock.

Kyle, coming in from the back, has gone dutifully downstairs once Lily tells him people are still in the basement.

Reed smiles, but she doesn't return it. All he wants to do is hug her tight, but it looks as though she's mad.

"What's wrong? I got here as soon as I could. You wouldn't believe what happened."

"I heard," she says curtly. "Roxy told me all about it."

"Roxy? She *is* here? She did all this?"

Reed takes a wider view and stands astonished by the wreckage. An inferno must have whipped through, super-heating the air, spawning winds that tossed anything not nailed in place. What hasn't been destroyed still bear scorch-marks. Yet, all the fire has gone. How is that possible?

Near Lily, a woman with blowing white hair struggles to breathe, and lain out at their feet is a man who appears not to breathe at all.

Reed bends to check the young man's vitals. "He needs an ambulance."

And considering the wheezing woman, he suggests she'll need to be checked for smoke inhalation.

The woman shakes her head, "It... will... pass."

He says, "I'm sorry about your house."

Lily says, "It's not hers. It belongs to the man who had the cure. Or a cure. Not the one we need." Besides her flat tone, her eyes don't meet his.

Reed nods, disappointed, but all is not lost.

In silent agreement that they should not stay in this house a second longer, they hurry out the back. Reed carries the man, Oliver, following Lily, and the woman.

The enclosed rear patio had caught much of what was blown out. A call for an ambulance is placed, but privately, Reed doesn't think the man's chances are good.

With Lily's profound thanks, the woman, Penny Sedgwick, agrees to keep Oliver company till the paramedics arrive. She'll be discreet and leave before questions can be asked. Lily insists that the woman take a portion of the cash intended for the cure, at least to cover cab fare, if not her invaluable assistance. With Lily, she has a customer for life.

Penny Sedgwick says they can settle up later.

"What the hell happened?" Reed asks.

"Nothing good," Lily says.

Her expression is hard for Reed to make out. "What?"

"Let's just get home."

***

In their apartment, Lily doesn't know what she's feeling right now, other than being desperate for a shower. She needs to shed her cloying clothes, which are damp and reek with her perspiration, and further fouled with smoke, which she doubts will wash out.

Reed hovers by her even till she's about to peel off her underwear and disappear into the steam. "I'm fine," she says, almost regretting her tone.

Reed nods and busies himself in the bedroom.

Under the spray, she has much to process: The dashed hope that tonight Reed would be human once more; the resurfaced memories of nearly being a meal for Jean-Paul; once again nearly being burned alive; Roxy's taunts that struck her deeper than she would have liked.

Physically, the shower has been almost restorative but did little to settle the convolutions in her mind.

Something is happening. Some kind of shift in her world is occurring that she can't understand or put into words. She doesn't even know enough to be disturbed or frightened with what it may signify or portend.

Entering the bedroom, she still feels the chill on her wrist from the woven bracelet Sedgwick had gifted her. Her fingers recall the icon hanging from her necklace. Another gift.

Reed looks her way, eyebrows raised with unspoken questions.

He has been arranging his clothes in their closet when she returns dressed in comfy cottony pajamas. From what she had packed in boxes and brought from his apartment, he has hung on hangers or placed on shelves. He also found a fresh white undershirt and teal track pants for sleep.

Being upset with him has washed away with the soap. Still, she will have her say.

"We need to talk." Her words turn him glum as he joins her reaching hands with his. She looks up to meet his eyes. After a breath she continues, "I suppose I understand why you felt you could confide in Roxy rather than me. She can help in ways that I cannot. But it hurts that there is still this distance between us and that you feel you need to keep things from me. That you have to hold back.

"So, I want to know, why is that? Are you afraid of what I will say, or that I'll fall apart, or that I'll run away from you?"

He says, "I don't—"

"Because I will never do that. And I'm not going to shatter when you tell me what you're feeling. I know some things will not be easy to hear, but you should tell me anyway. I'm here for you."

With a shake of his head, he breaks from her to pace, his hand raking his hair. When he speaks, she hears frustration and pleading, "It's not what I want, Lil. I don't like it any more than you do. But I have to. I have to protect you from all of this. From me. How can you trust me if I don't even trust myself? If I'm not careful, I'm afraid I'll hurt you. You have no idea. You shouldn't have to know what I know or what I've seen. Or what I have to do."

He flings an arm out, a vague indication, as he says, "They're predators. The deadliest kind out there. They've got jars of blood. Human blood. Liters of blood. Gallons of blood. As party refreshments. I don't want you anywhere near that."

He returns to her, speaking with emphasis, "I don't want you to take risks for me. I know you want to help. I love that you do and I wish you could. But—"

Lily shakes her head, "No, no. You don't get to decide for me, Reed. This is all horrible, I know. I can't pretend anymore that shadows are just people like anyone else. What Jean-Paul had wanted to do to me if Marie had let him—I saw that again. There are real monsters around us. Out there. Not in here. This is our home. A place only for us. It's our sanctuary."

She touches her hands to his cheeks, her eyes on his, "I want to be absolutely clear, I have never, not once, ever saw you as anything other than my dear husband.

"And I'm not afraid." She catches herself, looking away a moment. They both know that can't be true. She looks back, "Let me put it this way: I refuse to let the fear control me anymore."

"What are you saying?"

"I am saying that I am not sorry for what I did last night or tonight. And I'm not going to stop, Reed. I am going to take risks. For both of us. Because what else matters? I'm going to find a real cure. And I'm not going to turn aside, or cross the street, or refuse to get involved if, and I hope it's if not when, a vampire tries to hurt someone. If I can do something, I will. I won't do anything stupid; I won't be rash. But I won't let any more Jean-Pauls have their way."

His expression turns doubtful, not liking, believing, what she's saying.

Something miraculous. Aleron's words.

She takes a breath, then says, soft but certain, "I can't explain it, but this is what I'm supposed to do."

Aleron had said that when she abandoned reason and confronted the pirate shadow, he had heard a double-voice. When she spoke, it was her voice but also not her voice. Like an echo just a half-syllable behind, but one that was full of compelling resolve. It was like a force, he said, almost tangible that he could see it. Thus, he was not surprised when the shadow did exactly as she told him to do and fled.

Then she thinks on earlier tonight when she was certain that the armoire would crush all of them. She hadn't misjudged its position above them. They should be dead. But impossibly, it missed. As though at the last second the furniture was deflected by an unseen hand.

"Kyle will not like that."

A wrinkle for sure. "He does not have to know. I'm going to search the Church libraries. If there's something to find, I will find it." She won't jeopardize Reed's probation. But neither can she let Kyle hinder her mission.

"It's not just you. This is not just happening to you. This is happening to us. And you will be honest with me. This only works if we tell each other what's troubling us. Show that you trust me. That you trust me with everything that you are."

"How?"

She had been thinking of the answer to that. She understands why he doesn't want to show this side of himself to her. This shadow side. Certainly, because he's afraid of hurting her, and maybe because he holds some shame as Roxy intimated, but he needs to get over it. He's making the situation more difficult than he needs to. He's carrying all of this to spare her the burden. But they're bound together now. Through fire, through faith, they're husband and wife. She can and will do her part.

Silently parting from him she makes a trip to the bathroom and back. He looks on curious.

She says, "We are in this together," then takes out a safety pin, undoes the clasp and pierces the tip of her index finger with it. A liquid ruby wells up.

He looks like he's about to argue.

"You're safe with me, Reed. As I am with you."

His jaw sets, then eases.

He nods and gently raises her finger to his lips and into his mouth. He nurses on her finger and by degrees she can see his expression lift into a smile. Equally pleased, she meets his smile with her own, withdrawing her hand then leaning up to kiss him. She can taste a metallic hint of her blood in his mouth. With fervent lips murmuring I-love-yous, and his sheltering arms around her she feels returned to her best friend, her man, her husband, her heart.

He's already warm, and she's soon right there with him, urgent in her wanting contact, skin-to-skin. Their clothing shed, she's beneath the reassuring weight of him, feeling the strength of his body. Her fingers run through his hair while he kisses along her jaw, the quick pulse in her neck, her shoulders. Kissing, teasing, coaxing one another, the distance between them vanishes. Her eyes settle closed. Her own body becomes softening wax as they meld into one flesh.

Dear Reader

Thank you for reading *Shadows and Ash*. To borrow a word from one of my readers, I am "gobsmacked" and humbled and grateful that, among so many books worthy of your time, you chose to read this one.

A big part of what I love about writing this series is sharing with you its characters and their world. They are its heart. I hope you enjoy reading their stories as much as I do writing them.

If you would, kindly leave a review.

And to get the latest on my writing, subscribe to my newsletter, The Scrapple. You'll receive a free story when you sign up at: jpcane.com/newsletter.

Thank you!

J.P. Cane

Acknowledgments

I am so blessed to have such amazing people cheer on my writing.

As ever, my love and gratitude to Monica, my sunshine. You inspire me beyond what words can say.

My hearty thanks to the cheer squad: Carole and David; Gary; Zach, Lauren, Curt, Rosie; Michelle, Seth, Harrison, Mikey; Lauren, Andy, Samantha, Lily; Alan, Steve, Rich.

For helping to make a deeper, richer, more heartfelt story, my thanks to early readers Bill Blume, Charles Long, Mary Miley Theobald, Julie Valerie, and Chris Williams for their discerning eye and expertise. Any inaccuracies are my own.

My deep appreciation to Harry Heckel and Chuck Tabb for introducing me to the Virginia Writers Club; and for their encouragement and support, not only of my own writing, but that of many of our fellow writers.

Many thanks to friend and editor, Erica Orloff, for not letting me get away with anything.

And thank you readers!

About the Author

J.P. Cane writes *The Shadowless* series and other stories. He and his wife live in Virginia.

Contact him at jpcane.com.